'We shouldn't see one another again, at least not like this.'

'Is that what you want?'

When she didn't answer he slipped his fingers beneath her chin and lifted her face, forcing her to look at him. 'I'm glad, because I couldn't bear that either.' He tried to imagine living and working in Pontypridd and not seeing her, and shuddered at the bleak thought.

'But you must never, never kiss me again. And when I visit the hospital you must take me straight home. If you want to talk to me, it must be in front of Bethan or Maisie.'

'Yes,' he agreed hollowly.

'Do you understand what I said?'

'Everything. But that's next time. Can't we stay to-gether for now? I'll tell you about Cuba, and America and my family and we'll pretend –'

'That I'm not married and you're not engaged?'

'Yes – no – and that there isn't a war and we're just two *compadres* – comrades, friends, who meet once a week to talk.'

'Only if we go somewhere where there are other people.'

'The New Inn?'

'The cafe,' she said, thinking of their bank balances.

'I think we should go to the New Inn. A little luxury would help me to forget the hospital for a while, and you the factory.'

'And that we kissed.' But as she grasped the bag of crumbs and followed him back to his bike she knew that she would never forget that kiss. Not as long as she lived.

Catrin Collier was born and brought up in Pontypridd. She lives in Swansea with her husband, three cats and whichever of her children choose to visit. Her latest novel in Orion paperback is *Finders & Keepers*, and her latest novel in hardback, *Tiger Ragtime*, is also available from Orion. Visit her website at www.catrincollier.co.uk.

By Catrin Collier

HISTORICAL

Hearts of Gold
One Blue Moon
A Silver Lining
All That Glitters
Such Sweet Sorrow
Past Remembering
Broken Rainbows
Spoils of War
Swansea Girls
Swansea Summer
Homecoming
Beggars & Choosers
Winners & Losers
Sinners & Shadows
Finders & Keepers
Tiger Bay Blues
Tiger Ragtime

CRIME *(as Katherine John)*

Without Trace
Midnight Murders
Murder of a Dead Man
By Any Other Name

MODERN FICTION *(as Caro French)*

The Farcreek Trilogy

Broken Rainbows

CATRIN COLLIER

An Orion paperback

First published in Great Britain in 1998
by Century
First published in paperback in Great Britain in 1999
by Arrow Books
This paperback edition published in 2006
by Orion Books Ltd,
Orion House, 5 Upper St Martin's Lane,
London WC2H 9EA

A CIP catalogue record for this book
is available from the British Library.

Printed and bound in Great Britain
by Clays Ltd, St Ives plc

The Orion Publishing Group's policy is to use papers that
are natural, renewable and recyclable products and made
from wood grown in sustainable forests. The logging and
manufacturing processes are expected to conform to the
environmental regulations of the country of origin.

www.orionbooks.co.uk

To John and Penny Pugh, good friends
who have done so much to preserve the memories of
old Pontypridd for future generations

Acknowledgements

I would like to thank all the people who have assisted me with the research of *Broken Rainbows*, especially the old soldiers who often caused me to wonder whether they fought the Germans or the GIs in the Second World War.

A grateful thank-you to Ruth and Larry Gulino and their daughters Lisa, Bonnie and Vicki of New York, for their friendship and hospitality to a young and naive visiting English student in 1968, and for all their generosity since. They gave me an invaluable insight into the GI invasion of Britain from the American point of view.

As ever, I owe an incalculable debt to Mrs Lindsay Morris and the staff of Pontypridd Library, especially the archivist, Mrs Penny Pugh, and Mr Brian Davies and the staff of Pontypridd Historical Centre for their unstinting professional assistance and many kindnesses.

All the members of Pontypridd and District Art Society, for using their talents to preserve so much of the town in oils, acrylic and watercolours, especially Mr Edward (Ted) Walkey whose vivid and unfailingly accurate memory has enabled him to depict so many well-loved Pontypridd buildings as they were before the demolition hammer struck in the sixties, seventies and eighties. I only have to stand before one of his paintings to be back in the town of my childhood.

My parents, Glyn and Gerda Jones, my husband, John, and my children, Ralph, Sophie and Ross, for their love, and for giving me the time to write this book.

Margaret Bloomfield for her friendship and continued help in so many ways.

Everyone at Random House for their support

especially Mike Morgan, Louise Hartley Davies and Kate Elton, and above all my manuscript editor Mary Loring for her patience, encouragement, all her suggestions and being at the end of the telephone whenever I needed to talk, and my agent, Michael Thomas, for his continued faith in me.

And a very special acknowledgement to all those who have taken the time to talk or write to me about their own memories of Pontypridd.

Thank you Mrs Mary Jarvis (for a work that is a book in its own right), Kay Downs, Mary Wheeler, Poppy, and all my friends old and new, and while gratefully acknowledging the assistance of everyone I would like to stress that any errors are entirely mine.

Catrin Collier
Swansea, August 1997

Chapter One

'YOU CAN SEE almost the whole of Pontypridd from up here,' Rhodri Williams, Pontypridd's billeting officer declared as Corporal Duval turned the military staff car on to the road that wound along the hill top in front of the Cottage Hospital.

'Stop the car,' Colonel Ford ordered.

Duval obediently slammed on the brakes.

Opening the door, the colonel stepped outside. Rhodri pulled his ancient overcoat and hand-knitted muffler closer to his shivering body and followed. Autumn had come early to the valleys. The wind was keen, carrying sharp needles of frozen moisture that stung as they whipped into the unprotected areas of their faces. Scattered over the slopes below them, miniature trees and bushes blazed fiery orange, rust and scarlet interspersed with every shade of green known to nature's palette, from funereal conifer to sickly, pale lime.

'That's the park,' Rhodri informed the colonel proudly, shouting to make himself heard above the din emanating from the chainworks directly beneath them. He pointed to a cultivated area sandwiched between the foot of the hill and the town centre. Covering an expanse of land almost as large as the town itself, its borders encompassed manicured playing fields and a small, flag-pockmarked golf course. A strip of tennis courts bordered the river on their left, a diminutive clubhouse set behind them. An uninspiring, institution-yellow mansion dwarfed a shrubbery in the northern corner; slate-roofed, covered seating surrounded a children's playground. 'Those patches of blue are the swimming pools. The one closest to the swings is the children's, the other is for adults. Both are closed for the winter, but they'll open again in May, and your men will be more than welcome to use the larger one.'

The colonel nodded as he stepped further along the bluff to gain a more comprehensive view.

'People walk in the park all the year around,' Rhodri continued to prattle heedlessly. 'In summer they come from miles around to spend a day there. Not many towns in Wales, or England, come to that, can boast a recreation area with this many amenities.'

The colonel continued to gaze at the vista of twisting rivers and railway lines, pitheads marked by the huge wheels of winding gear and narrow, grimy streets. Lifting his head he studied the surrounding hillsides, their windswept summits cloaked in coarse, yellowed grass, the lower slopes ribboned with steep terraces and sprawling puddles of black slag and coal waste.

'It's a real people's park,' Rhodri shouted, acutely aware that his babbling was boring the colonel, but the American's reserve had unnerved him to the point where he felt that any sound, even that of his own voice, was preferable to a silence punctuated only by the noise of the chainworks and the gusting of the wind.

Maurice Duval thought otherwise. The eight weeks he had spent driving the colonel around Britain had taught him to keep conversation to a minimum during working hours. It wasn't that the CO was unfriendly, he simply preferred to limit communication to the essential. The corporal only wished that the billeting officer who had insisted on showing them Pontypridd understood as much.

'Ynysangharad estate was bought and landscaped with public donations, principally pennies from ordinary working men and women who wanted to build a Memorial Park as a tribute to the soldiers who lost their lives in the Great War.'

'Have you plans for another collection when this war is over, Mr Williams?' David Ford enquired drily.

Uncertain whether the colonel had made a joke or not, Rhodri laughed anyway.

2

'The mansion in the park? Is it privately owned?'

'A clinic. An essential facility for the mothers and babies of the town,' Rhodri informed him quickly, hoping the colonel wouldn't try to requisition that building along with those he had already earmarked. It was going to be difficult enough to administer the town's affairs as it was, with half the civic accommodation in military hands. The Americans might be allies, but after months of preparing for their arrival it was beginning to feel more like invasion than alliance. 'As you see, the town is quite compact. The drill hall and chapel vestries where the majority of your men will be billeted are either centrally situated or within easy walking distance of most of the facilities Pontypridd has to offer. And Mrs Llewellyn Jones will have accommodation organised for yourself and your officers by tomorrow morning. She is very efficient.'

'After meeting her, I don't doubt it.'

'The local WVS would be lost without her. Although she relinquished her position as chairwoman before the war, she's still very much a driving force within their ranks. She volunteered their services to take charge of, and find lodgings for all the evacuees sent to the town. It was no mean task. We were inundated when the London blitz began.'

Turning up the collar on his overcoat the colonel strode back to the car. Concerned that he hadn't done justice to Pontypridd and all it had to offer, the billeting officer trailed dejectedly in his wake. As soon as they'd closed the doors, the driver hit the ignition. Rhodri clutched the door handle as he perched on the edge of the rear bench seat. The boy behind the wheel was wearing a corporal's uniform but he looked too young to be out of short trousers, let alone be in charge of a car. He also talked funny, even for an American.

The accent Rhodri had such difficulty in deciphering was broad Southern. A native of South Carolina, Maurice Duval had recently celebrated his twentieth birthday, but to his constant chagrin, his skinny five-

3

feet-five frame, curly, ginger hair and boyish, freckled features made him look more schoolboy than soldier. Before being drafted he had helped his father manage a run-down automobile shop. Smarter, and quicker to pick up on things than most draftees, he was an excellent driver who knew what it took to keep an automobile on the road, just two of the reasons he had been picked out to be an officer's chauffeur.

He glanced in the mirror as he steered down the hill towards the town centre. The colonel had a look of profound concentration on his face, as though he were plotting out a defence against German attack. Maurice shivered. Ever since the regiment had landed in Liverpool and seen the bombed-out buildings and rudimentary, barbed-wire, coastal defences, they'd been expecting Jerry to materialise. Like everyone else in his unit, he couldn't understand why the enemy hadn't arrived ahead of them.

'Council offices, sir?' he asked, as the landmark old bridge came into view.

'Yes, Corporal.'

Two people were waiting in the doorway of the building. A short, plump, middle-aged woman, who was so tightly corseted, Maurice expected her to burst out of her green costume at any moment, and a tall, slim, blond lieutenant in immaculate dress uniform. Rhodri said his goodbyes and opened the door, stepping on to the polished shoes of the officer who'd caught the door to stop it from blowing back.

'I'm so sorry . . .'

'Not at all, sir.' Lieutenant Kurt Schaffer tipped his hat as he grimaced in pain. 'Nice to meet you again, Mr Williams. I'm looking forward to getting better acquainted with you and all the townsfolk. Mrs Llewellyn Jones.' Lifting her hand to his lips, he kissed it before climbing into the car and taking Rhodri's seat in the back alongside the colonel.

'Remember,' she panted breathlessly, before he closed

4

the door. 'Now that you have the key, you're welcome to move your things in any time, day or night.'

'Thank you, ma'am. That's most generous and hospitable.'

'Anthea will be so pleased to meet you.'

'I will be honoured to make her acquaintance, ma'am.' Sensing, rather than seeing the colonel's impatience, he closed the door, returning her wave as Maurice headed down the road.

'And who is Anthea?' Colonel Ford enquired.

'Mrs Llewellyn Jones's daughter, sir.'

'Age?'

'She didn't volunteer it, sir, and I didn't ask.'

'Occupation?'

'Bank clerk, sir.'

'You know army policy on billeting in private houses, Lieutenant. Only officers of the rank of major and above to be accorded that privilege.'

'With respect, sir, Mrs Llewellyn Jones insisted that there was more than enough accommodation for all the officers, including the lieutenants. And she offered . . .'

'You're a charming bastard, Schaffer. Just make sure those Hollywood looks and gentlemanly manners don't get you into trouble.'

'Sir?'

'Take that innocent expression off your face. You know exactly what I mean.' He glanced through the window as they overtook a stationary tram in the narrow main street. 'Do you see what I see out there, Lieutenant?'

'Buildings that could do with a damn good clean, sir?'

'With the dust generated by all this coal production there'd be no point; half an hour later they'd be just as black. Look again?'

'Empty shops, long queues and shabbily dressed civilians, sir?'

'They've had three years of war, Schaffer. Have you any idea what that does to a country's economy, not to mention morale? Do you think your South Carolina would have had the guts to stand alone against Hitler?'

'They had the guts to stand against the Yankees, sir.' Kurt realised he'd made a mistake as soon as the words were out of his mouth. David Ford was a Northerner, a graduate of West Point and a fourth-generation career army officer. A member of the fit, young, capable school of regulars who'd gained rapid promotion since George Marshall had been appointed Army Chief of Staff in '39. Rumour had it he'd been a captain only three years ago. At thirty-seven he was one of the youngest full colonels in the army. He was certainly up to the job, but he was not renowned for his tolerance or sense of humour. The lieutenant dropped his gaze as the colonel stared him coolly in the eye.

'As you're unable to see what's in front of you, Lieutenant, I will explain. If you look out of that window,' Ford enunciated every word slowly and clearly as though he were addressing an idiot, 'you will see far more women than men, and the few men you do see will be either too young or old for military service.'

'Sir.' Schaffer tried to put contrition as well as respect into his voice.

'That means that most, if not all, of the healthy, eligible men in this town are either away fighting, or have already been killed.'

'Sir.'

'Therefore we have to keep a close eye, a very close eye,' he reiterated slowly, 'on our boys, and make damned sure that they treat every woman between the ages of twelve and ninety in this town like ladies, no matter what their social position or marital status. *Every* GI in my command will show the utmost respect at all times. The same kind of respect they show their mothers and sisters: no more, no less. Do you understand?'

'Yes, sir.'

'Good, because I am ordering you to enforce that policy. As of now you are liaison officer to the town. I will hold you personally responsible for smooth and peaceful relations between our boys and the locals. You will organise social events. Large-scale events,' he added

6

caustically. 'Parties for the town's children and socials that old ladies will be comfortable attending.'

'I understand perfectly, sir.'

'The only seduction will be by the regiment of the entire civilian population, male as well as female. Old as well as young.'

'Sir.' Ford squirmed uncomfortably under the colonel's unflinching gaze. There had been a minor scandal involving a sergeant's daughter back in training camp. One he thought he had succeeded in keeping quiet; now, he wondered if it was quite the secret he had believed it to be.

'Officers lead by example, Lieutenant. I don't care how many girls throw themselves at you while we are here. You'll put that seductive charm of yours under lock and key for the duration. And in case I'm not making myself quite clear, here it is in plain English. Hands off the women, and that goes double for the daughter of your host family. That's an order.'

'Sir.'

'I'm glad we understand one another so well.' Lifting his briefcase on to the seat, Ford opened it, extracted a file and handed it to Schaffer. 'You have the accommodation details, sort the units into billets. This time tomorrow evening I want every man installed in his own space and ready for training.'

Bethan John slowed her car as she reached the top of Penycoedcae Hill. After checking the mirror, she swung sharply to the left of the narrow lane turning between a pair of imposing posts that had been devoid of gates since the Ministry of Supply's drive for scrap metal in 1940. Her heart sank when she saw the car parked in front of her substantial, three-storey villa. Only one person in Pontypridd had a Daimler, a semi-retired chauffeur to drive it and the petrol ration to run it: Mrs Llewellyn Jones, doyenne of the WVS and self-appointed administrator of the war in Pontypridd. Why did she have to come on a Thursday of all nights when *It's That Man Again* was on the radio at eight-thirty?

Bethan checked her nurse's fob watch. When Mrs Llewellyn Jones visited, she *visited*. She'd be lucky to get rid of the woman in under two hours, and she'd been looking forward to spending the time before her favourite programme playing, bathing and reading to her two children.

Gathering her coat, nurse's bag and handbag from the back seat, she left the car. Maisie, the unmarried mother she'd taken out of the workhouse to keep house and help with the children, was waiting at the front door.

'Mrs Llewellyn Jones . . .'

Bethan nodded as she hung her cape on the beech-wood stand. 'I saw her car.'

'Mr Williams is with her. They insisted on seeing Liza and her sisters. I don't know what they said to them but the girls have been crying ever since. They won't talk to me. They've shut themselves in their bedroom and . . .'

'Whatever it is, I'll sort it out, Maisie. You've put our visitors in the drawing room?'

'And taken them tea and cake.'

'Thank you. Tell the children to keep the noise down in the kitchen. They can play in the drawing room after Mrs Llewellyn Jones and Mr Williams have gone. And as soon Rachel and Eddie have finished their tea send them in to me please.'

'Even if Mrs Llewellyn Jones is still with you?'

'Even if the king and queen decide to join us. They are my children and I want to spend every minute I can with them.' Bethan gave her a reassuring smile as she crossed the hall. For all of her housekeeper's domestic capabilities she couldn't help thinking of her as a young girl, although they had been in the same class in primary school.

Steeling herself for a dose of Mrs Llewellyn Jones's imperious superiority, she opened the door and walked into the spacious drawing room that her husband, Andrew, had spent a great deal of time, money and care in furnishing when they had moved into the house. Before taking in evacuees she had packed his beloved blond wood, art deco furniture and ornaments into the stables. Now, the wallpaper and paintwork were as shabby as the second-hand pieces she had acquired to replace them. Despite Maisie and Liza Clark's eagle-eyed supervision, six evacuee children plus her own two, and Maisie's little girl had wreaked havoc, not only on the drawing room, but the entire house.

'Mrs Llewellyn Jones, this is an unexpected visit.' Bethan glanced at the tray Maisie had set out with an embroidered linen tray cloth, the best china and a plate of home-made dripping cakes. She hoped Maisie hadn't been over-generous. Rationing and wartime shortages meant there were never enough cakes and biscuits for the children, whereas Mr Llewellyn Jones's position as bank manager brought him into contact with enough black-marketeers to ensure that neither his wife nor his daughter went short of luxuries.

'Bethan.' Mrs Llewellyn Jones inclined her double chin but made no attempt to leave the battered but comfortable chair she'd sunk her bulk into. Rhodri Williams compensated for her lack of courtesy by leaving his seat and offering his hand.

'I believe you know Mr Williams?' Mrs Llewellyn Jones crumbled the cake on her plate with pudgy, ber-inged fingers.

'We're old acquaintances.' Bethan shook his hand. 'How is your wife?'

'Fine, thanks to you and Nurse Evans, Nurse John. You did a magnificent job of caring for her after that nasty fall. She still can't walk without a stick, but she is moving a lot easier.'

'And she'll continue to mend as long as she doesn't go dusting the tops of any more blackout curtains.'

'The trouble with blackout material is that it shows every speck of grey dust and spider's web.' Mrs

Llewellyn Jones stared pointedly at the curtains draped around the rails of the twin bay windows.

'Doesn't it?' Bethan agreed, straining to keep her voice even.

'And my maid never thinks of cleaning anything until I prompt her. I have to remind her to do even the most basic, routine housework. It's been impossible to find, or keep, good staff since the beginning of the war.'

The hinges squeaked as the door opened and Bethan's two children peeped into the room, three-year-old Rachel leading twenty-one-month-old Eddie by the hand. Managing to ignore Mrs Llewellyn Jones's presence for a moment, Bethan smiled broadly and opened her arms. Neither child needed further encouragement. They rushed in, Eddie climbing straight on to her lap, Rachel standing at her knee, eyeing the visitors shyly from beneath a thick fringe of straight, dark auburn hair.

'Say hello to Mrs Llewellyn Jones and Mr Williams.'

Rachel managed a shy 'How do you do?' but Eddie buried his head in her cardigan.

'I hope you don't mind, but as I'm on duty most days and some nights, I try to spend every minute I have at home with my children.'

'I don't know how you manage, working the hours you do.' Mr Williams leaned forward and tickled Rachel beneath her chin, driving her even closer to Bethan. 'My wife told me you're on the go from early morning until late at night. Then you're on call – '

'Bethan has plenty of help,' Mrs Llewellyn Jones cut in abruptly. 'And despite labour shortages, no mother of young children has to work.'

Bethan took a deep breath. Mrs Llewellyn Jones had made her opinion of working mothers known on numerous occasions, and generally in front of Andrew's already disapproving mother.

'Surely you haven't come to billet any more evacuees on me, Mr Williams?' she asked in the hope of bringing the unheralded visit to a speedy conclusion.

'Not evacuees.' Pressing his fingertips together he stared at the ceiling as he struggled to sort classified from unclassified information in his mind. Mrs Llewellyn Jones seized the opportunity to take over the conversation.

'We're here to lighten your load of the Clark girls.'

'We'd find it difficult to run the house without Liza's help.'

'She has three younger sisters who must make more work than she can possibly do.'

'They are no trouble.' Bethan helped Rachel up on to her knee next to Eddie. If she had been talking to almost anyone else she might have added, 'unlike the boys'. The three small cockneys were in constant trouble either with the school, or the neighbouring farmers.

'Their father has been killed. In North Africa. We received the telegram yesterday morning.'

'And you haven't come to tell them until now?'

'Time was hardly of the essence. Besides, arrangements had to be made, and I have been extremely busy with other matters.'

Bethan gritted her teeth at the arrogant assumption that no one's time, business or feelings were more important than Mrs Llewellyn Jones's own.

'I don't know if you're aware that the army ceases to pay dependants' allowance from the date of death, which in this particular case was fourteen days ago. So I am legally obliged to inform you that you will have to forfeit your next payment for the girls, and you will receive nothing to cover expenses incurred during the last fortnight. You can of course appeal – '

'Where are you taking them?' Bethan interrupted.

'The homes. I've arranged immediate admittance. It wasn't easy. Between munition factory accidents and service losses there are more orphans in the town than there've ever been. Strictly speaking the Clarks are the responsibility of Lambeth Council, not Pontypridd, but we can hardly send them back there. It will be a different matter once the war is over.' She removed a file from her bag. Opening it, she shuffled through the papers it contained. 'Now let me see, Liza, the oldest is nearly seventeen. A girl of her background should have been put into service years ago. You say she is useful around the house?'

'I couldn't manage without her.'

'She will have to go to the workhouse,' Mrs Llewellyn Jones declared officiously, 'but given your recommendation and the shortage of domestics I doubt she'll be there long. I could probably find a place for her myself.'

'She wants to be a nurse.'

'A laudable ambition, but hardly a feasible one for the daughter of an East End docker. I see there's a fourteen-year-old too.'

'Who has already completed her matriculation certificate. She will be leaving school at Christmas.'

'I see no reason for her to remain there if she has already sat her examinations. She will go to Church Village Homes, but again, hopefully not for long. These days more and more households are prepared to put in the effort required to train young girls. I can't overemphasise the shortage of domestics, but then you must be aware of that, having to take an unmarried mother.' She frowned as she turned back to the file. 'That leaves a girl of eleven who will also go to Church Village and a nine-year-old for Maesycoed Homes.'

'I think given the circumstances we could bend the rules and send them to the same home, Mrs Llewellyn Jones, don't you?' Mr Williams ventured timorously.

'Bend the rules for one and you find yourself having to do it for all, Mr Williams. The regulations on age are quite specific. Infants from six weeks to three years to be housed in J ward in the workhouse, three to ten years, Maesycoed Orphanage, ten to sixteen years, Church Village Homes and sixteen plus, back to the workhouse.'

'But Church Village is miles from Maesycoed. They'd never see one another, or the oldest in the workhouse.

They lost their mother in the blitz, and now their father has made the supreme sacrifice.'

'As have the fathers of many other children. Several of whom have siblings in institutions other than the one they are accommodated in.'

'Have you already told the girls that their father has been killed?' Bethan asked suddenly.

'Of course, as soon as we came in. We wanted them packed and ready to move into the homes.'

'There's no need for them to go anywhere at this hour.'

'But you're no longer getting paid to keep them. You're out of pocket as it is.'

'I'm more concerned about the girls than my pocket.'

'The sensible housewife puts practical considerations first in a time of national emergency. You have more than enough to do with full-time nursing, the other evacuees, your own children, and worry over poor Andrew. Every time I think of a fine doctor like him being held prisoner by those barbarians I want to go over there and tackle Adolf Hitler myself.'

'At least he's alive.'

'I'm glad you can take comfort in that thought. His poor mother is suffering dreadfully. I doubt she's had a night's sleep since Dunkirk.'

Setting Rachel down, Bethan lifted Eddie in her arms and rose to her feet. Exhausted after a long, hard day, she couldn't trust herself to keep her temper if she remained in the same room as Mrs Llewellyn Jones a moment longer. 'I'm sure the parish can have no objection to my keeping the girls for the time being. After all they've been with me for two years.'

'But you'll receive no payment.'

'They are welcome to stay as my guests until something better than the workhouse and orphanage can be arranged.'

'I have to warn you that the parish won't even cover your expenses.'

'I wouldn't expect it to.'

'You don't understand. It's not just a question of the girls, we need the accommodation.'

'For more evacuees?' Bethan glanced at Mr Williams who seemed to be engaged in trying to swallow his Adam's apple.

'Adult personnel,' Mrs Llewellyn Jones answered evasively.

'Munition workers?' Bethan pressed, giving Rachel's hand a reassuring squeeze. The frown on her daughter's face grew more pronounced every time Mrs Llewellyn Jones opened her mouth.

Mr Williams cleared his throat, but still no words came.

'I have a right to know who you intend to billet in my home.'

'Military personnel,' Mrs Llewellyn Jones said curtly.

'How many?'

'We're not sure.'

'You must have some idea.'

'Possibly three, maybe five.'

'The Clark girls share one bedroom. Surely you don't expect five adults to move into one room?'

'Mrs John mentioned that Andrew never got around to furnishing the top floor of this house. There has to be at least five rooms up there. With accommodation at such a premium in the town, it seems incredibly selfish of you not to put them to good use.'

Furious with her mother-in-law for discussing her domestic arrangements, Bethan struggled to keep her temper. She dare not give free rein to her thoughts. Mrs Llewellyn Jones wielded considerable power in the town, especially over evacuees like the Clark girls. 'Then if it is just the top floor you wish to requisition, you won't need the girls' room.'

Mr Williams couldn't believe what he was hearing. In three years of war he had never seen anyone, man or woman, dare to question Mrs Llewellyn Jones's authority or judgement.

'But there is just the one bathroom,' she replied testily. 'You're twelve in the house already.'

'There is an outside ty bach, and we have enough washstands and china to furnish all the children's bedrooms.'

'It sounds far from satisfactory to me.'

'Mend and make do, Mrs Llewellyn Jones. Isn't that what we've all been told?' Bethan's face muscles were aching from the strain of smiling.

Mrs Llewellyn Jones set down her plate, cup and saucer and rose majestically to her feet. 'We'll need to inspect the top floor and see what's needed in the way of furniture and fittings.'

'All you'll find are bare walls and floorboards. I closed off the rooms when Andrew left and haven't opened them since. Maisie?'

Sleeves rolled above water-reddened arms, the house-keeper appeared in the doorway.

'Show Mrs Llewellyn Jones and Mr Williams the top floor of the house, will you please?' She turned to Mr Williams. 'I hope you will excuse me for not accompanying you, but I'd like to talk to Liza and her sisters.'

'Shall I send a car for them tomorrow?' Unsure what, if any, decisions had been made regarding the future of the Clark girls, he looked from Bethan to Mrs Llewellyn Jones.

'I'll telephone you in the next few days.' Bethan gave him a warm smile before nodding to Mrs Llewellyn Jones. 'If you need anything, just ask Maisie. Goodbye.'

'Liza's crying,' Rachel said in a small voice as the sound of sobbing echoed down into the hall.

Bethan shifted Eddie higher into her arms as they climbed the stairs. 'Let's see if we can make her stop, shall we, poppet?' She knocked on the door of the girls' bedroom before walking in. All four were huddled together on the double bed the three youngest shared. The cheap cardboard suitcase they had brought with them lay open on Liza's bed, the contents of their meagre wardrobes strewn around it.

'I know about your father,' Bethan said softly. 'I'm so very sorry.'

'He promised that we'd all go home after the war. That he'd get his old job back on the docks, rent another house, and furnish it just like the old one. And now we've got no one. We've got to go to the workhouse . . .' Liza faltered as her younger sisters began to cry again. Bethan looked at them and realised they were too overwrought to discuss anything sensibly.

'Liza?' she beckoned to the older girl.

Fighting back tears, Liza followed her into the corridor.

'We have to talk. Can you help me bath Rachel and Eddie, please?'

'Yes, Mrs John.' Squaring her thin shoulders, Liza followed her into the bathroom. She put in the plug and turned on the taps as Bethan peeled Eddie's clothes from his small, plump body.

'I am really sorry about your father, Liza, but right now we have to be practical and sort out your future.'

'Yes, Mrs John,' Liza answered mechanically as she tested the bath water.

'You wanted to be a nurse? Well, I might be able to help you get a position as a nurse's assistant in the Graig Hospital until you are old enough to begin training. That way you can earn some money while gaining useful experience.'

'Would I earn enough to pay for my sisters' lodge?' she asked eagerly.

'No, but you'd earn enough for your own. I warn you, it will be long hours and hard work.'

'I can't leave the others. I promised Dad I'd take care of them, no matter what . . .' Her protestation ended in another flood of tears.

Helping Rachel pull her vest over her head, Bethan double-checked the water temperature before lowering first Eddie, then Rachel into the bath.

Liza struggled to regain control of herself. ' . . . when Ma was killed I thought I'd never be able to keep us together, then you took us in and I hoped we'd be all right until the end of the war. But that woman said that now Dad's gone you won't get a penny . . .'

'I'll do whatever I can to stop you from going into the workhouse, Liza, but keeping you together might be a bit of a tall order. Now that Mary's got her certificate she can leave school. Mrs Raschenko was telling me only yesterday that she was looking for someone to live in and help her with the baby and the shop. Supposing I recommend Mary for the job?'

'Mrs Raschenko's nice. She'd see Mary all right. And we'd be able to visit her, wouldn't we?' Liza's smile reminded Bethan of a rainbow after a storm.

'Whenever you have time, and she could spend every Sunday here.'

'That wouldn't be like getting separated. But what about Polly and Nell? It will be years and years before they can work.'

'Three years and five years isn't years and years. Supposing we carry on as we are for the time being?'

'They can stay here?'

'With two of you working and keeping yourselves, it won't be that much of a drain.'

'We could chip in from our wages.'

'Wait and see how much you and Mary earn before giving any of it away. Besides, Polly is almost as good at housework as you and Mary, and Nell is learning fast. I know it won't be like having you here full time to help Maisie, because Polly will be in school, but when Rachel goes into the babies' class at Christmas, there'll only be Eddie at home so there won't be so much to do.' The more Bethan thought about it, the more she realised she couldn't expect Maisie to cope on her own. Not if Mrs Llewellyn Jones had her way and billeted military personnel on her as well. But if extra help was needed in the house, it was her problem, not Liza's.

'So none of us will have to go into the homes?' Liza

crouched beside the bath and soaped Eddie who was splashing water into Rachel's face.

'No, Liza,' Bethan said firmly. 'That never was an option.'

'But that woman . . .'

' . . . doesn't run my home or your lives.' Bethan dabbed at Rachel's face with a towel. 'I can manage here. Why don't you go and see what your sisters think of our plans?'

Chapter Two

A S FAR BACK as she could remember Bethan had hated the transition from the long, warm, sunlit days of summer to the gloomy mornings and evenings and uncertain weather of autumn; and she had liked the change even less since the imposition of blackout regulations. Rising in darkness, she dressed herself and Eddie by lamplight and was checking that Rachel had fastened the buttons on her pinafore dress correctly when she heard wheels crunching over the gravel drive below her bedroom window. Switching off the light, she pushed aside the curtain just as an enormous, canvas-sided truck backed in close to the house.

'Mrs John?'

'I see it, Maisie,' she called back, wondering if this unexpected arrival was Mrs Llewellyn Jones's revenge for her insistence on keeping the Clark girls. Someone knocked on the front door, but refusing to hurry, she helped Rachel to negotiate the stairs while carrying Eddie on her arm.

Liza opened the door before she got there.

'Ma'am.' A redheaded boy who looked as though he should have had a school satchel instead of a gun slung over his shoulder, removed his cap.

'Can I help you?' she asked, as Liza stepped aside.

'Sorry to break in on you this early in the morning, ma'am. I'm Corporal Duval, Maurice Duval,' he drawled in a lethargic voice that sounded as though it would take him a full day to complete a sentence. 'We've come to move the colonel's things in.'

'Here?'

He pulled a paper from his pocket. 'This is Ty Twyfe?'

'I've never heard it pronounced quite that way before.'

'Sorry, ma'am, I didn't mean to insult your house, but according to this you have five rooms set aside for the use of American military personnel?' He glanced past her into the hall.

'On the top floor.'

'They said they were empty?'

'They are.'

'We have a truckload of supplies and furniture.'

'It might be easier if you carry the smaller items up the back staircase. There's a door that opens directly on to it at the side of the house. You have help?'

'Yes, ma'am, there's three of us.'

'I'll show them the way,' Liza volunteered.

'How many of you are moving in?' Bethan asked as Liza exchanged her slippers for her boots.

'Only four that I know of, ma'am. The colonel, his cook/batman, his aide, and me. I'm his driver.'

'So you'll be living here?'

'Yes, ma'am.' The boy grinned at Liza, who responded with a shy smile of her own.

Bethan's heart sank as Liza closed the front door behind them. It had been hard enough to assume responsibility for the girls in a town denuded of young men. Almost any presentable man, in or out of uniform, was enough to turn most married as well as single women's heads. She dreaded to think what an influx of Americans would do to Liza, Maisie – and Pontypridd.

'Oh my God, will you look at what's just stepped into station yard? I think I'm going to die!' Turning from the counter of Ronconi's cafe, Judy Crofter gazed, mesmerised by the sight of two men walking past the deserted taxi rank.

Tina Powell pushed a couple of cups of tea across the counter before glancing out of the window. 'Have you never seen a man before?'

'Not one who looks like either of those two.'

'Come on, Tina. You've got to admit they're a man-famished girl's dream come true,' Jenny Powell who worked with Judy in munitions chipped in from the corner table.

'They're not bad, but from what I can see, mostly uniform. I wonder where they got ones that look that good.'

'Or shoulders that broad. That fair one looks like a young Leslie Howard.' Jenny craned her neck in an attempt to see around the cocoa advertisement that blocked out most of the window. 'Prepare to die, Judy. They're coming this way.'

Handing Jenny her tea, Judy left hers on the counter and pulled up a stool just as the door opened.

'Good morning, ma'am.' Kurt Schaffer tipped his hat to Tina, before looking to Jenny and Judy. 'Ma'am. Ma'am.'

They had heard the accent before, but only in the pictures.

'You're American?' Jenny stared him in the eye as she carried her tea to the counter and climbed on to a stool.

'Guilty.' He beamed at her as he studied her slim figure and cool, blonde features. The colonel's directive was already proving difficult to obey. 'Lieutenant Kurt Schaffer, US Army at your service.'

'Isn't that a German name?' Judy demanded suspiciously, scanning the KEEP MUM, SHE'S NOT SO DUMB poster Tina had pasted on the kitchen door. Given the dearth of men in Pontypridd, it didn't take much imagination to picture the handsome American as the blonde siren, and replace the crowd of infatuated servicemen with admiring women.

'My German grandfather emigrated to the States in 1890. I hope that's far back enough for you to think of me as one of the good guys.'

'Just about. What can I get you?' Tina enquired brusquely.

'From where I'm standing I can think of a whole lot of things, ma'am.'

'Can you now?' Fully aware of the effect she was

21

having on him, Jenny deliberately hitched her skirt higher as she crossed her legs.

'Isn't your friend coming in?' Judy asked, watching the second officer, who was hovering outside the shop.

'Tea, coffee, cocoa?' Tina interrupted, giving Jenny a hard look.

'At the moment I'd settle for information, ma'am. Can you point us in the direction of the Council Offices? I was there yesterday afternoon, but we came in from the other end of town this morning and I seem to have lost my bearings. I tried asking in the train station, but they weren't at all helpful.'

'Probably thought you were spies.' Jenny smiled seductively.

'Are you looking for anyone in particular?' Tina picked up Jenny and Judy's cups, wiped the counter beneath them, and replaced them closer to the edge, but neither girl took the hint and moved to a table.

'The billeting officer, Mr Williams, and a – ' he reached into the top pocket of his shirt and pulled out a slip of paper – 'Mrs Llewellyn Jones? I can never remember which order to put those names.'

Taking no chances, Tina gave clear and precise instructions that would lead directly to the police station. She glared at Judy and Jenny, daring them to tell him otherwise as he opened the door.

'The billeting officer?' Jenny raised her eyebrows as she lifted her cup. 'Does that mean Americans are moving into Pontypridd?'

He pointed to the poster behind her. 'You guys have been in this war longer than us. What's that saying you have? "Careless talk costs lives." '

'Is that a yes?' Judy called after him as he stepped outside.

He flashed another smile. 'That's a maybe, or a maybe not, ma'am.'

'Imagine a whole regiment like him in Ponty.' Judy went to the window so she could watch them walk down the street.

'I can imagine what the thought might do to the men at the front,' Tina commented tartly.

'Not all the women in Ponty are married or spoken for, Tina.' Judy started guiltily when she saw Jenny walk back to the table. Jenny's husband, Eddie Powell, had been killed at Dunkirk, but because Jenny never mentioned him, Judy generally forgot that he had ever existed until embarrassing occasions, like now.

'It's about time we had some fun in this town.' Jenny sat down and stirred her tea.

'That depends on your definition of fun.' Picking up an enamel bowl full of dirty dishes Tina pushed backwards through the swing door that led into the kitchen. Dumping the bowl in the stone sink she shouted to the cook to stop reading the paper and start washing.

She hesitated for a fraction of a second before walking back out into the cafe. Just long enough to open the gold locket that hung around her neck and look at the smiling image of her husband, William. If a regiment had to be billeted in Pontypridd, why couldn't the powers that be have chosen a Welsh one?

'Why they had to inflict a regiment of Americans on a backwater like Pontypridd, or billet them in a household of women and children like yours, is beyond me,' Dr John, Bethan's father-in-law grumbled as she restocked her medical bag in the surgery.

'Because they're fighting on our side?' she suggested mildly, taking two crepe bandages out of a box before replacing it in the cupboard.

He gave her a wry smile. Relations between them had thawed into mutual respect since she had answered his plea to return to work after Eddie's birth. The shortage of qualified and experienced nurses was acute, not only in the town but in the country, and her presence had considerably reduced the workload of the second district nurse and the only two doctors left in Pontypridd: himself and the elderly Dr Evans who was well past retirement age.

'They should house them in barracks. With most of our men in North Africa or the East there must be hundreds of empty camps.'

'Obviously not enough.'

'They'll play havoc with the health of the women in the town,' he prophesied grimly. 'Be warned, two months from now we'll be in the throes of an epidemic of venereal disease and cleaning up after double the number of botched, backstreet abortions.'

'I hope not.'

'It's inevitable. Damned war. That case you referred from Station Terrace died last night.'

'Oh, no!' She dropped the box of dry dressings she'd been opening. 'She had four children . . .'

'And was three months pregnant with a husband who hadn't been home in a year.'

'What did you put on the death certificate?'

'Septicaemia. But the neighbours know the truth. I think she must have asked half the women in the town for advice before going to the butcher who finished her off. I spoke to the sergeant last night. The police haven't a clue who's doing it. That makes nine cases this year.'

'What's happening to her children?'

'Her sister's taken them in, but she has five of her own so we know how long that will last. I hate this war.'

'Don't we all.' She snapped her bag shut.

'Heard from Andrew?'

'Not for two weeks, but you know what prisoner-of-war mail is like.'

'Unfortunately.' He looked up at her as she went to the door. 'We will win now that the Americans are finally here.'

'Two minutes ago you were complaining about them.'

'Only because they want to fight from Pontypridd instead of the continent.' He flicked through the pile of paperwork on his desk. 'The sooner the blighters get into Germany, free the prisoners and send them home, the sooner Andrew can shoulder some of this load. But they'd better hurry up. I'm not sure how much longer I can carry on working at this pace.'

'The only question I've got, Bethan, is when can Mary start?' Alma set a couple of enamel mugs on the scrub-down table in the kitchen at the back of her cooked meats and pie shop, and reached for the teapot.

'Tomorrow soon enough for you?'

'Wonderful. She'll need a taxi to bring down her things. Tell her to book it. I'll pay the driver when she gets here.'

'I'll drop her off before I start work, and as for things, a carrier bag will hold all her possessions with room to spare.'

'You're not the only one to have had a visit from Mrs Llewellyn Jones. She came round here this morning.'

'Don't tell me she wanted to billet Americans on you too?'

'She tried, but I wouldn't have it. You know, she actually had the gall to suggest that a war widow, like me, should welcome the opportunity to have an American officer living in my home. I told her absolutely not, and reminded her that Charlie's posted missing, not killed.' She pushed the sugar bowl towards Bethan.

The *Presumed dead* that had been on the telegram still burned in Bethan's mind. She knew it was useless to remind Alma that Charlie had been missing for over fourteen months. When a letter from the War Office had arrived the regulation three months to the day after the first telegram, to inform Alma that Charlie had been declared officially dead and she could wind up his affairs, she had burned it, and continued to talk about him and make plans for their future as though he was about to walk through the door at any moment.

'So, Mrs Llewellyn Jones went away disappointed for the second time in two days,' she murmured, thinking of the argument she'd had with her over the Clark girls.

'As disappointed as I could make her. Where does that woman get her cheek from? She told me that with a kitchen this size in the shop I didn't need an upstairs living room or kitchen and it was my patriotic duty to turn them into bedrooms, then if you please, I could house *two* Americans. I told her all my rooms were earmarked – my living room for sitting in after a hard day's work, one bedroom for the girl I intended to hire, the other for Theo and me, and my kitchen was staying exactly as it was.' Alma looked to the playpen she'd set up in the corner next to the door that led into the shop, where Theodore, her nine-month-old son, a miniature version of Charlie, right down to his white-blond hair and deep blue eyes, was sitting contently playing with a wooden spoon and battered baking tin.

'I'm surprised she didn't suggest that the three of you should share.'

'She did. She even hinted that live-in help would prove to be an ideal chaperon for me and these officers, and silence tongues before they wagged, but I pointed out that if Charlie is being held prisoner by the Germans, he will need peace, quiet and his own bedroom to rest in when he's released.'

'I wish I'd thought of that one.'

'She has only billeted this colonel on you, hasn't she?'

'And his aide, his cook and his driver.'

'Bethan, how could you! You're too soft for your own good. Seven evacuees if you include Lisa, Maisie's daughter and now four Yanks.'

'It's Andrew's fault for buying a house that size.'

'It's yours for not using the word "no" more often.'

'It's difficult, Mrs Llewellyn Jones is Andrew's mother's best friend.'

'That's no excuse for allowing her to treat your house like a hostel for every waif and stray who wanders into the town.'

'You're probably right.' Bethan glanced at the clock. 'What do you want me to tell Mary about the job?'

'That it's hard work. She'll start at six every morning and probably won't stop or get much in the way of a break until the shop closes at six at night. Sunday and one half-day off a week. I'll pay her a pound a week while she's on a two-week trial, and put it up to thirty shillings if she can cope, but warn her that I'm looking for a general worker who could find herself cleaning the flat one day, working in the shop the next, and looking after the baby once I'm satisfied he's happy with her.'

'I think you'll find her only too glad to do anything that will enable her to stay close to her sisters.'

'You're determined to keep the others?'

'Yes. I saw the matron in the Central Homes before I came here. She's agreed to take Liza on as a ward maid in maternity, so there's really only the two younger ones. And I've already made an appointment to see the Parish Guardians to ask if they can stay with me, at least until the end of the war.'

'I'd be happy to pay half their keep.'

'I can manage.'

'I know you can, but if we take joint responsibility for them, then it's the two of us against the old bag. Given the respectability of Andrew's surname and the money the shops are bringing in, the parish can hardly object to our keeping the Clark girls, no matter what Mrs Llewellyn Jones says. We could even go for formal adoption.'

'The war won't last for ever and things are bound to change when the men come home. They may not be happy at us taking on a family of orphaned girls.'

'I know Charlie won't mind. Will Andrew?'

'As I've already gone ahead and done it, he's got little choice in the matter.'

'You can always blame it on Mrs Llewellyn Jones. After all, she billeted the Clark girls on you in the first place.' Alma reached for the teapot. 'Want a refill?'

'Much as I'd like to, if I don't start my rounds I won't finish before midnight.' Bethan rose from her chair. 'See you on Sunday?'

'Unless I get a better offer.'

'From an American?' Bethan joked.

Alma looked to her son again. 'A homecoming,' she

said softly, so softly Bethan couldn't be quite sure she'd heard her correctly.

'Thank you for sending me to the police station, ma'am. They were most helpful.' Kurt Schaffer smiled at Tina as he stood before the counter of Ronconi's cafe.

'I thought they would be. What can I get you?'

'Coffee would be good.' Slipping his hand into his pocket he pulled out a notebook. 'I was hoping to find the other ladies here.'

'They work, like everyone else around here.' Tina filled a cup and slammed it down in front of him. 'That'll be sixpence.'

He took half a crown from his pocket and handed it to her.

'Any chance of cream or sugar?'

'Cream exists only in the imagination and memory. You can have milk, but I warn you now, it's household.'

'Powdered?'

'What else?' She poured a little – a very little – into his cup. 'And sugar's rationed. Haven't you heard there's a war on?'

'I could pay extra.'

'I've heard that you Yanks are rich.'

'We're well paid.'

'Overpaid compared to the British Tommy, but money can't buy everything in this country, especially extra rations in this cafe.'

Still hoping to circumvent her hostility he gave up on the sugar and flashed her his most charming smile. 'It's official, we're staying in Pontypridd.'

'Who's we?'

'Me and a few fellow Americans. Colonel Ford thought we should mark our arrival by throwing a party for the natives. A sort of "getting to know you" affair. I was hoping for some friendly advice.'

'You'd be better off asking someone who has time to spare for parties.'

'I was hoping you'd come, ma'am.'

28

'I'll be busy.'

'You don't even know when it is.'

'I run this place.'

'Every night?' He lifted a sceptical eyebrow.

'Every day and night,' she reiterated firmly.

'No time off for good behaviour?'

'If we took time off, Hitler would be here instead of stuck on the other side of the Channel.'

'We've reserved the blue and silver ballroom in the New Inn. Here's the date and time.' Scribbling a note in his book he tore out the page and handed it to her. 'The tickets will be distributed just as soon as we can get them printed. I hope you won't mind me dropping some off here?'

'Suit yourself.'

He made a face as he sipped the coffee. 'We're only trying to lighten the load you British have been toting, ma'am.'

'I would have thought you'd do that best by joining in the fighting.'

'And we'll be doing that the minute we've finished training our troops. See you around, ma'am.'

Tina screwed up the paper he'd left on the counter and tossed it into the bin.

'Didn't you like the tip the Yank left?'

'Ronnie!' She started at the sight of her brother sitting at the corner table behind the door. 'How long have you been there?'

'Long enough to see the hard time you were giving that poor man. They are here to help, you know.'

'What are you doing here at this time of day?'

'They were short-handed in the factory, so I did a twenty-four-hour shift.'

'You look as though you haven't slept in a week.'

'It was a toss-up whether to come in here to eat, or crawl up the hill to bed.' He leaned against the wall and closed his eyes.

'After only a month of married life I would have thought bed would have been a better option.'

Opening one eye, he shot her a warning glance not to press family familiarity too far. 'Diana's opening the new shop in Treforest today. Come on, woman, I'm starving. Less talk more action, what have you got in the way of food?'

'Pie and chips.'

'Alma's pie?'

'Where else would I get pies?'

'I dread to think.'

She shouted the order through the hatch, before rooting in the bread bin. Taking a couple of slices, she scraped a knife over a margarine wrapper, finding just enough to colour the greyish national loaf pale yellow. 'So how's the happy couple?'

'Happy when we're together.'

'Don't try and tell me about separation. You don't even know the meaning of the word.'

Realising there was even more of an edge to Tina's voice than usual, Ronnie changed the subject again. 'What was on the paper you threw in the bin?'

'Nothing much.'

'Do I have to drag it out of you?'

'If you must know, the date and time of a party the Yanks are throwing to impress everyone in the town.'

'You don't want to go?'

'They can keep their party.'

'From what Dai Station's been saying, they've got food and drink we haven't seen since before the war.'

'So?'

'Haven't you heard from Will lately?' he asked perceptively.

'Not a bloody word. And Bethan called in earlier. The Clark girls' father's been killed. He was stationed in North Africa, just like Will.'

'William will be fine, Tina.'

'You keep saying that, but you can't know. No one can.'

'He came back from Dunkirk, didn't he? Believe me, whatever he's landed in, he'll come up smelling of roses.'

'And if he lands in a minefield?'

'Carry on thinking like that and you'll end up crazier than you are now.'

'It makes me mad,' she raged. 'The Yanks walk in, lording it over the whole town, although the closest they've come to fighting is seeing the newsreels in the pictures, and everyone falls over backwards to fawn all over them while the poor sods at the front get forgotten.'

'The Americans might be good for business,' he suggested as the cook came out with his meal.

'What's the use of more customers if I've no food to sell them? For all the good they're doing they might as well have stayed at home. At least then I wouldn't have had to listen to their stupid accents.'

When Bethan walked into her house that evening she found Maisie, Liza and the children crowded into the kitchen singing 'Ten Green Bottles' at the tops of their voices while a stout, balding, middle-aged man with a chef's apron tied over his uniform, poured batter into two frying pans set on the range.

She stood back, looking in from the hall while he flipped pancakes high in the air, occasionally tossing a finished one on to a plate Maurice held out for him. The younger children were all laughing, even Polly and Nell, she noted with relief. And Eddie was so excited by the party atmosphere, he would have fallen out of his high chair if Maisie hadn't been restraining him.

The noise they were making had masked her entrance, so she could continue to watch. When the pile of pancakes had grown high enough to be in danger of toppling over, the chef dredged the topmost one in syrup and sugar, deftly rolled it, slid it on to a plate and handed it to Rachel. As he turned back to start on the next one, he saw her.

'Sergeant Dino Morelli of the US Armed Forces, ma'am.' He tipped his cap. 'Hope you don't mind me taking over your kitchen this way?'

'Looks like I'd be outvoted if I tried.'

'It's a thank-you party for inviting them to live with us,' Rachel chattered, as she carried her plate to the table.

'So I see.' Bethan helped her climb on the bench before turning to Maurice. 'Did you move in all right?'

'Fine, thank you, ma'am. Those are large, airy rooms you have up there. The colonel's right pleased.'

'And you have everything you need?'

'Everything, ma'am. The colonel's upstairs in his office with Lieutenant Rivers. He wanted to pay his respects as soon as you came in. I'd better tell him you're here.'

'I have some paperwork to do.' She looked to Maisie as the corporal left. 'I'll be in the study.'

'I've put your letters on Dr John's desk, Mrs John.'

'Thank you.'

'Can Eddie eat some of my pancake?' Rachel asked.

'After Maisie's tied on his bib.' Slipping off her cape, Bethan lifted Eddie out of his high chair, hugging him close for an instant before setting him next to his sister on the bench.

'Shall I bring them in when they've finished?' Maisie asked, watching Bethan carefully to see if she was angry at the way the Americans had been allowed to commandeer the kitchen.

'When the fun's finished, not before. It's not often they get a chance to enjoy themselves like this.'

Hanging her cape in the hall, she walked into the study and sat at Andrew's desk. There was a pile of letters, one she noted with relief, from Andrew. She laid it on the blotter before opening her bag and taking out her visiting lists. Business first, pleasure later. She knew from experience that Andrew's letters were best left to last thing at night, when she could go straight to bed after reading and answering them.

She was checking the lists against her notes and diary entries when a tap at the door disturbed her.

'Come in.'

She'd expected a crusty army veteran with a grey

32

moustache and receding hairline, not a tall, slim, athletic-looking, fair-haired man in his thirties.

'I'm not sure whether I should call you Mrs or Nurse John?' He held out his hand. 'I'm Colonel David Ford.'

'Mrs will be fine. Pleased to meet you.' She left the desk, shook his hand and sat on the sofa in front of it, indicating the easy chair beside her.

'It was good of you to offer us accommodation. It was an offer?' he enquired, as he sat down.

'Let's just say I had five rooms going to waste up there.'

'I'm sorry if you were press-ganged. I guess people like Mr Williams and Mrs Llewellyn Jones can be overwhelming.'

'Mr Williams?'

'I assumed he'd talked you into it?'

'Not exactly.'

'We'll try to be as little trouble as possible.'

'There are four of you?'

'Myself, my aide, Lieutenant Rivers, my driver Corporal Duval – I think you met him this morning?'

'And Sergeant Morelli now.'

'He'll be doing all our cleaning, washing and cooking so we won't make any extra work for you. I hope you won't mind him occasionally using your kitchen? We'll be supplying our own rations and fuel, but there won't be much for him to do here. We've already set up our own canteen in town and we'll eat as many meals there as possible.'

'There'll still be breakfast and supper.'

'It might help if we work out a schedule. Perhaps there are times when he won't disturb anyone?'

'As you can see,' she indicated her uniform, 'I work, so he will have to talk to my housekeeper.'

'They seem to be doing that already.' Colonel Ford sat back in his chair and gazed at her with incisive, navy-blue eyes. 'If it's all right with you, we'll use the back entrance and staircase.'

'Perfectly.'

'I take it they were once part of the servants' quarters?'

'Not since I've lived here, Colonel Ford.'

'We'll try and stay out of your way as much as possible, but with the kitchen and bathroom on the lower floors I am afraid we won't be totally unobtrusive.'

'I didn't expect you to be.'

'About the bathroom. There is a special fund to adapt and furnish accommodation for the use of army personnel. If you have no objection I could arrange for a plumber to install a second bathroom in the small room above your existing bathroom.'

'Wouldn't that be horribly expensive?'

'Only for the American army. There'll be some disruption for a day or two, but on the plus side we won't be able to take it with us when we go.'

'In that case, how can I refuse?'

'You have quite a family.'

'Only two of the children are mine.'

'Rachel and Edward. We've been introduced.'

She looked up as the door opened. Maisie walked in with a tray.

'I thought you'd like tea, Mrs John.'

Bethan stared in surprise at the biscuits on the plate.

'Sergeant Morelli made some chocolate cookies for the children. These were left over.'

'Just make sure the children don't eat too much rich food, Maisie,' Bethan warned sternly, feeling that she was rapidly losing control of her household. 'They're not used to sweet things.'

'They only had one each, Mrs John.'

'And pancakes?' Bethan reminded as Maisie retreated.

'You're strict with your children,' the colonel observed as Maisie closed the door.

'Routine and discipline are essential in an extended family of this size, but I wouldn't want to bore a soldier about either of those things.'

'From what I've seen, you could teach the average GI

34

something about both.' He glanced at the photograph on the desk. 'Your husband?'

'Yes.'

'He's on active service?'

'He was captured at Dunkirk.'

'That means he's been a prisoner for . . .'

' . . . two years and five months.'

'I'm sorry. You must miss him.'

'I'm too busy, Colonel Ford,' she interposed briskly, negating any intended sympathy.

'I can see that I'm taking up your time.'

'I can spare a few moments, especially as Maisie has gone to the trouble of making tea. Would you like a cup and one of your biscuits?'

'Just tea please.'

'Milk and sugar?'

'Milk, thank you.'

She poured out two cups and handed him his. 'Colonel, as you're going to live here, presumably for some time . . .'

'Until we finish training our troops,' he interrupted, giving her no hint as to how long that might take.

'Perhaps we should lay down a few rules to ensure that all our lives run smoothly.'

'Such as?'

'I'm responsible for Maisie and Liza as well as the children. Given the shortage of men in Pontypridd it would be very easy for your staff to turn their heads.'

'I have already given my officers a lecture on respecting the young ladies of the town. It will be passed down to the men.'

'I'm glad to hear it.'

'As for my immediate staff, Sergeant Morelli is forty: he's a volunteer and wanted to ensure that he'd be in this war to the bitter end. He's old enough to be Maisie and Liza's father so I don't think you need fear he'll start chasing them.'

'There's still Maurice.'

'An extremely naive twenty-year-old.'

35

'I hope you'll ensure he stays that way.'

'I can't promise that. I drove past station yard last night. There seemed to be an extraordinarily large number of ladies waiting to meet the trains.'

'Every town in Britain has its station yard, Colonel Ford. It's Maisie and Liza I'm concerned about, not the ladies waiting to meet the trains.'

'Any problems, Mrs John, please feel free to discuss them with me.'

'Thank you.'

'And if you don't want my staff mixing with the girls or the children . . .'

'I didn't say that.'

He looked into her eyes as he set down his cup and rose to his feet. 'We're strangers, far from home in an alien land, Mrs John. And your kindness is greatly appreciated.'

Chapter Three

FOR THE FIRST time since they had started work in the munitions factory Jenny Powell and Judy Crofter didn't call in at either Ronconi's cafe or the pub before going home. Turning under the railway bridge, they began the long haul up the Graig hill halting outside Jenny's corner shop at the top of Factory Lane.

'Pick you up here at eight?' Judy asked, as Jenny opened the door of the shop she had entrusted to an assistant's care for the duration.

'That gives me enough time to turn from a dust-coated frog into a princess.' Jenny looked at her sister-in-law, Jane. 'Coming with us?'

'Not tonight, thanks.'

'Your Haydn wouldn't give up the chance to have a good time,' Judy taunted. Jane's husband, Haydn Powell, was one of the leading lights of ENSA and the newspapers were constantly printing 'morale boosting' photographs of him in uniform with his arms wrapped around scantily clad chorus girls.

'I'm looking forward to putting Anne to bed. She's growing up so fast I feel I'm missing out on her childhood.'

'Babies!' Judy wrinkled her nose in disgust. 'I learned all I ever want to know about them from my younger brothers. Thank God they're in the army now. There's nothing like a kid hanging round your neck to cramp your style. You won't catch me having any.'

'I'll talk to you when you're married. See you tomorrow, Jenny.'

'See you,' Jenny called after them as she walked inside. Pushing past the crowd of women and children waiting to be served, she murmured a brief hello before diving through the door that led to her private quarters, closing it quickly lest she be roped in to help out. Running up the stairs she stopped and sniffed the air.

'The lady of the house returns.'

'I thought I could smell paint.'

Alexander Forbes, a former university lecturer, museum curator and conscientious objector who'd been conscripted to work in the pits, was standing in her living room dressed in a pair of khaki overalls, a brush in one hand, a pot of paint in the other.

'You said you wanted to brighten the place up.'

'How did you get in?' Kicking off her shoes, she tossed her coat over the banisters.

'I told Freda you'd asked me to decorate the living room. She took quite a bit of convincing.'

'I've given her strict instructions not to let anyone up here when I'm at work.'

'Blame me, not her. I can be very persuasive.'

'Not that I've noticed. Why aren't you working?'

'Even "bloody conchies" get a day off now and again.' Setting the tin on the dustsheet he'd laid over the lino and square of carpet, he stamped on the lid.

'I thought paint was rarer than bananas these days.' Jenny stepped tentatively forward, checking the cloth around her feet for paint splotches before examining the walls.

'I asked Ronnie Ronconi. He knew a man . . .'

'Ronnie always knows a man. If you're not careful you'll find yourself standing in the dock alongside him charged with black-marketeering.' She glanced back at him as she walked around the room. He'd gone to a lot of trouble, and done a first-class job of covering the walls. Suddenly aware that she hadn't even thanked him, she added, 'You've certainly brightened the place up. Wherever did you get a light shade of green like this?'

'If you must know it's institution paint mixed with white.'

'It's worked. I can't see a trace of the pattern on the wallpaper.'

'You did say you were tired of overblown roses.' He eyed her warily, uncertain whether to expect gratitude or an outburst for invading her privacy. He adored Jenny, every delectable, beautiful inch of her body and every erratic, unpredictable facet of her sharp, intelligent mind, but he wasn't too besotted to realise that he loved her far more than she did him.

'I was,' she answered carelessly. 'And now, I suppose you'll expect me to show some appreciation?'

'That would be nice.'

Unpinning her hat, she threw it on to the sideboard before walking through to the kitchen. Wiping his hands on his overalls, Alexander followed.

'Finished for the day?' she asked as he lifted an empty jam jar from the windowsill and filled it with turpentine.

'I thought I'd finished the job.'

'What about the skirting boards and doors?'

'The stain's sound enough, it just needs a good clean.'

'You volunteering?' She filled the kettle and lit the gas.

'I could do it on my next day off.' Waiting until she moved away from the sink he pulled a bar of sugar soap from his pocket and began scrubbing his hands under the cold tap. 'I don't suppose . . .'

'What?'

'Never mind.'

'Alexander Forbes, you can be the most infuriating man.'

'I wondered if my next day off might coincide with yours?'

'I doubt it.'

'If you tell me when it is, I could swap shifts.' Checking his hands to make sure they were clean, he dried them on a rag he'd tucked into his pocket. 'I didn't just bring paint with me this morning. I also managed to get a bottle of whisky. Real whisky.' He closed his hands around her waist.

'You'll get me all messy.'

'I've cleaned up.' Bending his head, he brushed his

39

lips over the top of her head. 'How about that thank-you?'

She glanced at her wristwatch. 'I'm meeting Judy in two hours.'

'That gives us plenty of time.'

'I need to wash and change.'

'Why? You look perfect to me.'

'I'm all sweaty and dusty from the factory.'

'Not so I've noticed.' Slipping his hand beneath her pullover he slid his fingers inside her bust shaper. 'Where are you going?'

'The cafe, or the pub. We haven't decided.'

He curbed his jealousy and the urge to ask if they were meeting anyone. His relationship with Jenny was a precarious one. In his blackest moments he saw it as a reversal of the philandering cad, virginal maiden fable so beloved of Victorian melodrama; but he could hardly cast himself as the innocent. He had made love to many women before Pontypridd, the Maritime pit and Jenny had turned his comfortable academic, middle-class life upside down. But in all of his thirty-five years, no woman had touched his heart the way she had.

An independent widow, who was growing more independent every day courtesy of the wages she earned in the munitions factory and the takings of the shop she managed for her sick, absent father, she prided herself on her self-reliance, and didn't hesitate to tell him to go to hell whenever she felt he was intruding into her private life. The one and only time he had mentioned marriage, she had refused to see him for two months. The most miserable months he had spent in Pontypridd.

He nuzzled the back of her neck and fingered her nipples beneath the layers of clothing, touches he knew she found difficult to resist.

'I suppose I could spare you ten minutes,' she muttered as his hand slid downwards beneath the waistband of her skirt.

Recognising the teasing note in her voice he pulled her round to face him.

'Half an hour.' He bent his head to hers and kissed her. It didn't take long to elicit a response. She returned his kiss, but hers held none of the tenderness he'd offered, only harsh, selfish passion.

Reaching out blindly, she turned off the gas.

'No tea for the worker?'

'You can make it afterwards,' she said as she left the kitchen for her bedroom.

Alexander stood at the head of the stairs as she moved towards the bed. Slowly, provocatively, aware that he was watching her through the open doorway, she stripped off her pullover and skirt. Her smile broadened as she looked into his eyes. Unable to resist any longer he stepped towards her. Slipping down the straps on her petticoat he allowed it to slide to the floor. The brush of the silky, sensuous fabric against his hands combined with the warmth of her skin sent his senses reeling. Pulling down her bust shaper he buried his face between her naked breasts.

'God, you're beautiful. You've no idea what you do to me . . .'

'Why do men insist on talking at the most inopportune moments?' Jenny pushed him away from the bed. He watched her peel off her workaday, thick, ugly stockings, suspender belt and artificial silk knickers as he struggled out of his overalls.

'The floor.' She moved towards him, her fingers already busy with the flies on his underpants.

'It will be uncomfortable.'

'Not for me.' Pressing him down on his back she straddled him, running her fingers through the mat of hair on his chest, kissing his ears . . . his eyes . . . his mouth . . .

Conscious of his work-roughened hands, he caressed her lightly, gently, his calloused fingertips barely touching her breasts and thighs. 'Jenny . . .'

Her hands reached downwards, stroking the soft skin around his groin, rousing him to fever pitch. 'More action less words, Alex. I like it that way, remember?'

*

'More potatoes, Lieutenant?' Anthea Llewellyn Jones coyly lowered her eyes as she pushed a dish of steaming mashed potatoes towards Kurt Schaffer.

'I really couldn't eat another thing, but thank you for the offer, Miss Anthea.' He looked at Mrs Llewellyn Jones. 'That was the best home-cooked meal I've eaten since I left the States, ma'am. I can't thank you enough for inviting me into your home.'

'It's our pleasure.' Mrs Llewellyn Jones discreetly elbowed her husband, who was working his way through the thickest slice of roast beef he'd seen in three years of war. He had been less enthusiastic at the thought of sharing his home with an American officer than his wife and daughter, especially when he saw the lavish meal his wife had ordered the cook to prepare. Her faith in his ability to provide extra rations was an embarrassment and, he suspected, a talking point in the town. Seeing her glaring at him in obvious expectation of a contribution to the conversation, he finally laid his knife and fork on his plate, and contemplated the stranger sitting at his table.

'Are you a professional soldier, Lieutenant Schaffer?' he enquired briskly, as though he were interrogating him for a loan.

Feeling suspiciously like a prospective bridegroom, Kurt pushed his chair out from the table in an attempt to distance himself from Anthea.

'I was at West Point, sir. The fourth generation of my family to graduate from the academy.'

'Never heard of it.'

'I believe it to be the equivalent of your Sandhurst, sir.'

'Then you must welcome this war?'

'Hardly, sir.'

'Doesn't it give you professionals a better chance of promotion?'

'I was doing just fine before the war, sir. I was commissioned First Lieutenant less than six months after leaving the academy. Until we entered the war I was stationed in a training camp close to my home town.'

'And where is home, Lieutenant?'

'South Carolina, sir. My family live in Charleston.'

'Your father is in business there?'

'He was retired until the war broke out. He's been recalled.'

'An officer like yourself?'

'A general, sir.' Kurt enjoyed the effect the revelation had on the Llewellyn Joneses.

'Do you have any brothers serving?'

'I am an only child, sir.'

Mr Llewellyn Jones nodded sagely. The man might be an American, but his manners were civilised, if effusive, and in all his years in the bank he'd never heard of a poor general, American or otherwise. Anthea was a splendid girl, but at twenty-nine, she had yet to receive her first marriage proposal.

Both he and his wife had assumed that Anthea would marry her childhood playmate, Andrew John. Indeed both families had expected the marriage to take place after Andrew completed his degree in London and returned to practise medicine in Pontypridd, but much to his own and Andrew's father's exasperation, the boy had insisted on marrying Bethan Powell, a nurse and nobody from the wrong side of town, and the daughter of a miner, to boot.

Boys like Andrew were scarce on the ground in Pontypridd. There were a few, a very few, others he might have considered suitable; young men destined to join their fathers in family concerns: solicitors – dentists – businessmen – but unfortunately none had presented himself as a suitor. An American officer would be a compromise, but better a compromise than the humiliation of spinsterhood and a dependent old age like his maiden aunt's.

He studied Schaffer as the maid cleared the remains of the entree. The man was certainly presentable. It might be worth making discreet enquiries as to his bank

43

balance and social standing. He was debating the best way to go about it, when his wife interrupted.

'We have rhubarb crumble for dessert, with fresh cream.'

'We were warned that food was in short supply in Britain, ma'am.' Kurt leaned back so the maid could place his helping on the table in front of him. 'I hope you haven't gone to any trouble on my account?'

'Don't think we eat like this every day, Lieutenant,' Mr Llewellyn Jones cautioned, as the young girl handed Mrs Llewellyn Jones the cream jug. 'My wife's killed the fatted calf on this occasion.'

'Then I thank you again, ma'am.'

'I just love your accent,' Anthea enthused. 'I could sit and listen to it all day long.'

'I only wish my colonel thought the same way, Miss Anthea. Then I wouldn't have to do any work, just talk.' Kurt shifted uncomfortably on his chair as Anthea's laughter filled the room. While he enjoyed flirtation and the thrill of the chase, he didn't need his colonel's warning to back away from his hostess's daughter. The adoration in her eyes every time she looked at him meant only one thing. She was hungry for a wedding ring. Something he didn't intend to slip on any girl's finger for a long, long time.

When the crumble and cream had been reduced to smears on the plates, Mr Llewellyn Jones took a key from his top pocket, left his seat and lumbered towards the sideboard. 'Brandy and cigars?' he offered expansively as he opened the door of the drinks cabinet.

'Just a small brandy, sir. Thank you.'

'Lieutenant Schaffer is organising a party for the town,' Anthea announced as her father poured modest measures into two goblets.

'A sort of thank-you for putting up with us,' Kurt drawled, as he searched his mind for an excuse to escape from the dining room – and Anthea.

'A party would be a most welcome gesture. Things

have been rather bleak around here since the war started.'

'People have so little to look forward to,' his wife agreed. 'Just sherry for Anthea and myself, dear.'

Mr Llewellyn Jones filled two smaller glasses with sweet sherry and handed them to the maid to pass down the table to his wife and daughter. Standing in front of his chair, he lifted his goblet in a formal toast. 'To the Anglo-American alliance and the demise of Hitler.'

Kurt rose to his feet and touched his glass to his hostess's and her daughter's. 'And Britain's fair and hospitable ladies,' he added with an insincere smile.

'You're welcome to join us in the drawing room to listen to our wireless, Lieutenant Schaffer,' Mr Llewellyn Jones offered.

'Thank you, sir, but I have to drive into town to check that the troop quarters are ready for the morning.'

'I could show you the way,' Anthea broke in eagerly.

'I wouldn't want to put you to any trouble, Miss Anthea.'

'It's no trouble. No trouble at all.'

'And such a good idea,' Mrs Llewellyn Jones purred. 'You certainly had a problem getting your bearings this morning. It's even worse in the blackout.'

'I'll get my coat.' Anthea was out of the room before he could make any further protest. He stood and waited in the hall, cursing the impulse that had led him to accept Mrs Llewellyn Jones's offer of a billet. Perhaps he should have taken the colonel's advice after all. If he'd gone into one of the chapel vestries he might have been plagued by the presence of the men, but at least his free time would have been his own.

It was past ten o'clock when Bethan finally finished her paperwork. Packing the completed forms into her nurse's bag she turned off the lamp, left the study and felt her way through the blacked-out hall to the deserted kitchen. Switching on the light, she lifted the hob cover on the range, put the kettle on to boil and prepared for a long wait because Maisie had damped down the coals for the night. The mixed fragrances of food and the warmth of the room closed comforting and familiar around her as she settled in her rocking chair listening to the silence. Only when she was certain that the house was quiet, did she reach into her pocket for Andrew's letter. Taking a knife from the drawer she slit open the gummed section and began to read.

My darling Beth,
Today is the second anniversary of the day we arrived in this camp . . .

Checking the date, she discovered that the letter had taken only three and a half as opposed to the customary four months to reach her.

Needless to say all of us 'Dunkirk veterans' are even more depressed than usual. It's exactly two years, two months, one week, four days and five hours since I last saw, kissed and touched you. Every morning I open my eyes, hoping that this will be the day that will bring the news that I can finally come home to you and the children. Sometimes, I think it's the uncertainty that's the worst. Criminals are better off than we are. At least they go into prison knowing their sentence. They can scratch a calendar on the wall of their cell and tick off the days. If only I knew that it was going to be one, two or six months longer. Surely to God it can't be another year!
I tried to cheer myself up this morning by imagining the journey home. Packing my bag. (About thirty seconds' work. If anyone had told me before the war that a man could survive with so few possessions I would have laughed at them.) Travelling through Germany in a real train instead of the cattle wagons that brought us here. Walking across the French docks and up the gangplank of a boat without a guard pointing a gun at my back, fighting for a chair inside rather than out on deck, sailing

*to Dover; getting on another train, arriving in London,
picking up presents for Rachel and Eddie as I cross from
Victoria to Paddington – that's if there are any toys in
the shops to be bought – or even any shops left after the
bombing. Do you realise I don't even know what sort of
things they'd like?*

*I've seen Rachel holding dolls and teddies in the photo-
graphs you've sent me, but what kind of new one would
she choose? Does she prefer dolls with black or blonde
hair? Big ones, or little ones? And Eddie? Does he like
toy cars yet, or does he prefer playing with lead animals
and farmyards as Mother said I did at his age?*

*Paddington – sitting on the train – a corner seat if
I'm lucky, looking out of the window at the countryside,
reading off the towns as we pass through the stations,
every one taking me closer to you. Changing trains at
Cardiff – I went through the whole rigmarole, step by
step, even down to checking whether or not I needed a
shave in the men's room while I waited for the Pontypridd
and Rhondda Valley train. Pacing up and down the
carriage while we passed through the local stations.
Running down the steps from the platform into station
yard to be first in the queue for a taxi. Driving up the
Graig hill to Penycoedcae, seeing the house bathed in
early morning sunlight and overshadowed by leafy trees
– I always imagine arriving on a bright summer's
morning, I have no idea what I'll do if the war ends in
winter.*

*You sitting with the children on the lawn, you look
up . . .*

Bethan started guiltily. She hadn't had the heart to write
and tell Andrew that there was no more lawn. Every
inch of garden had been dug up by her, her father and
Maisie in the months after Dunkirk when food rationing
had really begun to bite.

*. . . will you be wearing essence of violets, the perfume
I remember from the day I left? And your hair? Do you*

*still roll it under at the nape of your neck? It's difficult
to see from your last photograph because of the hat. In
my daydreams you're always wearing the dark blue frock
you bought for that last Christmas we spent together in
1940.*

*Then I open my eyes, look around and realise that I
am lying on a straw mattress on a hard, wooden bunk;
one of sixteen built in four tiers in a cramped compartment
no bigger than my mother's larder, set in this overcrowded
wooden hut and likely to be here a while longer. I dare
not even hazard a guess as to how much longer lest I go
raving mad.*

*After reading this I realise that I'm suffering from yet
another dose of acute self-pity. Don't worry, it's not
terminal, or fortunately for us, contagious. For every
depressed prisoner or 'kriegie' as the German guards call
us, there's always one who can muster a modicum of
optimism to cheer the rest, and because we have to do all
our own housework, cooking, washing, cleaning and in
my case, nursing as well as doctoring, we have plenty to
keep ourselves busy.*

*What I can't understand is how a woman, any woman,
has time to do anything other than housework. It seems
to take us the best part of half a day to collect food from
the XXXXXXXXXXXXXXXXXXXX*

Bethan stared at the lines obliterated by the censor's
heavy pen. Guessing that Andrew had mentioned the
rations the Germans allowed them in addition to the Red
Cross parcels, and suspecting just how scant they might
be, she read on.

*XXXXX and make lunch. And no sooner have we
washed our tins and pans than it's time to start on supper.*

*In my free time I attend as many of the classes my
fellow inmates have organised as I can. I'm learning
languages. It's quite a little United Nations here between
the Canadians, Australians, South Africans, French,
Poles, Dutch XXXXXXXXXXXX and ourselves. We*

have a choir, but when I tried to join, the conductor unkindly diagnosed me as tone deaf. On that point, my love, he agrees with you. The drama group I wrote you about goes from strength to strength and they've finished building the theatre at the back of the church. We have a reading club (which would greatly appreciate any spare books no matter how old or decrepit) an art group, and even I've been roped in to run first aid classes. I've also taken up carpentry in the hope that it will help me with those odd jobs you keep threatening me with. So you see, I am busy if not happy. But then I could never be that again without you and the children.

I realise that you are facing problems too, my love, and from my father's last letter I also know you're working as many hours as there are in a day and night. He said that he and Doctor Evans couldn't manage without you. I feel so bloody useless locked up in this cage. All I want is to be home with you, working, helping, living but most of all loving. I really can't see that keeping thousands of men penned up in compounds all over Germany is contributing to the war effort of either side.

There I go, moaning again. Please, whatever else you do, don't worry about me. Food is no longer a problem since the Red Cross parcels started coming in regularly, and we are supplementing those by cultivating vegetable gardens between the huts. My swedes, cabbages and turnips have to be seen to be believed, Rachel could probably play with them in her dolls' house, but they are growing every day. I only hope that none of us will be here in the autumn to harvest our crop. Our hopes have risen since the XXXXXXXXXXXXXXXXXXXXX XXXXXXXXXXXXXXXXXXXXXXXXXXXXXX you see – news gets through even to us. Some of the gamblers are even taking bets as to when the first Yank will arrive.

Bethan smiled as she wondered at the censor's command of English, didn't he know the English nickname for Americans?

Thank you for the photographs of the children. You can have no idea how much they mean to me. I have pinned them alongside my bunk, starting with the one of you and Rachel I had in my wallet when I was captured, and carrying on with the ones you have sent every month since.

I have missed out on their entire babyhood and all of your pregnancy with Eddie, years that I will never be able to recapture. I only hope that when we are finally together again, there will be other children. What do you think? Could you give up caring for half the town after the peace treaties have been signed and settle for just our family and me?

I love you, Beth, and miss you every waking moment. I look forward to the night when I can close my eyes, because then you are with me. You haunt my dreams. Do you ever think of those magical, peaceful hours we used to spend alone together in our bedroom before going to bed? I do, constantly. I will be with you again the moment the war is over, I promise. Take care of yourself and the children until we can be together again.

   All my love
     your Andrew

PS: I'm sure you know, but just in case you didn't, Mother and Father write regularly. I am so glad you seem to be getting on better with both of them.

Bethan found it difficult to set aside her irritation at Andrew's habit of always finishing his letters with a PS about his parents. And as if that wasn't enough, there were the plans he was making for both of them after the war. Plans centred around a third pregnancy and her return to domesticity.

Knowing she was being unfair didn't quell the ugly thought that he intended to make up for missing out on Eddie's babyhood by replacing him with another child. He loved her and missed her and the children, but then he had nothing else to think about. Would he miss them as much, or write as often, if he'd been incarcerated somewhere more interesting than a wooden hut in an all-male prison camp in northern Germany?

Two and a half years was a long time. She knew she had changed. Become confident and assured enough to confront Mrs Llewellyn Jones – and win. The woman she was now bore little resemblance to the shy, uncertain, newly qualified nurse Andrew had courted and married. Would he recognise her, or more to the point want her, once he became acquainted with her new independent personality? Could she make room for him in her life again? Did she still love him?

She hated herself for daring even to think otherwise. But their life together seemed such a long time ago. Almost as though it had been lived by someone else. Why couldn't she concentrate on the happy times and weave those memories into their future instead of the problems they might or might not encounter if they were ever reunited?

Doubts crowded in on her as she set aside the letter and spooned cocoa into a cup. There were so many things she couldn't forget, no matter how hard she tried. The death of their first child a few months after his birth, a tragedy that had almost destroyed her and their marriage. Andrew's selfishness that she had always attributed to his mother's doting upbringing; never deliberate, always thoughtless, but as capable of wounding as if it had been.

Gingerly touching the side of the kettle and deciding it was hot enough, she poured water on to the cocoa powder. Returning to the rocking chair, she began to read again, this time trying to imagine Andrew as he had been when he'd written the letter. He had changed too. Just as increased responsibilities had lent her confidence, being imprisoned had sapped his. He would never have committed thoughts like these to paper before the war. Then, his emotions had been something to joke about, not reflect on in a letter.

He so obviously needed to believe that nothing had

changed. That everything would be exactly the same as when he'd left, including her, frozen in time to the extent that she'd be wearing the same dress, hairstyle and perfume. Was he secretly afraid, like her, that their marriage wouldn't stand the test of years of separation?

Lifting the cup she glanced up, and almost dropped it in surprise when she saw David Ford standing in the doorway.

'I'm sorry, I didn't mean to startle you. I assumed everyone was in bed.'

'I've just finished some paperwork.'

'They make civilians do that too?' His tone was dry, but there was a spark of humour in his eyes that she hadn't noticed when they'd spoken earlier.

She held up her cup. 'Would you like some cocoa?'

He pulled a tin from his pocket. 'I've brought my own coffee.'

'The water's hot but not boiling.' Returning to the stove, she set the kettle back on the hob.

'I don't want to keep you up.'

'You're not.' She pushed Andrew's letter into her pocket, but not before he saw it.

'From your husband?'

'Yes.'

He handed her his tin as she took another cup from the shelf. 'He's a lucky man.'

'To be in a German prison camp?'

'To be alive and have you and your children to come home to.'

'It would be nice to know when that's likely to be.'

'As long as it takes us to get organised, over there and destroy the German army.'

'My father thinks that they are going to take some beating, even with Russian and American help.'

'Your father is right.'

'I'm sorry, I'm forgetting my manners. Please, sit down.'

Leaving her the rocking chair, he sat on the end of

one of the benches placed either side of the scrub-down table.

'I don't want to get your hopes up, Mrs John, but have you considered that your husband could be home before the end of the war? There are prisoner exchanges and there's always the chance of escape.'

'Not for Andrew. He's a doctor, and from what little in the way of details the censor allows through in his letters, I think the only one in his camp.'

'And he wouldn't leave the men unattended?'

'He has a strong sense of duty.' She tried to make it sound like a compliment. 'When he drew the short straw at Dunkirk a medical officer who wasn't married offered to take his place. Andrew wouldn't hear of it. He stayed with the wounded in a field hospital. I didn't know for three months whether he'd been captured, wounded or killed.'

'Then it must be a relief to know he's safe now.'

'Safe? With the RAF dropping bombs all over Germany? Surrounded by armed guards who might shoot him at any moment . . . I'm sorry.' She picked up the kettle and poured water on to the coffee essence. 'I'm not usually like this. It's been a long day. Would you like milk and sugar?'

'Milk please, if you can spare it.'

Taking the jug from the pantry she ventured a personal question. 'Are you married, Colonel Ford?'

'I was.'

'I'm sorry.'

'I didn't lose my wife in the funeral sense. She divorced me.'

Bethan stared at the cup not quite knowing what to say.

'By the time the papers came through it was no longer a catastrophe for either of us. I hope I haven't shocked you. I've heard that divorce is more common in the States than here.'

'Not many women in Pontypridd can afford to leave their husbands.'

'My wife had independent means.'

'Do you have any children?'

'A son. He's sixteen now. You want the war to end so your husband can come home; I want it to end so Elliot won't have to fight.'

'Surely it can't last another two years?'

'Let's hope not, Nurse John.' He lifted his cup. 'To victory.'

'A quick victory,' she echoed, her imagination painting a future as bleak and lonely as the years that lay behind her.

'I could come in with you.'

'Civilians aren't allowed into military billets.'

'But . . .'

'I can't allow you, Miss Llewellyn Jones.' Kurt's voice was firm. 'And what goes for civilians goes double for pretty girls,' he added in an attempt to mollify her. Leaving the Jeep, he switched on the torch he was carrying, pointed the beam at his feet and gingerly negotiated the steps that led down to the basement of Penuel Chapel.

The cry, 'Watch the blackout!' greeted him as he pushed open the door. Fighting his way through the curtain, he saluted two senior officers who were inspecting the neat rows of army cots that had been set around the perimeter of the low-ceilinged, damp and freezing vault.

'Not like you to be working at this time of night, Schaffer.' Major Reynolds turned back to his list.

'With the men coming in tomorrow I thought someone should check everything was ready.'

'We already have. I hear you've sorted yourself a more comfortable billet than this,' Captain Reide needled him humourlessly.

'That depends on your notion of comfort, sir.'

'Women to do your cooking and cleaning?'

'One of you want to swap?' Kurt asked hopefully.

'For you to make an offer like that, there has to be something seriously wrong.'

'Nothing. I've got the lot. My own bedroom with a gas fire, carpet and comfortable feather bed. Full maid service, meals with the family, offers to do my laundry . . .'

'What's up?' Richard Reide pressed.

Kurt glanced over his shoulder before whispering, 'The daughter.'

'She's too young, old or ugly to seduce?'

'Not at all. Quite passable in fact.'

'She's a nun?'

'Or a lunatic?'

'Quit joking, you two. I had a lecture from the old man this morning on keeping my nest clean.'

'Quite right too. So, you leave her alone: what's the problem?' Charles Reynolds counted the number of cots and ticked off the last item on his inventory.

'She won't leave me alone. You've no idea . . .' Before he could finish the sentence, a 'Cooee' echoed down the steps.

'Cooee? Lieutenant Schaffer?' Anthea pushed aside the blackout.

'Watch the blackout, Miss . . .'

'Llewellyn Jones, Anthea Llewellyn Jones.' She posed self-consciously on the step, smiling coquettishly at all three men. Richard Reide winked slyly at Kurt before holding out his arm.

'Please join us, Miss Llewellyn Jones. Now that we've finished here, perhaps you'll be kind enough to show us where a man can get a drink in this town?'

Chapter Four

'WE WON'T GO unless you come with us, and that's our final word.'

'That's ridiculous.' Alma frowned in exasperation as Bethan sank down on to one of the easy chairs. 'You're going to crease that velvet,' she warned as Bethan folded the long skirt of her pre-war, midnight-blue evening gown around her ankles.

'No matter. There's no one to see it here.'

'Jane, talk to her?' Alma appealed to Bethan's sister-in-law. 'Just about everyone you two know will be there.'

'Except you.' More careful of her dress than Bethan, Jane perched on the arm of Bethan's chair.

'It just doesn't seem right.'

'What do you think Charlie would say if he could see you sitting here, moping alone night after night?'

'Probably that I should have got used to living without him in the last year and a half.' Alma smiled in a vain attempt to disguise her tears.

'I haven't become accustomed to living without Andrew in two and a half,' Bethan warned, her voice tinged with bitterness.

'I can't stop thinking about him. Wondering if he's in hiding, or locked up in a German prison unable to tell anyone his real identity. Everyone knows that soldiers out of uniform are shot as spies.'

'You're that sure he's still alive?' Bethan probed gently.

'That sure.' There was no anger in Alma's voice at the intimation that Charlie could be dead. 'He's alive. I'm certain of it. I'd know if he'd been killed. I'd feel it, but just as I'm certain he's alive, I also know that he's suffering. How can I go to a party, knowing he is pain?' Her eyes were dark, anguished.

'Because if you don't, you'll go mad sitting here thinking about him. Come on, Alma, Mary's been working for you for over a month now. Theo loves her, she's every bit as capable of looking after him as you are, and it's not as though we're going to the ends of the earth. The New Inn is less than five minutes' walk away. If he wakes she can telephone reception, they'll pass on a message.'

'I know.' Alma glanced at her husband's photograph on the mantelpiece. His presence was with her, so real, so tangible, she felt as though he were in the room with them. She could even smell the soap he used, the cologne he brushed through his thick white-blond hair . . .

'Then why don't you get ready?'

'Because – '

'We're all in the same boat, Alma,' Jane asserted forcefully. 'Bethan might know that Andrew is alive, but he's still locked away for the duration, however long that will be. And although I know where Haydn is, most of the time,' she qualified drily, 'he's only managed one three-day leave in the last year and I have absolutely no idea when he'll be home again. If we live like nuns until the end of the war we'll go crazy, or even worse, forget how to have a good time and become as dull as ditchwater. We can't stop living just because our husbands are away, and no one with any sense will think any the worse of us for going to a dance.'

'You really won't take no for an answer, will you?'

Bethan shook her head.

'I've ironed Mrs Raschenko's green dress, Mrs John.' Mary stood in the doorway, the long skirt of Alma's one and only evening dress draped over her arm. 'What do you want me to do with it?'

'Lay it on Mrs Raschenko's bed, Mary. You don't mind staying here on your own?'

'Of course not, Mrs John.'

'And you'll telephone the New Inn the minute Theo wakes?'

'Yes, Mrs Raschenko, but you know he never does.'

Jane looked at Alma. 'What are you waiting for?'

'Have you heard about the new brand of knickers the Americans brought with them?' Judy shrieked into Jenny's ear as they stood back, buffet plates in hand watching the American forces' band take their places on the podium. 'One Yank and they're down.'

'Did you make that up?'

'Overheard Alexander Forbes telling it to Ronnie in the cafe.'

'He would,' Jenny murmured caustically. Alexander had watched her like a hawk for the last month. She had no doubt that he would have been standing behind her now if he had been able to get a ticket, but the invitations Lieutenant Schaffer had sent to the pits had been snapped up by the Pontypridd born and bred miners; none had found their way into the pockets of the conscientious objectors who'd been conscripted in from outside.

She glanced around the room. The New Inn's blue and silver ballroom was brighter and more crowded than she'd seen it since before the war. All the lamps had been lit in defiance of energy-saving directives, the walls were decked out in bunting and miniature Union Jacks and Stars and Stripes. The buffet table that stretched down the entire length of one wall groaned with mounds of delicacies that had long since disappeared from the shops in the town: iced cakes, jellies, sugared buns, buttered beef and ham sandwiches, cheese straws, as well as peculiar American dishes and punch bowls liberally decorated with fresh fruit, most of it out of season.

All the town's councillors had turned out, a fair number of businessmen, and a few, mostly female few, munitions workers. Also just about every attractive girl in Pontypridd. Marriage had been no barrier to getting on to the ticket list, but an absent husband had certainly

58

helped. She wondered just how many girls had been left for the enlisted men's dance in the Coronation ballroom which presumably had been organised on a less lavish scale than this affair.

'Ladies?' Kurt Schaffer greeted them. 'Can I help you to some punch?'

'You can help me to whatever you like,' Judy giggled, already tipsy after a couple of double gins in the White Hart. Leaning forward, she kissed his cheek, smearing his face with lipstick.

'Mrs John?' Colonel Ford glared at Schaffer and Judy as he went to the door to welcome Bethan. 'I'm glad you came.'

'My friend, Mrs Raschenko, and my sisters-in-law, Mrs Jane Powell and Mrs Jenny Powell,' she added, drawing Jenny into their group as Judy began to flirt even more outrageously with Kurt.

Colonel Ford shook hands with all of them before leading them to his table set as far away from the noise of the band, and as close to the buffet and bar, as could be arranged.

'My adjutant Major Reynolds, Captain Reide, my aide Lieutenant George Rivers.' The officers rose to their feet as they were introduced. 'I believe you know the Mayor and his wife, Councillor and Mrs Llewellyn Jones, and their daughter, Anthea, Dr and Mrs John – '

'My mother- and father-in-law, Colonel,' Bethan interrupted, before he could recite the names of everyone at his table.

A glance in Captain Reide's direction secured extra seats and Bethan, Alma, Jenny and Jane found themselves squashed between the colonel and Major Reynolds.

'Sherry, ladies?' Major Reynolds took a bottle from the centre of the table and filled their glasses as a waiter appeared with more plates and a selection of food from the buffet.

'Sir?' Looking suitably contrite, Kurt Schaffer approached, his cheek scrubbed of lipstick and Judy nowhere in sight. 'Everyone is waiting for you to formally open the proceedings.'

Excusing himself, David Ford went to the stage. Taking the microphone from the band leader he tapped it, waiting for silence before speaking.

'Thank you for accepting our invitation. I hope this occasion will mark the beginning of a warm and mutually beneficial friendship between your town and the American armed forces. Let the dancing begin.'

The band struck up a waltz. He returned to the table and asked Bethan for the first dance. One look at Mrs Llewellyn Jones's downturned, disapproving mouth was enough. Bethan took his hand and followed him on to the floor.

'Bang goes my reputation,' she murmured as they joined the half a dozen couples who had braved the stares of the rest of the guests.

'With only one dance, Mrs John?'

'You don't know the gossips in this town.'

He looked back at Mrs Llewellyn Jones. 'I believe they're the same the world over.'

'You're probably right.'

'It's good to know there's a smiling woman beneath the starched uniform and efficient expression you usually wear.'

'We haven't much to smile about these days.'

'All the more reason to do so.'

'How are your men settling into the town?'

'I'd be lying if I said they were happy to be here. Most have left wives and sweethearts back home. They are just as lonely as I suspect most of the women are here.'

'It's bizarre when you think about it. You're here, and don't want to be. Our men are in North Africa, the East or imprisoned in Germany and they don't want to be . . .'

'That's war for you, Mrs John.' He swirled her around so she couldn't see her mother-in-law's or Mrs Llewellyn Jones's face.

*

'Would you like to dance, ma'am?' Major Reynolds asked Alma as Kurt Schaffer commandeered Jenny and Richard Reide escorted an ecstatic Anthea on to the floor.

'I don't dance very well, Major.'

'Truth be told, neither do I, so let's make a pact not to get riled if we tread on one another's toes.' Pushing back his chair he rose to his feet and offered her his hand.

'This feels peculiar,' Alma said as he whirled her out into the centre of the room.

'To be dancing with someone who isn't your husband?'

'You know?'

'I've left a wife and small son back in Tennessee, ma'am.'

'You must miss them?'

'Like hell, if you'll pardon the expression. But your son helps. I've seen him in the shop. He's not far off Chuck junior's age.'

'Chuck . . . that's your son's name?'

'Mine too. It's American for Charles.'

'Now you're teasing me.'

'I wouldn't dream of it, ma'am. Tell me, is Theo very difficult to manage on your own?'

'You know his name?'

'We live next door.'

'Above Frank Clayton's shop?'

'Richard and I have that privilege.'

'Is it very uncomfortable?'

'Not any more, thanks to Uncle Sam's home improvement fund, and Richard's talent for scavenging. You must visit some time. With your friends,' he added, to avoid any possibility of a misunderstanding.

'We'd like that.' To her surprise she realised she meant it.

'Chuck junior is seven months old, and according to my wife, almost, but not quite feeding himself, sitting

61

up unaided, and just beginning to crawl. Your maid was telling me that your Theo is nine months old, so that must make him more advanced.'

'Mary isn't my maid. She just works for me. And I'm no expert on babies, Major, only Theo, but the one thing I have learned is that they all develop at their own pace.'

'That's what my wife says. When Chuck junior was born, I bought a book that had all these tables telling you when a baby should be sitting up, standing and walking. She took one look at it and threw it away.'

'She sounds like a sensible woman.'

'I think you'd like her. When I was sent here she went back home to stay with her folks. They own a general store that sells a bit of everything, something like your corner shops only bigger. I've written her about your shop to see if it gives her any ideas about expanding the butchery counter. That's quite a business you have there. Queues around the block every morning.'

'If I could lay my hands on more supplies I could make a fortune.'

'The boys tell me you have more shops.'

'The boys?'

'The men . . . troops.'

'I have a couple of partners, we've opened six more shops between us, but the only one I – my husband – ' she corrected swiftly, 'own, is the one by the fountain.'

'He's in the army?'

'Where else?'

'Raschenko sounds more like an American than a Welsh name.'

'Charlie's Russian.'

'Then he's fighting with them?'

'He lived here for seven years before war broke out, so he enlisted here. He was posted missing fifteen months ago.'

'I'm sorry. Trust me to go and put my big foot in it. I had no idea.'

'The worst thing is having to deal with people who

believe he's dead. I know he isn't,' she insisted a little too forcefully.

The dance ended and they separated to applaud the band.

'At the risk of boring you, Mrs Raschenko, how would you like to sit down and have a drink with me so I can show off the snapshots I carry of my wife and Chuck junior?'

Alma took the arm he offered her. 'I'd like nothing better, Major Reynolds.'

The colonel put a smile on Mrs Llewellyn Jones's face by asking her for the second waltz. By the time the band had left the stage to take a break, he had danced with all the women at his table and the evening was going better than he had anticipated. Lubricated by American beer and whiskey, and filled with American food, the 'crache' (the first Welsh word he had learned) of the town were in a genial and charitable mood, even towards the interlopers who had butted into their territory and war.

The atmosphere at his table had livened up considerably since Bethan John and her sisters-in-law's arrival; and her friend, Alma, was doing sterling work with Reynolds. Every man on board the troopship that had brought them to England had been subjected to his collection of photographs, and not many were anxious to repeat the experience; principally because the sight of Chuck's attractive wife and child, coupled with his commentary, was enough to make even the most cynical officer homesick.

As he signalled to Rivers to replenish the guests' glasses his gaze rested on Bethan. Outwardly cool and self-assured, he noticed her hands tightening into white-knuckled fists every time her mother-in-law or Mrs Llewellyn Jones spoke. Her sister-in-law Jane, a skinny, little half-pint-sized thing, who looked about twelve years old despite the wedding ring on her finger, was laughing at something Richard Reide had said.

63

He frowned. If anything, the captain was worse than the lieutenant. At least Schaffer was honest about his womanising. A girl would have to be stupid not to see through his line, but Reide was more subtle. He'd heard some odd stories about the man, mostly from reliable sources. Making a mental note to give him the same lecture he had given Schaffer, he was just about to ask Bethan to dance again when the doors burst open behind them.

'It's D'Este. Hi, D'Este, over here,' Chuck shouted, waving at the officer who stood framed in the doorway.

Heads turned, the women's eyes widening at the sight of the exotically handsome officer. Dropping his kitbag in the corner he waved back.

'Is he . . . is he a Negro?' Mrs Llewellyn Jones enquired in a stage whisper that carried around the table.

'Negroes are generally a lot darker than Captain D'Este, ma'am,' Chuck replied, when he saw the colonel had no intention of answering her.

'He's a spic,' Richard Reide declared contemptuously.

'I don't think I've heard of them. Are they an African tribe?'

'Hispanic. Of Spanish origin. In Captain D'Este's case, Cuban,' Chuck explained, giving Richard a warning look.

'Probably with a touch of Indian, maybe even the tarbrush.' Reide reached for the whiskey bottle.

'Leave the liquor alone if you can't hold it, Captain,' David Ford warned brusquely as he rose to his feet. 'It's good to see you again, Captain D'Este.' He turned to the table, eyeing Mrs Llewellyn Jones in particular. 'Captain D'Este is one of our best surgeons.'

'A doctor.' She extended her hand warily.

'You've come to work in the RAF hospital in Church Village?' Dr John asked.

'There and Pontypridd and District Hospital, sir.'

'I'm one of the local doctors . . .'

'It's been such a lovely evening. Must we spoil it

by discussing medical matters?' his wife complained irritably.

'Sir. Ma'am,' the captain shook both their hands. 'I'm pleased to meet you both.'

'We must get together, Captain – '

His wife interrupted by tapping him sharply on the arm with her fan. 'The band's starting up again and I'd like to dance.'

Sensitive to her mother-in-law's lack of courtesy, Bethan held out her hand. 'I'm Bethan John, one of the district nurses.'

The captain murmured 'Pleased to meet you', in a tone that suggested his mind was elsewhere. Taking the chair the waiter brought for him, he turned to the colonel. 'I only got my orders this morning, sir. They told me you'd be able to sort out a billet for me when I reached here.'

'No room with us,' Richard Reide said firmly.

'We could manage,' Chuck Reynolds contradicted strongly.

'No need. That's if you have no objection to a fifth man moving into our rooms, Mrs John?'

'Not at all, Colonel.' Aware that something was wrong, but uncertain exactly what, Bethan smiled at the captain.

'Thank you, ma'am.' D'Este looked up as an officer escorted Jane back to their table. She was smiling, her thin face flushed with the heat of the room, her gold silk dress clinging to her scrawny frame. She saw the captain the same instant he saw her. Bethan glanced from one to the other, convinced that everyone else at the table must have sensed the change in the atmosphere. It was almost as though an electric current had charged the air linking them.

'Captain D'Este, Mrs Jane Powell.' David Ford effected the introduction with the slightest of stresses on the word, Mrs, and Bethan realised that he too had seen the attraction.

65

Recollecting himself, the captain held out his hand. 'Mrs Powell.'

'Captain D'Este.' Jane's cheeks darkened from pink to crimson as she took her seat.

'You're a surgeon?' Bethan asked, breaking the awkward silence that had fallen over the table.

'I was studying at a unit that specialises in the facial reconstruction of accident and burns victims when I was drafted.'

The band stopped playing and conversation ceased as applause filled the room.

'Mrs Powell, may I have the next dance?' He held out his arm to Jane.

'He's certainly very good-looking for a darkie, and he's obviously done well for himself,' Mrs Llewellyn Jones observed to no one in particular as D'Este led Jane on to the floor.

Anthea's frown turned to laughter as Richard Reide whispered in her ear before leading her away.

Bethan watched Jane dance with the captain. She hadn't seen her sister-in-law smile quite so broadly since Haydn's last leave. Perhaps it was time to write to her brother and suggest he press for another one.

'Begging your pardon, ma'am, I would have knocked if I'd known someone was sitting in here.'

Megan Powell lifted her slippered feet from the hearth of Bethan's kitchen range and turned to see a plump, middle-aged man standing in the doorway.

'And I thought all the Americans were at the parties.'

'I'm a bit long in the tooth for socials.'

'Join the club.' Megan set the Marie Corelli novel she'd borrowed from the library on the table. 'I've just made some tea, would you like some?'

'Colonel Ford's got strong views on us eating into the natives' rations.'

'Oh, I think we can manage a cup of tea.' Megan lifted crockery down from the dresser. 'I'm Megan Powell, Bethan's aunt and babysitter for the evening.'

'Nurse Powell?'

'My, you fellows are formal, aren't you?'

'The colonel's warned us not to impose on the family.'

'From what the children have been telling me, your imposition involves making bucketloads of biscuits and pancakes, and spoiling them at every turn.' She set the cup on the table and poured the tea. 'Are you the cook?'

'Sergeant Dino Morelli, ma'am.'

'I'm not a ma'am, I'm a Megan, and if you don't mind me saying so, the American army must be more desperate than the British, conscripting a man of your age.'

'I'm a volunteer and I'm forty.'

'And I'm twenty-one next birthday.' Megan settled back into the rocking chair. 'Well sit down, there's no point in standing up to drink tea.'

'Thank you . . . Megan.' He took the easy chair opposite hers.

'It's warmer in here than the sitting room. I never could understand Andrew John buying a place this size for Bethan. The rooms are so big they were always cold even before fuel rationing. He should have known he'd married a girl with simple tastes, but then that's the crache for you. All show and no comfort, that's what I always say.'

'I take it the "crache" are the blue bloods of Pontypridd?'

'You pick up fast.'

'This is a fine house,' he commented looking up at the high ceiling, and the two vast dressers filled with painted china.

'If you have the money and servants to run it and the coal to heat it. Bethan's found it tough going the last few years.'

'She's a nice lady.'

'She is.'

'I have a niece about her age. I left her in charge of my diner . . . a sort of cafe,' he explained in answer to her puzzled look.

'You have a business?'

'Back in a small town on Cape Cod. You heard of Cape Cod?'

Megan shook her head.

'It's in Massachusetts. Pretty place, and as you'd guess from the name, surrounded by sea. My wife fell in love with it. She used to summer there every year with her folks, and when we married she decided we should settle there. By that time I'd learned not to argue with her. We worked in a seafood restaurant until we got enough money together to open a place of our own. Didn't do too badly either.' He stared down into his cup, lost in a time and place she could only guess at. It took him a few minutes to recollect her presence. 'Aside from the diner we opened a small restaurant on a prime piece of real estate overlooking the beach. It was the kind of place Bostonians and New Yorkers didn't mind paying to eat in. We made enough money to buy a house with sea views, a car and a boat. You can't be a someone on the Cape and not own a boat. But, we never found the time to go out in it.'

'Sounds like you miss your home?'

'That I do, Megan.'

'So why volunteer for the army? No one could criticise a man your age for taking it easy.'

'It seemed the right thing to do. I don't like bullies, and this fellow Hitler's certainly behaving like one.' He made a wry face as he set his cup on the table.

'You don't like tea?'

'I prefer coffee.' He emptied his pockets of tins. 'As you see, I brought all the ingredients except hot water.'

'Help yourself.' She pushed her chair away from the range as he picked up the kettle.

'You got anyone fighting in the war, Megan?'

'My son, William. As far as we can tell he's in North Africa.'

'You must be worried about him?'

'Me and his wife. You have no idea how much. I lost my husband in the last war.'

68

'You must have been widowed young.'

'Twenty.'

'I thought the end of the world had come when I lost my wife three years ago. At least we had twenty-two years together.' He shook his head as he opened up the hot plate with the tongs and set the kettle to boil. 'Such a waste of young men's lives.'

'And it's still going on.'

'Auntie Megan?' Rachel opened the door and peeped around the corner, her nightgown trailing around her ankles, a doll clutched in her hand.

'What are you doing up, poppet?' Megan opened her arms and Rachel ran into the room and climbed on to her lap.

'I can't sleep, and Mam's bed is empty.'

'She'll be back soon.' Reaching for the blanket folded on the brass log box, Megan wrapped it around her great-niece and began rocking the chair.

'You've got your hands full.'

'The way I like them filled.' Megan returned his smile.

'I hope everyone's having a good time.'

Megan thought of the excitement on Maisie's and Liza's faces as they'd left the house, and remembered her own girlhood. 'I'm sure they are,' she murmured, hugging Rachel closer.

'I think we should go straight home,' Liza suggested primly, as Maurice led the way out of the Coronation ballroom.

'We have to,' Maurice agreed. 'I've got to get back to the New Inn at twelve to pick up the CO.'

'Come on, five minutes ain't going to make no difference,' Manny Rodriguez coaxed as he tightened his grip around Maisie's waist.

'You know what a stickler for punctuality the old man is.'

'Tell you what, how about I take the girls home with you?'

'I don't think so. Colonel Ford gave me permission to take the ladies home in the car, but no one else.'

'Who in hell is going to see us in this blackout?' Manny demanded. 'There isn't even a moon. There and back. It's not as if anyone else is about. You had to be the first to leave.'

'So I could take Liza and Maisie home. I promised Nurse John that I'd . . .'

'OK, Duval, keep your hair on. Where's the car?'

Maurice hesitated, relenting only when Liza's small, cold hand slipped into his. 'All right, just this once, but if the old man catches us . . .'

'He won't. God you're a worrier, Duval.' As soon as they reached the car, Manny opened the back door and pushed Maisie inside, following quickly before either of the girls could suggest that they sit together in the back.

Maurice climbed into the front seat and hit the ignition. After flicking the switch that illuminated the single, heavily hooded headlight he set off cautiously into the darkness.

'So, Maisie, we are going to be friends, aren't we?' Manny whispered close to her ear so neither Maurice nor Liza could overhear him above the noise of the engine.

'I hope so,' she said warily, moving as far from him as the seat would allow as he tried to slide his hand under her skirt.

'How about me picking you up tomorrow evening around seven?'

She clamped her hand firmly over his. 'There'll be none of that.'

'Have a heart. I'm a lonely serviceman far from friends and home, and you're a gorgeous girl . . .'

'Once more and I'll slap you.'

'Tomorrow?' he repeated, peering through the gloom as Maurice changed gear in preparation for the steepest part of the hill. 'You'll meet me tomorrow? I've got a pass, and the money to take you wherever you want to go.'

'I don't like fast men.' Maisie dug her nails into the back of his hand as his fingers strayed once more to her knee.

'Ouch!'

'You all right in the back?' Maurice asked as he slowed to a crawl, looking for the entrance to the driveway to the house.

'Fine, just hit my hand on something sharp.'

'Check it out, will you? The old man . . .'

' . . . won't have my problems.' Manny retreated to suck his wounds.

'Here we are.' Maurice turned the car into the drive and pulled up outside the front door.

'Thank you for bringing us home.' Liza fumbled for the door handle.

'Give us two minutes, pal.' Manny followed Maisie, who'd been quicker than Liza, out of the car.

'Two minutes is all you've got,' Maurice called back softly. Leaning across Liza he opened the door for her, starting back nervously when he accidentally brushed his arm against her breast. 'I'm sorry,' he apologised, glad of the darkness that concealed his burning cheeks.

'That's all right. You didn't mean to do it.'

'No.' The silence closed in on them, tense and suffocating despite the chill in the air. He tried to distinguish Manny and Maisie's shadows in the darkness that shrouded the front door, but it was impossible. They had merged into the grey-black mass of the house. 'Thank you for coming to the dance with me.'

'I enjoyed myself.'

'So did I.'

'It's the first real dance I've gone to,' Liza confided shyly.

He reached out and touched her hand. 'I don't suppose . . .'

'What?' she asked, his diffidence lending her confidence.

'That I could kiss you?' he blurted out uneasily.

'I haven't had much practice at that sort of thing.'

'Truth be told, neither have I. Have you got a boy-friend?'

'No.'

'Neither have I. A girlfriend I mean,' he amended hastily as she smothered her laughter. Leaning forward, he gripped her arms, held her close and pressed his lips against hers for an embarrassing instant. 'I don't suppose you'd consider being my girl while we're here?' he asked as he released her.

'What would that mean?'

'Coming out with me once in a while. To dances. Perhaps the movies . . .'

'I'd like that.'

'Really. You mean it?' He bent his head to hers again. The pressure of his lips was harder, more confident now; then he remembered the time. Releasing her abruptly he pressed the ignition. 'The colonel's going to be madder than hell if I don't get back into town to pick him up in the next few minutes . . . begging your pardon, Liza.'

'That's all right.' She swung her legs out of the car.

'Manny?' he hissed as Liza walked towards the house.

'I've been waiting for you.' Manny slammed the back doors and climbed into the front seat.

'Goodnight, Maurice,' Liza called as she opened the front door.

'Goodnight, Liza.' He reversed the car carefully, trying to recall the exact location of the trees and bushes that bordered the drive.

'Looks like you got a bad case of the hots there, boy.' Manny reached for his cigarettes, pushed two into his mouth and lit them.

'Liza's a nice girl.'

'And may the good Lord protect me from nice girls. Me, I'm far from home and out for all I can get.'

'With Maisie?'

'Word is she's got a kid and no wedding ring. She might be playing hard to get now, but she'll come round. A girl like that knows the score, and that's the sort I like.'

'Who told you she has a kid?' Maurice asked sharply as they headed back down the hill.

'I heard. Man, the boys are right. The only thing cheap in Britain is the women.'

'Maybe that was true back at base . . .'

'Back at base nothing. A pair of nylons, a couple of cigarettes or a Baker's chocolate bar, and they're anyone's.' He handed Maurice a cigarette before leaning back in his seat. 'It sure does feel like I've landed in a bargain-priced whorehouse, and as I don't have my mother or the local priest peering over my shoulder, and money in my pockets for the first time in my life, I intend to make the most of my good fortune.'

'What about the girls?'

'I'm a democrat. I don't mind sharing my pleasure with them.'

'Maisie might have a kid, but she's a decent girl.'

'Who says?'

'I know, I live in the same house as her.'

'Have you asked her to drop her knickers?'

'Of course not.' Manny's crude question shocked as well as disgusted him.

'Buddy, are you slow. She's had a taste of what a man can give, and she's desperate for more. I can always tell.'

'Horseshit.'

'Well, one thing is certain: she won't have to wait for you to make a move. Decent or not, Uncle Manny'll put a smile on her face before long, never fear. Drop me off at station yard?'

'You heard the doc's lecture. You'll get a dose.'

'You know your trouble, Duval? You've seen so many propaganda films, you're actually beginning to believe them.'

Maurice set his mouth into a hard line as he dropped Manny off. Maisie might have a daughter and no husband but she was a kind, thoroughly nice girl who reminded him of his oldest, married sister. He wondered if he knew Liza well enough to ask her to warn Maisie that Manny was only out for what he could get.

Chapter Five

JANE WALTZED AROUND the ballroom in an aura of romance and excitement that blotted everyone and everything except Tomas D'Este from her mind. All she could see, all she could think of, was his heartbreakingly handsome face. She imagined herself back in his arms, dipping and swaying to the lilt of the music, his arm wrapped around her waist, the warmth of his hand radiating through the thin silk of her dress to the small of her back, the touch of his fingers as they held her own . . .

She glanced up from beneath lowered lashes, starting in surprise when she saw Lieutenant Rivers staring back at her. She turned away disconcerted by the ridiculous feeling that he had read her thoughts.

'You're very beautiful.'

His voice grated harsh and discordant after Tomas D'Este's musically accented tones.

'I'm anything but beautiful. Small, mousy-haired, mousy-eyed, skinny.'

'But what a mouse.' His smile became a leer.

'Will you be in Pontypridd long?' she asked, taking refuge in commonplace enquiries.

'Long enough to get to know you better.'

She blushed, suddenly conscious of Bethan and Colonel Ford dancing behind them. 'That kind of talk doesn't impress me.'

'It wasn't meant to. I confess, I'm smitten. You've bewitched me. I'm yours, body and soul.'

'It's more like you're handing me a line.'

'You already speak American?'

'I don't know what you have been told about Welsh women, Lieutenant Rivers, but we're not that gullible.'

'I'm not interested in Welsh women. Only you.'

'You didn't know I existed five minutes ago.'

'I've always known you existed. I've been waiting all my life to meet you.'

'Which Hollywood picture did you get that from?'

'So beautiful and so hard-hearted.'

'And what would your wife say if she could hear you now?'

'I have no wife.'

'I can understand why, if this is an example of your courting technique.'

'How can you be so indifferent to the plight of a lonely man?'

'Because I have a husband at the front.' She moved back as he tried to pull her closer.

'He's in Africa?'

'He was two weeks ago, but he'll be home soon.'

'I thought leave was hard to come by for your boys.'

'Haydn is a singer, an entertainer with ENSA.'

'I've heard of ENSA. An English officer warned us about the organisation in holding camp. Don't the initials stand for "Every Night Something Awful"?'

'Not the shows Haydn plays in.'

'It was a gag.' He breathed beer fumes over her as he bent his head closer to hers. 'Not much of one, but I will try to do better next time.'

'There won't be a next time, Lieutenant Rivers.'

'Oh, but I think there will, with me living in your sister-in-law's house.'

'I hardly see Bethan.'

'You don't get on with your family?'

'Very well, but as we both work, neither of us has much time for visiting.'

'You're a nurse too?'

'I'm in munitions.'

'You work in a factory?'

'That shocks you?'

'It's hard, manual work.'

'But necessary, and one way I can help us to win this war.'

'It's a sad state of affairs when a ravishing girl like you has to slave away in a factory.'

'There is a sad state of affairs in this country, Lieutenant Rivers. Haven't you been here long enough to see it?'

The dance ended. Slipping from his grasp, Jane applauded the band. She saw the frown on Bethan's face, and knew that her sister-in-law had seen and understood exactly what the lieutenant had been trying to do, and judging by the amount of whispering going on at their table, so had Mrs John and Mrs Llewellyn Jones.

'It is time for you to practise your lovemaking techniques on some other girl, Lieutenant.'

'Please call me George.'

'Well, George, I think it might be as well if I pointed you in the direction of the unmarried ones. It might save you embarrassment as well as effort.'

'As we've only just met, I'll forgive you that. Love at first sight can rattle a girl, particularly when she's married.'

'I don't believe in love at first sight, Lieutenant.' Looking around she realised that they'd been left, marooned on the dance floor. Leaving him she began to walk back to their table.

'I think you do, Mrs Powell.' He grabbed her wrist.

'Let me go! If I talk to you any longer, people will gossip.'

'Not now the band is about to play again.' He jerked her back into the centre of the floor as she continued to struggle to free herself. 'Stop it, you're making a scene.' He glanced over his shoulder to see if the colonel was watching.

'And you've had too much to drink.'

'At the fountain of love.'

'That is not funny, and you don't understand Pontypridd. Two dances with the same man are enough for

76

gossips to have the couple walking down the aisle, or in my case, committing adultery.'

'Now that's an idea. With your husband away you need someone to practise on. I am healthy, ready, willing and . . . ouch!'

Stamping on his foot a second time, Jane turned on her heel and collided with Tomas D'Este and Chuck Reynolds.

'We were coming to rescue you, but it doesn't look as though you need our help.' Tomas took her hand for the foxtrot as the major clamped his hand on the lieutenant's shoulder and steered him towards the door.

'A little late, but thank you anyway,' she replied heatedly.

'George Rivers isn't a bad fellow. Just young and let loose away from home for the first time in his life.'

'And drunk.'

'I'm not making excuses, but it's not been easy for us. One minute we were home with our families, the next, shipped across the Atlantic into a strange country with even stranger customs, and thrown into the society of a lot of pretty women with hardly a man in sight. It's enough to turn the head of even the most sensible guy.'

'Most of the pretty women in this room have husbands, Captain D'Este.'

'And most of the servicemen have wives, Mrs Powell, but that doesn't mean we can't be friends.'

'No, I suppose it doesn't,' she allowed grudgingly.

'Is your husband at the front?'

'With ENSA. I hate this damned war!' She had never meant it more or missed Haydn so much. She longed for peace so she could become a part of his everyday life again; from the moment of waking in the morning to sleeping at night. To live like the families in the children's stories she read to Anne. To enjoy simple things like shared meals and outings, to go shopping with Anne tucked into her pushchair and Haydn at her side. And she couldn't help feeling that if it wasn't for the war she would be doing just that, instead of dancing with dangerously attractive strangers and listening to crazy protestations of instant love from the likes of George Rivers.

'Do you always look as though you're ready to kill someone? . . . No you don't, you can smile.'

'Sometimes,' she conceded, blushing at the memory of her earlier thoughts about D'Este.

'You can't have been married long.'

'Three years.'

'You must have been a child bride.'

'Hardly, I have a two-year-old daughter.'

'It must be difficult to bring her up on your own.'

'I live with my father-in-law and his wife. I wouldn't be able to work and look after Anne without their help. Are you married, Captain D'Este?' She willed him to say yes, feeling that if he was, it would somehow cancel out her attraction to him.

'I've been too poverty-stricken and too busy studying to think of a wife.'

'Perhaps you'll find one here?'

'My family has other ideas. They are very traditional. I have been betrothed . . . engaged to my cousin since we were children.'

'An arranged marriage?'

'It is difficult to explain to someone who is not accustomed to our ways. We don't see it as "arranged". We have the same philosophy towards life and respect one another.'

'And love?'

'My mother didn't see my father until their wedding day. It was the perfect marriage of convenience: he had the money, she the aristocratic Spanish blood. They were forced to leave everything they owned in Cuba in 1934 when Antonio de Guiteras was hunted down and murdered by the military. They had supported him and his ideals of political freedom and democracy and if they hadn't fled to America we would all have been arrested and possibly murdered too. Especially me. Antonio was a close family friend and I was named

78

Tomas Antonio de Guiteras D'Este after him. When we set foot in America we had only the clothes on our backs, but my mother insisted that as we were all alive and healthy she had riches. I think that if my father had been killed like Antonio, she would have lain down and died alongside him, so perhaps you can forgive me for thinking, like them, that love is something that comes after marriage.'

'Perhaps they were just lucky.'

'Perhaps.'

'It must be wonderful to have seen so many different countries. I'd love to travel.'

'I think travel in the comfort of a cruise ship's stateroom must be a very different affair to fleeing as a refugee, or being shipped out as a soldier in cattle quarters, and that is the only travelling I've ever done.'

'But you have seen America and Cuba.'

'And Haiti, and England and now Wales.'

'After the war there could be other places. A doctor can work anywhere in the world.'

'I am only a doctor because my family made many sacrifices so I could continue my education.'

'I still can't imagine anyone telling me who to marry.'

'Is this so much better?' he asked. He didn't have to elaborate. The lights had dimmed. Under the cover of darkness half the couples were dancing so close, it was difficult to see where American uniform began and evening dress ended. 'I doubt that many of these people met before this evening, and looking at them now, I think there's something to be said for the respect of the old Spanish colonial ways.'

'In peacetime,' she agreed, thinking of her own rushed marriage, and Eddie and Jenny's. 'But few people can afford the luxury of a slow courtship these days.'

'I only hope that their marriages survive when the guns fall silent.'

'Mine will,' Jane said determinedly.

'Tell me about your daughter. I have six brothers and sisters. I never thought I'd miss them, but every time I see a little girl about my youngest sister's age, I get unbelievably homesick.'

'It's odd to finish the evening with two National Anthems,' Alma observed as they queued in front of the cloakroom hatch.

'Isn't it?' Bethan agreed absently, as she collected her own, Jane's and Alma's coats. 'I'll give you a lift back up to the fountain.'

'There's no need. Chuck – Major Reynolds – has offered to walk me home. He's billeted above Frank Clayton's shop next door,' she added when Bethan gave her a knowing look.

'I'm pleased for both of you. He can tell you all about his wife and baby, and you can tell him about Charlie and Theo.'

'Were we that boring?'

'No one had to listen if they didn't want to. I think it's wonderful that you've found a new friend to talk to.'

'Do you think it's wrong of me to let him walk me home, Bethan? After all, Charlie . . .'

'Charlie and Chuck Reynolds's wife might not have been sitting at our table tonight, but they were certainly there in spirit. I'm sure that if they could have seen you two together, both of them would have been proud to be married to such loyal people.'

'Do you really think so? I'm not so sure. I saw the way Mrs Llewellyn Jones was looking at us.'

'Mrs Llewellyn Jones would look at any man and woman who'd bumped into one another in the street and assume they were about to commit adultery.'

'Do you mind if I get to the counter, Bethan?' Anthea Llewellyn Jones snapped from behind them.

Taking a deep breath, Bethan stepped aside. Handing Jane her coat, she smiled and nodded to Chuck Reynolds who was waiting at the top of the stairs, before kissing Alma on the cheek. 'I'll see you tomorrow. If the major's free why don't you bring him up for tea as well?'

'I don't know if that's a good idea.'

'He can always visit Colonel Ford if he finds the children too noisy. Tell him he's welcome if he has nothing better to do.'

'I will.'

'That's the first time I've seen Alma smile since Charlie was posted missing,' Bethan said to Jane as they walked to the top of the staircase.

'Ladies, I only have a motorbike which is most unsuitable for evening dresses, but perhaps I could arrange a lift for you?' Captain D'Este stood halfway down the stairs shouldering his kitbag.

'We have our own car thank you, Captain. A handsome man with ten times the charm of Lieutenant Rivers,' Bethan whispered as they headed through the passages to the old coaching yard at the back of the hotel, where she had parked her car.

'That's not difficult. George Rivers is an idiot.'

'Both of them had eyes for you.'

'And my eyes are firmly fixed on Haydn.'

'Even when he hasn't been home in nine months?' Bethan asked as they climbed into her car.

'If you're trying to tell me something, why don't you come straight out with it, Bethan?'

'I'm not trying to tell you anything. Just having a private moan that I hope won't go any further. Tonight I saw more men than I've seen in the last three years, but as I looked at all those young American officers I couldn't help wondering if I'd recognise my own husband if he had been standing among them.'

'At least I've got Haydn's photographs in the *Sunday Pictorial* to look at,' Jane muttered apologetically, in an attempt to make amends for misunderstanding her sister-in-law.

'Andrew told me in one of his letters that he's going grey. Next year he'll be thirty. Since we married we've spent as much time apart as we have together. Do you want to know my worst nightmare?' She slammed the car into low gear as she negotiated the corner that led out on to Gelliwastad Road. 'That this war is going to go on for ever and we're going to waste our whole lives waiting for it to end, only to die before it's over.'

'You don't really think it's going to last for ever, do you?'

'I don't know. I'm sorry, I shouldn't have started this. All I've succeeded in doing is depressing you as well as myself.'

'Most of the time I try not to think about anything except what's in front of me. It's easy enough in work when there's endless bins of empty shell casings waiting to be packed with explosives. All I have to do is pick them up and fill them, but when the whistle blows at the end of the shift and I go home to Anne and read her a bedside story, it's always from the books that you, Haydn, Eddie and Maud had when you were little. Books about normal families where Mummy looks after the children, Daddy goes to work and comes home . . .'

' . . . in a suit and bowler hat, to a semi in Croydon.' Bethan laughed at the memories Jane evoked. 'That way of life was as alien to us as Hindu princesses and Baghdad caliphs in the *Arabian Nights*. There was my miner father going out every day looking like a tramp and coming home as black as a Negro . . .'

' . . . and still doing the same.'

'Are he and Phyllis all right?'

'Very happy as far as I can see.'

'I wish I had more time to talk to him, really talk to him the way I used to when I lived at home.' Bethan reached out and touched Jane's hand. 'I'm sorry. I know how much you miss Haydn.' She slowed the car, turning under the railway bridge that marked the beginning of the Graig hill.

'I have his letters, and unlike Tina with William, I know he's unlikely to be sent close enough to the front to be put in any real danger. The War Office would never risk a hair on the head of the chorus girls he travels with. Can you imagine the fuss the papers would make if any of them were hurt by a bomb or hit by a sniper?'

'Those girls don't mean anything to him. I know Haydn, he wouldn't have married you if he hadn't loved you.' Bethan crossed her fingers under cover of the blackout. The man who came home on all-too-brief, intermittent leaves was very different from the younger brother she had grown up with. She might have known the old Haydn, but she certainly didn't know the present one.

'I'm lucky. When I think of Eddie getting killed at Dunkirk I can't understand how Jenny bears it – or you and Haydn, come to that. I can't even begin to imagine what it was like to have grown up with brothers and sisters only to lose them the way you lost Eddie and Maud.'

'We have our memories, one another, and my father. He's the real mainstay of the family.'

'I worry more about what will happen when the war is over, than about it going on for ever. Can life ever go back to what it was? With so much destroyed, so many people dead . . .'

'We're getting far too maudlin. Let's go to sleep on a happier note.' Bethan cut the engine and coasted up outside her father's house. 'Have you heard from Haydn lately? Is he likely to be coming home?'

' "Soon", according to his last letter. Whenever that will be.'

Bethan leaned forward and hugged her sister-in-law. 'Let's hope this time the War Office isn't stringing him along.'

'You coming in?'

'And disturb Phyllis and my father and the lodger at this hour? No, I'll see you all tomorrow. You still have tomorrow off?'

'My first free Sunday in two months. You didn't think I'd give that up, did you?'

'Isn't it time you took a break from the factory? You

don't have to hand in your notice, just take a couple of weeks' holiday.'

'If you did the same we could take the children away for a few days.'

'I can't, not right now . . .'

'You really fell for that one, didn't you, Beth? I will take some time off, I promise. Just as soon as Haydn gets home. And thanks.'

'What for?'

'Being honest. It's good to know there's someone I can tell the truth to. I'm fed up to the back teeth of trying to pretend that everything is wonderful.'

'It was a good party.'

'I'm glad you enjoyed it, ma'am.'

'The name is Mrs Powell, Jenny to my friends.'

'Jenny, ma'am.' Kurt Schaffer pulled up the hand-brake of the Jeep as he stopped at the white cross Jenny had painted below the window of her corner shop. 'It's just as well they blacked out the coastal areas of the US of A before we came over here. At least we're used to finding our way around in the dark.'

'But not some of the other aspects of war like rationing, judging by the amount of food and drink on offer tonight.'

'Uncle Sam looks after his own.'

'And looks after them very well.'

She didn't resist as he pulled her into his arms, or find any difficulty in returning his kiss. His lips were cold, but proficient, and in the event it was he who moved away from her.

'Would you like to come upstairs?'

'Ma'am?' he murmured, unsure he'd heard her correctly.

'For tea?'

'What about your folks?' he asked, wary not only of her family, but the colonel's directive.

'My mother's dead, and my father's in hospital and likely to be there for some time.' She omitted the word

84

'psychiatric' in front of hospital. Not everyone understood mental illness, and some of her more outspoken neighbours had already asked if she was likely to inherit her father's condition.

'That's a damned shame.'

'It all happened a long time ago.' She deliberately kept her voice light. Glancing up she saw a flicker of movement in the window above the greengrocer's across the road. 'But if you're coming in, you'd better move the Jeep. Mrs Evans opposite has nothing better to do than watch my comings and goings. She'd love to see an American car parked outside my house all night.'

'All night?'

'Tea can take a long time to make, and then we have to drink it.'

His mouth went dry and his hands clammy. He wondered if he'd picked up a professional. Usually he knew exactly where he was with women. In his extensive experience they fell into two distinct categories: the 'good' and invariably inexperienced and naive whose seduction required protestations of undying love and promises of marriage, and the whores, who no matter what price they initially quoted, had always cost him dearly. He'd placed Jenny Powell firmly in the former category. Although she was a widow, what else could the sister-in-law of Colonel Ford's landlady possibly be?

Deciding she was joking about the 'all night', he asked, 'Where do you suggest I hide it?'

'Lower down the hill, on the right-hand side of the road outside the chapel,' she directed mischievously. 'When you come back, turn down the lane at the side of the shop. There's a back entrance. I'll be waiting behind the storeroom door. If you've got a torch, bring it. I don't want you crashing into the ash bins, but whatever you do, don't switch on the light until you're behind the yard door.'

'Afraid I'll get hurt?'

'Afraid of the neighbours hearing you.'

He climbed out of the Jeep and walked around to

help her out. She kissed him goodbye for Mrs Evans's benefit before he scrambled back into the driving seat. Waiting until he'd driven off, she didn't open the gate that led into the yard until she saw the blinds move a second time in Mrs Evans's window.

Lifting the latch Jenny unlocked the stockroom door. There had been a time when she would have found Alexander waiting for her, but she had relieved him of his keys to her house after his last fit of jealousy. Kurt Schaffer wasn't long. Less than five minutes later the gate creaked. Opening the door, she heard him call out softly.

'My torch battery is flat, and it's as black as a pig's nose in here.'

'Can you feel my hand?'

'Got it.'

'Walk towards me ... careful there's a step. I'll put the light on as soon as I've closed the door.'

'Floundering in the dark can be fun,' Kurt muttered as he crashed into her.

'Not as much as floundering in the light.'

He breathed in sharply, as her hand brushed across the fly on his trousers.

'There.' She clicked the light on in the shop, locked the back door and opened the side door to reveal a staircase. 'Switch off the light behind us, will you?'

She ran up the stairs, lifting the long skirt of her evening gown above her knees. 'The living room is through there.'

'What's this?' He opened the door in front of him.

'The kitchen. If you're good at doing dishes, there's a pile in the sink.'

'What's a sink?'

'I can see where your expertise lies.' She leaned back against the bedroom door. He kissed her again, his hand caressing her breasts through the lace bodice of her dress.

'Don't!'

'Sorry.' He stepped back, kicking himself for mis-

reading the signals. Resorting to the well-worn excuse
he had employed in similar situations, he murmured, 'I
lost my head. It's been a long time since I've seen a girl
as beautiful as you.' His eyes widened as she pulled
down the sleeves and low-cut neckline of her dress,
exposing her breasts.

'This frock shows every mark, Lieutenant, especially
finger marks.' Her blue eyes sparkled with suppressed
humour as she savoured the shock on his face. Slipping
her hand behind her, she opened her bedroom door and
walked backwards into the room. Still gazing at him,
she stepped out of her dress and petticoats and laid
them on a chair. With her left foot on the bed she
unclipped and rolled down one stocking, then the other.
Holding them up to the lamp at the top of the stairs,
she shook her head. 'They're laddered, and they're my
last pair.'

Swallowing hard, he muttered, 'I can get you more.'

She unhooked the suspender belt at her waist, pulled
it free and flung it on top of her clothes. Standing before
him naked, except for a pair of lace-edged, cream silk
knickers, she held out her arms. 'Are all Americans so
tardy?'

He stepped towards her, hardly daring to believe his
luck.

'You do have a French letter?'

'A . . .'

'I don't mind spending the night with you,
Lieutenant, but I don't want your baby.'

He unbuttoned his top pocket, praying that he still
had one of the American rubbers left. The English ones
were so damned small and tight. His luck was in. He
kissed her again as she began to peel off his jacket.

Afterwards Jenny tossed restlessly on her pillow while
Kurt slept soundly beside her. Unable to endure the
thoughts swarming through her mind, she switched on
the bedside lamp, sat up and lit a cigarette. What was
she trying to prove? That sex with one man was very

like sex with another? At least Alexander cared for her, loved her, even wanted to marry her, but this man was no different from a hundred others. Anything for a quick, cheap thrill: she, or a common prostitute, either would have done. She had seen through him the moment she had met him – so why had she allowed him to take her home and invited him into her bed?

Since she'd received the telegram telling her that Eddie had been killed, nothing had felt real or touched her emotions. It was almost as though she'd been sleep-walking since that moment, trying to convince everyone, especially herself, that the only way to live was minute by minute. Justifying her more outrageous actions with the excuse that as all pleasures were fleeting, she should take what came while it was there for the taking.

Alexander – Kurt – what was the difference? Now she had discovered that making love to either was just like drinking a bottle of Alexander's good wine. Once finished, she felt just as flat, lonely and despairing as she had done before.

It hadn't been like that with Eddie. Or had it? Was her memory playing tricks, painting an idyllic portrait of the physical side of her marriage, because the rest of it had been so disastrous?

Eddie had abandoned her on their wedding night believing, with good reason, that she loved and wanted his brother Haydn, not him. By the time she realised just how deeply she did love him, he had joined the Guards and left for France, and there had been no time to make amends other than one brief, two-day, compassionate leave after her mother's death. Did he . . . could he have known how much he had meant to her? Fighting back tears, she reached out to reassure herself that she wasn't alone.

'Baby . . .' Kurt mumbled thickly as her hand caressed his naked back.

Crushing her cigarette in the ashtray beside her, she switched off the lamp. Bending her head she kissed his neck, her fingers seeking pulse spots that had aroused

Eddie. As Kurt responded to her touch, it was enough to know that for the moment, there was someone lying beside her who could dispel the black thoughts crowding in on her. Tomorrow she would be alone again. But then, tomorrow was hours away.

Chapter Six

BETHAN WOKE EARLY to the sound of voices drifting up from the garden. Throwing back the bedclothes she went to the window and lifted a corner of the blackout in time to see David Ford climb into his car. Lieutenant Rivers and Sergeant Morelli were with him. Sunday or not, the Americans were working. She was glad. The rare free days when she was able to organise a family tea had become all the more precious since they had introduced round-the-clock shifts in the munitions factories and pits in an effort to step up production.

She returned to her bed and looked at the box on the side table. It contained all the letters Andrew had written to her since he'd left for France. Five short notes before he'd been captured at Dunkirk, and over a hundred longer epistles since.

She reached for them, then, changing her mind, she replaced the box on the cabinet and opened the drawer in the table. Taking out one of the blue letter/envelopes the authorities insisted on for prisoner-of-war correspondence, she unscrewed the top from her fountain pen, sucked the end thoughtfully, and began writing.

Dear Andrew,
*   It is six o'clock on a Sunday morning and our new lodgers . . .*

She hesitated. If she told Andrew there were Americans billeted in the house, the censor would not only blank out the relevant sentences but could even impound her letter.

*   . . . who have taken over the top floor of the house have*

*left for work. Their company doesn't make up for your
absence. It never could, but at least I have new people
to talk to in the winter evenings when I am not on duty.*

   *I saw your parents last night, they are both well and
anxious for news about you. Unfortunately Mrs
Llewellyn Jones was with them. I'm sorry, darling, I
can't like that woman even for you and your parents'
sake.*

She wished she could write something reassuring about
the party. He knew the Americans were in Britain, but
did he and his fellow prisoners know about the success
the Yanks were having with British women? How could
she tell him that she was immune to their charms
without worrying him? It was easier to write about the
children.

   *Eddie and Rachel continue to thrive. Both of them are
very sociable, but no matter how many hours I work, I
make sure they know exactly who their parents are.
Eddie's vocabulary is quite extensive, and he certainly
recognises his daddy. If anyone mentions you, he runs
straight to your photograph. Rachel is going to start
in the nursery class in Maesycoed primary school after
Christmas, much to your mother's disgust. I think she
would have preferred a private school, but I hope you
agree that it is important for our children to be able to
mix with people from all walks of life. Your father does.
He says that after the war, class differences won't matter
so much. How can they when labourers are working
alongside public schoolboys in the most unlikely situations?*

   *I also want to tell you how much Maisie and Liza
Clark, the eldest evacuee I took in, help me to run the
house. I couldn't manage without either of them. I suspect
that you may get a letter from your mother about my
insistence on keeping the Clark girls. Their father has
been killed and Mrs Llewellyn Jones wanted to put them
in the workhouse. No matter what your mother says, they
are not much of a drain on our resources as the two*

eldest are working and Alma and I are sharing the cost of the younger girls.

I know this may be difficult for you to understand, but I dare not look too far into the future. Like most people in Pontypridd I live one day at a time. I have to, Andrew. Work takes up most of my time, my few free hours are spent with the children, and although Maisie and Liza are marvellous, I still have to watch that everything runs smoothly and do the household accounts. (That's one job you can have back the minute you walk through the door.)

Everyone in Pontypridd keeps talking about 'when the war is over'. They assume that everything will return to what it was in 1939, but sometimes, like Jane, I wonder if life can ever go back to what it was? Most of the evacuees can go home, but what about the ones who have no one and nowhere left to go to, like the Clarks? If it finished tomorrow, Liza and Mary will be earning barely enough to support themselves let alone the other two. And then there's Maisie. I know your mother disapproves of my employing an unmarried mother to look after the children, but she has no one else and I can hardly put her and her daughter back into the workhouse . . .

She leaned back on the pillows and read what she'd written. What was she thinking of? There was no way she could burden Andrew with her problems with the Clark girls, Maisie, and especially her fraught relationship with his mother and Mrs Llewellyn Jones. Regretting the loss of the pre-paid envelope, she tore it up, took another from the drawer and began again, this time without voicing a single complaint or criticism of his mother or Mrs Llewellyn Jones, a mention of the Clarks or giving him the slightest cause to worry about her, the children, the house or what was going to happen at the end of the war. She even finished with a white lie.

Eddie has just toddled in. He sends you a kiss, but

*unfortunately demands all my attention. I will write
again soon, darling. I love you, yours as ever, Bethan*

She looked up at the closed door. Her letters were
getting shorter, but what else could she write about?
Day-to-day problems he wouldn't understand, and even
if he could, was powerless to help her solve. Given the
choice over the Clark girls would he have sided with
her, or his mother and Mrs Llewellyn Jones?

The most painful thought was not that he might do
so, but that she couldn't be sure what he would do. He
was her husband, and she didn't even know him any
more.

Jenny fastened the last button on her blouse, leaned over
and poked the comatose figure in her bed. 'Wake up!'
When he refused to stir she prodded him again, harder
this time. 'Come on, wakey wakey!'

Kurt Schaffer opened his eyes, screwed them against
the glare of the electric bulb and peered up at her. 'Hi,'
he mumbled sleepily, smiling at the memory of their
uninhibited lovemaking and the night they'd shared.

'Hi,' Jenny said brusquely. 'You've five minutes to get
dressed and out of here.'

'What time is it?'

'Five-thirty.'

'Jesus H. Christ! I should be in combat gear and on
manoeuvres.' Leaping out of bed he dived for his dress
uniform which was still scattered over the floor where
Jenny had thrown it the night before. 'Hell! I have to
go back to my billet to change. What do I tell the old
battleaxe if she asks where I spent the night?'

'That you were praying in a chapel?'

'She'll never believe me.'

'I don't care what you tell her as long as you don't
mention my name or the Graig hill. And while we're on
the subject, make sure no one sees you leaving.'

'Who's watching your door at this time in the
morning?'

'Nosy parkers.'

'I just love your language. What exactly are parkers?' he asked as he heaved on his pants.

'Out!' She folded the blankets to the foot of the bed and stripped the sheets.

'All right, so you don't want to talk. I can understand that at this unholy hour. I'm not feeling so good myself. See you tonight?'

'I'm busy.'

'Tomorrow?'

'Busier.'

'Give a guy a break?'

'I've given you all I'm going to.'

'Come on. Last night – '

'Last night was fun,' her blue eyes took on a frosty glaze as they gazed into his, 'but let's not turn it into something it wasn't.'

'You don't want to see me again?' he asked incredulously, his ego shattered by the first rebuff he'd experienced.

'The very next time you organise a party.'

'That could be months away. I thought after what happened last night, you'd be my girl.'

'I'm my own girl.'

'You really don't want to see me again?'

'How many ways are there of saying no?'

'You weren't like this last night.'

'Last night I wanted your body.' She blanched when she realised how true that was. Last night, almost any young and presentable man would have done to alleviate her loneliness. Picking up his jacket she thrust it at him. 'We'll go out the back way. Wait in the yard for five minutes after I'm gone. Mrs Evans should have pulled her blackout back by then.' Handing him his boots, she herded him through the door and down the stairs.

'Do you mind if I call in later in the week? You could change your – '

'I won't.' She strode through the shop and unbolted the storeroom door.

'Am I allowed to talk to you if I see you in the town?' he asked caustically.

'That depends on who I'm with, Lieutenant.' She pushed him into the yard.

'The name is Kurt, Kurt Schaffer, and it's freezing out here,' he protested, hopping from one foot to the other.

'Nice to meet you, and thank you so much for stating the obvious,' she replied, adopting his sarcastic tone.

He threw his boots to the ground, sat on the step and tried to push his numbed and frozen feet into them. 'Goddamn it, it's impossible to dress out here.'

'Ssh, keep your voice down.'

'I need a bathroom.'

'There's a ty bach in front of you.'

'What in hell's that?'

'Open the door and find out.' Stepping around him, she locked the storeroom door, and opened the gate. Walking through it, she slammed it in his face. He was left staring at the planks of wood in the early morning gloom, wondering if he'd broken any peculiar Welsh rule of conduct that no one had thought to tell him about. For the first time in his life a girl had used and abandoned *him*. Until now, he'd always been the one to cut and run and he discovered that the taste of rejection, like bile, lingered sourly in the mouth, and he didn't like the sensation. Not one bit.

Bethan sat back in her chair watching Eddie stagger on chubby, unsteady legs from her father's knee to her own. He collapsed in a fit of giggles as Ronnie reached out and tickled him.

'That one's going to run in the Olympics one day, mark my words,' Megan predicted as she brought in a plate of sandwiches from the kitchen.

'Mam always sees a glowing future for the Powell children.' Diana's dark eyes shone warm with love as they rested on her husband.

'What about Ronconi children?' Ronnie asked in mock indignation.

'They'll count as Powells.'

Megan gave her daughter a sideways glance. Ronnie and Diana might have been married only a few weeks but there was a dreamy look about her Diana made her wonder if she was already pregnant.

'Reeses are important too.' Catching hold of his small stepson, Billy, Ronnie swung him high in the air.

'Careful! That's my grandson you're about to drop.'

'I wouldn't drop you, would I mate?'

'Dada,' Billy chanted, grinning cheekily at Megan.

Taking two sandwiches from his mother-in-law, Ronnie handed one to Billy, and demolished the other in a single bite.

'Looks like you've got your work cut out keeping those two in order, Diana,' Evan smiled, happy for his niece. Both she and Ronnie had been married before. Diana's marriage had ended in tragedy when her husband had been killed in an explosion in the munitions factory. And when his younger daughter, Maud, had died of tuberculosis, her husband, Ronnie, had seemed inconsolable. Ronnie and Diana's wedding had been the one bright spot in an otherwise bleak year.

'They gang up on me all the time.' Diana pulled a wriggling Billy from Ronnie's lap. 'Go and play with your cousins.' She set him down and pushed him in the direction of the hall where Rachel, Eddie and Anne were playing a complicated game of tag that was beyond adult comprehension.

'If the noise is anything to go by, the next generation of Powells are likely to be even wilder than the last.'

'If you and Ronnie want some peace, Dad, why don't you sit in Andrew's study?' Bethan suggested.

'And miss the chance of being nagged by my wife and mother-in-law?'

'You don't know what nagging is, my boy,' Megan threatened as Ronnie went down on all fours and growled at Eddie and Billy who were creeping towards the door pretending to be bears.

'What do you say to some peace?' Evan asked his youngest son, Brian, who was sitting in the corner lost in an old book of Andrew's.

Brian was too engrossed to answer. Although he was only four years older than Rachel, he already had a reputation as a bookworm. Evan's common-law wife, Phyllis, looked fondly at her son. 'He's always the same. Once his nose is in a book you can't get a word out of him.'

'Just like his big sister.'

'Was I really that bad?' Bethan asked.

'You can't remember?'

'Any sign of Haydn or William coming home?' Ronnie said as he returned to his chair; the boys had tired of the game.

'None that I know of,' Jane said flatly.

'Tina was going spare yesterday.' Megan bustled in with another tray and began setting cups out on the table. 'She hasn't heard from that son of mine in weeks. I'll brain him when he comes home. How long does it take to write a postcard?'

'Not as long as it takes a mail bag to get from North Africa to here.' Evan pulled out his pipe.

'Tina'll be up later with Alma. You never know, something may have come in today's post, but I wouldn't bank on it. Andrew writes at least two letters a week, some take six months to get here, others only three and a half. The post is in a right mess. Everyone you talk to who has family serving overseas complains about it.'

'If there'd been trouble with either of the boys we would have heard.'

'I suppose you're right, Evan.' Megan walked to the window. 'Your Americans are back, Beth, and Alma and Tina are with them.'

'And Alma's major?'

'Alma has a major?' Ronnie raised his eyebrows.

'A married man who talks even more about his wife and son than she does about Charlie.'

'That's impossible.' Evan frowned as he remembered a letter Charlie had left with him. A letter he would have given Alma months ago, if she had been prepared to accept the possibility that her husband was dead.

Bethan went into the hall and opened the front door. 'Tea's made and you're all welcome to join us.' She smiled at the Americans as Alma carried Theo in.

'That's very generous, thank you. We'll be happy to join you, Mrs John.' David Ford stood back to allow Tina to walk in ahead of him.

'How about I make some American coffee to go with the tea, sir?' Dino Morelli asked.

'Good idea, Sergeant.'

Ronnie went to fetch more chairs from the dining room that Bethan had rarely opened since Andrew's departure.

'Looks like you're running a nursery here, ma'am.' Chuck stepped warily around the marauding toddlers.

'And here's one more to add to them.' Alma handed over Theo as she unbuttoned her coat.

'There's usually more, but my evacuees and house-keeper are helping out in the Sunday school. They've organised a tea and entertainment for your soldiers.'

'And very welcome it will be, Mrs John, after the manoeuvres we've put them through today. I've never seen so many pained faces. Running up and down your hills has exercised muscles they didn't know they had.'

'Lieutenant Rivers?' David Ford prompted as they entered the drawing room. 'I believe you have something to say to the ladies?'

'I would like to apologise for my ungentlemanly conduct last night.' He was too embarrassed to meet Jane's eye.

He looked so sheepish, Bethan almost felt sorry for the man. Leaving her father to make the introductions she followed Dino into the kitchen. He was mixing flapjacks and Megan was greasing pans, both of them chatting away as though they'd known one another for years.

'We met last night, he helped me babysit,' Megan explained.

'I hope you don't mind, Mrs John, but as hard tack rations aren't great, I thought I'd cook up something for the officers and give the children a treat at the same time.'

'I don't mind, and you don't have to apologise every time you walk into my kitchen.'

'But I am trespassing.' He reached down a pitcher of syrup from the cupboard Maisie had cleared for his use.

'Trespass away.' Scooping up Eddie who was threatening to hit Billy with a wooden car, she returned to the drawing room where George Rivers was holding forth as though he were on a soapbox.

' . . . and I get mad every time I think of the Jerries chaining our men like common criminals . . .'

'Chains? On our men?' Bethan looked to David Ford.

'I've heard rumours.' Evan realised that the colonel was annoyed by George's outburst. 'But I assumed they were just stories. So many unsubstantiated claims of atrocities have been made by both sides since the war started it's difficult to sift truth from propaganda.'

'Impossible,' David Ford concurred. 'But unfortunately this particular rumour is true. I saw the Red Cross report myself. But didn't you tell me that your husband was captured at Dunkirk, Mrs John?'

'What difference does that make?'

'The only confirmed reports of chaining relate to Canadian, Free French and British prisoners captured after the Dieppe raid.'

'But now the Germans have set a precedent, how long will it be before they start chaining all the prisoners of war?'

'The Red Cross are working to calm the situation. They believe the Germans only began to use chains after receiving false reports that the British and Canadians were chaining German prisoners.'

'What next? They hear we shot their men so they start shooting ours?'

'I doubt even the Germans are capable of shooting unarmed men,' her father interposed.

'No? What about the reports of atrocities in the Warsaw Ghetto? Not only men died there, but women and children.'

'Bethan, no one has cause to hate the Germans more than me, but they're men not monsters,' Ronnie interrupted. 'I know, I've seen them. They have two eyes, two arms, two legs and one head, exactly the same as us.'

'And guns. And they are trying to take over the world.'

'If we'd moved over and let them get on with it, there wouldn't be a war for us to fight.'

'Are you saying that we should have let the Germans take over Europe?' George Rivers demanded belligerently.

'I believe that is an example of what is known as British humour, Lieutenant,' David Ford informed him as everyone else in the room burst out laughing.

'Bad taste, but meant as a joke,' Ronnie smiled disarmingly.

'Well I'm ready to kick Jerry's ass . . . begging your pardon, ladies.'

'That's some military machine you're ready to take on.'

'And what would you know about the Germans, stuck here in Pontypridd, Mr Ronconi?'

'Ronnie fought with the partisans in Italy,' Diana asserted, furious at George's assumption that the Americans were the only fighting men in the room. 'He was badly wounded . . .'

'Not that badly.' Ronnie took the coffee Megan handed him. 'This smells wonderful,' he complimented her, hoping to change the subject.

'Do you speak Italian?' David asked.

'What do you think, with a surname like Ronconi?'

'My sergeant is a Morelli, but his Italian isn't up to first-grade standard.'

'We spoke it at home,' Tina volunteered. 'Both our parents were Italian born.'

The conversation moved on, but Bethan caught David Ford looking at Ronnie more than once afterwards. She had a feeling that he'd filed away the fact that Ronnie was bilingual and had fought with the partisans, but with the front in North Africa she really couldn't see what possible relevance the information might have.

After the younger children had been bathed and put to bed, the evacuees returned from Sunday school and followed them upstairs. George Rivers and the colonel disappeared, David Ford to work, George out of the house, but Maurice Duval and Dino Morelli stayed in the drawing room. Tina opened the piano and roped the Americans in for a sing-song. Using her lack of musical talent as an excuse, Bethan cleared the dishes. She was crossing the hall with a loaded tray when Tomas D'Este walked in.

'You look exhausted,' she said.

'I confess I'm beat. I'd forgotten just how tiring a fifteen-hour stint of surgery can be.'

'I'll make you something to eat, sir,' Dino offered, as he walked through with a second tray.

'As you're the only one with any pretence to a voice, don't you dare leave the drawing room,' Bethan said. She had noticed that the sergeant hadn't left her aunt's side all afternoon, and anyone who could take Megan's mind off William's protracted silence for more than five minutes had to be a miracle worker. 'I'll make the captain something. I'll be glad of the excuse to talk shop and brush up on my knowledge of surgical techniques.'

'It's my job.'

'And I'm relieving you of it, Sergeant. This way, Captain.' She opened the kitchen door.

'Anything will do. As soon as I've eaten, I'm for bed. In ten hours I start all over again.'

'There's that many casualties?'

'Not so many recent ones, thank God, although we've had a few in from the Dieppe disaster.' He sat at the table. 'The boys with burns are the worst. Your flyers paid dearly for the Battle of Britain victory.'

'But you can do something for them?'

'We can't repair blinded eyes, but we can mend damaged bones and graft new skin over the worst disfigurements. Success depends on the degree of injury. Hello again,' he greeted Jane as she walked in with a fistful of enamel mugs.

'Sorry, I didn't mean to interrupt, I've just collected these from upstairs.'

'It looks as though they've had a party up there. Be an angel and wash them for me please, Jane, while I heat up some of Maisie's rabbit stew for the captain?'

'It's Tomas, and I don't want to eat into your, or the children's rations.'

'It's to even things up. Sergeant Morelli uses any excuse to make treats for the children. And before you say anything about the meat, it's off the coupon. The farmer's son trapped them and gave Maisie a pair. Just between us, I think he'd like to start courting her.'

'She's twenty-five and he's seventeen,' Jane remonstrated as she ran water from the boiler set in the range into a jug.

'That's the age they get it worst,' Bethan said, opening the pantry door. Ladling a generous portion of the stew from a large saucepan into a smaller one, she set it on the hob. 'I'm fascinated by what you do.' She opened the breadbin and extracted a gritty national loaf. 'Just the idea of rebuilding a face seems like something out of H.G. Wells.'

'Tremendous advances have been made in reconstructive surgery since 1939, but for every man we help, there's half a dozen more we can do nothing for.'

'But it is wonderful that you try,' Jane interrupted. 'I know I shouldn't be telling you this – Official Secrets Act and all that – but I'm sure you've already heard that there was an explosion in one of the munitions factories here last year?'

'Not only heard. I've seen some of the casualties.'

'Jane was caught up in the blast,' Bethan explained.

'You weren't hurt?'

'I was one of the lucky ones.'

'She only broke both her legs.'

'At least I recovered. I just wish there was something I could do to help the ones who weren't so fortunate, like Megan's brother's wife, Myrtle.'

'There is.' Tomas sat back as Bethan placed a tray on the table in front of him. 'We're desperate for volunteers to befriend the servicemen who haven't any friends or relatives living close enough to visit them. Not just the Americans but the Canadians and British.'

'I'd love to help too, but . . .'

' . . . you're working twenty-four hours a day as a district nurse, twenty as a mother and sixteen as a foster mother for evacuees, Mrs John?'

'Not quite those hours, although sometimes it feels like it.'

'What about you?' He turned to Jane.

'I only get one day off a week, and I can't be certain when that's going to be from one week to the next.'

'But you could spare an hour now and again?'

'As long as no one relied on me.'

'That would be fine. I could put you down as a casual.'

'What would I have to do?'

'Talk to the patients.'

'I'm not much of a conversationalist.'

'Just remind them that there's an outside world. Tell them about yourself, your daughter, anything, as long as you let them know that someone appreciates what they've done, and still cares what happens to them. The trouble with reconstructive surgery is that it's usually a long job involving several operations. Anything that takes the patient's mind off what's happening to him has to be good. Even if it's only for an hour a week. When's your next day off?'

'A week tomorrow.'

'I'll work out some transport.'

'Shanks's pony,' Bethan suggested.

'Pony?' he looked up, confused.

'Walking?'

'A charabanc picks up the volunteers in town every day, and I'd be only too happy to bring you home on my motorbike, Mrs Powell. That is if you don't mind riding pillion?' He smiled at Jane as Bethan laid the stew in front of him.

Chapter Seven

A GREY, JANUARY Sunday afternoon was threatening to turn into an even colder, murkier Sunday night as Captain Richard Reide escorted Anthea down the steep hill that led from the Common into town.

'That was some meal your mother organised.'

'Christmas leftovers.'

'Didn't taste like any leftovers to me.' He shifted the umbrella he was holding over both of them, pushing it against the wind that was driving the rain into their faces. 'What are these church socials like?'

'Boring.'

'Then why are we going?'

'Because there's nothing else to do in Pontypridd on a Sunday night. Nothing respectable, that is.' Anthea brushed an imaginary fleck of dust from Richard's great-coat as she tightened her hold on his arm.

'What if we looked for something else?'

'You trying to corrupt me, Captain Reide?'

'Most definitely. But what about your parents? We told them that we'd be at the social.'

'If they ask, I'll say we got sidetracked.'

'Won't they be mad at you?'

'Possibly, but I can handle them.'

'I'm not so sure. Your father watches you like a hawk, and me like a buzzard. And with good reason. I know that if I was ever lucky enough to have a daughter like you I'd do exactly the same, and God help the fellow who dared ask her for a date. Every time I'd look at him, I'd remember the way I'm feeling about you right now.'

'Then you'd frighten him off and your daughter

would die an old maid. She wouldn't thank you for that.'

'I suppose she wouldn't.' Richard stopped. Drawing the umbrella closer to their heads he unbuttoned his greatcoat and reached for his cigarettes. Tapping two out of a pack he offered her one.

'On the street?'

'Live dangerously. Besides, no one else is crazy enough to walk out in weather like this.'

She smiled up at him as he lit it for her. 'Do you know my father thinks you're a fine officer and a trust-worthy fellow?'

'You sure he was talking about me?'

'Absolutely. He said it the first time you came to dinner.'

'Nice to know that your folks think as well of me as I do of them.' Richard closed his gloved hand over hers and gave it a light squeeze as they turned the corner opposite the old bridge and entered the top end of Taff Street.

'That's better. Rain is bad but rain and wind like that is disgusting. I'm soaked through.' Turning down the collar on her coat, Anthea shook the worst of the icy raindrops from her scarf.

'Now we've decided to play hooky from the social, we have to find something else to do, preferably out of this rain.' Richard looked up and down the deserted, blacked-out street. The only sounds were the rain teeming in the gutters and the hymn singing resounding from Tabernacle Chapel behind them.

'You're the gentleman, you decide.'

'You're the native. How about a drink?'

'The pubs only serve travellers on Sundays.'

'So the boys have been telling me. But we could be travellers.'

'Only in the pubs a lady wouldn't go into. Try it in the New Inn and we'd get thrown out. They value their licence too much to bend the rules.'

'I've spent so much time in your house since I've

been here I haven't had time to explore the town. Are there any good but quiet bars?'

'No, and none of any kind that open on a Sunday.'

'The movies?'

'The cinema, you mean. Not open on Sunday.'

'Something has to be open on Sunday.'

'The cafes, chapels and churches.'

'We've already discounted the churches, and the cafes are out, they're full of enlisted men. It's bad enough facing them during working hours without socialising with them. Unfortunately Chuck's taken our transport. The colonel's sent him into Cardiff to – sorry, classified – so I can't even drive you anywhere.'

'There isn't anywhere to drive.'

'And it's too cold and wet for a walk. Who suggested we leave your cosy parlour?'

'You did.'

'So I did. Well, as I said, Chuck's out. I have a bottle of bourbon stashed in our rooms. I don't suppose you'd consider keeping a guy company?'

Anthea caught her breath at the outrageousness of the suggestion. Every warning her mother had ever given her about putting herself in compromising positions with men flashed into her mind. But then, 'men' didn't mean Richard. He was different – an officer and a gentleman – and it wasn't as though she didn't know him. He'd called on her at least once a week since the party. Her parents knew and approved of him. And, after all, she was a mature twenty-nine-year-old working woman with a responsible job, not a sixteen-year-old schoolgirl.

'Maybe,' she answered hesitantly, 'but only if he behaves like a gentleman.'

'You could tie my hands behind my back.'

'Would I need to?'

'You can trust me with your honour and your life, honey.' He kissed her, grazing her cheek with his moustache. 'Well, what are we waiting for?' Taking her by the arm he walked her briskly up towards the fountain and his billet.

Damning British licensing laws that didn't allow for Sunday opening, Kurt Schaffer sipped his fourth luke-warm cup of tea in Ronconi's cafe and continued to watch the door. Darkness had fallen, the blackout was in place, and half the lamps had been switched off to comply with fuel-saving regulations; but in his mind's eye he was back, dancing with Jenny in the brilliantly lit ballroom in the New Inn. Her blonde hair gleaming silver under the lamps, her lace dress glittering like a Christmas fairy's as she dipped and swayed in time to the music. Her lips curved upwards in a smile, her blue eyes gazed into his, sending his heart pounding in anticipation of the night to come . . .

The dream world he'd manufactured out of that one short evening and night was more beguiling and romantic than anything he'd seen on or off a movie screen, and much more real than the cafe and the people around him, but he realised it wasn't the time or place to wallow in imaginings.

Snapping out of his reverie he reached for his ciga-rettes. Since the night of the party he'd become obsessed with Jenny. All he could think of was seeing her, kissing her – making love to her again. And convinced that all he had to do to rouse her passion to the same fever pitch as his own was to confront her, he'd spent every free moment since the party plotting out ways to meet her again. But despite endless visits to the cafe, dance halls and pubs frequented by the munitions workers, weeks had passed without him seeing her, until that morning, and then he had been unable to talk to her. He had been racing through town in a Jeep with Chuck and Rick Reide and she'd been heading into station yard with a crowd of girls. He'd seen and recognised her silver hair even through the gloom of the blackout. Knowing that she worked in a munitions factory, and having heard somewhere that the girls were on twelve-hour shifts he realised she'd be back in town about the time he'd finish for the day.

The minute training manoeuvres were over he'd raced up to the Common to change out of his combat dress. Mrs Llewellyn Jones had been less than cordial since the evening of the ball, despite his lying assurances that he'd had to sit up all night with a sick man. A week later she'd dropped a heavy hint that of choice, she'd exchange him for Captain Reide, who had been cultivating the entire family with the assiduous attention of a salesman out to make the 'big' kill.

Subsequently, she, her husband and Anthea had grown noticeably cooler towards him, with the result that he now spent as much of his off-duty time as he could out of the house. Christmas had been especially dismal. He had whiled away most of the day with the enlisted men in the basement of the Tabernacle Chapel that had been turned into a 'British Restaurant'. But even then it had been Jenny, not his family, who had occupied most of his thoughts.

Seeing her that morning had honed his desire to the point when he physically ached to be with her. One night, and all he had been able to think of since was her. Colonel Ford had bawled him out twice on manoeuvres for not paying attention, and that was after Chuck Reynolds had covered a couple of his mistakes.

After washing and changing in record time he had spent all evening in the cafe, sitting, watching and waiting. A few girls had approached his table and spoken to him, but none had silver blonde hair, or could hold a candle to Jenny. He was debating whether finally to put himself out of his misery and risk another rejection by driving up the hill and knocking on her door, when the curtain moved and she walked in with a man. A tall, well-built, fair-haired man he hated on sight. He left his seat.

'Hi,' he greeted her, unable to conceal his resentment.
'Hello.'
'It's Lieutenant Schaffer. Remember?'

'I remember. Alexander, this is one of the American soldiers I told you about. Lieutenant Schaffer, this is Alexander Forbes.'

'How do you do?'

Alexander's politeness, polished BBC accent and well-cut, though shabby clothes only served to fuel Kurt's irritation.

'Not so well. This country takes some getting used to.'

'Is there anything we can do to make you feel more welcome, Lieutenant?'

'Explain why you drink such disgusting tea and warm beer. And you can't even get the beer on a Sunday night. There's no movie theatres open, no dance halls, nothing for a man to do after a hard day's work.'

'Sundays in Wales are for chapels and churches. I'm sure you'd be made welcome in any one of them.' Jenny took Alexander's arm. 'If you'll excuse us, Lieutenant, we've friends waiting.'

Kurt watched them walk into the back room where they joined another, younger couple. Tossing enough coins on to the table to cover the cost of his tea and a tip, he went outside. The rain had stopped, the moon had risen, but a chill, damp wind began to bite as he fastened his greatcoat. Hating the town – the weather – the country – the war for exiling him from the States – but most of all hating Jenny Powell – he pushed his hands into his pockets, pulled his cap over his face and headed across the road towards station yard.

'Want a good time, Yank?'

'If you do I'm the one to give it to you . . .'

'Not if you like redheads.'

He peered into the darkness. 'How much?'

'A pound?' answered the nearest voice.

He did a swift conversion into dollars. 'Where's your room?'

'No room, but I know a quiet doorway.'

'Forget it.'

'All right, ten bob.'

'No room, no go.'

'My, aren't we the picky one.' Cackles of laughter followed as he walked away. Furious he kicked a ball of newspaper from his path.

'Kurt?'

He turned around. 'George?'

'Meet Vera and her younger sister . . . what is your name, sweetie?'

'Harriet.' The voice was muffled.

'I met them at a chapel social.'

'George persuaded us that there were better things to do than go to chapel on a Sunday.' Vera managed to giggle and slur simultaneously.

'You found somewhere to drink?'

'All you have to do is knock on the back door of the right pub. Isn't that so, ladies?'

'George has bought a bottle of sherry.'

'To go with the one of whiskey. How about it, Kurt, want to join us?'

'Where are you going?'

'I've got rooms in a house on Broadway.' Harriet swayed as she clung to George's arm.

'Lead me to them,' Kurt said carelessly.

George hesitated for a moment. Making a decision, he pushed Harriet towards Kurt. 'Two are one too many, even for me, buddy.'

Richard checked the blackout before switching on a second lamp. 'Another?' He picked up the bottle and waved it in front of Anthea.

'I shouldn't.'

'Why not? You deserve a good time after years of austerity.' He poured a generous measure before moving next to her on the sofa.

'You've made these rooms really comfortable.'

'Thank you. You do realise that I'm not just out for a casual fling, don't you, honey?'

'You've never said otherwise.'

'It might be wartime and all that, and soon I'll be

going away to fight and I may not be coming back, but the minute I saw you, I knew, I just knew, something special was going to happen between us.' He abandoned his glass on a side table and took her hand into his. 'Don't tell me you didn't feel it as well?'

Bewildered, she gazed mutely into his eyes.

'Of course you did,' he continued, answering for her. 'You're a gorgeous and unusual girl, Anthea.' Leaning forward he cupped her face in his hands. 'There isn't anyone else, is there?'

'No one in particular,' she breathed headily.

'I'm selfish enough to be glad.'

'Why selfish?'

'It's a bit much to ask you to be my girl when I could be sent overseas at any moment.'

'You could go any time?'

'Any time,' he reiterated. 'I'm fully trained, unlike some of the other officers, and most of the men.' He lifted her fingers to his lips and kissed the tips one by one. 'Would you be prepared to wait for me?'

'Of course I would, Richard.'

'I hoped you'd say that.' He moved closer. Slipping his hand behind her neck he pulled her face to his and kissed her. A long, slow, unhurried kiss that ended only when he tried to put his tongue into her mouth. 'Chuck won't be back until tomorrow,' he reminded her, slipping the buttons on her blouse.

She closed her hand over his, trapping his fingers.

'I'm not doing anything we haven't done before,' he remonstrated.

'We've never been alone in your rooms before.'

'You feel safer in the Jeep, or the front porch of your father's house?'

'There was no risk of you getting carried away there.'

'I promise I won't do anything you don't want to.'

'And I don't want to do this. Not here.'

'Come on, honey. Just a few memories to look back on when we're apart? That's not much for a fellow to ask from his girl.'

'But I'm not that kind of a girl, Richard.'

'You're the kind of girl I love and respect. The kind I want to marry.'

'Marry!' Her eyes sparkled as they gazed into his. 'But we only met a few weeks ago.'

'Do you think I want to cram years of loving into weeks? I'd like nothing better than to carry on calling on you, enjoying a slow, leisurely courtship while I get to know you and your folks properly. But there isn't time, honey. Besides, don't you feel as though we've known one another all our lives?'

'Yes, but . . .'

'Honey, I respect you. I love you. Come here.' He kissed her again, his fingers busily flicking open buttons as he crushed her against his chest, so she couldn't feel what he was doing. 'My, but you're beautiful.' Pushing her blouse open he pulled down her bust shaper, exposing her breasts.

'Richard!'

'Even when I felt them I never dreamed they'd look this fabulous. No pin-up could hold a candle to you, honey. One glimpse of these would be enough to make any man take on ten armies and win.' He bent his head and kissed her nipples, teasing them with his tongue.

'Richard . . . no . . . at least turn the light off,' she begged.

He lifted his head surprised to see that she'd turned crimson. 'Is this is the first time you've done this?'

'What do you take me for?'

'My special girl.' He lay back, pulling her on to his chest, freeing his hands so he could continue to caress her. 'If it will make you any easier, we could get a ring.'

'An engagement ring?'

'You do want to get engaged, don't you?' He slipped her blouse further down her arms.

'I want it more than anything else in the whole world. But there's Daddy and Mummy . . .'

'I thought they liked me.'

'They do. But marriage is such a big step. Where would we live? What would we do?'

'For now, carry on as we are. But after the war we'll live in Georgia. It's a beautiful state. My family has a farm there. You'll love it. Soft clean air, green trees, rolling acres of tobacco and cotton.'

'You're a farmer?'

He burst out laughing. 'Do I look like a farmer?'

'No.' In her limited experience farmers were part of the rough, uneducated, labouring class her mother had taken pains to shield her from; and farmhouses were badly furnished, rudimentary buildings that smelt of chickens and sour milk.

'We've rented out most of the land, but we've kept on the big house.'

'A plantation house? Like Tara in *Gone With The Wind*?' she broke in, suddenly realising that an American farm could be a very different affair from a few windswept acres carved out of the open hillsides and scrubland of Wales.

'It's prettier and bigger than Tara. A real, old, family house. We have a lot of get-togethers there, but although I love the place, and we own it and all the land around it for miles, I have no interest in farming. I'm a lawyer, honey. A partner in my father's firm in Atlanta.'

'So that's where we'll live?'

'We'll get a great, big, modern apartment in the city for the week, and a house in the country for the weekends. One by a lake where we can swim and I can fish. I love fishing, don't you?'

'I've never tried.'

'I'll teach you. We could get a boat too. An oceangoing vessel so we can go out in the Gulf. Nothing beats the thrill of fighting a big fellow on the end of a line. I once caught a six-foot shark. It was touch and go for a while whether we ended up on land or in the water.'

'There's sharks in America!'

'Only in the sea, honey.' He bent his head and kissed

her again. 'So, you'll marry me?' he murmured, pulling her blouse down to her wrists.

'Of course. But you'll have to talk to Daddy.'

'He'll probably think we're crazy for allowing things to move so fast.' Finally succeeding in removing her blouse, he laid it on the arm of the sofa. Kissing the hollow below her neck he drew the straps of her petticoat and bust shaper to her waist.

'Richard . . .' Too embarrassed to look at him, she turned her head.

'I never thought I'd have a wife who looked like you.'

'You really think I'm beautiful?'

'The most beautiful girl I've ever seen.' He fumbled with the buttons that fastened her skirt.

'Richard, no!'

'I told you I respect you, honey. Far too much to do anything you don't want, but just a little peek? What harm could that do? Think of me a few months from now, out there fighting for you? What we'd both give then, to be back here. Look, I'll make it easy for you. I'll take my shirt off first.'

'I . . .'

'There shouldn't be any secrets or modesty between engaged couples. Here.' He handed her his glass as he removed his jacket. 'Drink that and you won't be scared any more.'

'What if I have a baby?' Her voice dropped to a whisper at the shame of even mentioning such a thing in front of a man.

'I want hundreds, don't you?'

'Not before I'm married. I've always dreamed of walking down the aisle in white.'

'And you will, honey.' He pulled a small packet from his shirt pocket as he laid it on top of her blouse. 'Thanks to Uncle Sam's, one hundred per cent foolproof, special issue.'

'What if something goes wrong?'

'What can go wrong with a girl like you?'

'You could hate me afterwards. Mother always says – '

' . . . and your mother would be right if it wasn't wartime.' He bent his head and kissed her lips. 'I promise, honey, I won't do anything you don't want.'

'The light?'

'How about I put the lamp down beside the sofa? That way I can still see you.'

'I have to leave soon.'

'I'll walk you home.'

'You'll speak to my father tonight?'

'If you want me to.'

'I do.' She closed her eyes as he pulled her back down beside him and continued to undress her. 'Do you think we'll marry soon?'

'The minute Uncle Sam gives us permission.'

'You have to ask the army for permission to marry?'

'Just a formality, honey.' He slipped his hand between her thighs, gently moving it upwards. 'We can't have undesirables moving into America now, can we?'

'Don't. You'll ladder my nylons.'

'There's plenty more where they came from.' He pulled her French knickers down to her ankles. Leaving her suspender belt and stockings, he sank back on his heels and looked at her.

Anthea clung to him mortified, hiding her face in embarrassment as his hands continued to roam freely over her body, stroking, caressing, and returning to what her mother had taught her was the most shameful part of a woman's anatomy.

'How about it, honey?' He continued to fondle her as he moved back and looked down into her eyes. 'I'm going to ask your father for your hand tonight. We'll be married just as soon as I can arrange it.'

A peculiar feeling coursed through her veins as his fingers continued to move, gently, insistently. 'Yes, Richard,' she breathed recklessly, seeing a golden future for herself as a lawyer's wife in a world she had only glimpsed on a cinema screen.

'This may hurt a little, but remember that I love you, honey, and you'll soon feel the pleasure, not the pain.'

'You've done this before?' She was shocked at the thought.

'It's different for men, honey. You wouldn't want an inexperienced husband now, would you?'

'No, but . . .' She winced as his fingers probed inside her. Clinging to his neck she closed her eyes tightly as he moved on top of her.

'I've never done it with a girl I love before. So this is sort of a first for both of us.'

'I love you too, Richard,' she whispered. 'With all my heart.'

Feeling sick and disgusted with himself, Kurt closed the front door and ran down the steps of the house the girls had taken him and George to. George's mocking comments at his insistence on leaving before the fun had started still rang in his ears. He could barely understand his behaviour himself. The house was grubby and shabby but he'd been in worse whorehouses in the States. The girls were drunk, but no drunker than others he'd had sex with. They were pretty enough and willing to strip but the minute the last of their clothes had hit the floor, he'd fled, leaving Harriet angry and George laughing. It was simply the contrast between them and Jenny . . . Damn the girl. She'd invited him into her bed when she was obviously seeing another man. She was no better than the two he had left behind. One had even mentioned a husband. Where was loyalty, faithfulness . . . the things a man had a right to expect in a wife?

It seemed as though all the women in Britain were using the excuse of war to behave like whores. No, not all the women – there was the girl in the cafe, Tina. Attractive, with the kind of figure that gave a man sleepless nights, and from what the enlisted men had been saying most of the regiment had tried it on with her, and none had succeeded in getting more than a cup of tea or coffee – and paying for it. Even a smile would have been rated a success.

He wondered about her husband. What kind of a man was he to inspire such devotion? He'd heard some funny stories about the cathouses in North Africa. Did Tina's husband frequent the brothels, or did he spend all his free time sitting in his tent writing letters home? Of course he went with other women. It was too much for a wife to expect a husband to be faithful. Men simply weren't built that way. Women – decent ladies like his mother – were different. No lady liked sex. Professional whores were something else, they revelled in it, or at least the ones he'd paid had. They never wanted it prettied up in lies and declarations of love like the daughters of respectable families he'd dated.

Suddenly he knew what was different about Jenny. Why he wanted to see her again. There was nothing false about her, including her modesty. She had behaved like a lady right up until the moment they had been alone outside her house. And in the privacy of her bedroom she had made love like a seasoned whore. What he wouldn't give to have that in a wife. He almost envied her husband. He might be dead now, but if his wife's performance was anything to go by, he would have done one hell of a lot of living before he went.

Bethan heard the quiet tread of David Ford's foot on the stair, and left the rocking chair to put the kettle on to boil.

'Tea or coffee?' she asked as he opened the kitchen door.

'My own coffee, please.' He handed her his tin before sitting in the easy chair set at the side of the range. 'You would tell me if you resented me intruding on you every night like this?'

'Of course. What makes you think that I do?'

'I've just remembered the first conversation I had with you.'

'I was being defensive.'

'To the point of attack.'

'I didn't know Americans were human then.' Pouring

out his coffee and her cocoa she sat in the rocking chair opposite him. 'To quote Ronnie, you all have two eyes, two arms, two legs and one head, just like us.'

'And just like the Germans.'

'Try as I may, even after what's happened to Eddie and Andrew, I find it difficult to hate a whole race. They can't all be bad.'

'Just don't go putting any thoughts like that into my men's heads, Mrs John. When the enemy starts pointing guns at their heads I want them to shoot back, not wonder if the man behind the gun is good or bad.'

'Don't you ever wonder why we're fighting this war?'

'Wonder and questions are luxuries soldiers dare not indulge in. They get in the way of what has to be done.'

'The killing,' she murmured, thinking of her brother.

'War is ugly, but occasionally necessary. Your politicians tried to talk Hitler out of trying to turn Europe into a German colony before he invaded Poland. Someone has to stop him before he annexes the whole world. And that's what my government is paying me and everyone else in the regiment to do.'

'And how many more will get killed before you succeed?'

'That doesn't bear thinking about, by civilian or soldier. Can't we talk about something more cheerful like the dinner dance being held in the Park Hotel in Cardiff for American officers and their ladies next Saturday? I was hoping you'd do me the honour of accompanying me.'

'I'd like to, but . . .'

' . . . I hate buts.'

'I'm afraid I have to refuse.'

'Gossips again?'

'If my mother-in-law got to hear of it, I'd never know another moment's peace.'

'If we leave after blackout and return before dawn, who's going to find out?'

'Mrs Llewellyn Jones. She has spies posted on every street corner.'

'Surely that's an exaggeration.'

'They masquerade as wardens.'

'We could ask Chuck Reynolds and Alma Raschenko to chaperon us?'

'Then tongues would wag at double the pace, because they'd have two loose women to talk about.'

'So the answer is definitely no?'

'I'm sorry.'

'Not as sorry as I am, Mrs John. I think both of us would have enjoyed the evening.'

Kurt Schaffer heard the unmistakable sound of a champagne cork popping as he fought his way through the curtain that covered the inside of the Llewellyn Joneses' front door.

'Kurt?' Richard Reide opened the door to the formal parlour, a room Kurt had only seen opened up for the maid to dust under Mrs Llewellyn Jones's eagle-eyed supervision. 'Just the man I need. Come and join us. You can be my best man.'

'Best man?' Kurt questioned dully, wondering if Richard was drunk. He walked in to see Anthea and her parents holding champagne glasses.

'Aren't you going to congratulate the happy couple, Lieutenant Schaffer?' The smile on Mrs Llewellyn Jones's face broadened into a veritable sunbeam.

Richard wrapped his arm around Anthea's shoulders. 'Kurt, meet the future Mrs Richard Reide the third.' He countered Kurt's astonished stare with a warning look.

Confused and bewildered by the turn of events, Kurt held out his hand to Richard. 'Congratulations.'

'We're going to be married as soon as the army gives us permission,' Anthea babbled, drunk on a heady mixture of whiskey, sex, love and the champagne her father had been keeping back for just such an occasion for the last ten years. 'I am so glad you're going to be our best man.'

'We'll have to start planning right away. A wedding

takes some organising, even a simple, wartime ceremony,' her mother warned. 'We'll have to have a cake, flowers and a dress. A dress . . . what about clothing coupons?'

'Join us in another toast, Lieutenant Schaffer,' Mr Llewellyn Jones interrupted his wife as he handed Kurt a glass half filled with champagne. 'To our daughter, her husband and her new life in America as a lawyer's wife.'

'To her new life.' Kurt gulped the champagne and almost choked. This time, he noticed, Richard had the grace to look away.

Chapter Eight

'LOOK AT THAT prop.' Alexander left the cage and crouched beside the steel roof support, shining his lamp on to a section that had buckled beneath the pressure of the thousands of tons of rock weighing down on the shaft. 'Since the government took over the mines last June, management no longer even pays lip service to safety. All they care about is trying to meet impossible production targets, and if half a dozen of us get killed in their attempt to put an upward curve on the Ministry of Labour's productivity graph, so what?'

'Steady, Forbes, that's dangerously close to treasonous talk. You don't want to be taken for a Fascist now, do you?' Viv Richards, Evan Powell's next-door neighbour, taunted. His support of the British Blackshirts before the war was well known, and had earned him the contempt of most of his fellow workers.

'I'd call it common sense rather than treason.' Evan Powell stooped and ran his hands over the steel brace. 'The base is warping just like the centre.'

'Look how many accidents there've been since June,' Alexander contended. 'Four dead, three injured and every incident avoidable.'

'What's the hold-up there, Powell?' Mogg, the shift foreman, shouted down from the cage.

'Ropey prop.'

'And it takes eight of you to stand around and look at it on a Monday morning when there's five rows of empty trucks waiting to be filled?' Mogg strode towards them. 'Don't you know there's a war on? Our boys are risking their lives in Africa this very minute while you lot sit back on your arses and contemplate a bloody prop as though it's a bleeding work of art.'

'Now that's an idea,' Alexander pronounced caustically. 'Donate it to a museum. It'll do more good as an exhibit entitled "A Fatal Accident Waiting to Happen" than it will as a roof support.'

'Who the hell do you think you are, Forbes?'

'A bloody conchie who wants to live to see the end of this war.' Alexander lifted his head, streaking the roof of the tunnel with dirty yellow pools of light from his lamp.

'Think you know it all just because you're an educated bastard, don't you? Well, I'm telling you now, the last thing this pit needs is a bloody smart alec like you. We've got you taped, Forbes. We all know you were too much of a coward to join in the fighting. I'm sorry, we don't have any gentlemen's clubs or rest rooms down here for you to take your ease, just coal to be dug out. And I suggest you start now before I have to dock your wages.'

'He speaks for all of us, Mogg,' Evan interposed quietly.

'Since when?'

'Since management slacked off on safety.'

'There's a war on. Our boys – '

'Our boys, Mr Jones, are risking their lives because they've no choice in the matter. They've been herded to the front like cattle.'

'And you were too bloody yellow to go with them, Forbes.'

'I don't see many German guns pointed at you, Mr Jones.' Couched in Alexander's English accent, 'Mr' sounded more insulting than 'bastard' to Mogg.

'I'm a reserved occupation, not a bloody conchie.'

'When you've finished shouting what you are, do you mind telling us what you intend to do about this prop, Mogg?' Evan interrupted.

'There's a bloody war on.'

'Which I've cause to know better than most.' Everyone fell silent. They all knew that Evan had lost a son at Dunkirk, a daughter in Italy and that his son-in-law was a prisoner of the Germans. 'But the war's no reason for management to make it as dangerous down here as it is at the front. What good would a cave-in do, other than to the Germans? If that prop collapsed it would bring production to a standstill. And if this one is like that, out here in the main walkway, what's the state of the others nearer the face?'

'He's right, Mogg,' Viv Richards concurred, dropping his pick to the ground.

'So you're abandoning the Fascists for the Communists now then, Viv?' Mogg crossed his arms over his ample chest.

'It's a free country.'

'Not in wartime.'

'Mogg,' Evan began patiently, 'we're not doing this to be difficult, we're all experienced miners . . .'

'What in hell do you think I am?'

'Experienced, before you became management.' Evan looked him in the eye, blinding him with lamplight. 'And neither of us have survived working down here for near as dammit thirty years by taking unnecessary risks. All we're asking is that you check out all the props.'

'We're twelve short on this shift as it is, Evan. Where do you expect me to find men to do extra?'

'I'm not management, so I don't know, Mogg, but what I do know is that if they aren't all checked and the damaged and weak ones replaced, we'll be forced to send an official deputation to the office.'

'Are you threatening to go over my head?'

'Just asking for a bit of common sense.'

'There's no point in going to management. You know what they'll tell you? There's a war on.'

'And that makes us expendable?' Alexander asked.

'Do you know what I hate most about this war, Forbes? It's brought the likes of you down here, pushing your noses in where they're not wanted, telling us how to live our lives.'

'It's his life now too, Mogg,' Evan reminded him.

'You wanted to be a boss, Mogg, so bloody well act

124

like one. Go and tell management about the state of these props or I'll . . .'

'You'll what, Viv? Strike?'

'Walk out. And you try and stop me.'

'That's not just suspension talk, Richards. They jail men and women who won't pull their weight for the war effort. Five in last week's *Pontypridd Observer*.'

'Viv doesn't want to walk out, Mogg. None of us do,' Evan maintained calmly. 'All we want are the props checked. Will you see to it, or do we go to management?'

'I'll see to it,' Mogg conceded irritably. 'But not today. There's – '

'Today,' Alexander insisted. 'Or we go to management at the end of this shift.'

'I'll put Robinson on to it. Will that do you?'

'When?'

'This afternoon.'

'If something isn't sorted for definite by knock-off time, we'll go to the office. Luke?' Evan nodded to his junior butty and set off up the tunnel to the coal face.

Viv glared at Mogg for a moment before following the others. Their footsteps echoed eerily in the narrow chambers. Evan wondered why the sound still had the power to set the hairs pricking on the back of his neck. Thirty years of working in filth, damp and gloom, and he still wasn't used to the conditions.

Rats scurried across his path, melting into the shadows that lapped at the borders of his lamp beam, their feet continuing to patter long after he could make out the shape of their long, thin bodies and stringy tails. The roof sloped abruptly, forcing him to stoop, but the closer he drew to the coal face, the easier he breathed. The new steel props were in short supply and despite Ministry directives, management had been forced to utilise the old wooden supports near the cutting edges. Evan wasn't alone in preferring them. They cracked before they collapsed, a warning sound that gave a man a fighting chance to run from a cave-in, unlike the steel props that bent and twisted slowly, and silently, until the actual moment when the roof fell . . . crushing . . . suffocating . . .

Forcing the images he'd conjured from his mind, Evan fell to his knees and looked at Luke. 'Let's start, boy.' He lay on the ground, crawling sideways beneath the seam he had opened up two days before. Luke wiped the back of his hand across his mouth, rubbing in more coal dust than he removed. He waited until Evan emerged from his check before swinging his pick. Evan glanced at the boy as they worked side by side. Luke was nineteen going on twenty but he looked younger. Like Alexander he had been a consciousness objector conscript, and also like Alexander, he was a careful and good worker. Closing his mouth against the dust, Evan decided that it wouldn't be fair to keep the boy much longer. Luke should be a miner in his own right. He'd have a word with Mogg, although he dreaded the change. It was never easy to break in a new boy to the ways of the pit.

Tomas D'Este stood at the window of the spartanly furnished cubicle that had been set aside for the doctors' rest breaks. Pulling the surgical cap from his head, he surveyed the hospital grounds. A black streak of newly tarmacked drive cut through the swath of lawn that swept down to the gates. Uniformed nurses shivered beneath their capes as they pushed bandaged invalids in wheelchairs over the uneven ground. To his right, a row of patients sat on open verandas tucked up in crimson blankets. He could only wonder at the matron's insistence on fresh air. The sky was leaden, heavy with unshed rain, the air damp and wintry. By rights, half the invalids should go down with pneumonia after exposure to these elements.

If they had been in his native Cuba he could have understood her obstinacy. At this time of year it would be wet, but warm enough for sea bathing, the bougainvillaeas would still be blooming in thick purple clouds, hanging over crumbling, white-painted walls . . .

An ancient charabanc edged through the gates, puffing and jerking sluggishly up the drive. Pushing his wire-rimmed glasses further up his nose Thomas studied the visitors as they streamed out. Frail old men, wearing medals that proclaimed them veterans of the last war; elderly women carrying baskets of home-made food and drink he doubted they could spare; and behind them the diminutive, waif-like figure he had been waiting for.

He took a deep breath to steady the pounding of his heart. He was lonely, that was all. A perfectly natural feeling for anyone who had left a large, close-knit family for life in a strange country. Working twelve- to fifteen-hour days didn't help; neither did being annexed to a South Carolina regiment, when most of the officers were strongly prejudiced about socialising with people who didn't have lily-white, Anglo-Saxon pedigrees.

Pushing his cap into his pocket, he checked his watch. He'd warned the theatre sister that he was taking an hour lunch break instead of his usual twenty minutes. There were fifty-five minutes left. Removing his glasses, he clipped them on to his coat, walked to the door, turned the corner and headed for the foyer.

Jane was alone, looking somewhat lost and forlorn as the other visitors filed off down the corridor behind the almoner. He noticed that her hat and coat were well cut, and of good-quality cloth. Both had undoubtedly been expensive, but they appeared to have been made for an older sister, making her look more like an orphan Annie than ever.

He smiled as she turned and saw him. 'You came?'

'I said I would in my letter.' Her brown eyes shone dark, apprehensive, and he realised she was as nervous as he was.

'I'm sorry I missed you on your earlier visits.'

'They said you were operating.'

'It's been like a madhouse,' he explained, thinking that 'butcher's yard' might be more appropriate. 'Would you like tea?'

'I thought I was here to visit the patients, not the doctors.'

'You are, but there's one patient in particular I'd like you to meet today, and you need to be warned about his mental state as well as his wounds.'

'The sister thought I managed fine with the others.'

'It's your past successes that have given us hope that you might make headway with this man. I'm on a meal break. There's a canteen where we could talk. I need to eat, and I'm sure you could manage something.' Anticipating, but hoping to brook further argument, he pushed open the door behind him. 'Please?'

'Just tea then, I've already eaten.'

'This boy is only eighteen,' Tomas said as he led the way down a corridor and up a staircase that led to the second floor. 'He was badly burned when his plane went down. The pilot and navigator were killed. He may seem frightening and aggressive.'

'I can imagine.'

'I'm not sure you can. We're used to bitterness, but his hostility even caught the ward sister unawares.' He led her into a large, square room that smelt of boiled cabbage and fish. What seemed like acres of wooden tables and chairs stretched across sixty feet of wood-block flooring, but few were occupied. Pulling out two chairs from a table jammed into a corner next to the window, he smiled at the girl manning the counter.

'I'll bring your meal over, Captain D'Este.'

'You are a mind-reader, Gaynor, thank you. And a tea for Mrs Powell too, please?'

'You remember the name of the skivvies?'

'Skivvy's a horrible word.'

Jane turned her head. The girl smiled at her. 'She's a personal friend?'

'Just being kind to an overworked doctor. I don't let it go to my head, she's the same with everyone.' He sat down opposite her.

'There's one thing we should get straight before you

say any more. I've been visiting here for weeks, and I don't need protecting from the harsher realities of life.'

'I haven't suggested that you do.'

'I know I look younger than I am . . .'

'How old are you?'

'Twenty-one. And I've worked in a theatre and a pub besides the factory. I've seen a lot of things . . .'

'And survived an explosion, which is one of the reasons I thought you'd be able to help this boy.'

'Are you being funny?'

'Funny?' He frowned at her. 'No, I'm not being funny, and as we're doing some straight talking, I wouldn't have asked you to be a visitor if I hadn't thought you were up to the job.'

'So,' she leaned back as the waitress brought his food and her tea, 'what is this boy like?'

'Facially, badly scarred, and mentally at the stage where he doesn't want to see or talk to anyone. His family lived in London. Both his parents were killed in an air raid. He has a brother, but he's serving overseas, and as yet we haven't managed to organise compassionate leave for him. There are a couple of aunts and uncles. The almoner offered to arrange travel warrants so they could visit him here, but he refuses to see anyone who knew him before the accident. He's been here two weeks, has had one operation and is scheduled for another at the end of this week. We're trying to rebuild his jaw with bone grafts taken from his hip. His nose and cheek-bones are going to be more difficult, and once the bones have been restructured, which probably means another five or six operations spread over a year, there's still the skin grafts. It's going to be a long, slow job. On the plus side, one eye is undamaged, and he will recover a degree of sight in the other. His body and hands are unscathed, which is unusual. Flyers usually try to protect their faces with their hands when fire breaks out. I wish I had time to talk to him, but with my surgery schedule it's impossible. Like all the doctors here, I barely have time to treat my patients' physical wounds let alone address their psychological problems. The nurses have told me they can't get through to him, and believe me if they can't, the task is almost impossible.' He poked at the mess of watery cabbage and minced meat that was mostly gravy on his plate. 'His name is Peter Greaves. He was a gunner in the RAF, and that's all I can tell you about him. If there's more he hasn't confided it to any of us.'

'What makes you think I'll succeed in getting through to him when the nurses have failed?'

He dropped his fork on to his plate. 'You don't know?'

'No.'

'The night we met . . .'

'In the New Inn?'

'I walked into that ballroom feeling as though I'd been exiled to the ends of the earth and wanting to be anywhere but where I was. Then you came up to the table and smiled and I felt as though I had arrived somewhere civilised after all.'

As the whistle blew, Alexander dropped his pick and pulled his snap box from his haversack. Crouching on hands and knees he made his way up the seam to where Evan was sitting with his back against the coal face. Sinking down alongside him, he opened his box and removed the metal flask of cold tea.

'Do you think they'll carry out the safety check?'

'They'd be fools not to.' Evan scrutinised the wooden prop in front of them with narrowed eyes.

'And if they don't?'

'We'll have to go to management.'

'I keep thinking back to my first day underground.'

'When you wanted to go up top to eat your snap,' Evan laughed.

'It seemed a normal thing to do at the time. I couldn't understand how anyone could eat in these conditions. Come to think of it, I couldn't even understand how anyone could work in this stinking hole, and here I am two years later accepting it as normal.'

'You'll be looking to eat your sandwiches in the coal

hole when you go back to your museum,' Luke suggested, with a rare flash of humour.

'Hey, Luke?' one of the other miners shouted across to him. 'You going to the boxing tonight?'

'Only if his missus lets him.' Viv Richards's quip raised a laugh. Luke had married Gina Ronconi when he was eighteen and she sixteen. Although they had been married for nearly two years, most of the men continued to rag him as though he was a newlywed.

'What time does the first bout start?' Luke rose to his feet, dusted off his trousers, and walked over to the others.

'That boy's shaping up nicely.'

'That boy's a man, Evan.'

'Something the matter, other than the state of the props? It's not like you to go off the deep end with Mogg.'

'Everything and nothing.' Alexander stared at his sandwiches.

'My daughter-in-law giving you grief again?'

'I love her. I've asked her to marry me more times than I can remember.'

'And she's still leading you a merry dance?'

'It never feels right to be talking about Jenny to you.'

'I often wonder what she would be like if Eddie hadn't been killed. They should never have married. They were far too young, but Eddie always was reckless as well as hot-tempered. On his last leave they both seemed happy, although it's impossible to predict if things would have stayed that way. You can't build a lifetime of marriage on one two-day leave. And looking back, that's all they ever really had.'

Alexander struggled to decipher the expression on Evan's face; it proved impossible given that the only lighting came from the lamps attached to their helmets.

'I thought they were married for a year before he was killed?'

'They spent precious little of that time together. Hasn't Jenny told you?'

'She never talks about Eddie.'

'That's not a good sign.' Evan bit into his sandwich and his teeth crunched on a sliver of coal that had fallen from the roof. Turning away from Alexander he spat it out.

'I thought Eddie lived in the flat above the shop with her?' Alexander hated pressing Evan for information, but he couldn't think of anyone else he could ask about Jenny's marriage to Eddie, as she had consistently refused to answer his questions.

'He took her back there after their honeymoon night in the New Inn. Her mother was alive then. He didn't stay. A couple of days later he enlisted. He only came home on leave once after that, as I said for two days.'

'So she was hardly married at all,' Alexander mused more to himself than Evan.

'I told her not to blame herself. Eddie always was headstrong.'

'He was a good-looking boy.'

'Of course, you met him on his last leave. Yes, he was good-looking, but as I've already said, on the wild side, and given Jenny's personality that made for an interesting combination. I think she feels guilty about his death, although I've no idea why. It was hardly her fault that he fell in with a bunch of murderous SS.'

'Thank you for telling me. It explains a lot.'

'If it's any help, Alexander, I think that if you can get her to marry you, you might make her happy. She needs stability.'

'It's good to have your blessing, even if I don't have hers.'

Alexander rose to his feet as the whistle blew again. Pushing his uneaten sandwich back into his box, he stretched his cramped limbs. He would visit Jenny tonight. Talk to her, tell her that no one could live in the past, but above all he would make her understand just how deeply he did feel about her.

*

132

'I wish I'd read as much as you.'

'Don't you belong to a library?'

'Now.' Jane looked down at Peter's left eye, all that was visible between the bandages that covered his face and head. 'But given my shifts in the munitions factory and looking after my daughter, there's not much time for reading other than children's books to her.'

'I loved Robert Louis Stevenson . . .'

'*Treasure Island* and *Kidnapped*, but my favourite has to be Captain Marryat's *Children of the New Forest*.'

'I always wanted to be Humphrey.'

'The farmer, not the soldier?'

'I admired the way he could turn his hand to anything. Whatever they needed, he built. Traps for game, a cow shed . . .'

' . . . fencing for extra fields.'

'Then Humphrey was your favourite too?'

'I liked the idea of living in a cottage and producing everything I needed to survive. Growing my own food, selling the surplus to buy clothes and essentials, cleaning, cooking, washing, sewing . . .'

'You actually like housework?'

'I loved it when I had a place of my own in London.'

'You'll go back there after the war.'

'It was bombed,' she said quietly, remembering what Tomas had told her about Peter's parents.

He turned away from her. 'That's rotten luck.'

'I have a good roof over my head now, even if it isn't my own. We're staying with my father-in-law. His house is very comfortable.'

'And you work in munitions?'

'I think a lot of people are doing things they never dreamed of before the war.'

'I wanted to be an engineer. Build bridges, carry roads and railway tracks across impossible places, like ravines and mountains in Africa and Australia.'

'You can still do that.'

'With a freak's face?'

'You don't build bridges with your face.'

He stared at her through his one good eye, amazed that she hadn't responded with the platitude that once his operations were over everything would be fine. 'No one will want to work with a monstrosity.'

'I grew up in an orphanage. We had to wear awful, grey-striped dresses. I used to stand behind the others and hope that no one would notice me. I was so ashamed of being a charity case and a burden on the parish.'

'It was hardly your fault that you were an orphan.'

'I wish that some of the people who looked after us had seen it that way. It took me a long time to learn to stand up for myself, and trust people enough to show them who I really was.'

'A very pretty girl.'

She recognised the bitterness in his voice. 'When this war is over there'll be lots of people with scars.'

'Don't tell me to be proud of them.'

'You could try not letting them get in the way.'

'My girl wouldn't see it that way.'

'She told you?'

'She wrote me a "Dear John" letter before we flew that last mission. There's some bloody Yank . . . sorry, I don't usually swear.'

'If she left you for an American she's not worth having.'

'Oh, she was worth having all right.'

'Have you tried writing to her since?'

'So she can see me like this and offer me her pity? No bloody fear.'

'Language,' a male voice shouted from lower down the ward.

'Sorry,' he murmured contritely. 'But just look at this place – nothing but Yanks.'

'Who've left their families to fight for us. They're not all after other men's girlfriends.'

'No? You're married, you've got a daughter, yet you came in with that Yank doctor.'

'He lodges with my sister-in-law.'

'So you're just good friends?' he sneered.

'Not even good ones, we've only met twice.'

'But you will see him again?'

'Possibly.'

'And your husband's at the front?'

Jane sat back wishing she could get Peter to talk about himself instead of asking questions about her. 'Haydn doesn't like being separated from our daughter, Anne, and me, any more than we like being away from him. But that's the war for you. He's a singer, with ENSA.'

'Every night something awful.'

'So everyone tells me.'

'I'm not being fair, they put on some pretty good shows back at base camp.'

'That's the first kind word I've heard a serviceman say about ENSA.'

'Haydn . . . Powell, your husband is Haydn Powell?'

'You've heard of him?'

'Who hasn't? Do you see him often?'

'Not for the last ten months.'

'This war is messing up everyone's life.'

'It'll be over some day,' she declared briskly before he could become maudlin again. 'You said you wanted to build bridges in faraway places. Have you ever travelled?'

'No, but I had an uncle, my father's brother, who lived in Africa. He went out there to farm just before I was born. I never met him, but he used to send us photographs and letters, and parcels at birthdays and Christmas full of strange things like wood carvings, and peculiar dried fruits. I always wanted to see the places he described. The jungles, the plantations, his bungalow, the native villages, the animals . . .'

Jane sat back enthralled as he told her about Africa as seen through his uncle's eyes. All she knew about the dark continent had been gleaned from an ancient Blackwell's reader in the Homes and a Tarzan film. Immersed in his stories, she forgot where she was and why she'd come. Together, they painted mental pictures of the jungle, stocked it with exotic animals and plants, submerged themselves in the romance of ancient and alien cultures, and wandered every track and byway around his uncle's farm.

'Short stint today, D'Este. You've been working round the clock for the last week, so why don't you knock off early?' the senior RAF surgeon suggested as Tomas dumped his surgical suit in the linen bin in the changing room.

'Thanks, I intend to.'

'You look happy. Dare I suggest you have a girl tucked away somewhere?'

'When have I had time to meet a girl?'

'Good point. God, what would I give for a social life that included women.'

'And you a married man.'

'Far from home.'

'Your home is in London, sir, not three thousand miles away,' Tomas chided him.

'It may as well be three thousand miles away for all that I see of my wife,' he grumbled.

Tomas opened his locker and reached for his clothes. Slipping his shorts on, he pushed his dog tags aside and pulled his vest over his head. As he picked up his shirt, he realised the senior surgeon was right: he was happier than he'd been since he'd left home. And all because he had something to look forward to.

Jane was still sitting beside Peter's bed. Tomas glanced at his watch as he stood back, watched and listened. She must have been there for the best part of three hours. Peter's pronunciation was difficult to understand, the result of burns that had affected his larynx and vocal cords, but there was more animation in his hoarse and cracked voice than he had heard before.

Jane looked up as Tomas walked towards them.

'Not come to take her away have you, Doc?' a boy called out from a bed on the opposite side of the ward.

'It's time Mrs Powell went home.'

'Can't we keep her? She looks pretty sitting there,

136

and she gives us something other than the walls to look at.'

'Bloody doctors get all the luck,' a flight lieutenant grumbled as Jane picked up her coat and hat from the foot of Peter's bed and joined Tomas.

'You will come and see me next week?'

Jane smiled at Peter, 'I promise, but as I warned you, I don't know what day it will be.'

'And you won't forget, any magazines, books . . .'

'I won't forget and I'll see if I can persuade some of the other girls to come from the factory.'

'Great, get them to bring some beer and we'll have a party.'

'That's all you ever think about, Eric,' Peter protested.

'Looks like you made a lot of friends,' Tomas said as he opened the door for her.

'You were right. They're a lot of nice boys, who just need someone to talk to.'

'I've finished for the day.' He thrust his arms through the sleeves of his overcoat as they walked into the foyer. 'So, you can ride back to town in the charabanc, or risk the pillion of my motorbike.'

'I've never ridden on a motorbike,' she said doubtfully.

'It's no different to a pedal bike, only faster. You'll need to pull your hat down, and button up your coat.' He stepped outside. The rain that had threatened all afternoon was finally falling, a steady, cold drizzle that clung to their coats and eyelashes. 'Do you have to go straight home?'

'I promised I'd be back in time for Phyllis and Evan to go out.'

'Your father-in-law and his wife?'

'They're going to visit Alma Raschenko. I think you met her at the party?'

'It's only four o'clock, what time are they going?'

'Half-past seven.'

'We could go for tea. A small celebration in view of your success, no expense spared. Do you know, I've never had afternoon tea. Does the New Inn do it?'

'At a price,' she warned.

'I feel extravagant.'

'It will be less extravagant if I pay my share.'

'I wouldn't hear of it. I invited you.'

'Dutch, or I won't go.'

'Dutch?'

'I pay my whack, you pay yours.'

'Stubborn creature, aren't you?'

Her eyes glowed as he climbed on to his bike. 'You have no idea how much, Captain D'Este.'

Chapter Nine

A QUEASY FEELING rose from the pit of Haydn Powell's stomach as the edge of the long platform of Pontypridd station came into view. Uncrossing his arms, he pushed his hat back from his face and rose to his feet to lift his kitbag from the string rack above his head. It slipped as he brought it down, almost hitting a young WAAC sitting opposite. She glanced up, and as recognition dawned, her eyes widened in amazement. Haydn had seen the same incredulous look on other faces. Most of them female.

'Haydn Powell?' she gasped.

The sick feeling escalated into full-blown nausea, but he managed a nod.

'And to think I've sat in the same carriage as you all the way from Cardiff. I wish I'd known. I love . . .'

The train groaned and shuddered to a halt. He opened the door and threw out his kitbag.

' . . . I don't suppose I could have your autograph?'

'I'd be delighted.' He gave her the full benefit of his well-rehearsed theatrical smile.

'We – me and the girls that is – listen to your show on the radio every week.' Her hands shook as she rummaged in her bag. 'Oh, thank goodness . . . I have it with me.' She handed him an autograph book. 'You'll be the first famous person to sign it. Please, use my fountain pen. It's got an ink reservoir.'

'Thank you.' Hastily scribbling his name and a cliche about the prettiest girl in the carriage, he handed them back to her before stepping outside.

'You can't be staying in Pontypridd?' she cried as he held the door open for her. 'What I mean is, people like you don't. Not in a town like this. I thought you only went to exciting places like London.'

'I live here. Or at least I used to.'

'My brother always said you were from around here, but I never believed him. Not a star like you.'

He tipped his hat. 'Thank you for the compliments, miss, but I'm not in the least important. Do you need help with that case?'

'I don't believe it . . . you're actually offering to help *me*!'

Heaving her luggage from the floor of the carriage he walked on ahead. There was only so much sycophantic adoration he could tolerate. Since the propaganda department had begun releasing photographs of him touring the fronts to every Sunday and most of the weekly papers, he had been unable to call his life his own. Simple things like buying a packet of cigarettes had become at best a marathon of autograph signing, at worst a riot that called for police presence. A casual visit to a pub was impossible: he was mobbed wherever he went; and he soon discovered that adulation was no substitute for friendship. Life was easier when he was touring with showbusiness people who had some understanding and sympathy for what he was going through. After being set upon twice in London by men who'd resented their girlfriends fawning over him, he'd taken to seeking out the company of older thespians who constantly bemoaned the fact that fame was a transitory state, and one he'd long for when it was no longer his. A platitude he didn't entirely believe but could take comfort in.

Dropping the WAAC's case at the foot of the steps, he looked around for a taxi. There wasn't a car or van in sight. Shouldering his bag, he walked across the road to Ronconi's cafe.

'Oh my God, look what the wind's blown in. I can't believe it, a big star . . .'

'Carry on like that, Tina, and I won't give you the parcel William sent.'

'Will!' She dropped the tea towel she was holding. 'You saw Will! Where . . . when . . . how was he? Is he all right?'

'One question at a time.' Trying to ignore the stares of the bus crews who were taking their break, he untied the string that fastened his kitbag and extracted a small, square package wrapped in greasy brown paper. 'There's a letter in there.'

'Is he all right?' she repeated, grasping the package with both hands.

'Missing you.'

'He really is all right?'

'Read his letter.'

'Something's happened to him, hasn't it?' Her voice rose precariously. 'I just knew it . . . he hasn't written in weeks. He's been wounded . . .'

'Let's go in the back.'

'Haydn!'

He opened the counter, took Tina's arm and gently propelled her through the door that led into the kitchen. The cook looked up in surprise.

'Could you go out front for ten minutes to cover for Mrs Powell?'

'Haydn – '

'Sit down.' He pushed Tina on to a stool. 'As you seem so determined not to open that package, I'll tell you. He has been wounded.'

'Oh my God!' She covered her mouth with her hands.

'But it's not even bad enough for him to be sent home. The last I saw, he was sitting in a chair, sipping brandy and lapping up the attention of the nurses.'

'Nurses!' Her dark eyes flashed with jealousy.

'Male nurses, before you crush whatever's in that parcel to smithereens. The bullet went through his arm. It didn't even stay there. He's probably back with his unit by now.'

'Getting shot at again?'

'It was a fluke, Tina. Someone tripped on night patrol, their gun went off . . .'

'Are you saying he was shot by our side?'

'Open your parcel and read your letter, that way you'll hear it all from him.'

She tore at the paper then suddenly stopped. 'I'm sorry. You must be starved. I didn't even ask . . .'

'I'll go into the cafe and grab a tea. I don't suppose you know when that wife of mine is due to finish her shift?'

'She's got a day off.'

'Great, I'll go on up to the house.'

'She's visiting the RAF hospital in Church Village.'

'She knows someone there?'

'Bethan's got a Yank doctor lodging in her house. He's been drumming up volunteers to visit the men who have no one living close by. Jane offered to help.'

'That's my wife.' He shook his head fondly. 'I didn't even know Bethan had a Yank staying with her?'

'Five of them. You can't move an inch in any direction without hearing their funny voices or seeing their uniforms. Don't tell me you haven't seen them?'

'Not in Pontypridd, but I've only just got in.'

'They act as though they own the town . . .' Tina finally broke through the surface layers of paper. An envelope fluttered to the floor. Dropping the box on to a work surface, she dived down to retrieve it. Tearing it open, she didn't even look up as Haydn returned to the cafe.

Jane had never been so terrified in her life. Screwing her eyes tightly, she buried her face in the back of Tomas's overcoat and clung to his chest as they tore along the road that wound back into Pontypridd. Rain soaked her hat and trickled down her neck, the roar of the engine and the wind deafened her, her skirt rode high above her knees. Paralysed with fear, it was as much as she could do to keep her grip on Tomas. When he finally turned into Market Square and slowed to a halt outside the side entrance to the New Inn, she was shaking too much to climb off the machine.

'Are you all right?'

She kept her eyes tightly shut as she nodded.

'We've stopped.'

'I know.'

'Perhaps I should buy you something stronger than tea? It looks like you'll need it before I take you up the hill.'

Jane finally opened her eyes. Half a dozen women were staring at her. Making a supreme effort, she pulled down her skirt, took the hand he offered and stepped on to the pavement. Her legs were trembling so much she would have sunk to the ground if he hadn't supported her.

'I'm not going on that bike with you ever again.'

He smiled. 'It's not that bad.'

'I thought I was going to die.'

'How about if I promise to slow down?'

'No!'

He steered her around the corner and through the main door of the New Inn. It took a moment for her to recognise the drenched, wind-blown scarecrow framed in the reception mirror as herself. She darted into the Ladies, hoping she'd remembered to pack a comb and powder into her handbag.

By the time she'd returned, still damp, but smoother around the edges, Tomas had commandeered a corner table in the lounge, and was sitting back while a uniformed waitress laid out a selection of cakes, crockery and cutlery.

'A taste of civilisation.' He pulled a chair out for her.

'I haven't seen cakes like this since the night of the American party.' Jane eyed the plate wishing she could take some back for the children, Phyllis and Evan.

'Only one covering per cake allowed,' the waitress declared as though they'd complained. 'Jam, mock cream or chocolate.'

'They all look wonderful to me.'

'I wish you could see the fresh fruit flans my mother makes,' Tomas said as he offered her first choice.

'I love fruit cakes.'

'Cuban fruits are very different to what you get here. We used to grow so many varieties in our garden. Oranges, passion fruit, pineapples, bananas, grapes. And vegetables – ' he kissed the tips of his fingers – 'and such vegetables. Sweet potatoes, yams, squash, okra, artichokes . . .'

'You lost me after oranges.'

'Sorry, homesick.'

'Tea?' she picked up the teapot.

'Please.'

'Most Americans don't like it.'

'I'm not most Americans.'

'You seem more Spanish.'

'One of the first things I learned in the States is that there are no Americans except the Indians, and they're even more socially unacceptable than the blacks and Hispanics. First, second, third sometimes even sixth or more generations of natives of every country in the world except America. It's immaterial if their family hasn't set foot in their homeland for over two hundred years, they are still Italians, Greeks, Germans, French, English, Chinese . . . I could go on for hours.'

Jane poured out two cups. 'Milk and sugar?'

'Black with sugar, please.'

'Tell me about Cuba.'

'The way Peter told you about Africa?'

'You were listening?'

'Only for a few minutes. It seemed a shame to disturb you.'

'I love hearing about other countries. I've always wanted to travel.'

'One day I'll go back to Cuba and reclaim our house and farm. Then you can visit me.'

'That's a wonderful dream.'

'Not a dream. When this war is over it will be possible to travel again, and Cuba is a fabulous country. Acres and acres of tobacco and cane fields, long beaches of white sand and deep blue sea. Bluer than any water I have seen since.'

'Are there a lot of farms there?'

'Thousands. But there is still some jungle left, and huge plantations of palms, coffee shrubs, bananas – and villages and magnificent cities. Beautiful cities with splendid buildings of carved and decorated stone. The rich live in palaces, with patios and fountains smothered with flowers, the poor have only crude bamboo and thatch shacks, but they still have the flowers. Whenever I think of Cuba I see enormous clouds of purple bougainvillaeas, white and pink magnolias, camellias . . .'

'And the sun? Is it hot there?'

He looked into her eager, shining face. He had never known anyone so thirsty for knowledge.

'Except when it rains. And believe me, when it rains in Cuba, it rains.'

'Like here?'

'Not cold and damp like here. Warm . . . warm and steamy.' He looked away. He had never wanted to kiss a girl more. Not even his fiancee. Deliberately avoiding her eyes he stirred his tea. 'You made quite an impression on Peter. That's the most I've heard him say.'

'I enjoyed talking to him as much as the others.'

'Admit it – when I first asked, you didn't want to be a visitor.'

'No.'

'You assumed you'd have trouble coping with the patients' injuries?'

'No, not that. I was set to work on the old people's wards in the workhouse when I was sixteen. There were a lot of men there who'd been injured in the pits. Some had lost arms or legs, and often their skin was ulcerated from old wounds. I used to help the sister and nurses to bathe and dress the open sores, so I knew I could cope with that. But I was afraid I wouldn't have anything to say to them that they'd want to hear. Most of your patients are officers. I didn't think they'd want to talk to an uneducated factory girl like me.'

'You can't be uneducated if you worked in a hospital. Were you thinking of a career in nursing?'

'More like fancying. And it wasn't a hospital it was a workhouse – a place where they put the poor who have no money and nowhere else to go,' she explained. 'I grew up in orphanages. When I was sixteen I was put back in the workhouse, that's when I worked with the old people.'

'No wonder you didn't have a good education. But everything's going to be different after the war. You will be able to do anything you want.'

'I'm a wife and mother. My career's mapped out for me.'

'Why did you marry so young?

'Living in the workhouse ages people. It certainly didn't feel young at the time.'

'I'm sorry, that was ill-mannered of me.'

'I met Haydn when I worked in the theatre I told you about. He was the star of the show and I was one of the usherettes. I fell head over heels in love with him, along with every girl in the cast and the rest of the house workers. Looking back, I can't believe he noticed me, let alone married me.'

'You don't have a very high opinion of yourself.'

'It's not easy to be self-confident, when you've spent the first eighteen years of your life being told you're a nobody and a burden to the honest citizens of the parish. But I've got over it,' she smiled, steering the conversation on to safer ground.

'I think I understand how you felt. I told you we had nothing when we went to America. It wasn't easy for my parents to accept charity, but it was the only way we could survive until my father and brothers found work.'

'Are they doctors too?'

'My father is, but two of my brothers are teachers, the other's a priest. You're not eating the cakes.'

'Neither are you.'

'I eat well enough in the canteen so I think I should leave my share for the natives.'

'And I think we can spare one for our noble allies.' She slipped a chocolate sponge on to a plate and handed it to him. 'It's funny to be sitting here again. Haydn and I spent our honeymoon here, but I felt like an impostor, not a guest. I kept expecting someone to order me to the kitchens or linen cupboards to skivvy behind the scenes.'

'How old were you when you married?'

'Eighteen.'

'Then you'd just left the workhouse?'

'I worked for eight months before I married.'

'Eight whole months?' He smiled as she looked at him. 'I was teasing you. Sorry, big brother's habit.'

'I am not your sister.'

'I don't know about you, but I'd like another cup of tea.'

'And I'd like to take some of these cakes home for Anne and Brian.'

'Then ask the waitress for a box.'

'Not allowed.'

He slipped his hand into his pocket and pulled out his wallet. 'I can see you're not used to being with Americans.'

Mogg was waiting for Evan at the entrance to the cage at the end of the shift.

'It's settled, you've no need to go to management.'

Alexander heard the word management, and joined them. 'You're going to check the props?'

'First thing tomorrow morning.'

'We wanted today.'

'No manpower.'

'How many men have you detailed to the job?'

'Three.'

'And you're going to examine the supports at the coal face as well as the main passage?'

'All of them.' Mogg lifted the lantern he was carrying higher so he could see Evan's face. 'Satisfied?'

'I'll let you know after it's been done.' Alexander shouldered his pick and entered the cage.

'I was talking to you, Evan.'

'It's the Ministry of Labour you have to satisfy, not me. It would have been a pity to close this pit because of a fall.'

'Well?' Haydn looked at Tina as she emerged from the kitchen.

'He insists he's not badly hurt and I'm not to worry. But I thought they sent all the wounded home.'

'Not if the wound's slight enough to be treated in a front line hospital.'

'He also says there's no likelihood of him getting leave in the foreseeable future.'

'What did he send you?'

'He didn't show you?'

'Yes, but I'm supposed to report back on how you liked it.'

She opened the box, displaying an ornately worked silver necklace, bracelet and earrings set with brilliant blue stones. 'It's beautiful.'

'Oh, Tina, wherever did you get those?' Judy asked as she walked in with Jenny and Ronnie.

'William. He's been wounded.'

'But he's fine now,' Haydn broke in quickly. He saw the moisture in Tina's eyelashes. If he knew women, that meant she liked the jewellery, but he'd already decided to write and tell William that his wife would have much rather had him home than a present that had set him back a month's card winnings.

'Do me a favour, Judy?' Tina's voice wavered with unshed tears. 'Nip down to the cafe and ask Gina to come up here when she closes the restaurant so I can go and see Megan. She's been half out of her mind with worry the last month.'

'Go now,' Ronnie suggested. 'I'll take over.'

'Do you mean that? You've been working all day.'

'I wouldn't have offered if I hadn't. It's a good time

148

to go, Diana was taking Billy to spend the afternoon with her mother and Myrtle, so you can all have a good cry together. Not that William needs, or deserves your tears. But don't forget to remind Diana I'm hungry and waiting for my tea.'

'You can have pie and chips here.'

'Women! Give them an inch and they take a mile,' Ronnie complained as Tina grabbed her coat and ran headlong out of the door.

'Speaking of which, it's time I went looking for my wife.'

'You haven't been home yet?'

'No.'

'Jane's visiting the RAF hospital.'

'So I've been told, Judy. Good to see you looking so well, Jenny.' Haydn bent his head and kissed his sister-in-law's cheek. 'You home for long?' Ronnie poured himself a tea.

'Three days, then I have to go to Bristol to record the next series of shows.'

'Can I buy you a tea, or a drink in the Hart?' Jenny asked. There had been an awkwardness between her and Haydn since Eddie's death that she was anxious to ease.

'No thanks.' He looked back at Ronnie. 'Judging by that smug look on your face there's no need to ask how you and Diana are enjoying married life.'

'Nothing like it.' Ronnie poured out two more teas for the girls. 'If you get a move on you might catch that taxi pulling into station yard.'

Alexander stepped out of the tin bath. Wrapping a towel around his waist, he opened the back door and heaved the tub into the yard, emptying the scummy water directly down the drain. Shivering, he hurried back into the washhouse, and ran a sinkful of cold water. Studying his face in the cracked square of mirror propped against the window, he soaped his flannel and washed it out well. When he was finally satisfied it was clean, he rubbed it around his eyes. No matter how thoroughly he scrubbed himself after a shift, vestiges of coal dust always lingered in his eyelashes, reminding him of a chorus girl's eye-black. He'd long since given up trying to remove the grit embedded in his hands and nails. He wondered how long it would take him to feel really clean after he finally finished working in the pit. Always supposing he managed to do so.

Hanging his filthy working clothes on a peg ready for the morning he reached for his clean underclothes, shirt and trousers. A splash of cologne, a fingerful of goose grease slicked through his hair – Vaseline had been impossible to find the last month – and another fingerful rubbed into the cracked and broken skin on his hands and he'd made himself as presentable as he knew how.

'Your meal's ready.' Phyllis carried the saucepan to the table as soon as he emerged.

'Just don't ask what it is,' Evan warned as Alexander sat opposite him.

'Austerity stew, and the children ate it without a murmur,' Phyllis asserted.

'They have no memories of anything better.' Evan pulled her to him as she passed, hugging her round the waist to show there was no malice in his teasing.

'I'm sure it's delicious, Phyllis,' Alexander said as he helped himself to a slice of bread,

'I wonder where Jane is?' She put the stew back on to the stove and unbuttoned the overall she always wore in the house. 'She promised she'd be back in time for us to go to Alma's.'

'And she will, love.' Lifting Anne from the playpen Evan sat her on his knee and handed her a lump of bread soaked in gravy. 'Why don't you leave the children with us for five minutes and go and get ready?'

Phyllis was walking down the passage when the door opened and Haydn walked in.

'Oh my God . . .'

He put his finger to his lips. 'I want to surprise everyone.'

'Jane's not back yet. She's – '

' . . . visiting in the RAF hospital. I heard in the cafe.'

'But Anne, Brian and Evan are in the kitchen. Oh, Haydn, it's so good to have you home in one piece.' Always a little shy with Evan's children, she hesitated for a moment before offering him her cheek to kiss.

'Phyllis?' Jane opened the front door, slamming it into Haydn's back. 'Haydn? What are you doing here?'

'That's a fine greeting for a husband after ten months' separation.' Haydn swept her off her feet, only to drop her when he noticed Tomas D'Este standing behind them.

'I can see this isn't the time to make your acquaintance – ' Tomas studied the insignia on Haydn's lapels – 'Captain Powell.'

'You've been promoted?' Jane asked, trying to hold Haydn at arm's length so she could look at him in the crowded passageway.

'Don't worry, it isn't a serious promotion.' He scrutinised Tomas before offering him his hand. He was too young, exotic-looking and charming for Haydn's liking. If Jane wanted to take up charity work in a hospital, why hadn't she approached old Dr John or Evans? 'You must be the doctor who's lodging with my sister?'

'Tomas D'Este. Pleased to meet you. And I'm sorry Jane's late. It's my fault. She had great success with one of my patients today. Quite transformed the man.'

'Please come on in, Captain,' Phyllis pressed him. 'I know Evan would like to meet you again.'

'No, really, I don't want to intrude.'

'You wouldn't be.'

'It's all right, Phyllis, you go and change. I'll see to everything.' Jane stood next to Haydn, wanting to kiss him, but holding back. A hundred and one questions crowded in on her, but it didn't seem to be the right time to ask, not in front of Phyllis and Tomas.

'We've eaten, but there's enough for you, Haydn, and you, Captain D'Este, if you'd care to join Jane and Haydn.'

'Oh God I didn't realise we were that late.'

'Stop apologising,' Phyllis called back as she ran upstairs.

Haydn led the way down the passage and opened the door. Tomas stepped back, and not only out of consideration for Haydn's homecoming. Used to the cool, open spaces of the hospital wards he was suffocated by the steamy, claustrophobic warmth of the kitchen. He looked around while he became acclimatised.

The kitchen was crammed with huge pieces of dark-wood furniture, more suited to an old-fashioned villa than the back room of a terraced house. Opposite the door an immense range belched out heat, its brass boilers and rails gleaming in the immaculately blackleaded iron frame. Above it hung a wooden rack draped with neatly folded clean clothes. Sandwiched in the corner next to a cupboard that filled an alcove, was a wooden playpen crammed with home-made toys. A single, small window covered with patchwork curtains was set above a chair to the left. Patchwork cushions and covers covered the only two easy chairs. The overall effect was of a clean, welcoming, orderly household where there wasn't much money to spare, and he felt not only a pang of homesick-ness, but envy. He knew instinctively that this was a real home, with all the attendant emotions that meant. How long would it be before he could embrace his father the way Jane's husband was hugging his now?

He watched as Haydn took Anne into his arms. Jane was right, there was something of the celebrity about him. The kind of extraordinary good looks he had seen in studio portraits of Hollywood stars. He found himself wondering about their life together. Did Haydn make all Jane's decisions for her, or was their marriage a real partnership, like that of his parents? The kind of mar-riage he wanted for himself.

'So you finally decided to pay us a visit?' Evan attempted to conceal his feelings by turning aside and tickling Anne.

'The minute they gave me leave.' Haydn smiled at his

daughter who promptly screwed up her face and began to cry.

'Hey, sunshine. I'm your daddy. You wait until you see what I've got for you in my kitbag.'

'She'll be fine in a moment, won't you, darling?' Jane relieved him of their daughter. 'Dad,' she turned to Evan, 'you remember Captain D'Este.'

Tomas stepped forward. 'Pleased to meet you again, sir. I'm sorry we didn't have much chance to talk last time.'

'You were sleeping on your feet, and I'm sorry I didn't see you standing there. You must think us an ill-mannered lot.'

'Not at all.' He shook Evan's hand.

'You will stay and eat with us?' Evan offered.

'Thank you but I have to get back to town. We have all been given orders to eat in the canteen.' He turned to Jane: 'Thank you for the sterling work you did today. I hope to see you when you can next spare an afternoon.'

'I'll look forward to it. Thank you for the ride home.'

'I'll see you out.' Haydn opened the door.

'Good-looking fellow,' Evan observed as Jane went to the stove.

'Is he?'

'Some women might think so.'

'Especially the ones who are American mad,' Alexander chipped in sourly.

'Good, you've found the stew, Jane.' Phyllis bustled in carrying her hat and coat.

'I've brought cakes from the New Inn.'

'Shouldn't they have been consumed on the premises?' Alexander enquired.

'Americans seem to have a way of bending the rules.'

'I've noticed.'

'Don't go doing any housework,' Phyllis warned. 'Make the most of Haydn's leave.'

'All three days of it.' Haydn closed the door behind him. 'Any chance of you getting the same, Jane?'

'I'll have to go in tomorrow to beg, but management's more sympathetic these days. I should manage it.'

'If we'd known you were coming we wouldn't have promised to go down Alma's. On the other hand, you could come with us,' Evan suggested, as Phyllis persuaded Brian to lay aside the book he was reading and put on his coat and shoes.

'I'll call in and see her before I go back,' Haydn said. He could hardly take his eyes off Jane as she walked around the kitchen with Anne on one arm, clearing dirty plates and setting out clean ones. He pulled a chair to the table as she returned Anne to her playpen so she could ladle out two portions of stew. He watched his daughter for a moment, before daring to lift her on to his lap. When her face crumpled again, he gave her a piece of bread and she sat back, dipping it into his gravy and sucking on it.

'That poor child is going to be as round as a barrel,' Alexander warned as he reached for his jacket. 'Every time someone eats a meal in this house they sit her on their lap and feed her.'

'Don't listen to nasty Uncle Alex.' Jane kissed the top of her daughter's head before taking her seat. 'He doesn't know what he's talking about, does he, poppet?'

'He's right,' Brian informed them solemnly. 'People who eat too much get fat. My teacher told me so.'

'And is she fat?' Evan asked.

'A little bit,' Brian admitted. 'She said that rationing may be one of the best things that's happened to this country.'

'Try telling that to your mother the next time she has to queue for two hours to get our allocation.'

Alexander fished in the pocket of his overcoat as he slipped it on. 'I found this today, and I thought you might like to share it with Anne and the rest of your cousins.' He handed Brian a triangular bag of boiled sweets.

'Alexander, you shouldn't,' Phyllis protested. 'That's your entire month's ration.'

'I don't want to get fat.' He ruffled Brian's hair as he opened the door. 'You've no idea how much Jane and your father miss you when you're away, Haydn. It will be good to have you home so they can talk about something else for a change.'

'Cheek!' Jane exclaimed indignantly as he left.

'Promise me now, no housework,' Phyllis pleaded as she took Brian's hand.

'You just go off and enjoy yourselves.'

'See you later, son?'

'Just one minute, Dad.' Haydn left the table and opened his kitbag. 'Give this to Alma.' He pulled out a small bottle of vodka. 'Tell her it's for Charlie when he comes home.'

'Haydn, this is very good of you, but . . .'

' . . . I know as well as you that he won't be coming home, but Alma wrote to me. She knows I meet a lot of people and she asked if I'd mention his name to anyone who'd been in Europe. She won't accept it, Dad. Not until the war is over and she finally knows the truth.'

'If anyone will tell her then.' Evan ran his hands over the sides of the bottle before pushing it into the pocket of his overcoat. 'This will only give her one more reason to hope.'

'Is that so bad?' Haydn looked at the photograph of him, Eddie, Bethan and Maud on the mantelpiece. 'Sometimes I wish we had as much.'

'See you later.'

'Have a good time,' Jane called out as they finally left. She dropped her spoon on to her plate and leaned closer to Haydn.

'Alone at last.'

Haydn looked down at his daughter on his lap. 'Not quite.'

Chapter Ten

'MRS JOHN?' DINO Morelli knocked on the open door of the drawing room where Bethan was bundling toys into cardboard boxes with Maisie's help and Rachel and Eddie's hindrance. 'Colonel Ford gave me a letter for you. It's a copy of confirmation received from the Red Cross this morning that the Germans are no longer chaining their prisoners. He was anxious that you should get it right away.'

'He's not coming back this evening?' She took the envelope and tore it open.

'Not tonight.'

'He's working?'

'Possibly.'

'Is this "possibly" something that I, or the doctors, should be aware of?'

'I'm only a dogsbody sergeant, Mrs John. No one confides in me.'

'If your regiment is invading, capturing and securing the town yet again . . .'

'If night manoeuvres are scheduled, Mrs John, they're classified.'

'As long as this particular classified doesn't result in any more blackout casualties. I treated three people this morning who were hit by your trucks hurtling around after dark last night. But, sergeant, I thank you, and Colonel Ford for this.' She glanced at the sheet of paper to confirm the information it contained.

'It's the least we could do in exchange for your hospitality. But, while we're in your good books I do have a favour to ask.'

'I'll make a start on getting the children ready for bed, Mrs John.' Maisie shepherded them to the door.

'Go with Maisie, darlings, I'll be up to read you a bedtime story.'

'The wolf one?' Eddie asked hopefully, wide-eyed in anticipation.

'No, silly. Cinderella?' Rachel countered with all the assurance of an older sister used to getting her own way.

'Both if you're good.'

'With all the words?'

'You know me too well,' Bethan laughed as Rachel skipped off behind Maisie. 'Well, Sergeant, if we're going to talk, how about doing it over a cup of tea in the kitchen?'

'We could make it brandy in here?' He pulled a small bottle out of his pocket.

'This must be a very big favour.'

'It is.' He waited until she brought two glasses in from the kitchen. 'Maurice would like to take Liza to the St Valentine's dance in Cardiff.'

'Liza's already asked me.'

'And you said no.'

'She's my responsibility. One slip from her, or me, in caring for her, and Mrs Llewellyn Jones would have her in the workhouse quicker than you could flip a pancake.'

'Maurice and Liza won't be alone, I'll be going with them.'

'Why didn't he tell me that?'

'Because I only decided today, after Maurice told me that you'd refused Liza permission to go with him.'

'You can hardly blame me. The dance doesn't finish until after midnight. And although Maurice is a nice boy . . .'

'It's a long dark road to Cardiff in the blackout?'

'Precisely.'

'But you'll let Liza go if I chaperon them?'

'If you give me your word that you won't leave them alone for a moment, Sergeant.'

'You have it. And please, call me Dino. I may be a GI but I'm hardly regular army.' He poured out two modest measures of brandy, and touched his glass to hers. 'Here's to the war effort, and all the prisoners coming home.'

'Is this dance going to be a big one?'

'Massive, if the grumbles of boredom from our boys are anything to go by.'

'Are you taking anyone?'

'I was thinking of asking your Aunt Megan, but there's a problem. I don't know where to find her.'

'I can give you her address.'

'She said she lived with her brother and his wife. She helps him to take care of her?'

'Myrtle was badly injured in an explosion in a munitions factory last year, but that isn't all Megan does. She also helps out in the shops that her daughter, son-in-law and Alma Raschenko own.'

'That's the Diana and Ronnie I met here?'

'You're getting to know the family.'

'Megan told me she's been a widow since 1918.'

'She hasn't had an easy life.'

'There's no one . . . no one special in her life?' he asked diffidently.

'That's something you'll have to ask my aunt. If she wants to go to the dance with you, Dino, she will; if she doesn't, she'll tell you, and knowing her, straight out. Are you going into town tomorrow?'

'Yes.'

'There's a small shop on the right-hand side at the bottom of the Graig hill that sells cooked meats, pies and pasties. She'll be there until midday.'

'Thank you, Mrs John.'

'Just more one thing, Dino.' Taking his empty glass she returned his bottle. 'If my aunt should go with you, don't forget to keep an eye on Liza, will you?'

'You should have left the dishes.'

'As I couldn't help you put Anne to bed, I thought I might as well do something useful to pass the time.'

'She'll soon get used to you.' Sensing how much

Anne's bedtime tears and rejection had hurt Haydn, Jane hugged him, but to her dismay he didn't respond.

'Before I have to leave?' he enquired acidly as he left her to sit in his father's chair.

Jane hesitated before answering. She recognised the irritation in his voice. There had been times when she had felt like taking out her disappointment and frustration at their separation on everyone around her; but the harsh regime and discipline of the workhouse had taught her that anger never helped any situation. Closing the door, she went to the easy chair. Slipping into the narrow space behind it and the wall, she massaged the back of his neck, dropping a kiss on his forehead as she did so.

He reached up and grabbed her hand. 'You could come to Bristol with me.'

'How long will you be there?' she asked, wishing she could see the expression on his face.

'I don't know, two . . . three weeks.'

The suggestion was unexpected, his tone casual, but an icy claw of suspicion raked through her mind. 'And then?'

'They'll probably send me on another tour. The powers that be seem to think that's all I'm good for.'

'Abroad?'

'That's a fair bet.'

'You're not allowed to say?'

'I never get told where I'm going until I get there.'

'The war won't go on for ever.' She wished she could retract the platitude as soon as she'd said it.

'I'd like a pound for every time I've heard that lately.' Closing his fingers on her wrist, Haydn drew her around the chair and pulled her down on to his lap. 'Have you thought, really thought, what's going to happen to us at the end of the war?'

'We're going to live happily ever after?' She smiled, willing him to see that she didn't want to continue with the conversation. Not now, not the first time they had seen one another in ten months.

He moved his head, avoiding her kiss. 'I'm serious, Jane. I talked to my agent before coming down here. He mentioned films. Musicals are booming, and everyone thinks that when peace finally comes there'll be even more demand for light entertainment because by then we will all have had our fill of misery. If I'm lucky, I could find myself working in America as well as Britain. And no doubt there'll still be tours.'

'So the end of the war won't change anything for us? Is that what you're saying?'

'Come to Bristol?' His blue eyes were dark, serious as they gazed intently into hers. 'Please?'

'Where would we stay?'

'They always find rooms for me.'

'Ones big enough for all of us, and suitable for Anne?'

'She doesn't take up much room.'

'Her things do. How many hours a day will you be working?'

'How do you expect me to answer that?' he retorted brusquely. 'Like every other soldier, my life isn't my own.'

'When we lived together in London, we had the mornings.'

'I can't make any promises, Jane. If you don't want to go, forget I asked.'

Locking her hands around his neck she forced him to look at her. 'Haydn, I'd like nothing more than to go to Bristol with you. But think about what you're asking. You want me to take Anne to a strange city where we don't know a soul, to live God knows where . . .'

'They'll be tidy rooms.'

'No doubt, but what will we do other than sit and wait for you to finish work? Here I have my job. Phyllis, Bethan, your father and everyone else for company. Anne has Brian and her cousins to play with . . .'

'So now you're married to my family, not me?'

'That's ridiculous.'

'I couldn't get you to leave London at the height of

the blitz when you were pregnant, but now you're here, you refuse to leave for a couple of paltry weeks.'

'Now we have a daughter to consider.'

'And she's more important than her father?'

Turning away so he wouldn't see her tears, Jane slipped off his lap and crossed to the range.

He left the chair and stood beside her. 'I'm sorry. I don't know what's got into me. My only excuse is that being away from you has driven me mad. Of course Anne's more important than me.'

'Not to me,' she whispered. 'Haydn, you and Anne are my whole world.'

'I know.' He wrapped his arms around her and held her close. 'I know, darling, and I'm sorry.'

He had to steel himself to touch her. How could he tell her that he wanted her to travel everywhere with him and never leave his side, because he could no longer trust himself? Because one dark, shell- and bomb-torn night in Africa the explosions had been closer, louder and more terrifying than ever before. And when death had seemed imminent, instead of thinking of her and Anne, he had clung to another woman. And that clinging had led to the breaking of a solemn promise he had given Jane on their wedding day. A betrayal that had plagued his every waking and sleeping moment since, until he had begun to wonder if he'd ever regain his peace of mind.

Alexander walked quickly down the hill and around Vicarage Corner. After three years of blackout he could have found his way to Jenny's shop blindfolded. Pausing outside, he ran his fingers over the knot in his tie to check it was straight, slicked back his hair with the palms of his hands, and debated whether to walk around the back to the storeroom or knock on the front door.

Deciding on straightforward attack, he braved the twitching curtains across the road and rapped the steel bar set below the letterbox. He had to knock twice before Jenny pushed up the casement above his head and shouted down, 'We're closed.'

'I know. I have to talk to you.'

'Alexander?'

'Yes.' He suppressed the urge to call out, 'Who were you expecting?'

'Go round the back, I'll be down in a moment.'

He could tell by the frost in her voice that she was angry with him for calling in on her unexpectedly. Feeling like a tradesman dismissed to the servants' entrance, he walked around the corner into Factory Lane and opened the high gate into the yard. After five minutes during which he almost – but not quite – gave up waiting, he finally heard the bolts being drawn back. The door creaked open on its hinges, but it proved impossible to see anything in the inky blackness of the yard.

'You wanted to talk to me?'

'Yes.' He turned his head towards her disembodied voice.

'Then talk.'

'I was hoping to be invited in.'

'After knocking the front door loud enough for the whole of Llantrisant Road to hear?'

He managed to keep his temper – just. 'If I can't come in, perhaps you'd like to go out? There's a musical playing in the Park Cinema.'

'I've seen it.'

'In that case we could go to the cafe, or the New Inn for a drink?'

'I have a headache.'

He was about to press her, when he summoned the remnants of a dignity he had almost forgotten he'd possessed. Suddenly tired of always being the one trying to please, he spoke quietly and sincerely.

'I came to ask you to marry me, Jenny. I know I've asked before, but this time it's different. I'm sick of pleading and begging, of sneaking in and out of this place like a thief. I love you. I want to live with you, but above all I want a wife who is prepared to accept my love and love me in return.' When she remained silent, he murmured, 'I take it that's your answer.' Turning his back, he felt his way across the yard.

She stood in the doorway, listening while he lifted the latch and stepped out into the lane. Suddenly beset by an irrational fear that she'd never see him again, she opened her mouth to call him back, but no sound came. She was frightened, but not enough to humiliate herself by running after him.

Fear was superseded by indignation and resentment as she took refuge in anger. How dare *he* give *her* an ultimatum! If she wanted to live alone it was her prerogative – and her punishment, she decided wretchedly, retreating into the storeroom where she and Eddie had made love so many times before they'd married.

Eddie – she had driven him away too. She'd had no business marrying him when she'd believed herself in love with Haydn. Or hurting Eddie by kissing Haydn on their wedding day. She'd ruined their honeymoon, and made a complete mess of her marriage. And now she'd succeeded in hurting Alexander by making him fall in love with her too and then taking that love for granted. Using it as a means to ease her loneliness, betraying their pathetic relationship – all she had allowed it to become – with an American serviceman out for a good time.

'*I came to ask you to marry me . . . I love you. I want to live with you, but above all I want a wife who is prepared to accept my love and love me in return.*'

Marriage! Peace, quiet, a man to love and be loved in return, wasn't that what every woman wanted? And Alexander wasn't just any man. He was tall, handsome, well educated – crache. A man she would never have met if it hadn't been for the war. Someone to be reckoned with, who had prospects that would be realised when the war was over. He'd go back to his museum and his lecturing and, if she let him, he could take her with him, out of the valleys, away from all the places that held such painful bitter-sweet memories. Together they could build a comfortable home, the kind she had always dreamed of. Maybe even have children. But was that what she really wanted?

Since Eddie's death she had set great store by her independence, but what had it brought her? The freedom to indulge in meaningless lovemaking with strangers like Kurt Schaffer; the freedom to sit alone and brood at nights?

Suddenly she realised she couldn't imagine life without Alexander. Without his sometimes savage, sometimes tender lovemaking. His thoughtfulness, his unexpected gifts, his company . . . did she love him, or was she using him? Did it matter, when he loved her?

She ran to the gate, opened it and stepped out ready to call him back. The blackout, blinding, suffocating, silent and bone-chillingly cold, closed around her. He must have turned the corner and carried on into town. It was too late.

Closing the gate, she returned to the storeroom. She could put on her hat and coat and go after him – but to where? There were pubs like the Horse and Groom that no respectable woman would enter, even taking the emancipation that the war had brought into consideration. But there was always tomorrow. He might think it was over between them now, but if she wrote to tell him she wanted to see him he wouldn't be able to stay away.

There hadn't been a man who hadn't come running when she had wanted him, even Eddie on that last leave. He might have returned to Pontypridd because the army had given him compassionate leave for her mother's death, but two days had been enough to convince him that their marriage had been worth saving. If he'd lived she'd still have him. She *had* to believe that much. It was all she had to cling to.

Just like Eddie, she'd get Alexander back, and when he came, she'd give him her answer. But first she'd tell him about her and the American lieutenant. If he could forgive her that, perhaps she could find it in herself to be a loving – and faithful – wife.

Perhaps it was finally time to settle down.

Alexander carried on walking down the hill, fingering the coins in his pocket. There were any number of things he could do. Call in the cafe and talk to Tina. See the picture in the Park Cinema, visit one of the pubs, it didn't matter which, there were bound to be far more men than women among the customers, and at this time of night, Yanks that the landlords would be more anxious to serve than him, simply because they had more money in their pockets. But whatever he did, one thing was certain: he had to put Jenny out of his mind, not just for this evening but permanently. If he didn't, he'd risk his sanity. Two years was a long time to be dangled on a string, even by a woman as beautiful and passionate as her.

'And here it is.'

'Richard, it's beautiful.' Anthea's eyes shone with delight as he opened a small, leather-bound box.

'Diamonds and sapphires. Nothing's too good for my girl. Here, let me.' Taking the gleaming, jewel-studded band from the box he slipped it on to the ring finger on her left hand. 'Well, honey, what do you think?'

'I love it. Absolutely love it. The girls in the bank are going to be green. And my mother will be over the moon. You'll come to tea tomorrow? Then we can show her together – that's if I can wait that long.'

'I won't mind you giving your mother a quick peek beforehand.' Dropping the box on to the table behind him, he slid his hands down the sides of her body. Catching the hem of her pullover he pulled it up and caressed her breasts through the tight band of her bust shaper and the fine silk of her petticoat.

'Where's Chuck?' she murmured nervously.

'Playing cards with some people in Alma Raschenko's. We've got the place to ourselves, so I took the liberty of

165

buying a bottle of champagne to celebrate the occasion. How about starting right now?'

'With the champagne?'

'I can think of a little preliminary.' He fingered her hand, turning the ring until the stones caught the light.

'My father's going to notice I'm wearing this when I go home.'

'Not if it's in your pocket.'

'You're being cruel.'

'How about I come in with you?'

'That would be wonderful, but it does mean I'll have to be back early. They go to bed at half-past ten.'

'Very wise, we'll have to adopt the same habit when we're married. And all the more reason for us to start celebrating right now.' Taking the champagne from a bucket of cold water, the nearest he could get to ice in wartime Pontypridd, he twisted the metal stay, popped the cork and filled their glasses. 'To us, and a long and happy life together.'

'To us.' she echoed, watching him over the rim of her glass.

'I have another bottle of champagne put away behind the bar in the New Inn.'

'I'll get my bag.'

'Later. As I said, Chuck's out. We may not have another opportunity to be alone for some time, and this evening is a very special one.' Setting down his champagne glass he began to unbutton her blouse.

Moving away from him, she clamped her hands over his fingers. 'Rick, I've been thinking . . .'

'Don't.' Bending forward he uncovered her breasts, caressing the tips with his thumbs.

'You know I can't think when you do that.'

'Who needs to think?'

'I'm afraid I'll lose my head again.'

'That's the idea. We're officially engaged now, honey. You have my ring.'

'But we're still not married. And I think we should

wait before we do . . . we do . . . what we did the other night again.'

'Ordinarily I might agree with you, although I'd still find it darned near impossible to keep my hands off you. But as I said, wartime is different, honey.' Lifting her on to his lap he kissed her. 'You know I love you and I'm going to marry you the minute permission comes through. Now about this – ' he slipped his hand beneath her skirt and into her knickers. 'You have no idea how much it means to me. How just the thought of you keeps me going from one free evening to the next. I've an idea,' he whispered when he'd succeeded in pulling down her bloomers. 'How about we do this properly. In bed?'

'Chuck's only next door, he could have forgotten something, and come in and find us.'

'Chuck! Never. Have you seen the way he looks at that redhead? He's got a terminal case of lust.'

'Rick, I can't help being afraid. What will we do if something goes wrong?'

'Believe me, honey, with me for a fiance, nothing can go wrong.'

'Mother's still saying that once a man gets his way with a girl he'll lose all respect for her.'

'But I've already had my way with you once, and you're wearing my ring. What more can I do to show my respect?'

'You promise you'll never leave me?'

'Only when Uncle Sam says I have to, and the minute I'm demobbed I'll be back.'

'You swear it.'

'I swear it,' he repeated solemnly, kissing her naked shoulder.

'My mother – '

' . . . lived in different times. Now come on, don't be shy like last time.' Taking her hand he led her into his bedroom.

Her eyes rounded in shock as she saw a tripod and camera set up at the foot of the bed. 'What's that?'

'What does it look like?'

'A camera.'

'Full marks.'

'You want to take pictures of us here, in your bedroom!'

'All the guys – the married guys,' he amended hastily, 'have photographs of their wives. I thought . . . I hoped you'd let me take yours.'

'But I gave you one.' She clutched the edges of her blouse together as she turned and faced him.

'I was hoping for something a little more intimate, honey. A special pose just for me?' He swung the tripod round, pointing the lens in her direction. She continued to stand transfixed, staring at him. 'I can't take you like that, you look as though you've seen a ghost.'

'You can't take photographs of me undressing,' she whispered, finally finding her voice.

'I'll remind you of that in twenty years.'

'Will you?'

Reaching up he pulled her down beside him. She lay beside him, trembling. 'They will just be for me, honey. To look at when I'm away from you.'

'What if anyone else sees them?'

'Who's going to see them when they're safely buttoned in my breast pocket, over my heart?'

'Someone has to develop them.'

'Me. I have a darkroom in the back.'

'I really don't want to, Rick,' she pleaded as he lifted her skirt above her stocking tops.

'How about we leave it until afterwards, then?' Unbuttoning his shirt he dived on to the bed. 'Last one between the sheets washes the champagne glasses.' Pulling off his trousers and shorts he threw them out on to the floor.

After last time she thought she'd discovered everything there was to know about lovemaking. Every time they'd met, they'd kissed, and he'd caressed her breasts, but lying naked alongside him in his bed was a new, shocking and incredibly exciting experience. She shivered as his legs moved over hers, pinning her down in the bed. His lips moved slowly over hers, his tongue exploring her mouth, his hands stroking, fondling every inch of her body.

'Tell me you don't like this, and I'll know you're lying.' Pulling the sheets back he rolled on top of her.

'I never thought it would feel this way,' she moaned, crying out softly as he entered her.

'You see you're already beginning to like it, honey,' he murmured as he continued to push himself into her. 'Just think about that ring, and what it means – to both of us.'

'You've an unusually long face on you tonight,' Tina commented as she left the counter to replenish Alexander's teacup.

'It's been an unusually long day.'

'I know the feeling.' Pulling out a chair, she sat opposite him. 'You seen Haydn?

He nodded. 'He seems happy to be home.'

'Lucky Jane. Right now I'd give five years of my life to have William home for an hour.'

'He might have something to say about a deal like that when the war's over.'

'Do you think it will ever end?' she asked dolefully.

'With what it's costing in men and money it has to.'

'When we're all old, grey and past it. And then everything will change again. You'll go back to where you came from . . .'

'And William will come home.'

'And the Yanks will leave. Sounds like paradise.'

'To be rid of me? Thank you very much.'

'Not you, to have William back and the Yanks gone.'

'You really hate them, don't you?'

'Only because they're here and William isn't. It's unusual to see you in here without Jenny. You haven't quarrelled, have you?'

'No.' He took a deep breath. 'We haven't quarrelled.'

'I'm glad to hear it. You two are perfect for one another.'

'Why?' He eyed her suspiciously, waiting for the sting. The only compliments he'd ever heard Tina pay were barbed ones.

'Because she likes using men as doormats, and you're happy to lie down and let her wipe her feet on you.'

'I am not.'

'Come on, Alexander, I've never seen a man crawl around after a woman the way you crawl around after Jenny. And while you are prepared to do it, she'll be only too delighted to let you. She likes to make out she's so self-sufficient and independent and doesn't need anyone or anything, but you must have seen past her hard-boiled image to have put up with her as long as you have. I doubt any other man would have stuck around as long. Eddie certainly didn't, but then, he had his reasons and his distractions. He was no angel.'

'I doubt any man is.'

'William had better be or I'll make a bow-tie out of his dangly bits.'

Alexander burst out laughing.

'You think I'm joking?'

'No, I just love your turn of phrase.'

'It's easy for you to laugh, you're in the same town as Jenny, and not likely to get separated.'

'We're not even engaged.'

'Only because you've both got all the time in the world to play silly games. Lucky devils. I've forgotten what it's like to have enough of that commodity to waste it in stupid arguments.'

'We haven't quarrelled.'

'Pull the other one. It's none of my business, but if you're that besotted with her, have you tried asking her to marry you?'

'And have you tried minding your own business?'

'Yes, but my life is so boring at the moment I'd rather not. And Jenny's not only my friend, but family.'

'Because her husband and yours were cousins?'

'In Graig terms that's family. I'd like to see her happy, and she's not at the moment for all her independence and the men running after her. So, I suppose that leaves it up to you.'

'I rather think it leaves it up to her.'

'So you have asked her to marry you?'

'I think it's time for another tea.'

'You don't want any more.'

'Now you're telling me I'm not thirsty?'

'The last tram crew has just gone out through the door. If I'm going to open up at five, I'd better get to bed.'

'I don't know how you work the hours you do,' he said wearily as he hauled himself to his feet. 'Twelve-hour shifts are enough for me.'

'That's the trouble with most men: no stamina.'

'Thanks, Tina,' he said as she went to the door to see him out.

'What for?'

'Tea and no sympathy. I couldn't have taken it. Not tonight.'

Jane left Haydn talking to his father and Phyllis and climbed the stairs. Moving quietly so as not to wake Anne, she filled the china bowl on the washstand with water from the jug. It was icy cold. Undressing quickly, she soaked her sponge, rubbed it against the soap and steeled herself for its touch. After washing and rinsing, she towelled herself briskly dry in an attempt to restore her circulation. Emptying the bowl into the slop bucket beneath the washstand, she reached for the small blue bottle of Evening in Paris Haydn had brought her on his last leave, and liberally sprinkled drops around her neck and wrists.

From the tallboy she removed a long, flat box. It held a negligé set Haydn had given her after his first tour. Feeling faintly ridiculous, she slipped on a cream silk and lace nightgown that accentuated every angle of her skinny frame. She surveyed herself critically in the mirror. She had put on weight since Anne's birth, but not enough to give her the Betty Grable curves she so desperately craved, curves that the chorus girls Haydn toured with possessed in abundance, if the photographs in the *Sunday Pictorial* were to be believed. She brushed her hair until it hung glossy and smooth over her shoulders. Was there anything else she could do? She heard Evan's familiar tread on the stairs closely followed by Haydn's lighter step. Picking up the scent bottle she pulled the stopper and dabbed another fingerful at the base of her throat as the door opened.

'Wow!' Haydn whispered.

She looked at him in the mirror. 'Now, are you going to tell me what's wrong?'

Unbuttoning his jacket, he sank down on the bed behind her. 'Nothing.'

'If that was the case, you wouldn't have started that argument downstairs.'

'Why did I have to marry a woman who can read me like a book?'

'Haydn, I know something's the matter.' She glanced anxiously at the cot as she lowered her voice. Fortunately Anne appeared to be fast asleep.

'It's nothing I can't cope with.'

'Being separated is bad enough. You shutting me out is a lot worse. Tell me, is it something to do with me – or Anne rejecting you? I know it must seem dreadful to you now, but it won't be like that when she's older.'

'It's nothing to do with Anne, or you.' Reaching out, he pulled her down beside him and kissed the back of her neck. 'You smell nice.'

'And you're changing the subject.'

'I just need time to remind myself of the important things in my life. God, you're freezing.'

Turning back the sheet and blankets Jane climbed into the bed as he carried on undressing. She watched him for a moment. He turned away, avoiding her eye.

'Who is she, Haydn?' Her voice was quiet, so quiet he couldn't be sure he'd heard her correctly.

'Who's who?'

'Don't try to fool me. I watched you work your way through the chorus of the Town Hall, remember? You've got the same guilty "little boy been at the honeypot" look on your face now that you had then.'

'There isn't anyone, Jane. I swear . . .'

'No please. Don't swear. Even if you haven't actually made love to another girl, you've come close to it. That's what all this is about, isn't it?'

Loosening his tie he sank down wretchedly on the end of the bed.

'Haydn?'

He nodded dumbly. 'It's the usual story. I haven't any excuses. She was there, you weren't . . .'

'So now it's my fault for not being there?'

'Of course not. It's mine. We – '

'I don't want to hear the details.'

His eyes clouded with guilt and misery as he turned to look at her. 'That's why I want you to come to Bristol with me. Jane, I need you.'

'As an excuse to keep predatory girls at bay, or a chaperon?'

'As my wife,' he insisted fervently.

'You promised me on our wedding day that there'd never be anyone else.'

'And there won't be ever again.'

'Please, no more promises, Haydn.'

'I've been an idiot. I've no right to ask, but please try to forgive me. All I have, all I care about, are you and Anne. I even invented a fictitious family crisis so I could get this leave.'

'Do you expect me to thank you for that?'

'I had to see you,' he murmured dejectedly.

'Why? To find out if you still loved me, or if I'd forgive you?'

'It's not like that.'

'Then what is it like?'

'I *do* love you.'

'For three days. And then you'll go back to this girl.'

'I've had her taken out of the show.'

'It's hardly her fault.'

'You'd rather I carried on working with her?'

'No! Of course not . . . it's just that . . . Oh God, Haydn, I feel dirty, betrayed . . . the one thing I've clung to for the past ten months is the thought of you coming back. Of us being together again. Now, in one day you tell me that there'll be no settled life for us at the end of the war, and as if that wasn't enough, that you've had an affair.'

'It was hardly an affair. It was one night. And it's over. She's gone.'

'And the next time a girl catches your eye?'

'It won't happen again.'

'If it's happened once, it can happen again.'

'I know "sorry" sounds inadequate. But if you'll give me a chance, I'll make it up to you.'

'You'll never be able to make this up to me, Haydn.'

'Don't say that. In the middle of this war, this awful bloody mess of bombs and bullets, there's only one thing I'm really terrified of, and that's losing you.'

'Then you shouldn't have done what you did.'

'Would it have been better if I hadn't told you?'

'You couldn't keep it from me.'

'I'll do anything you want if you'll forgive me.'

'Like what?'

'Anything. I might belong to the army now, but when I'm demobbed after the war, if you want to settle down in one place I'll give up my career.'

Her eyes rounded in amazement. 'With your voice and acting ability, you'd give up your career? What would you do?'

'Run a pub, keep a shop, what does it matter as long as we're together? I'll do whatever it takes to prove that to you.' Tentatively he touched her fingers. 'If you want me to, I'll sleep downstairs in a chair.'

'And what would that prove?'

'That you forgive me enough to punish me.'

'I'm not sure I do.'

'If you let me I could spend the next three days trying to show you just how much I do love you.'

'It will be a very long time before I trust you again, Haydn.'

'And forgiveness?'

'I don't know. I honestly don't.'

He brushed his hand across the silk bodice of her neglige. 'Pretty nightie, but I wish I hadn't bought it. Skin is so much better.'

She moved as far from him as the bed would allow. 'I'm tired. You can sleep here, but no more. Not tonight.' Turning her back on him she folded the pillow beneath her head and faced the wall.

'And tomorrow?'

'I need to think. Not just about tomorrow, but all our tomorrows, Haydn.'

Chapter Eleven

SNOW FELL SOFTLY and silently, flecking the blackout and icing the landscape with a shimmering coat of white that gleamed through the darkness, highlighting roofs, roads and the tops of the surrounding mountains. Evan paused as he opened the front door. Breathing in the sharp, clean smell of wintry air he trod warily down the steps to street level.

'Careful,' he called back to Alexander who was closing the door behind him. 'There's ice beneath the snow.'

'This is all we bloody need,' Viv Richards grumbled as he joined them.

'Nice for the kiddies,' Evan murmured from the depths of the scarf he'd wound round his neck.

'Damn the kiddies, roll on summer, that's what I say.'

'Don't we all.' Evan clutched at the wall, skidding on his hobnailed boots as they rounded Vicarage Corner on to Llantrisant Road.

The muffled sound of tramping feet reverberated around them as they joined the stream of miners flooding out of the terraces and heading down the hill towards the Maritime. Alexander walked stolidly behind Evan, his mind still numbed by sleep despite the freezing temperature. As they passed the turn to Factory Lane, he couldn't resist glancing up at the cushion of snow that lay across the windowsill of Jenny's upstairs sitting room.

'Girlfriend not out to wave you on your way?'

Resolutely ignoring Viv, Alexander carried on down the hill.

'Not talking today?'

'Too busy wondering how many props management can check in one shift.'

'That will depend on how many men they put on the job,' Evan pronounced logically.

'And in the meantime we're at risk.'

'Bloody cannon fodder, just like the poor buggers in the trenches in the last war. That's all we are to the bastards sitting in their safe, cosy offices up on ground level,' Viv muttered darkly. 'All they can think about is tonnage, not the miserable sods who have to dig it out for them . . .'

Evan clamped his hand on Alexander's shoulder as they entered the gates of the Maritime. They'd succeeded in their objective. They'd managed to draw Viv's attention away from Alexander's private life.

'Where's Mogg?' Viv asked no one in particular as they joined the queue shuffling into the long brick shed where the helmets and tools were stored.

'Keeping out of the way if he's got any sense,' someone called down from further up the line. 'The men Mogg put on checking the props have just been told they're working on the face.'

'Someone's going to have to go to management.' Alexander had to shout to make himself heard above the mutters of rebellion rippling through the ranks.

'I'm bloody going to management.' Viv slammed down the pick and helmet he'd collected and marched past the men to the door.

'Steady. Watch the blackout,' Evan warned as he pulled aside the curtain.

'To hell with the bloody blackout.'

'You won't be saying that when Jerry lobs a bomb at us.'

'Bloody Jerry doesn't need to blow us up. Not with management doing their damnedest to kill us.'

'Cage going down in five minutes.' Mogg blocked the exit at the end of the shed closest to the shaft.

'No one's going down, Mogg,' Viv proclaimed theatrically, milking the situation for every ounce of drama. 'Not until every prop has been checked and all the damaged ones replaced.'

'Management's doing it.'

'When?'

'They're arranging it now.'

'Management couldn't arrange a bloody piss-up in a brewery.'

'Language, Viv. I could report you for that.'

'Go ahead, report me,' Viv taunted. 'I meant every bloody word. And I'll – '

'Steady, Viv.' Evan stepped between him and Mogg as a hush descended over the shed. 'He only wants what we all want, Mogg. An assurance that the props are going to be checked out today.'

'And I told you, management's doing it.'

'Who in management?'

'Me for one.'

'I wouldn't trust you to recognise a weak prop if it hit you between the eyes . . .'

'Who else, Mogg?' Evan interrupted Viv.

'Dan Howells and Joe Plummer.'

'Joe's all right,' Alexander asserted, in an attempt to defuse the escalating tension.

'He's worked on top for the past three years. I doubt he even remembers how to put a helmet on, and I'd sooner trust a snake than Dan. He's management's man through and through.'

'Who would you trust, Viv?'

The assembled miners turned as a clean-shaven, suited, middle-aged man stepped into the shed behind them.

'Myself,' Viv stated contentiously.

'Just as you find Dan unacceptable, management would find it difficult to work with you.'

'How about Evan Powell, Mr Williams?' Alexander suggested, knowing that most of the men admired and respected Evan, both for his cool head and for his long service underground.

'Viv?' The manager looked at him.

'All right,' he said grudgingly.

'Right, Evan, Joe and you, Mogg, start checking the props right away.'

'What about my butty Luke, Mr Williams?' Evan asked.

'Is he capable of working alone?'

'He's ready for it.'

'Then perhaps it's time he started. He'll get miner's pay from today, and you'll get full shift allowance plus bonus. All three of you report back to me on the state of the props at the end of the shift.' He studied Mogg for a moment, looking for further signs of insubordination before turning and walking out.

Evan handed Luke his pick. 'It's sharper than yours. You can borrow it for today, but you'd better see about getting yourself a new one.'

Luke took it. 'Thanks, Mr Powell, and thanks for speaking up for me.'

'It's something I've been thinking about for a couple of weeks. It's high time you worked on your own. Stick close to Alexander, he knows what he's doing and what's even more important underground, he's careful.'

'Looks like you'll be training your own boy next week,' Alexander said as he picked up his own tools.

Luke grinned. 'Gina's not going to believe it. She told me I didn't stand a chance of becoming a fully fledged miner before my twenty-first birthday.'

'Married life must have put muscles on you sooner than most,' Viv sniggered.

'Cage going down in one minute. Anyone not on it, misses a day's pay,' Mogg shouted impatiently.

'Check those props well.'

'Don't worry, Viv.' Evan picked up an extra lantern. 'I intend to.'

Jane lay still and rigid for a full ten minutes after Evan and Alexander left the house. Finally, she reached out and silenced the alarm five minutes before it was due to ring. Lowering the lamp to the floor she pulled it close to the bed before switching it on, muting its glow so as not to disturb Haydn.

She glanced across at him. His eyes were closed. If any nightmares had disturbed his rest there were no visible signs. Resenting his peacefulness, she checked the clock. Anne was due to wake any moment. Usually she looked forward to early morning. She made a game of washing and dressing both of them and cooking and eating breakfast. The beginning and end of the day were the only times she felt like a real mother. Just as Haydn's leaves were the only times she could feel like a real wife. But now . . .

Turning her back on her husband she slipped out of bed. Lying next to him all night had been pure purgatory. Every time he had moved close enough for her to feel the warmth emanating from his body she had inched away, until she had ended up clinging to a few inches of mattress. Shattered by his confession, and tortured by images of him, naked, in the arms of another woman, she couldn't bear the thought of touching him. Sleep had proved impossible. She couldn't remember ever feeling this depressed, bone weary and unwilling to face the world. Not even during her most dismal days in the workhouse.

She peeped into the cot. Anne was curled on her side, her tiny fists half closed above her head, her face flushed in sleep. Shivering, Jane checked the jug on the washstand. The water had frozen. Picking up her own and Anne's clothes, she lifted Anne from her cot, wrapped a blanket around both of them and padded softly out of the room and down the stairs.

As soon as he was certain he was alone, Haydn opened his eyes. He stared at the door. He could go after her, but after the night they had shared there seemed little point. Confession might be good for the soul, but it certainly played havoc with marriage.

*

'You're up early.' David Ford walked into Bethan's kitchen where she was curled into the rocking chair, pencil in hand and an open notebook in front of her.

'I couldn't sleep so I thought I'd make out a list of things for myself and Maisie to do. We won't get through half of it, and no doubt I'll lose the list before the end of the day but I feel virtuous for trying.'

'I know that feeling.'

'You saved the town from invasion again last night?'

'Someone has talked. Dino?'

'Don't blame him. I guessed. I'm worried about the casualty rate among the natives.'

'The only people injured last night were our men.'

'Anything serious?'

'Sprains, cuts, bruises, a couple of sore heads. Nothing drastic.'

'That's good to know. Tea's made. It's on the hob if you'd like some.'

'Thank you.' Taking a cup and saucer from the dresser he picked up the teapot. 'Would you like another?'

'Yes please.'

'I'm in danger of getting to like this stuff.'

'That would be terrible. You might even end up trying to make the regiment drink it instead of coffee.'

'I'd be on to a loser. The army couldn't march without its cup of Joe.' He sat in the chair opposite Bethan as she put aside her pencil and paper. 'Living in wartime England is like living in a gopher hole,' he observed, staring at the closed blackout.

'Wales, not England, please,' she corrected.

'You people are so touchy. One state back home could swallow the whole of England, Wales, Scotland and Ireland and still have land to spare.'

'Then it's a pity Hitler didn't set his sights on America before Europe. Looks like he could have got all the room for expansion he wanted there.'

'I said they were big, I didn't say they were all desirable.'

'That isn't what your men are saying. They're doing a first-class job of convincing the local girls that everything is bigger, better and more splendid in America. The legendary land of milk and honey and all they have to do to gain admittance is hook an American husband.'

'Do I detect a note of complaint?'

'Not exactly complaint. Just concern about Maurice and Liza.'

'Ah, love's young dream. Dino's keeping an eye on them for me.'

'So it was you who suggested that he should take them to the dance?'

'I hinted that it might be a good idea for all the enlisted men to go together.'

'And what happens when Dino's not around?'

'Liza works long hours and I do my best to keep Maurice occupied.'

'And when they're not working?'

'I've talked to Maurice. He's promised to behave like a gentleman. And speaking of gentlemen, and lonely ones, I don't suppose you'd reconsider your policy of non-fraternisation and accompany me to an officers' ball in the Royal Hotel in Cardiff on St Valentine's Day?'

'Sorry, much as I'd like to, I've already given Maisie the night off.'

'You let Maisie go to the dance without a chaperon and not Liza?'

'Maisie's not going to the dance, not that it would make any difference if she were. She's the same age as me and her free time is her own. Liza's only sixteen and my responsibility.'

'Can't your aunt look after your children?'

'Not on St Valentine's Day. Dino's taking her to the dance.'

'So you'll be alone on the most romantic night of the year?'

'I have my memories, and,' she smiled, 'now that you Americans are here and optimism is in the air, the hope that this might be the last St Valentine's I'll be spending by myself.'

'I think that might be a little too much optimism, Mrs John. Even for the Allies,' he said grimly as he finished his tea and carried his cup to the sink.

The winding gear turned as the cage creaked, groaned and shuddered its heavily burdened way to the floor of the shaft. Mogg pushed the doors open and stood back, watching as the mass of men shouldered their tools and headed for the coal faces.

'Got paper and pencil, Joe?' Evan asked as they waited for everyone to leave.

Pulling a pencil from behind his ear, he nodded.

'So have I. It might be an idea for both of us to keep a tally.' Stepping carefully around a pile of horse manure Evan made for the twisted steel prop that had attracted Alexander's attention the day before. 'Shall we start?'

'I didn't expect to see you in today, Jane,' Jenny commented as they fought their way through the crowds in the station, past the booking office and up the steps to the platform.

'I didn't fancy a fine.'

'Management's not that strict. Sally took five days off when her husband was given leave. They didn't even know where she was until she came back after he'd gone, and no one seemed to care. Her pay just got docked for the days she didn't work. She said it would have been worth it at twice the price. And like her, you can't be that desperate for the money.'

'No.'

'Haydn told me yesterday he's only got three days.'

'He has.'

'Then you shouldn't have come in. I would have told them he was home.'

'It's all right. He's tired and could do with the sleep anyway.'

Jenny eyed her sister-in-law, but the blackout

shrouded her face. 'It can't be easy only seeing him now and again,' she murmured as the train came in and they pushed into a carriage.

'It's the same for every forces wife.'

'Jane, what are you doing here?' Judy plonked herself into a narrow gap on the bench seat opposite her, wriggling until she'd forced the two girls on either side of her to make room. 'I saw Haydn in the cafe last night.'

'Don't tell me he's abandoned his chorus girls? What will the *Pictorial* do on Sunday?'

'Not print a picture of you, Maggie, that's for sure,' Judy retorted tartly.

'Ooh, nasty. What's the matter? A Yank keep you up all night?'

'Actually, sad thoughts of pathetic old maids like you.'

'Ladies, it's too early in the morning to quarrel,' Jenny yawned. 'Surely you're only going in to ask for leave, Jane?'

'I thought I'd ask for tomorrow and the day after off.'

'What about today?'

'Haydn's tired.'

'I bet he is.' Having come off worse in her exchange with Judy, Maggie turned her attention to Jane. 'All that prancing around with chorus girls must take it out of a man.'

'If you must know, Maggie, it does,' Jane bit back viciously.

'Hey, I was only joking.'

'Sometimes you push it too far, Maggie, and,' Judy smiled maliciously as she flung the final insult, 'what you should remember is that you haven't even got a man for us to joke about.'

'You're not taking Anne out in this?' Phyllis asked as Haydn lifted his daughter's coat down from the hooks behind the front door and carried it into the back kitchen.

'All kids like snow.'

'Snow maybe, but not a blizzard.'

'I thought I'd call in on Megan and see if Diana's around, or telephone Bethan's to find out if she's home.'

'And Anne's dinner?'

'We'll go to the cafe. Want to come?'

'It's my baking day.'

'Take a break for once?'

Phyllis looked out of the window at the snow that was still falling, thick and fast. She shook her head.

'Coward.'

'I always have been.' For all the banter, she couldn't help feeling that Haydn's attention was elsewhere. 'If you see Bethan, Megan and Diana, invite them and the children up for tea. It would be nice to have a family party to celebrate your homecoming.'

'What about food?'

'I can see you're not used to living in the real world. They'll bring a contribution.'

'Here, snookems.' Haydn put away the wooden jigsaw he had used to play with Anne all morning as part of his strategy to become reacquainted with his daughter, and held out her coat. 'Want to come to town with Daddy?'

'No.' She stepped back, eyeing him warily from under her eyelashes.

'Come on, I thought we were mates now. We could meet Mam from the train. She's in about four, isn't she?' he asked Phyllis.

'About then,' Phyllis concurred, wondering why Jane hadn't taken the day off. Reaching down she caught Anne who was trying to hide behind her skirt. 'Daddy will take you to the cafe.'

'See Auntie Tina?'

'You bet. And I'll buy you whatever they're selling.'

'Surprise pies?'

Haydn looked quizzically at Phyllis.

'That's all Tina says she can offer on the menu these days, because no one, least of all her, knows what's in them.'

'OK, sweetheart, I'll buy you the biggest surprise pie Auntie Tina's got.'

'I'll get the pram out of the front room,' Phyllis offered as Anne ran to the washhouse to exchange her slippers for her boots. 'No need. I'll carry her.'

'She's heavy.'

'Not to me.'

'And if you slip?'

'Good point, I'll get it.'

'Don't forget the rubber sheet to put over the blankets or she'll be soaked to the skin.'

Phyllis watched as Haydn, all fingers and thumbs, strapped Anne into the pushchair. When he'd finally succeeded in covering her to Phyllis's satisfaction he wheeled the chair down the passage and out through the front door. Carrying it carefully, he negotiated the steps and set off down the road. He wasn't even sure why he'd insisted on going out in a snowstorm. He only knew that he had to see Jane, and the sooner the better. He needed to assure her that their marriage was worth saving, and himself; that she would give him another chance.

A glimpse of the top of Anne's fur-trimmed bonnet was enough to rouse his guilt. He'd been a fool, and a stupid one at that, but he was determined that it was for the first and last time, and if Jane would only let him, he would never do anything to hurt her or Anne, ever again.

Richard Reide surveyed the bank. It was solid, substantial, the walls panelled in dark wood, lending the atmosphere a sombre, hallowed air, almost like that of a church. Soberly suited men past military age sat at desks in a large well behind brass-trimmed mahogany counters, while women manned the cashiers' points. He glanced along the row of clerks. Anthea was perched on a stool next to the wall that divided the public area from the private offices, her head bent over a ledger, a pile of notes in her hand.

He walked up and rapped the counter in front of her with his knuckles.

'I'd like to complain about the service in this place.'

'Richard.' She flushed in surprise, conscious of the other girls listening in. 'What are you doing here at this time of day?'

'Seeing my girl.'

'It's still on for tonight, isn't it?'

'Of course. I've just found myself free for an hour and I wondered if you'd like lunch. We could go to one of the cafes.'

She glanced at the clock. 'I'm not due to take my break for another hour.'

'I thought you had special pull with the boss?'

'Daddy hates me asking for favours in work.'

'Just this once? I have something to show you.'

'What?' she asked excitedly.

'Come with me and find out.'

'Richard, are you viewing the bank with a view to investing with us?' Mr Llewellyn Jones left the exclusive precincts of his private office and crossed the floor.

'Not today, sir. Uncle Sam likes his troopers to put all the dollars they can spare into US of A stock. I was hoping to persuade my fiancee to lunch with me.'

'Now?'

'Afraid it's now or never, sir. The army waits for no man.'

Ignoring the stares of the staff, Mr Llewellyn Jones turned to Anthea. 'You may take an early break, Miss Llewellyn Jones.'

'Thank you, sir.' Knowing how her father hated any familiarity when he was working she'd been taken aback by his cordial attitude towards Richard, but she was still careful to observe the formality he insisted on in the office. 'I won't be a moment, Richard. I'll just get my coat.'

'You brought Anthea home late last night,' Mr Llewellyn Jones murmured as she left them.

'I'm sorry, sir, it won't happen again.'

'I quite understand. I saw the ring.'

'You approve, sir?'

'I do. You are coming to dinner tonight?'

'Wild horses wouldn't keep me away, sir.'

'Good.' He nodded to his daughter as she lifted the flap in the counter. 'Back in one hour, Miss Llewellyn Jones.'

She nodded, beaming with pride as Richard offered her his arm, revelling in the envious glances of the other girls as they headed through the door.

'Where are we eating?'

'An exclusive little restaurant. I persuaded the cook to grill us a couple of steaks.'

'Steaks . . . real beef steaks?'

'Is there any other kind?' He looked around to make sure no one was close enough to overhear their conversation as they crossed the road by the fountain. 'I figure that it will take us ten minutes to eat them and five minutes to get you back on time, which leaves us forty-five minutes.'

'For what?'

Opening the door at the side of Frank Clayton's shop he pushed her into the passage. 'I'll give you one guess,' he murmured, before kissing her.

'Rick . . .'

'Sorry, honey, but after last night I couldn't wait another minute to be with you. Properly, that is.'

'You said you wanted to show me something?' she protested as he propelled her up the stairs.

'And I do.' Drawing a small box out of his pocket, he handed it to her. 'Open it. I want to see you wearing them on Saturday.'

'Oh, Rick!'

'Like them?'

'They're beautiful.' She fingered a pair of sapphire and gold drop earrings as she removed them from the box.

'And you will wear them on Saturday?'

'I can't wait.'

'And now?'

She rushed to the mirror. Unscrewing the gold studs her parents had given her on her eighteenth birthday, she replaced them with his present. 'What do you think?'

'I think I'd like to see you in those and nothing else.'

'Rick, the curtains are open. Anyone can see in.'

'Not in the bedroom, honey. Come on, I hate to rush you, but we've no time to waste.'

'You're the last person I expected to walk in here today.' Ronnie lifted his stepson, Billy, on to the counter so he could see Anne.

'And I thought you were working in munitions?' Haydn shook the snow from his overcoat and hung it on the stand. Crouching down he removed the rubber cover from the pushchair, careful not to spill any of the snow on to Anne or the blankets.

'Day off.'

'And you spend it working here?'

'Tina and Diana thought that as the weather was so foul it would keep all the other shoppers away so they've gone to Cardiff to look for girl things, though I doubt they'll find anything other than empty shelves and snow. Hello, sunshine.' He looked down at the pushchair, and winked at Anne who responded by giving him an enormous smile that made Haydn idiotically jealous.

'She knows her uncle.'

'I should hope so. After all, I am her uncle twice over. What can I get you intrepid explorers?'

'I'll have tea. What would you like, Anne?'

'Cocoa,' Ronnie pronounced decisively, 'milky and sweet and the same for Billy,' he decreed, smiling at the small boy still perched on the counter.

'You've got a way with kids.'

'You try growing up as the eldest of eleven. It's easier to learn to control them than suffer their tantrums. Not that you ever do anything like that.' He tickled Billy affectionately before handing him over to Haydn. 'Set him down next to Anne, they can sit at the corner table.

It's the safest place for them while I heat up the milk. Household milk!' He made a face as he mixed the powder with water. 'So, how come you're here instead of cuddled up in bed with your wife?'

'My wife went to work.'

'They probably need her in the factory.'

'Probably,' Haydn murmured noncommittally. 'Hopefully she'll get tomorrow and the day after off.'

'And then you're returning to the glamorous world of showbusiness?'

'It never was very glamorous behind the spotlights, even before the war, and it's got a sight worse since I've been touring in khaki. Sometimes it feels as though the whole bloody world has been dipped in camouflage. The trucks we use to tour the desert, the tents we sleep in, the clothes on our backs, even the canvas buckets we wash in.'

'That bad?'

'No,' Haydn replied sheepishly. 'Nowhere near as bad as what William and your brothers face every day, or what Eddie faced before he bought it at Dunkirk. Just tiring and tedious. Sorry. Forget I complained. I've no right to gripe at my lot when I see what everyone else is going through, and that includes you back home.'

'As Churchill says, we're all in this together.'

'I suppose so.' Haydn lowered the half-filled cups of cool cocoa to the table where Anne and Billy were sitting, perched on the edges of their chairs, their tiny legs drawn up beneath them as they drew indecipherable pictures with stubs of pencil on the backs of the old bills Ronnie had piled up for them.

'Homecoming not what you expected?' Ronnie asked astutely.

'It's not easy after being away for so long. Anne didn't stop screaming at the sight of me until an hour ago.'

'She's with you now.'

'And as soon as I get to know her I'll have to leave again.'

'There's always next time.'

'I suppose so.' Haydn took a packet of cigarettes from his breast pocket and offered Ronnie one. He took it and pushed it behind his ear.

'Is anything else bothering you? . . . Well, is it?' Ronnie pressed when Haydn didn't answer.

'Nosy bugger, aren't you?'

'I hate to see people miserable.'

'It's Jane.'

'Things are bound to be strange between you. You haven't been home in months.'

'Ten, and it was six before that.'

'There you are then. Take a tip from Uncle Ronnie, leave Anne with Phyllis tonight and take Jane out. Go to the pictures, or the Town Hall and cuddle up in the back row. It's amazing how quickly you can recapture that early courtship feeling in a darkened fleapit.'

'I think we already have. When we first met, Jane used to spit and claw like a cornered cat whenever I went near her, and she's doing the same now.'

'Then you're really in trouble?'

Haydn nodded as he pulled a stool close to the counter. He lit his cigarette, holding the lighter out to Ronnie, watching as he lowered his face to the flame. He had known Ronnie all his life, but the Italian was a good eight years older than he. And although he'd married his sister, Maud, they had left for Italy straight after the wedding and there hadn't been any time to get to know him, not then, nor since his return after Maud's death. But he had to talk to someone. There was no way he could tell his father what he had done, and he sensed that Bethan, despite the very real affection between them, would quite rightly be furious with him for cheating on Jane. If Eddie had been alive, or his cousin William had been there or even, as an absolute last resort, Bethan's husband, Andrew, he would have turned to them. But they weren't and Ronnie was.

'There was a girl . . .' he hesitated, searching for the right words.

'I take it Jane found out about her?'

'I told her.'

'You what!' Ronnie almost dropped the cup he was holding.

'She knew something was wrong. I couldn't keep it from her.'

'If you'd had any sense you would have lied through your teeth.'

'You think it would have been better if I had?'

'Frankly, yes. You're a complete idiot, you do know that?'

'Yes.'

'Where is this girl now?'

'It was a one-night thing. I couldn't face her afterwards. As soon as the tour finished I had her taken out of the show.'

'You must be feeling really proud of yourself.'

'I saw that she was given another job. A good one. It wasn't serious. It was just that . . .' his voice trailed away lamely as he realised there was no way he could justify what he'd done.

'You hadn't been home, and she was there?'

'So you do understand?'

'I understand that this war is playing havoc with people's lives.'

'Can't you see that I had to tell Jane the truth?'

'No. Sometimes, just occasionally, it's better to tell a lie. And I bet if you ask Jane tonight which she'd have preferred to hear she'd settle for a whopper over that kind of truth any time.'

'Thanks for the advice, but it's a bit late.'

'Do you still love Jane?'

'Of course.'

'And you told her?'

'She still wouldn't come near me. She said she needed time to think. Which is presumably why she went to work.'

'Put yourself in her place,' Ronnie advised. 'How would you feel if you'd come home and she'd told you she'd been having an affair?'

'I'd want to kill him . . . and her,' he added slowly.

'So what makes you think she should feel any different?'

'Because she's a woman and a better person than me?' Haydn said cuttingly.

'You really have got yourself into a hole, haven't you?'

'And only two days left to dig myself out of it. Any suggestions would be gratefully received.' He looked hopefully at Ronnie.

'Other than crawl on your hands and knees and give her everything she wants and everything she didn't know she wanted, I'm afraid I can't be much help.'

'I don't suppose you've ever got yourself into a jam like this?'

'Not when I was married to Maud, and when she died I lived like a monk until Diana came along.'

'Then you must think I'm a right bastard?'

'No more than any other man who succumbs to the mood and the moment, including me before I fell in love with your sister. Maud and I weren't apart for more than an hour or two from the day we married until the day I buried her. So quite apart from the love aspect, there wasn't any opportunity for either of us to indulge in any shenanigans. And now, I can't imagine not waking up beside Diana in the morning. That's not to say I wouldn't be tempted if I ended up in your situation. But,' he shrugged his shoulders, 'I hope to God I'd have more sense. And if that's too sanctimonious for you, I'm sorry. The one thing life's taught me is that there's nothing better than marriage to a good woman.'

Chapter Twelve

'IT WAS HARDLY fair. He got fined forty bob for having the cigarettes and fifty bob for the matches. Two weeks' wages gone just like that and it wasn't as if it was his fault. He forgot he had them in his pocket. They should have been picked up in the search at the top of the cage. Besides, there's no bloody gas in this pit. Everyone worth their salt knows that.'

'You playing devil's advocate again, Viv?' Alexander queried, as he helped his boy shovel coal into a truck.

'And what's that supposed to mean?'

'You know as well as I do – one spark down here and we'd all be blown to kingdom come.'

'Or hell,' Luke murmured, the Quaker upbringing he'd almost, but not quite abandoned since he'd been sent to Pontypridd, surfacing.

'You suggesting that I'm destined for hell, boy?'

'No more than the rest of us, Mr Richards,' Luke replied cheerfully as he sank his pick into the coal face again.

Hearing footsteps, Alexander pushed his shovel deep into his pile of coal. 'Here comes management.'

'The day I recognise that bloody turncoat, Mogg, or Joe Plummer as management is the day I give up on life.'

'All talk and no work as usual, Richards?' Mogg goaded as he passed by with Joe and Evan.

'I make twenty replacements needed out of three hundred examined so far.' Evan stopped to consult his list.

'I make it the same,' Joe agreed after totting up his figures. He shone his torch towards the junction of the face with the main tunnel. 'Thirteen in this shaft, then

I think we should check off the areas we've looked at on the plan, and decide where to go next.'

'The north face?' Evan examined the prop in front of him. 'Look at this support. It was split before it was put up. The top and bottom don't even meet. This is no crack, I doubt the two halves were ever married together . . .' He faltered, sniffing the air. A distinctive smell permeated the close, fetid atmosphere. One he recognised, but couldn't quite place. A familiar, sulphurous reek. Then he heard Alexander shout . . .

'You bloody idiot, Viv.'

Fire flashed through the tunnel, blinding, searing in its intensity. It was as dazzling as it was fleeting. The tunnel exploded. Coal and rocks ricocheted off the roof, walls and floor. Thick, choking dust filled the air along with the desperate shouts and screams of men. When it settled there was only darkness, and silence.

Ronnie raised his eyebrows as they heard the wail of the siren in the cafe. 'The Maritime?'

'It's close enough.'

'Your father on day shift?'

'Yes.' Haydn's voice sounded strange, even to his own ears, as foreboding numbed his senses.

'You go up, I'll look after the kids.'

Haydn reached for his coat.

'There's been a run of small accidents in all the pits lately,' Ronnie did his best to sound nonchalant. 'Men getting caught in winding gear and coal cutters. You know the sort of thing?'

'I know the sort of thing,' Haydn said grimly. 'I grew up here, remember?'

'Accident in the Maritime.' Dr John dropped the telephone receiver back on to its cradle. 'Want to come up, Bethan?'

She abandoned the list of patients she'd been compiling. 'Is it bad?'

'A flash fire, fall and explosion. You know as well as

I do that could mean anything from one man injured to fifty trapped.'

'I'll get my bag.'

'Good girl. Leave your car here, we'll go in mine.'

Bethan started shaking when she heard the full blast of the siren as she stepped outside the door, and once she started, she couldn't stop.

'Your father will be fine,' Dr John reassured her with more conviction than he felt. 'He's experienced, and from what I've seen, the older miners have a sixth sense about accidents. He'll have reached safety before the first rock hit the tunnel floor.'

Bethan couldn't answer. She only knew that if she opened her mouth her teeth would start chattering. She hadn't felt quite so cold or panic-stricken since she had received the news that Andrew was missing.

'Close relatives to the left. Come along now, there's nothing to see. Relatives only, over here.' Constable Huw Davies stood between the gates and the crowd of people massing in Albert Road.

'Is there any news, Uncle Huw?' Haydn demanded breathlessly, staring up at the wheels of the winding gear as he pushed his way to the front.

'A hundred and fifty men are already up, safe and sound. We'll know more when the cage comes up again.'

'What happened?'

Huw beckoned him closer.

'It's all right for the relatives of the coppers then? They get to know what's going on,' a woman with a baby in a shawl screamed hysterically from the back of the crowd.

'My orders are to lead anyone with first aid experience through to the shed, Daisy,' Huw said quietly. 'And any able-bodied men to the office. They may be needed.'

'Seven hundred men down there and you're . . . oh my God.' The crowd fell silent as the implication of Huw's words sank in. A sprinkling of fit, young men in uniform started forcing their way towards him. When the crowd saw what was happening they allowed them through.

'In here, boys.' Huw opened the gate a couple of feet.

'I worked underground for ten years before I was conscripted,' a short stocky man announced proudly. 'What do you need us for?'

'Hopefully nothing, lad.' The police sergeant joined them as the cage doors opened. Two men on stretchers were handed out. As Haydn scanned their blackened faces and those of the men who filed out silently behind them he saw Dr John and his sister examining the injured. He'd been so preoccupied with his father he hadn't even spared a thought for Bethan.

'Your father wasn't amongst the first lot either.' Huw turned back to Haydn as soon as he'd made certain that Evan wasn't with the survivors.

'Where are they now?'

'In the tool shed. As far as we can make out they were all working some distance from the site of the explosion. As soon as they heard the blast and felt the tremors they made a run for the cage. The manager's sending a man down now to make a tally of those waiting at the bottom.'

'Has anyone questioned the ones in the shed?'

'Not properly.'

Haydn charged across the compound.

'Hey you . . .'

'His father was down there, sir,' Huw explained to his superior.

'That still doesn't give him the right to barge in there.'

Siren wailing, an ambulance charged up to the gates.

'Let it through.' The manager nodded to the solitary figure waiting in the cage. 'Send it down again,' he ordered flatly.

Haydn leaned against the doorpost at the entrance to the packed tool shed and looked across the heads of the blackened miners. Dr John, white coat shining like a beacon through the gloom, was standing at the far end superintending the loading of the stretchers into the ambulance. Bethan was behind him, talking to one of the miners. Pushing his way forward, Haydn went to her.

'Any news of Dad?' he interrupted.

'None.' She clasped the grimy hand of the man she'd been talking to. 'Thank you, Mr Davies.'

'Don't you worry about your father, Nurse John. He knows his way around down there better than any of us. He'll be fine.'

She nodded before turning back to Haydn. 'Some homecoming.'

'Never mind me. Has anyone seen Dad?'

'None of these men. They were in the shafts closest to the cage, but they all agree that the explosion seemed to come from the direction of the face Dad was working on. Only he wasn't working on it today. He was checking props.'

'Alexander, Luke?'

'The cage is coming up again!' The shout echoed through from outside.

'I'll go, sis.' Heart thundering, Haydn broke out into a cold sweat as he went to the top door. The silence at the pit head was palpable as all attention focused on the winding gear, everyone trying to gauge the exact moment when the cage would reach the top.

Finally the doors opened and men flooded out. After checking to see if any of them were injured the manager ordered them into the shed to down tools for the day. Haydn peered into the grim, blackened faces as they passed. He would have recognised his father in a mudbath, but Evan wasn't among them. He searched for other familiar faces – his next-door neighbour, Viv Richards, the lodger, Alexander, Luke – but to no avail. Huw came and stood next to him.

'Most of the men are accounted for.'

'Except Dad?'

'It looks as though the explosion and fall affected just one small area.'

'And he was there?' Haydn's blood ran cold as he looked to Huw.

'There's more men waiting to come up, but no one I've spoken to saw your father among them. That doesn't mean that he was caught up in the fall, only that he was some distance from the cage when it happened.'

Haydn wanted to cling to the straw of hope Huw offered, but try as he might, he couldn't. A horn blasted. An open truck packed with miners holding picks and shovels waited outside the gate. They all had blackened faces, which meant they'd been taken off shift in another colliery.

'Rescue team from the Albion,' Huw explained. 'They'll assist the team from here.'

'Mr Powell.' The manager walked over and offered Haydn his hand. 'I recognised you from your photographs in the newspapers. Your father isn't the only one who's proud of the way you've put Pontypridd and Wales on the map.'

'Is there any news of him?'

'The under-manager's been down to make a tally. There's twelve men unaccounted for, your father among them. We think they could be caught behind a fall. But don't worry, if they are, we'll soon get them out.'

'Is there a chance that any of them are still alive?'

'There's always a chance. Mr Powell. And those – ' he nodded to the miners climbing out of the truck – 'are good men. If anyone can get them out, they can. They'll be going straight down. If you'll excuse me,' he held up a piece of paper, 'I've a list to post, and I think your sergeant would like you to make some house calls, Constable Davies,' he warned Huw.

'Are you going to stay here?' Huw asked Haydn.

'I'll talk to Bethan. If they let me, I'll stay as long as she does, which will probably be until we know one way or the other.'

'I'll see you later.'

'Oh God, there's Phyllis . . .'

'I'll tell her, mate. You just see to Bethan.'

At first Bethan had no time to think. There were too
many minor scrapes, contusions and bumps on heads
that needed dressing to worry about her father. But
when the final eardrum had been checked for perforation
and blast damage, and the last cuts and bruises bathed,
and most of the shift had left early for once, all she, Dr
John and Haydn could do was sit in the office, smoke
their way through their combined rations of cigarettes
and wait . . . and wait . . . and wait . . .

At blackout time, boards were fixed over the window
panes in the office. The night shift were turned back at
the gates and still the clock on the office wall ticked
inexorably on. Just before midnight the manager
appeared, followed by a clerk with a tray of tea.

'Anything from the rescuers?' Bethan asked anxiously.

'Nothing as yet. But we should hear something by
morning. We've put six fresh men on to the fall as well
as a new shift from the Albion.'

'Only six!' Haydn exclaimed in disgust.

'The space is too confined for more, we're changing
them over every hour. Believe me, we're doing all we
can.'

'Has there been any sound? Any signals?' Haydn hesitated as the fixed expression on the manager's face
quashed his hopes.

Dr John glanced at his watch. 'Why don't you two
go and get something to eat,' he suggested.

'Good idea,' the manager concurred. 'Nothing's going
to happen here for a couple of hours.'

'I'm staying,' Bethan said firmly.

'You should look in on Rachel and Eddie,' her father-
in-law asserted quietly.

'Phyllis might appreciate a visit,' Haydn pointed out.
'We could both go, have a meal, and be back in an hour.'

She looked to the manager.

'I promise you, Nurse John, nothing much is going to happen before morning.'

'They could get close enough to hear a sound, a cry . . .'

'If that does happen, I'll send someone up to you right away.'

'My car's still in town.'

'Take mine.' Dr John handed her the key. 'The Infirmary's only across the road. I'll check on the men we sent there, and see what the sister has in her food cupboard. She always seems to find a sandwich or two.'

'We could bring you something back.' Reluctantly Bethan left her chair.

'No need, but thank you for the thought.' Her father-in-law hugged her as she walked to the door.

The kitchen in Graig Avenue was hot, steamy and crowded. Phyllis sat white-faced and dry-eyed, staring at the door, while Jane, Diana and Megan moved between dresser, stove and table, pouring out cups of tea and emptying ashtrays. To Haydn's surprise, Jenny was sitting amongst the throng of neighbours, nursing a fretful Anne. Mrs Richards was hunched in the corner crying in inconsolable hysteria as Luke Grenville's young wife, Gina, very obviously shell-shocked and trauma-tised, absently patted her hand. Lines from an old folk song sprang to his mind,

'*Married at sixteen, widowed at seventeen*'

·He only hoped they wouldn't prove true in Gina's case.

Phyllis jumped up as soon as they walked through the door. She looked mutely from Bethan to Haydn.

'They've got two rescue teams trying to dig them out.'

'Huw said they were trapped. Are any of them alive?'

'They don't know, Jenny,' Bethan answered, won-dering if her sister-in-law's relationship with Alexander was more serious than she had thought.

'You must be starved.' Phyllis walked blindly towards the pantry door.

'I don't want anything, thank you, Phyllis.' Bethan caught her by the shoulders and led her back to her chair. 'I'm going to drive home, check everything's all right up there and change.' She looked across at her brother above Phyllis's head. 'I'll be back in half an hour, but you don't have to return with me.'

'Yes I do,' he said flatly, seeing her to the door.

'I'll get you something to eat, Haydn,' Jane offered, refusing to meet his eye when he returned.

'There's a cheese and onion pie in the pantry that just needs heating up.' Phyllis's voice was husky with unshed tears.

'I'll get it.' Jane went into the pantry while Haydn closed the door of the washhouse behind him.

Gripping the thick, cool, solid sides of the Belfast sink, he bent his head and closed his eyes. The door opened behind him.

'I'm sorry, Haydn. I know how much your father means to you . . . to all of us,' Jane said simply.

Tears fell from his eyes, splashing down into the basin as he leaned further forward. He felt Jane's small hands on his shoulders. Turning, he caught hold of her, pulling her close.

'Thank you for being here.'

'I don't have any other place to go.'

'I'm sorry. I left Anne in the cafe. I wanted to meet you from work. I thought . . . I hoped . . .'

'Ronnie managed to get us a lift up the hill in a bread van.'

'I wanted to make it all right between us.'

'Now isn't the time, Haydn. We've other things to think about. You'll want to wash. I'll get you a clean towel from upstairs.' Slipping from his arms she went to the door. 'Your meal will be on the table when you've finished.'

The sound of Mrs Richards's sobs wafted in as Jane opened the door. Jenny's voice rose, sharp, impatient, and the noise subsided. Pushing the plug into the sink he filled it with cold water and plunged his head into it. Two days, barely two days since he had come home and he felt as though his whole world had caved in around him.

The sound of the wheel turning on the winding gear woke the manager. Stirring himself, he blinked rapidly as he looked around his office. Dr John was snoring softly, his head thrown back against the side of the chair at an awkward angle. Bethan John and her brother were slumped either side of a table in the corner. Leaving his chair he went to the window and lifted a blackout board from one of the panes. Dawn was breaking. He switched off the lamp and removed the rest of the boards, but no one else opened their eyes.

He'd had good reason to allow Dr and Nurse John to stay in his office, but he found himself wondering why he had permitted Haydn Powell to sit with them. It was a dangerous precedent. Allow one relative on to the premises during a disaster, and in theory, he had to accord them all the privilege.

He opened the door. Cold air gusted around him, blowing away the last vestiges of sleep and the cosy warmth of the coal fire that had warmed them during the night. He had never allowed rationing restrictions to interfere with office heating.

He stepped out quickly, closing the door behind him. Rain drizzled steadily from heavy skies, pockmarking the few remaining drifts of snow. Shivering from a combination of lack of sleep and a chill that had seeped into his bones, he walked stiffly down the steps that led to the pithead. As the cage reached ground level he saw that both teams were in it.

'There's been another fall, sir.' The leader of the Albion's rescue team was the first out. 'It's in front of the last. We were lucky not to get caught up in it.'

'How thick?'

'A good few tons. It's put another four, maybe six feet

between us and the original collapse. We've worked all night for nothing. The face those men were working on is well and truly buried.'

'I'll put out a call for more shoring and fresh teams.'

'If you want my opinion there's not much point, sir. We haven't heard a peep from the other side. If they were alive there would have been some sound. Twelve men, most of them experienced miners. They know the drill, sir.'

'We should make an effort to bring out the bodies.' Mr Williams didn't have to say any more. As a breed miners were a superstitious lot. Too many corpses had been left down after falls in the past, giving rise to ghost stories of spirits trapped underground, striving to escape the filth and darkness they had been forced to work – and die – in.

'Bethan?'

Standing barefoot in her hall, Bethan wrapped her dressing gown around her as she lifted the receiver closer to her ear.

'Have they found Dad, Haydn?'

'It's not Dad, but I think you should come down. Now, if you can.'

Bethan glanced up at the grandfather clock. It was two o'clock. She had been in bed for only three hours. 'What's wrong?'

'I'm in the Graig Hotel. I've got to get back.'

'I'll be there as soon as I can.'

'Make it quick, Beth.'

'Have they found your father, Mrs John?'

'I don't think so, Maisie, but I've got to go down to Graig Avenue. If anyone from the surgery or my father-in-law telephones, take a message, please?'

Bethan could hear her mother's voice as soon as she opened the front door, then she understood why Haydn hadn't wanted to talk to her over the telephone with the landlord and probably half the temporarily laid off miners from the Maritime listening in. She closed the door and leaned back against it, mustering her remaining strength.

After making her father's, her brothers' and sister's and her own life a misery, her mother had finally left them for her Baptist minister uncle's house in the Rhondda. She hadn't seen her since she had driven up there to break the news of Maud's death. Even then her mother had shown no sign of grief, merely reiterated that she had warned all of them often enough that they would go to hell for their sins, and the early deaths of Eddie and Maud only served to confirm her prognostications.

Why had she come now, of all times, when she had sworn never to set foot over the doorstep again? Was it to gloat? Then she thought of Phyllis. Much more her father's wife than her mother had ever been. The door opened at the end of the passage and Haydn looked at her.

'Mam's back. She's moving in.'

'She can't do that.'

'Unfortunately she can. I rang Spickett's the solicitors before I telephoned you. If she wants to move back into the matrimonial home, she's entitled to whether Dad's alive or dead.'

'Dad made a will.'

'Which Mam has already said she'll contest.'

'But what about Phyllis and Brian?'

'You know Phyllis. Self-effacing to the point where she blends in with the wallpaper. She loves Dad but she's always hated being his fancy woman, and that's one of the kinder names Mam has called her. When Mam and Uncle Joseph walked in through the door she went upstairs to pack her own and Brian's things. She's with Mrs Richards.'

'What about you, Jane and Anne?'

'Mam said she has no intention of running a common lodging house. She wants all of us out. If we don't go peacefully, she's threatened to call in the bailiffs.'

'She can't do that at short notice.'

'Legally perhaps, but would you want to live with her again, Beth? Believe me she has no intention of leaving now she's here.'

'But this house is Dad's. It was his father's before him. He paid the mortgage.'

'And she insists that as his widow she's entitled to his estate.'

'Widow! We don't even know he's dead.'

The door opened wider to reveal Elizabeth's gaunt frame. She stared dispassionately at her daughter. 'Your Uncle John Joseph telephoned the manager of the Maritime as soon as we heard the news. There's been another fall in the pit. They've suspended the rescue operations.'

John Joseph's voice thundered down the passage from the kitchen. 'Evan Powell got the death he deserved. He'll writhe in eternal damnation for his sins. The mark of Satan was upon him . . .'

'Give us an hour to move everyone's personal possessions out of the house.' Bethan recognised, as Haydn already had, that it was futile to argue with her mother or John Joseph while they were in their self-righteous, Bible-quoting mood.

Haydn returned to the Graig Hotel to telephone removal firms. When none was able to do anything at short notice, Alma sent up her boy, and he helped Haydn carry Phyllis's furniture and china into Mrs Richards's house. After years of shaking her head at Evan and Phyllis 'living in sin' next door to her, Elizabeth's sudden return and the eviction of the family from their home had brought Mrs Richards's sympathies firmly down on Phyllis's side, and she even managed to set aside her grief over Viv long enough to make tea for Phyllis and Brian.

While Haydn and the boy were busy with the furniture, Elizabeth and her uncle supervised Bethan and Jane's packing to ensure that they didn't take anything that belonged to the house Elizabeth now termed 'hers'.

Bethan drove Brian and Anne, along with the high

chair, toys and dismantled cot, up to her house. Leaving the children with Maisie, she returned for Jane, Phyllis and their suitcases. Phyllis was distraught, principally, Bethan suspected, because her mother had allowed her acid tongue free rein on her arrival in Graig Avenue. But by forcing Phyllis to concentrate on practical matters, she succeeded in coaxing her back to the dry-eyed, pale-faced, shocked state of the previous evening.

The domestic arrangements proved comparatively easy to sort out. By giving up her own bedroom to Phyllis and Brian and carrying her children's and Anne's cots into Andrew's old dressing room, laying a mattress on the floor of the children's room for Haydn and Jane, and relegating herself to the sofa in Andrew's study she managed to fit everyone in.

She regretted the loss of Andrew's dressing room much more than her bedroom. When she had taken in evacuees she had turned it into a tiny sitting room for herself, and now she realised she hadn't a corner of the house to call her own, except perhaps Andrew's study. Which in the middle of a harsh winter of coal rationing was a cold and cheerless room.

Once the last bed had been made up and everyone ensconced in the kitchen where Maisie was making tea, all she felt like doing was curling up and having a good cry. But there was more to do. Squaring her shoulders she drove back down the hill to Graig Avenue. It was the first time she had seen the key out of the door and she was forced to ring the bell. The door was opened by her uncle.

'I'm here to pick up Haydn.'

'And your mother?'

'Pardon?' She stared at him in bewilderment.

'I haven't heard you, or your brother, offer one single word of condolence on her loss. You didn't even let her know about the accident. She had to find out the fate of her husband from strangers. Have you no sympathy for her suffering?'

'She didn't even live with Dad.'

'That's it, decry his unnatural state of sin to the entire world.' He opened the door wider and stood beside her on the doorstep. 'Your mother was driven out by your father's whoring and drinking . . .'

'Not before she'd driven us all mad with her misery and moralising,' Bethan snapped, strain and lack of sleep shortening her temper.

Beside himself with rage, he pointed his finger at her. 'How dare you! Your mother is a God-fearing Christian, which is more than can be said for any other member of this family. A respectable woman living under her dead husband's roof. A roof that is rightfully hers . . .'

Knowing that her uncle would carry on sermonising as long as she provided him with an audience, she pushed past and walked down the passage into the kitchen. Haydn was crouched in front of the dresser. Her mother was standing over him watching his every move.

'Those photograph albums are mine, Haydn,' she lectured as he lifted out books crammed with photographs Evan had taken with his ancient Box Brownie.

'These are the only photographs we have of Maud and Eddie. Could we borrow the negatives to make copies?' He picked up a pile of envelopes marked with his father's writing.

'I know you, I'd never see them again. Neither they, nor the albums are leaving this house.' She turned to Bethan. 'I thought I heard your uncle talking to someone.'

'I've come for Haydn.'

'As you can see, he's still here.'

Haydn looked at the pathetic pile of objects he'd piled next to his feet. Brian's first pair of shoes, a highly coloured, hand-painted plate that Phyllis had brought with her and was particularly fond of for some reason. As he picked them up, Bethan went to the mantelpiece. He father's tobacco pouch and pipe were propped in the corner closest to his chair, just where they always were. She picked them up.

'Leave those,' her mother snapped.

'They're Dad's.'

'They *were* your father's. Now they're mine.'

'Taken to smoking a pipe, Mam?'

Elizabeth's hand flew in the air as she aimed a slap at Bethan's cheek. Haydn's fingers closed around her wrist, holding it firmly he looked at his sister. 'Come on, Beth, there's nothing left for us here.'

'So we won't hear anything before morning?'

'It will probably take longer than that, Nurse John.'

'Thank you for keeping in touch, Mr Williams.'

'I only wish I had better news.'

'So do I. Thank you again for telephoning. Goodbye.' Bethan turned her face to the wall as she replaced the receiver, wishing that the house wasn't full of people who needed her. Steeling herself, she swallowed her tears and walked into the kitchen. The tea Jane had made was growing cold, untasted in the cups as Haydn sat next to Phyllis, holding her hand. Avoiding the look of despair in Phyllis's hollow eyes, Bethan shook her head.

'Mr Williams said they'll be reopening the pit in the morning, and the first ones down will be another rescue team.'

'Then they haven't given up?' Phyllis's eyes shone bright with unshed tears and burgeoning hope.

'Not yet.'

'As none of us slept last night, I think it's time we all went to bed.' Jane left the table and collected the cups.

'Leave them. Maisie will do them in the morning,' Bethan said as she left her chair.

'Or me, come to that.'

'You're not working tomorrow?' Haydn looked at his wife.

'I took two days off for your leave, remember?'

'You have to go back tomorrow, Haydn?' Bethan asked.

'I rang the office from the Graig Hotel and tried to

get an extended leave on compassionate grounds, but they've booked the orchestra and the studio. There's so many people involved . . .'

'There's no question about it. I think you should go back.'

Both Haydn and Bethan turned to Jane.

'In which case you two should spend what little time you have left together,' Bethan suggested.

'If you're sure I can't do anything, I'll see if Brian is all right.' Phyllis rose to her feet.

Bethan took two pills from her pocket and handed them to her as she passed. 'They'll help you sleep.'

'I don't want to take anything.'

'Just for tonight. Brian's upset, he needs you, and you need your rest.'

'And Evan will need me if they find him tomorrow.'

Neither Bethan nor Haydn could find the strength to say any more to reassure Phyllis as she left the room.

'It might be a good idea for you to take a couple of those pills, sis,' Haydn advised as she switched off the kitchen light.

'I don't need them.'

'None of us are indestructible.' He kissed her cheek before following Jane up the stairs. The house was in shadows; the only light shone soft and low on the landing. Despite all the fuel-saving directives Bethan kept it burning all night in case any of the children needed to go to the bathroom.

Jane opened the bedroom door and walked in ahead of Haydn. Children's drawings had been pinned to the wallpaper. A mattress had been made up into a bed on the bare floorboards, with a rug laid beside it. Haydn closed the door behind him. Jane lifted the case she had brought on to a chest of drawers and opened it.

'Do you want to go to the bathroom first?'

'No, you go.'

She took her toilet bag and dressing gown and left the room. He sank into a wicker chair in the corner. The politeness between them was worse than a full-blown quarrel, but he had no idea how to break through the barrier she had erected between them. A good argument might have cleared the air, but they could hardly shout and scream with the house crammed full of people.

Jane returned and he rummaged through his kit for his own toilet bag then went along to the bathroom. He could hear movement and water running overheard and he remembered Bethan telling him that the American quarters had been as good as self-contained since they had installed a bathroom on the top floor; that he was only likely to see them if they came down to use the kitchen.

He returned to the bedroom to find the lamp switched off and Jane already in bed. Undressing, he folded his uniform and placed it on the chair, then crept on to the mattress beside her. She moved away from him.

'I know you're awake,' he whispered. 'I'm sorry I have to leave tomorrow.'

'The early train?'

'Six o'clock.'

'Then you'd better get some sleep.'

He reached out and laid his hand on her. He could feel her shrinking from his touch. 'Jane please . . .' he rested his hand on her waist. She didn't remove it and he dared to leave it there. 'I need you. From now on . . .'

'No, Haydn,' she whispered dully, conscious of the people sleeping close by, 'there'll be no more "from now ons".'

'Then we have now. Please, turn towards me?'

'No.'

'Why not?'

'Because if I did I might lose control.'

'Maybe that's what we both need.'

'It might not be in a way you'd want.'

'Slap me if it will make you feel any better.'

'That would be too easy. I'd like to do a lot more than slap you.'

Touching her shoulder he gently drew her towards

him until her back nestled against his chest and her legs lay against his.

Despite the anger churning inside her, his touch was so familiar, so comforting, she finally allowed herself to relax.

'You're freezing.' He rubbed her arms lightly, all the time longing to tear the silk neglige from her body. After a few moments he dared to whisper, 'I love you.'

'And I love you, although right now I wish I didn't.'

He kissed her lightly on the back of her neck. She turned to face him, returning his embrace with an intensity that sent the blood pounding through his arteries. Her teeth sank into his lips biting, cutting, tearing until he could taste the salt tang of his own blood.

There was no tenderness in her lovemaking. Her nails dug, sharp, scarring, into his back, but there was something purifying and cleansing in her ferocity, and afterwards, absolved and exhausted, he slept.

But she didn't. She lay back staring blindly upwards, imagining Haydn making love to the chorus girl. She pictured her soft, blowsy body, visualised the coarse texture of her peroxide hair, saw the kisses he bestowed, heard the whispered endearments, smelt the cheap perfume . . . and it was as much as she could do to stop herself from clawing her husband's eyes from his skull and every inch of skin from his body.

Chapter Thirteen

BETHAN UNDRESSED, WRAPPED herself in an ugly, thick flannelette nightgown and lay in the makeshift bed she'd made up on the sofa in the study. Too exhausted to sleep, she tossed and turned as her mind conjured hideous images of her father buried alive in a pitch-black hole, dying infinitely slowly for lack of water, heat and light. When she could stand her imaginings no longer she slipped on her robe and left the freezing atmosphere for the warmth of the kitchen.

Switching on the light she peered at the clock. Four. Another hour and Haydn would be downstairs. She picked up the kettle and filled it, setting it on the range without thinking what she was doing. Pacing mindlessly, she returned to the darkened hall, starting when she caught sight of herself in the mirror opposite the door. Barefoot, tall, thin she resembled wraith more than living person in her pale, floor-length gown and robe, with her hair hanging loose around her shoulders.

She shivered. Was this her future? Her life after Rachel and Eddie had grown up and left home to carve out lives of their own? Andrew still incarcerated in a prison camp, her father dead and her, left alone in this great big house a pathetic, abandoned, old woman drifting from room to lonely, empty room.

Scarcely knowing what she was doing, she opened the door to the drawing room and stepped inside. Moving slowly, she tried to recall the position of the toy boxes when she had last seen them. She had hated having to move out Andrew's treasured pieces. He had taken such pleasure in overseeing the decorating of this room. What would he think of it now?

When she reached the window she tore open the

blackout. Moonlight flooded in, painting everything silver. She stood back, staring at the chair her father usually sat in when he visited. She could almost hear his voice, quiet, soft-spoken as he expressed opinions that never seemed radical until she considered them afterwards.

The cold, the silence and the full horror of being buried alive closed in her. Slowly, silently, the first tears began to fall, and as they trickled, cold and wet down her cheeks, the emotions she had been so careful to keep penned up finally erupted.

Falling to her knees, she lowered her head, wrapped her arms around her legs and wept, harsh, rasping, bestial sobs that tore from her throat and lungs.

'If you're going to cry, wouldn't it be better to do it where you won't catch pneumonia?' Strong arms lifted her from the floor, and led her out of the room through the hall, into the kitchen. Weakening waves of warmth swept over her. Dizzy and lightheaded she allowed David Ford to help her to the rocking chair. Picking up the blanket from the log box he tucked it around her legs before taking the boiling kettle from the stove.

'I'll try my hand at making tea.' He reached down cups and saucers from the dresser. 'I'm not promising it will drinkable, but as they say in Wales, it will at least be warm and wet.' Passing her his handkerchief, he spooned tea into the pot. 'Dino told me what happened to your father. If you ever need a shoulder to cry on, you only have to knock on my door.'

'I'm sorry,' she apologised feebly, finally finding her voice. 'I'm not usually like this.'

'Perhaps that's the trouble. You British have such stiff upper lips, they don't bend, only crack. Frankly, with all you've had to cope with, I wonder that you're still sane.' Pouring out the tea, he handed her a cup. 'Milk and sugar?'

She shook her head.

'I'm not sure I've done it right. You people have

turned teamaking into a ritual. Doesn't the spout have to face north when it infuses?'

'It's fine.' She looked up at him. He was in shirt-sleeves and braces. It was the first time she had seen him without his jacket. 'I'm sorry, I didn't mean to wake anyone.'

'You didn't. I was working.'

'At this time in the morning?' Bethan brushed her hair back from her face, and as her fingers became knotted in damp tangles, she understood his reference to sanity. Between her wild hair and tear-streaked cheeks, she must look deranged.

'Joys of command. About your father. If there's anything I, or for that matter my men can do, just say the word. Some of them may not be over-bright, but if brute strength is all that's required, they can furnish it.'

'Experience counts for more than strength down the pit, and the manager of the Maritime is doing all that can be done. This isn't helping, I'm behaving like a spoilt child.'

'No one can be strong all the time.'

'My father was . . . is,' she corrected swiftly. 'And the bedrock of our family's existence. I can't imagine him not being here.'

'From what I heard, there's still hope.'

'I wish I could believe it, but I've lived in Pontypridd all my life and I've seen this happen more times than I can count. The lucky ones are the families that have a body to bury.'

He made a face as he sipped his tea. 'This is foul.'

'Only because you made it when the water was off the boil.' She tried to smile but her face was cold and stiff, and as he looked down at her, she began to cry again, softly and silently this time. He took the cup from her trembling fingers and placed it on the table. Helping her to her feet he cradled her in his arms, the way her father would have done, if he had been there.

'It can only get better.'

'I wish I could believe you.'

'And I wish I could convince you, but you're too intelligent to believe platitudes, no matter how well meant.' He stroked his hand across the top of her head as her tears soaked through his shirt. Emotions stirred inside him that he hadn't allowed to surface since his wife had left him. Wary of taking advantage of her grief, he reminded himself that he was far from home. There hadn't been any time for socialising – or women – for years, because he'd been too busy building a career. It was simply her need, the unfamiliar scent and texture of her skin and hair beneath his fingers that was making him feel this way. He was confusing compassion with desire, a natural enough mistake considering the way they had been thrown together. Bracing himself to release her, he glanced up and saw Haydn watching them from the hall.

'So, it's true what they say about Yanks.'

Bethan lifted her head, saw her brother and extricated herself from David's arms. 'It's not what you think.'

'It's none of my business.' Haydn walked past them and picked up the kettle. 'Mind if I make tea before I go?'

'I found your sister crying, I was trying to comfort her.'

'Looks like you succeeded.' He eyed David Ford coolly as he filled the kettle but Bethan could sense hostility between the two men.

'David provided a shoulder for me to cry on and that's all.'

'You could have called me.'

'And disturb your last few hours with Jane? Stop playing the outraged brother, Haydn, and make yourself some breakfast while I dress, then I'll take you down the station.'

'There's no need to put yourself out.'

'Please, I have enough to worry about, without you being difficult.'

He opened the bread crock. 'Toast, anyone?'

'No thank you. It's time I was going.' David Ford went to the door.

'Don't worry,' Haydn called after him. 'Your secret is safe with me. I won't tell cashmere coat.'

'Cashmere coat?' David looked to Bethan as she picked up the blanket from the chair.

'My brothers' nickname for my husband. I'll be ready in five minutes, Haydn.'

David watched her collect her clothes from the study and walk upstairs to the bathroom. When he was sure she couldn't overhear him, he turned back.

'There's nothing going on between your sister and me,' he said firmly.

Haydn shrugged his shoulders. 'As I said, it's none of my business.'

'This war isn't easy for her . . .'

'Or you, stuck back here in nice safe Pontypridd while the rest of us go out and get killed.'

'My men will get killed soon enough.'

'And you?'

'I'll be with them.'

'Leading from the front or sitting safe in some dugout, Colonel?'

'Give me credit for one thing, Captain Powell.' David's grip tightened on the door handle. 'Knowing how and when to retreat. I couldn't give a damn what you think of me, but I am concerned what you think of your sister. And you are doing her one hell of an injustice if you think her capable of cheating on her husband.'

Bethan drove down the hill in silence. She crouched behind the wheel, peering into the blackout, framing sentences that she lacked the courage to voice, while Haydn sat tense and preoccupied alongside her. It was the thought of Eddie and Maud, and how she hadn't been able to say goodbye to either of them that finally drove her to speak.

'Did you wake Jane to say goodbye?'

'No.'

'Haydn, what you saw . . .'

'It's all right. Your fancy man explained what I saw.'

'There's nothing between us. You don't have to be so – so – big-brotherly about this.'

'Big-brotherly?' Haydn exclaimed as she slowed to a crawl before turning left into station yard. 'Is that what you think this is about? I find my sister in a Yank's arms . . .'

'And that's all you did find. Colonel Ford holding and comforting me. As we tried to tell you, he heard me crying in the drawing room, took me into the kitchen, made me tea and when I didn't stop crying, he hugged me. I was miserable, afraid, lonely and looking for sympathy. He just happened to be around.'

'Can't you see that's just the problem? He's here and I'm not. I want to be here all the time. For you, for Jane, for Anne, for Dad – and don't talk to me about the war. I'm fed up to the back teeth with the bloody war.'

Turning off the ignition she sat back in her seat. 'We're all fed up of the bloody war, Haydn. Andrew in his prison camp, the Americans away from their families, Jane facing hard, manual labour every day in the factory when all she really wants is to be with you and Anne.'

'But we've just got to get on with it, is that what you're trying to say?'

'That's what I am saying. It can't go on for ever.'

'No it can't. But have you thought what will happen if the wrong side wins?'

'It won't.'

'And I never thought we'd lose Dad.'

'We haven't, not yet.'

'Bethan . . .'

'I don't want to hear it, Haydn. Dad told me about the bottle of vodka you gave him for Alma. You found it in yourself to give her hope that Charlie is still alive, why can't you do the same for us? Dear God, haven't we lost enough with Eddie and Maud?' She opened the door. 'Come on, I'll buy a platform ticket and walk you up to the train. And try not to make it so long before coming home again.'

'I'll do my best. You'll take care of Jane and Anne and Phyllis and Brian?'

'You don't have to ask.'

'About money, I have plenty. I made quite a bit before the war, and although I'm on an officer's pay now, I still get royalties from my records, and I've done one or two private shows. Jane has access to the account. It's in joint names. Take whatever you need for Phyllis and Brian. There's more than enough to buy them a house. Graig Avenue, if Mam will sell it.'

'You don't know Phyllis if you think she'll take charity from us.'

'She has to live.'

'She's already talked about taking a job in munitions.'

'And Brian and Anne?'

'Don't worry, we'll sort something out. Whatever else, the children will be well looked after.'

'Jane doesn't have to work.'

'She knows. Weird, isn't it? For the first time in our lives the two of us have enough money to leave some in a bank, and it's useless. It won't buy Andrew out of his camp . . .'

'Or Dad back . . .' The noise of the train pulling in drowned out the rest of his sentence. Kissing her cheek, he murmured, 'I forgot to tell you to take care of yourself. You won't always have to rely on Yanks for comfort. And enjoy what you have, while you have it. That's what I do, sis.'

She looked at him, wondering exactly what he meant.

He climbed on to the train. 'It's good advice.'

'Just come home again, safe, sound and soon,' she called after him.

'You sure?'

'Heard it myself from George Rivers. He's billeted with someone in the family, isn't he?' Linking his hands behind his head, Richard Reide leaned back behind his desk, propped his feet up on a filing cabinet and looked at Kurt Schaffer. 'He said that Jenny Powell's fancy man was caught up in the same pit fall as Nurse John's father. And as that was three days ago, he reckoned that made the delicious and very desirable Jenny free, and ripe for the harvesting. I would go in there myself, but my hands are full with the ardent and appreciative Anthea. There's nothing like the adoration of an erstwhile virgin who's been shown just how good a good time can be.'

'Is Jenny upset?' Kurt asked, deliberately ignoring Richard's mention of Anthea.

'How would I know? George thinks he's in there with a chance, but I saw the way she looked at you in the New Inn. If anyone should jump in there quick, it should be you, boy,' he drawled. 'Take a tip from Uncle Rick, a widow never forgets her way around a mattress. And just like tumbled virgins, they're so grateful afterwards.'

'You're disgusting.'

'This coming from Mr Morality himself?'

'At least I don't go peddling photographs of my girl-friend in the nude.'

'Only because you don't have one.'

'If her father ever finds out . . .'

'How's he going to do that when I sell exclusively to US army personnel?'

'It's a small town.'

'Or someone could tell him?' Richard narrowed his eyes.

'Don't look at me. Your sordid little affairs are your own concern.'

'Just remember, Lieutenant, only a complete moron would cross a superior officer. And,' he ran his tongue over his lips, 'when you succeed with the blonde with the big knockers, my camera is yours. I'll even market the product for you for a straight ten per cent. You could make a packet. I've cleaned up two hundred bucks on Anthea, but that blonde – ' his eyes glittered in antici-pation – 'she's got a lot more, if you know what I mean?'

'I know exactly what you mean. And forget the superior officer. I'm warning you, man to man, Reide. Stay away from Jenny Powell or I'll reshape your face.' Kurt walked to the door.

'Is that a threat?'

'A warning.'

'First man to take the photographs wins the loot, Schaffer,' Reide called after him.

After she saw Haydn off at the station, Bethan felt as though she'd moved into a limbo where time no longer held any meaning. Minutes . . . hours . . . days . . . nights . . . passed in a blur, and all she could do was go through the motions of living, waiting and watching – waiting and watching – for news that she dreaded hearing and that might never come. In her bravest moments she tried to determine what she feared most: the rescue teams finding her father's body, or conceding defeat and sealing off the shaft.

Since Andrew's capture she had often likened herself to the tin man in *The Wizard of Oz* who had been searching for his heart. Now she felt like an ancient Greek who had come face to face with the Gorgon and been turned to stone.

Unable to think about anything other than her father, she stopped writing to Andrew without even realising it. She did only what she had to, driving from one patient to another, bandaging and cleaning wounds, cauterising ulcerated legs, delivering babies, laying out the dead, filling in endless forms, but she avoided calling into the cafe where she would see Tina. She didn't want to hear how Gina was coping, or run the risk of meeting Jenny or Mrs Richards and seeing her grief mirrored in their eyes.

Every time she drove up or down the Graig hill she made a detour along Albert Road so she could stop outside the gates of the Maritime Colliery, but one look at the grim-faced men moving around within the confines of the pithead was usually enough to make her drive on. She had to stop herself from telephoning Mr Williams as soon as she reached home at night, and on waking, first thing in the morning. If there was news, he had given her his solemn promise, she would be the first to know. But it was hard to simply wait, especially when she saw lines of strain and anguish etch daily deeper into Phyllis's face and Brian grow more and more withdrawn. They had told him that his daddy was 'lost' underground, but he couldn't understand why he wasn't allowed to go down and find him, or why he'd had to leave the familiar surroundings of Graig Avenue.

In an attempt to distract herself, she confided in Dr John, telling him about her mother's appropriation of her father's house. He made an appointment for her with his solicitor, but the old man only confirmed what Haydn had already been told, that the only way to get Phyllis back into Graig Avenue was to buy the house from her mother. After checking the funds in her own and Andrew's bank accounts she instructed him to make an offer, but she wasn't surprised when her mother didn't reply.

The telephone call she'd been dreading, yet longing for, finally came at three o'clock in the morning of the seventh day after the fall. She was in the study, reading, having given up on trying to sleep yet again. Charging barefoot into the hall she picked up the receiver.

'Mrs John?'

'Mr Williams?'

'They've broken through . . .' he paused; it could have been no more than a few seconds but to her it was an eternity. 'Your father is badly injured but alive. They're taking him to the Graig Hospital now.'

'I'll be there.'

'There's no visiting.'

'I'm a nurse, Mr Williams.'

She dropped the receiver. Hearing a noise she looked up to see Phyllis and Jane standing on the staircase. Clinging to the banister for support, she whispered, 'He's hurt but alive, Phyllis. He's alive.'

Dr John came looking for her as soon as he left the operating theatre. Sitting beside her on the bench in the corridor he took her hand.

'I had to amputate his right arm. I had no choice, Bethan, the bones were crushed to pulp, but the good news is that there's no sign of infection or gangrene. He's a strong, essentially healthy man. If he hadn't been, I'd be telling you something different now. He'll need a lot of nursing care, but I think he'll live.'

'Can I see him?'

'Only if the sister doesn't catch you, but there's little point. He's still under the anaesthetic.'

'He really is going to be all right?'

'As all right as anyone can be after a week trapped underground with a ton of rock on top of him. He was lucky that his head was free and the boy found the snap boxes. Clever lad, he fed him, rationing out the cold tea, but it was just as well the rescuers broke through when they did. It had all but gone.'

'Boy?'

'Luke Grenville. Isn't he the one married to Gina Ronconi?' He didn't wait for her to answer. 'Well, she'll be happy. I've checked him over. Hardly a scratch on him. I want to keep him in at least until morning, but he insists on going home.'

'Does Gina know he's alive?'

'Not yet. Huw Davies is doing the rounds of the families, but Luke refused to allow him to go up Dany-coedcae Road to tell her.'

'What about the others . . . Alexander Forbes . . . Mr Richards . . .?'

'Your father and Luke were the only survivors.'

'Mrs John, I thought I heard your voice.' Luke padded towards them in a skimpy workhouse nightshirt that revealed the blackened bruises on his legs and arms.

'Dr John just told me you saved my father's life, Luke. How can I begin to thank you?'

'I wish I could have done the same for the others.'

'It's a miracle you and Evan Powell survived, boy,' Dr John said gruffly.

'Please, ask them if I can go home, Mrs John? You know me. You can see I'm all right.'

'You're in shock . . .'

'Supposing I keep an eye on him and check up on him every couple of hours,' Bethan suggested.

'Haven't you got enough to do?'

'Not until my father is discharged.'

Luke looked hopefully from the doctor to Bethan.

'See if someone can find you something more substantial to wear, Luke. We'll set the whole town talking if I take you up the hill looking like that.'

While Luke dressed, Bethan stole into the cubicle next to the sister's office. Her father's face was ashen, bleached by the subdued lighting and the startling, pristine whiteness of the bedlinen. She laid her hand on his forehead noticing the traces of coal dust ingrained in the stubble on his chin and the lines of his face. Folding back the bedclothes she checked the cage that had been placed over his shoulder to take the weight of the blankets. Replacing it after she had noted the extent of the damage, she smoothed his hair away from his temples and bent her head to kiss him.

'He's going to need a lot of care, Bethan, you do know that?'

'And he's not going to make an easy patient.' She smiled awkwardly at Dr John. 'He's used to getting his own way. Doing what he wants, being active.'

'Take some time off.'

Squaring her shoulders, Bethan set her face, determined not to break down as she had the night David Ford had found her. 'When he leaves here I might take you up on that offer.'

'Not before?'

She shook her head.

'Bethan . . .'

'I'm all right. I'd better take Luke home. I'll see you in the surgery tomorrow.'

He watched her walk away. She had lost weight since the accident and she looked as though she hadn't slept in a month. He couldn't even write to Andrew to ask him to tell her to slow down. It would only make him worry all the more about what was happening back home. Possibly even drive him over the edge. There had been some disquieting reports about deaths in German POW camps. Quite understandably. He couldn't imagine being locked up as long as Andrew had been with no sign of a reprieve.

'Thank you, Mrs John. I really appreciate you getting me out of there.'

'I'm not sure I've done you a favour. You still look in shock to me. I could have brought Gina down to the hospital.'

'I don't want anyone to tell her I'm all right except me. Have you seen her? How is she?'

'How do you think? Upset. Bearing up because there was nothing else she could do.'

'That's why I have to see her. To convince her that I really am all right. All I want is to be with her. Mr Williams has given me a few days off.'

'That was big of him.' Bethan couldn't keep the sarcasm from her voice.

'It could be longer, I have to see Dr John at the end of the week.'

'You're quite a hero, Luke.'

He clenched his fists. 'I didn't do anything to save the others.'

'Did they die in the fall?' She hated asking the question, but she had to know.

'I think Alexander died yesterday. Mr Richards the day before. I'm not too sure about the exact time, it was difficult to tell what day it was. I had the foreman's watch, but when I slept I lost all track. I couldn't tell if it was day or night. And when the batteries failed in the last of the lamps it was hopeless. Only four of us survived the fall, and apart from me they were all badly injured. I tried to do what I could, but I couldn't even dig the others out. They were trapped under the rocks and I was afraid that if I tried to free them, the whole lot would come tumbling down on top of us.' Guilt, raw, choking, lay behind his simple explanation.

'I can't even begin to imagine what it was like down there. Not knowing whether you would be rescued or not. It says a great deal that you found the strength and courage to save my father.'

'And myself,' he added drily.

'You can't take the blame because you survived and the others didn't.'

'No, but I don't have to feel good about it either. If you want to talk about heroes, talk about Alexander. He was crushed from the waist down. An intelligent, educated man like him must have known it was hopeless from the start, yet he kept us all going. Talking, making suggestions about rationing out the food in the snap boxes. Even cracking jokes.'

They passed the shadowy figures of the first miners going out on early morning shift as they turned the corner into Danycoedcae Road. Turning off the ignition, she pulled on the handbrake.

'Would you mind coming in with me, Mrs John?' he asked diffidently. 'I didn't like to tell Dr John, but Gina could be having a baby. She's not sure yet, or at least she wasn't a week ago. I don't want to risk her getting upset. My mother lost her third when her brother was killed in a farm accident, and the midwife put that down to shock.'

'Would you like me to go in first?'

'What do you think?'

'How about we go in together?'

Gina's cries of relief and joy were still ringing in Bethan's ears when she left Danycoedcae Road ten minutes later. She had two more calls to make before returning to her own house and she hoped that Phyllis would forgive her the delay. Heading back down Llantrisant Road she turned right into Graig Avenue, spotting the gleam of the white flashes on Huw Davies's helmet and armbands as she drove up the road. When he heard the engine of her car, he stopped. She parked outside her old house, and opened the door.

'Is that you, Bethan?'

'Have you been to see my mother, Uncle Huw?'

'Not yet. I've only just left Mrs Richards.'

'Is she all right?'

'No, but I left Mrs Morris and Mrs Evans with her. They both know what she's going through, having lost their own husbands.'

'Then I suppose it's up to me to call on Mam. Do you want to come with me?'

'After what she did to Phyllis and you? Try and stop me.'

Bethan ran up the steps and knocked on the door. She knocked half a dozen times, but it was Huw's cry of 'Police' that finally prompted Elizabeth to leave her bed and walk down the stairs.

'Who is it?' she called from behind the closed door.

'Huw Davies, Elizabeth.' He placed a reassuring hand on Bethan's shoulder. 'We have news about Evan.'

'Who's we?'

'Bethan is with me.'

Drawing the bolt, she switched off the light, opened the door and peered out at them.

'Dad's alive, Mam, but he's injured. He's going to need a lot of nursing. You'll need us to give you a hand to pack up the things in the parlour and move a bed in there.'

'I enjoyed that,' Huw said as Elizabeth closed the door on them.

'I didn't.' Bethan had hoped that her mother would invite them in. But she hadn't. Merely told them that she'd be returning to her Uncle John Joseph's house in

Tonypandy by midday and they could move Evan in then. Bethan hadn't told her that it would be weeks before Evan could leave the Graig Hospital. Elizabeth had shut the door without giving her a chance to say any more.

'Have you been to see Jenny?' she asked.

'No. Should I?'

'There was something going on between her and Alexander Forbes. Phyllis said he wanted to marry her.'

'Poor Jenny,' Huw mused, remembering the day he'd read her the telegram telling her that Eddie had been killed. There were times when he hated his job. Jenny would be his sixth call that night. Could he really go through another four?

'I'll tell her.' Bethan opened her car door.

'You don't have to. It's my job.'

'I know I don't have to, Uncle Huw, but I feel I should.'

'Bethan . . .'

'Eddie was my brother. And despite everything I think he loved her. I'll tell her.'

Elizabeth pushed the bolt across the front door, dropped the blackout and switched on the light. She walked slowly down the flagstoned passage into the kitchen. Her brain was pounding inside her skull, throbbing unrelentingly as though it was about to burst free.

Resignation and acceptance of God's will. That was the lesson that had been drummed into her from birth by her minister father and, after his death, by her uncle. How often had both of them warned her never to question the wisdom of the Supreme Being? That her life was significant only in that it was an infinitesimal part of a greater plan she could neither begin to understand nor question, because to even attempt to do so would jeopardise her immortal soul.

She laid her hand on the latch of the kitchen door and pushed it open. This was *her* home. She had cleaned every corner of this room more times than she could remember. Polished every inch of brass rail in the range, blackleaded every corner of the ironwork. She had sewn plain, serviceable, grey cotton curtains, and chair covers that had been discarded. And in their place was evidence of Evan's whore's work. In *her* home.

She knew she should pray for guidance and above all forbearance. But for the first time in her life, the words refused to come. Why was she being put to the test? Why had God destroyed Sodom and Gomorrah, yet allowed the filth of those cities to live on, here, in her home?

Her home – *she* would never have sewn patchwork curtains, or patchwork covers for the chairs. She would have put the hours it had taken to make those garish patterns out of rags to better use. She ran her fingers above the door frame, disappointed when she found no dust.

She stepped inside the room. She had a right to remain here, but she couldn't stay, not with Evan. Never again would she allow a man to do such filthy things to her. The fruit of his loins – their children – stared back at her from a photograph on the mantelpiece. *Her* children – not the whore's. But Evan's whore had put the small posy of artificial flowers next to the frame. An offering commemorating their father's vulgar, morbid grief. In His infinite wisdom God had chosen to take their younger son and daughter, and for their sins, He had given them no grave in their home town, no marker, where they could be mourned by their family. So why make a memorial here? In the house their mother had been ousted from by a whore.

She continued to stare at the smiling faces. Bethan, with her arm around Maud; Haydn and Eddie standing behind the girls. Suddenly sweeping her arm across the mantelpiece she sent the frame and the china ornaments surrounding it crashing to the hearth. Still the photograph stared up at her. Slowly, deliberately, she pulled the broken glass, shard by shard, from the frame, heaping the fragments into the coal bucket. Opening the door on the range she pushed the photograph and the frame on top of the coals. She sat back on her heels and watched it burn. When it was no more than a smudge of white ash on the glowing coals, she opened the dresser cupboard and took the first photograph album. When she had transformed it into a pile of curling, flaking, black ash, she took the next . . . and the next . . . until the cupboard was bare. Then she turned her attention to Evan's books. Books she would never have allowed in the house. Marxist filth, Russian novels penned by degenerates who wrote about things decent people would never think of, much less study.

She pulled down the curtains, ripping the pole from the wall; the covers from the chairs, the rag rugs, the pictures from the walls. Looking down at the pile she'd made on the floor, she realised it would take for ever to burn it all. Picking up the workbox she reached for the scissors and attacked the cloth, not only the loose covers but the chairs themselves. Emptying the shelves on the dresser she dropped the plates, cups and saucers that had belonged to Evan's grandmother on to the flagstones where they shattered into slivers too small to mend. She looked at the dresser itself, big, solid and heavy. There was an axe in the coalhouse. She glanced up at the clock. She had until midday. It would be time enough. Then Evan could have his precious house back. If he still wanted it.

Bethan had prepared herself for an outburst of grief, but Jenny sat, dry-eyed and white-faced. There were no tears, screams, or protestations of anger, only a calm acceptance that sent shivers down Bethan's spine.

'Alexander survived the fall but he died before the rescuers could reach him. He saved Luke's and my father's life with his suggestions for rationing the food. He even made jokes to keep up their spirits.'

'He would have.' There was no bitterness or rancour in Jenny's voice. Leaving the sofa she walked to the window and pulled back the curtains.

'The blackout,' Bethan warned.

'I forgot.' Dropping the curtain she glanced at the clock. 'I have to be in work in an hour.'

'They'll understand if you take the day off.'

'There's no need.'

'Jenny, you have to give yourself time to get over this.'

'There's nothing to get over,' she murmured flatly. 'It wasn't as if we were married. It's not like losing Eddie. Alexander wasn't my husband, only my lover. I'll find another.'

Bethan laid her hands on Jenny's shoulders, forcing her to look into her eyes. 'Give yourself time to grieve. If you don't, you could have a nervous breakdown.'

'I'm fine.' Jenny smiled, but her blue eyes remained cold, dead. 'You see. I'm fine, Bethan. There's nothing to get over. Nothing at all.'

Chapter Fourteen

KURT SCHAFFER BUTTONED his greatcoat as he waited in station yard. Winter was slowly but surely giving way to spring, but it was a cooler spring than he was accustomed to, and in early evening the damp air still had the power to penetrate layers of uniform. When he saw the blonde head he'd been waiting for, he took a deep breath and stepped forward.

'I was hoping to see you.'

'Were you?' Jenny stood back and watched the crowd of girls she'd travelled with walk on without her.

'Some people get all the luck,' Maggie shouted.

'Don't eat all of him, Jenny,' Judy called back over her shoulder. 'Leave some for me.'

'I wanted to tell you how sorry I was about your boyfriend,' Kurt murmured, glad when Jenny's companions moved out of earshot.

'Alexander wasn't my boyfriend, Lieutenant Schaffer. He was my lover.'

Kurt stared at her completely lost for words.

'I've embarrassed you?'

'Not exactly. It's just that I've never met anyone quite as direct as you.'

'And?'

He continued to gaze at her blankly.

'Is this an accidental meeting, or did you meet my train to offer your condolences?'

'I've been hoping to see you for some time.'

'Let me guess – ever since Alexander was killed, because you'd like to move in and take his place?'

He whistled under his breath. 'Ma'am, there's honesty and then there's brutality.'

'Let's settle for the unvarnished truth, shall we? My

guess is that you want a girl to sleep with while you're in town. Someone who's willing, able, not too demanding, and won't make a scene when you wave goodbye?'

'No,' he protested hastily. 'I don't want that at all.'

'That's a pity, Lieutenant Schaffer.' She took his arm and led him across the road towards the White Hart. 'If you had, you might have been in luck. And then again you might not have been. I'm looking for a lover, you've already presented and proved your credentials, so as far as I'm concerned you fit the bill. But, I'd be very careful what I was getting myself into if I were you. My price may prove to be a high one.'

'Price?' He glanced back at the professionals standing outside the booking office. 'I don't understand.'

'My husband was killed at Dunkirk, and now Alexander's body has been shipped back to his parents. You've heard of the kiss of death?'

'Come on . . .'

'I'm deadly serious, Lieutenant. Some women are cursed. Ask any RAF pilot if you don't believe me. Make love to me again, and it may be the last thing you do.'

'I don't believe all that superstition bullshit,' he retorted irritably.

'No? You'd be a fool not to.'

He pushed open the door of the Hart, and stood back to allow her to walk ahead of him. 'Can we start by forgetting what you've just said and have a drink?'

'Don't ever say I didn't warn you.'

As he watched her enter the back room he wondered if she'd had some kind of a breakdown following Alexander Forbes's death. After what had happened to her husband it would be understandable.

All he knew was, no other girl had ever made him feel the way Jenny Powell did, and he wanted to put a smile on her face. Just like the one she had worn when he had first met her in the cafe.

*

'Home.' Bethan stopped the car, turned off the ignition and looked across at her father in the passenger seat.

Opening the car door awkwardly with his left hand, he stepped outside. Phyllis was standing on the doorstep, waiting, an apprehensive smile on her face.

'Daddy!' Brian shouted. Charging out from behind his mother he ran down the steps to meet them.

Evan turned back to Bethan. 'There's no party?'

'No, Dad, I promised there wouldn't be, and there isn't,' she reassured him. 'Maybe we'll organise one later when you've had time to settle in.'

'To life as a cripple?'

'To consider your options,' she countered, as he crouched down to hug Brian. He wasn't the only one having difficulty in adjusting to his injuries. The calm, even-tempered man she had trusted and relied on all her life had been supplanted by a bitter, self-pitying amputee capable of seeing offence in the most innocuous remark.

She took a steadying breath before following him and Brian up the steps. Standing back, she watched Phyllis hold out her arms, but her father only kissed her cheek, before stepping into the house. Bethan saw Brian looking at the pinned up, empty sleeve on his father's coat as they walked down the passage. Wanting to comfort him, she took his hand.

During the past month she had studied every textbook she could find that documented reactions to amputations, but nothing she read had helped. If her father had been simply another patient she could have chivvied him along in the standard, brusque, professional manner. But he wasn't just a patient. He was the guiding force she counted on to solve her problems. The one person who had always been there when she, or her brothers and sister, had needed someone; and now, when she needed him most, she couldn't turn to him.

Before the accident she hadn't realised how much of his strength stemmed from his physical fitness. Since the moment the anaesthetic had worn off he had seen himself as a useless cripple. A burden on his family and friends. A man with nothing more to offer.

He hadn't threatened suicide. He hadn't needed to. She had recognised the signs. The lethargy, the indifference to people and life. He had barely spoken to Phyllis on her twice-weekly visits. And when she had seen the ward sister giving orders for her father's food to be cut up on his plate before serving, and the nurses to shave him rather than entrust him with a razor, she knew she was not the only one to have considered the possibility that he might try to kill himself.

Even as they were leaving the hospital, Dr John had called her back to warn her to dispense her father's painkillers carefully when she got him home, giving him no more than a single day's supply at a time.

Phyllis pushed open the door to the kitchen and hesitated, waiting for an outburst. It came.

'What the hell's happened here?' Evan demanded furiously as he looked around the room. Ever since he could remember there had been far too much furniture. A massive Welsh dresser and long table and chairs that his father had inherited from his farming grandparents. Victorian easy chairs that his mother had been given as a wedding present. A sideboard she had been bequeathed by an elderly aunt, and that had never really fitted in.

Now there was only an impractical, delicate china cabinet Phyllis had been left by her landlady. A small round table and three spindly-legged chairs that belonged in a parlour, not a kitchen, and two dainty upholstered chairs in place of the substantial, comfortable easy chairs that had stood either side of the range. The familiar ornaments had gone, as had the pictures and photographs from the walls. Phyllis's dainty blue and white shepherdesses stood on the mantelpiece instead of his mother's dogs. Even the patchwork cushion covers and curtains had been replaced by a print that looked suspiciously like Bethan's dining room curtains.

'We had a bit of a clear-out,' Phyllis confessed nervously, looking past Evan to Bethan.

'Clear-out! All the furniture's gone!'

'Sit down, Dad, and I'll tell you what happened.' Bethan virtually pushed him into the chair that stood where his had been. 'Mam came back.'

'When?'

'When you were trapped underground. Unlike the rest of us, she thought you were dead, and decided to claim the house.'

'I made a will. She had no right to walk over the doorstep.'

'Unfortunately she did. In law, apparently even an estranged wife has the right to live in the matrimonial home. Haydn checked with a solicitor. In his opinion, as your legal wife, Mam was entitled to a share of your estate. If she'd gone to court the chances were she'd have got everything and Phyllis nothing.'

'So you let her walk in and take what she wanted?' He glared at Phyllis who murmured something about tea, took the kettle, and retreated into the washhouse with Brian.

'It wasn't Phyllis's fault, Dad. Put yourself in her position. Whichever way you look at it, without you, she has no right to be here.'

'She's my wife in all but name.'

'I agree, she's more your wife than Mam ever was. But the courts wouldn't see it that way.'

'Or your mother,' he muttered grimly. 'I can imagine some of the things she said.'

'It wasn't just her. Uncle John Joseph came with her. Haydn was still here, he tried to stop them but they ordered all of us out.'

'And you went like sheep?' His face was dark with anger.

'What choice did we have? The situation was impossible for Phyllis. And Haydn and Jane wouldn't stay without her, even if Mam had invited them to, which she didn't.'

His anger began to subside when he realised that his children had rallied around his common-law wife, not their mother. 'So, where did Phyllis and Brian go?'

'They moved in with me, as did Jane, Haydn and Anne. Jane and Anne are staying for a while. It's easier for Maisie to look after two toddlers than one,' she added tactfully, hoping he wouldn't realise that she and Jane had decided on the new arrangements to make things easier for Phyllis, now she had him to nurse as well as the house and Brian to look after.

'I'm surprised you found room.'

'We managed.'

He leaned wearily against the back of the chair. 'That still doesn't explain the furniture.'

'The night they found you, Uncle Huw and I came here to tell Mam you'd survived. We mentioned you were injured, but she assumed you'd be back the next day. We didn't disillusion her. It was the middle of the night, she said she'd move out by midday. Giving her those few hours' grace was a mistake. She, or Uncle John Joseph, took an axe to the furniture in here.'

'The china?'

'Smashed, but worst of all was the photographs.' Bracing herself for another bout of rage, Bethan decided that her father might as well hear all the bad news at once. 'She burned them.'

'All of them?'

'And smashed your camera.'

'All the pictures I took when you were children? Maud . . . Eddie . . .'

'Mam destroyed everything in here, but I got together with Ronnie and Jenny. Between us we had quite a few copies. I've put them into an album for you.' She opened the china cabinet, removed a book and handed it to him. He flicked through its pages without really looking at the photographs it contained. 'Before we left, Haydn carried Phyllis's furniture around to Mrs Richards. If he hadn't, you'd be sitting on the floor right now. It's practically impossible to buy furniture these days.'

'This is going to take some getting used to.' He glanced at the corner shelf where he'd kept his books.

'The good news is, Mam didn't do anything to the bedrooms, or Alexander's room, so we were able to box his things up and send them on to his parents.'

'That must have been a comfort to them.'

She chose to ignore his caustic tone. They'd all been fond of Alexander, but since the accident, concern for the living hadn't given them much time to mourn his, or Mr Richards's passing.

'But she did empty the parlour, and she must have arranged to take the furniture with her. There was no wreckage left like here.'

'Everything in the parlour was hers, she had a right to take it.' He glanced up at the mantelpiece. 'Even my pipe?'

'I tried to take it. Mam wouldn't let me.'

'I've been a fool, Bethan. A bloody fool. When Phyllis moved in I thought everything would be all right. But it won't be. Not until this mess is sorted once and for all between your mother and me. We can't carry on the way we have been, not after this. Can you take me down to the solicitor's?'

'Now?'

'Right now. I'm going to divorce your mother and marry Phyllis. She needs security. She has a right to know that this can't ever happen to her ever again. I won't have her relying on charity from you and Haydn.'

'Phyllis is family so it's hardly charity, and, Dad, I hate to say this, but you may find it difficult to divorce Mam when you're the guilty party.'

'Your mother left me.'

'Whatever, but the one thing I do know is that a divorce will cost a lot of money.'

'Thank you for reminding me I've no way of earning any more.'

'Yet,' she said, refusing to get involved in a discussion on his prospects straight after dropping the bombshell about the damage. 'Haydn and I talked about this before he left. We made an offer to Mam for the house. She wouldn't sell it to us. But you could. Your name is on the deeds. You're the sole owner, so how about it? We'll give you a fair price.'

'More charity?'

'More like a good investment for us. House prices will go up after the war.'

'And you two can afford it?'

'We can, and we'd put a clause into the contract that will give Phyllis the right to live here as long as she wants. Brian too if you like.'

'Brian will have to make his own way when the time comes, just like the rest of you. But I won't take hand-outs, Bethan. Not from you or anyone. If I sell you the house, Phyllis and I will move out and find a smaller, cheaper one to live in.'

'Was it charity when you kept us when we were children?'

'Everyone looks after their children.'

'Not everyone.'

'If we stay we'd have to pay you rent.'

'We'll ask the solicitor to fix a fair one,' she suggested, wondering if she could have a word with him first. 'And perhaps he could give you some advice on investing the money. You might be able to buy an annuity that would give Phyllis and Brian an income if anything happened to you.'

'But it still doesn't solve my problems with your mother. In spite of this,' he looked around the room, 'and everything else that's happened over the years, I can't help feeling that I'm the guilty one. I had no right to marry her. Not feeling the way I did about Phyllis.'

'It happened, Dad. You're happy now with Phyllis.'

'And your mother? Don't try telling me she's happy.'

'Sometimes I wonder if anything could have made her happy.'

'Her father's at fault. A God-fearing chapel minister who saw fun and laughter as the work of the Devil.'

'She didn't have to adopt his beliefs, or make our lives quite so miserable.'

'No. But we owe her our understanding, Beth, if nothing else. And,' he smiled wryly, 'when all's said and done, she did give me four quite remarkable children.'

'Come on, honey, just a couple of drinks with the boys?'

'I don't know, Richard. Going to the New Inn is one thing, but the White Hart has a reputation for attracting people who aren't quite respectable.'

'It'll be fun, honey.' Taking Anthea's hand he tucked it into the crook of his elbow. 'The New Inn is so stuffy,' he declared, glossing over the real reason for not taking her there – the upmarket prices. 'And both George and Kurt go to the Hart.'

'Don't mention Kurt. He's hardly said two words to me since we got engaged.'

'Only because he's jealous, honey. And who can blame him? He lives in your house, sees you every day, and knows I've beaten him to the post. He obviously wanted you for himself.' Richard pushed the door open and ushered her in. As she walked down the dingy passage towards the back room, the stench of sour beer, stale tobacco smoke and male sweat crowded in on her, making her even more uneasy.

'It's full and noisy,' she complained, retreating as he opened the door.

'Lively, not noisy, honey. Hi, fellows.' He waved to Kurt, Jenny, and George Rivers who were sitting at a round table in the centre of the room. 'Can we join you?'

'Can we stop you?' Kurt enquired drily. The quiet drink he'd hoped for with Jenny hadn't materialised. George Rivers and his floozie, Vera, had parked themselves at their table less than five minutes after they'd arrived, rendering any serious attempts at conversation impossible, and now Richard and Anthea had appeared, it was hopeless. He would have made for the door if he and Jenny hadn't had full glasses.

'Hello, Anthea. How are you?' Jenny reached for the gin and pep Kurt had bought her.

'Quite well, thank you, Jenny,' Anthea replied primly, blanching when Vera Collins appeared and sat next to George. Barely eighteen, Vera was married to the middle-aged owner of a dairy stall on the market. Anthea had heard that he'd thrown her out for consorting with American servicemen, but assuming officers to be gentlemen, she hadn't realised that one of the consorting servicemen was George Rivers.

'Hello, Anthea.' Vera took the cigarette George offered her. 'How is your mother?'

'Quite well.' Anthea looked to Richard, who studiously ignored her as he went to the bar.

'You're engaged, Anthea?' Jenny was amazed to find that she actually felt sorry for the girl. Just like her mother, Anthea was a stuck-up snob, but as she saw her blush and squirm, she realised she lacked the courage to 'cut' Vera and didn't know how else to deal with Vera's new-found notoriety.

'At Christmas,' Anthea gushed. 'Would you like to see the ring Richard gave me?' She held out her hand.

'Very pretty.'

'So, when's the wedding?' George winked broadly at Vera as though they shared a secret joke.

'Just as soon as Uncle Sam gives us permission.' Richard laid a tray full of glasses on the table. 'Drinks all round, boys and girls?'

'We have to go.' Kurt downed the remainder of his half-pint and picked up Jenny's coat from the chair.

'But I've just bought you two drinks.'

'And if I have another on an empty stomach, I won't be able to stand up straight.' Jenny allowed Kurt to help her on with her coat.

'Who wants to do that?' Vera giggled.

'Some of us have to stand up to work, Vera,' Jenny said coolly, tired of her innuendo. 'See you, Anthea.'

*

'Remind me never to go into the Hart again when Vera's there,' Jenny said as Kurt led her outside.

'I'm sorry, I didn't even know George had a pass tonight. Can I buy you dinner?'

'I've stew at home. If you're hungry you can eat with me.'

'I am hungry.'

'Kurt, I meant what I said about me being the kiss of death.'

He helped her into his Jeep. 'For a home-cooked meal, I'm prepared to take my chances.'

'Do you still work for your father in the bank?' Vera asked Anthea as Richard and George disappeared into the Gents.

'Yes.'

'Cushy number.'

'It may not look as though I'm contributing to the war effort, but by working, I've freed a man to go to the front.'

'Whoever he is, I bet he's grateful,' Vera observed snidely.

'Do you work?'

'Of course.'

'What do you do?'

'Vera's in charge of morale-boosting for American servicemen, aren't you, sugar?' George beamed as he returned.

'Drinks?' Richard plonked two more gins and two more beers on the table.

'It's getting late, we should be going,' Anthea said primly.

'It's not that late.'

'It is in my book.'

'Is anything the matter, honey?'

'She can't wait to get you on your own, Richard,' Vera suggested. 'And if your talents run in the same direction as George's, I can understand why.'

Anthea gathered her handbag and coat from the chair. 'I'm going.'

'Can't we finish our drinks?' Richard asked.

'I don't want to stay.'

'Boy oh boy, it's easy to see which one of you wears the pants,' George commiserated.

'When they have them on. I know all about engaged couples.' Vera wagged her finger at Anthea.

It was one remark too many. Holding her head high, Anthea stalked out through the door.

'When you get it from her, it must be so bloody refined I wonder you recognise it.'

'And what would you know about refinement, Rivers?' Richard polished off Anthea's gin as well as his beer.

'About the same as you I guess, after comparing Anthea's snaps with Vera's here.'

'Shut your mouth, or . . .'

'Or?' George rose unsteadily to his feet.

'I'll see your name on the first list of combat troops to ship out of here, Lieutenant.' He fingered his captain's insignia.

'Gentlemen, please.' The landlord left the bar and walked over to their table. 'Is there a problem?'

'Lieutenant Rivers and his companion have had a few too many, Mr Hunt.' Richard buttoned on his greatcoat. 'I wouldn't serve them any more before the MPs do their rounds if I were you.'

The landlord looked down at Vera. 'You, out of here.'

'Come on . . .'

'I warned you, one wrong move and you'd be out. Well, you've just made it.'

Richard took advantage of the altercation to slip out through the door. It had been a mistake to bring Anthea to the Hart. Broke or not, he should have taken her to the New Inn. If she caught a whiff of the way the boys were talking about her, he'd have a lot more than her displeasure to contend with.

Never mind Rivers; perhaps it was time to put his own name on that list.

'How could you?' Anthea ranted as Richard caught up with her outside Woolworth's. 'Whatever you think of me, I'm not that naive. I understood what Jenny said about standing up to work. Vera Collins is nothing more than a common prostitute.'

'I didn't know, honey. I swear it. Until this evening, I just assumed she was George's girlfriend.'

'You've met her before?'

'Once or twice.'

She whirled around to face him. 'You've been with her?'

'I'm a one-woman man, honey. You know that.' Grabbing her arm, he tucked it into his own.

'Let go of me.' She struggled free.

'Please, you're making a scene.'

'I don't want you near me.'

'It's hardly my fault if one of my fellow officers likes the common type.'

'We don't have to socialise with them.'

'No we don't, and I'm sorry, honey. My mistake. I'll never take you there again.' He walked her quickly round the corner along Bridge Street towards the park gates. 'Come on, don't be mad,' he pleaded.

'Go away.'

'Honey, please, don't let's quarrel.' He pulled her close to a gap in the park railings. 'It's not that late, let's go somewhere and make up.'

'I want to go home.'

'And I refuse to let you go anywhere until you've calmed down.'

A mixture of anger, irritation and frustration seethed inside Anthea as he fondled pressure points that he knew aroused her. 'Chuck's in your rooms,' she reminded him peevishly.

'But not in the park.'

'It's closed.'

'Only to those not in the know.' He looked up and down the rapidly darkening street before pushing aside a railing that had been sawn through. Ducking his head, he stepped through the gap and dragged her after him.

'Richard . . .'

'Ssh, quick, before anyone sees us.' Pulling her by the hand he led her through the trees to a secluded, covered seating area that he'd marked out earlier. 'Our very own private place.' Sitting on the bench he drew her down on to his lap and slid his hand beneath her skirt.

'Richard, we can't. Not here.'

'No one can see.'

'But here, in the open air!'

'It's not that cold.' Hooking his hand into her knickers he tugged them down to her ankles.

'Someone could come.'

'They won't see anything in this light.'

'No . . .' the protestation died in her throat as he kissed her, ' . . . we should wait.'

'I can't, honey. I've told you men aren't built like women.' Pushing her down on to the bench he unbuttoned his trousers. 'A quick one, honey, just to tide me over until tomorrow lunchtime. Oh boy, do you know how to turn a fellow on.'

'That was good.'

'It was terrible.' Jenny piled her own and Kurt's empty bowls on to a tray. 'The meat was tough and stringy, there wasn't enough of it, there was too much barley . . .'

'I could get you extra food from the canteen.'

'No. Thank you, but no.'

'Why not?' he asked as he picked up the bread plate and followed her into the kitchen.

'Because I'd rather not be tarred with the same brush as Vera and Anthea.'

'I like you. I . . .'

'Want me to be your girl?'

'You remembered?'

'You don't have to pay for sex with food, Kurt. Not with me.'

'I wasn't trying to.'

'Come to bed?'

'Now?'

'Don't you want to?'

'Yes, but . . .'

'But what? You want it prettied up with visits to the pictures and walks in the park? Some women have the same needs as men. I thought you would have realised that the night of the dance.'

'I don't want it to be like this between us, Jenny,' he said slowly, wary of blowing his chances with her.

'Like what?'

'Cold, calculating sex.'

'You want hearts and roses, love and romance?' she mocked.

Taking her hand he drew her towards him and kissed her. She reciprocated with a warmth and passion that told him she wanted him every bit as much as he wanted her, but for all her talk of no emotional ties, when he finally released her he saw that her eyes were wet.

'How about we go back to your living room, sit down, talk and get to know one another?'

'What's the point when you'll soon be dead?'

'I have no intention of dying.'

'Neither did Eddie or Alex.'

'Why don't you tell me about them?'

'No.' She shook her head violently and turned away from him.

'Then tell me about yourself?'

'There's nothing to tell.'

'In that case you've no excuse for not allowing me to monopolise the conversation. I've led an extremely interesting life and you're going to hear all about it, in great detail, starting with the day I was born in my mother's hairdresser's with a full head of hair and one tooth.'

'You're being absurd.'

'Maybe, but if that's what it takes to get you to smile, I'm prepared to carry on making a fool of myself.'

246

Wrapping his arm around her shoulders, he kissed her cheek. 'The living room and my life story?'

'All right.'

'And tomorrow, if you're good, I'll meet your train again and take you to the movies.'

'I don't want a courtship.'

'We'll make it a quick one.' He kissed her again.

'Very quick or I might move on,' she threatened as he led her towards the sofa.

Chapter Fifteen

'HELLO, STRANGER,' ALMA called out as Bethan walked into the kitchen of her shop early one mid-June morning. It was already warm, and the long-sleeved, blue uniform dress Bethan was wearing looked prickly and uncomfortable. 'Tea?' She lifted the teapot from the back of the stove where it had been warming.

'Please.' Bethan sank into one of the chairs. 'The last two days have been horrendous.'

'Finding it hard to get back to work?'

'Harder than I thought after being part-time for three months, although why six days a week feels like ten times more than three is beyond me.'

'Possibly because you're trying to run your home and look after your father in one day instead of four?'

'Dad's no trouble,' Bethan protested.

'Who are you trying to kid?'

'He's been much better since Mr Williams offered him a position covering safety in the pit. Mind you, we had the devil's own job convincing him that management wasn't just being kind. Even now, he's not sure that he'll be doing a real job.'

'When does he start?'

'Next Monday.'

'Then why don't you go on holiday? A real one,' Alma suggested, concerned by Bethan's pallor. 'Your in-laws have still got that summer place on Gower, haven't they? Steal some petrol, drive down there with Rachel and Eddie and let the world go by for a week or two.'

'And you'll come with me?'

'I can't leave the business.'

'And I can't expect everyone else to keep covering for me. I should never have cut down on my days after my father's accident. We're rushed off our feet at the surgery. Half the town seems to be down with summer colds and sore throats. There've been more accidents than ever in the munitions factories and pits the last month, and every other woman I meet seems to be pregnant.'

'Courtesy of the Yanks?'

'I refuse to calculate back to husbands' last leaves.'

'It's a good job accents aren't inherited.'

'If they were, there'd be a lot of men disowning their children when this is over. But is it any wonder?' Her brown eyes clouded over as she took the tea Alma handed her. 'Haydn hasn't been home in six months, William for nearly two years . . .'

'Andrew for over three and Charlie for two years and four months. How is Jane coping?'

'Why Jane especially?'

'Something she said to Maggie the last time they were in here. She almost bit her head off when she mentioned Haydn and chorus girls in the same breath.'

Bethan frowned. 'She hasn't said anything to me, but then she's hardly mentioned Haydn since his last leave. Like the rest of us she seems to be marking time until the war's over.'

'And that may come sooner than you think.'

'You know something I don't?'

Alma looked into the shop and closed the door before moving her chair closer to Bethan's. 'Most of the Americans are moving out tonight.'

'Tonight!'

'Ssh. Not so loud. Chuck told me in absolute confidence, but I know you won't tell a soul and tomorrow everyone in town will have noticed that they've gone.'

'Colonel Ford hasn't said a word to me.'

'He's staying. Someone has to train the next lot.'

'Is it France?'

'Do you think Chuck would have told me that?' Alma took a packet of cigarettes from her apron pocket. 'I doubt even Chuck knows where they're going, but now we've pushed the Germans out of North Africa, and the Russians are driving them out of the Soviet Union we can hope.'

'They still control most of Europe.' Bethan's hand shook as she took the cigarette Alma offered her.

Bracing herself to hear an unpalatable truth, Alma asked, 'Are you thinking what I'm thinking?'

'That if we land troops in France they'll take it out on the prisoners. Line them up and shoot them?' Once Bethan had put her fears into words she unaccountably stopped trembling. Lighting the cigarette with the match Alma struck, she sat back and inhaled deeply.

'The British POWs are protected by the Geneva Convention. The Germans wouldn't dare harm them, not when we're holding so many of their men prisoner here.'

'But you're concerned about the Russian prisoners?'

'I've always thought that Charlie could be hiding among the Russians in a German prison camp. And the papers are always full of some new atrocity that the Nazis have committed against the Poles, the Jews or the Russians. I couldn't bear to have him survive this long only to get shot now, so close to the end.'

Like everyone else who knew Alma well, Bethan had long since given up trying to convince her that Charlie was dead. She took her hand and held it tight.

'Charlie is far too sensible to do something as stupid as die at the end of the war.'

'I couldn't bear to live without him. I simply wouldn't want to. And there's Theo . . .'

'And plenty of friends to take care of both of you until Charlie does come home.' As a district nurse, Bethan had seen several women succumb to nervous breakdowns during the last three years. Women whose husbands had been killed in action or the pits, or died slowly and painfully of lung disease, inflicting lingering mental torture as well as grief on their families. Some of the most traumatic cases she'd had to deal with had been those whose husbands had simply run off, leaving them in rented rooms with no means to provide for themselves or their children.

Despite all the hysterical protests and suicide threats, most eventually allowed themselves and their children to be carted off quietly to the workhouse. But Alma was different. She had no financial worries, proving the old adage that money wasn't everything. But her absolute conviction that she couldn't go on living without Charlie terrified Bethan. There was a quiet composure and finality in her words that held more menace than any hysterical threat.

'And here's your ma.' Chuck Reynolds flung open the door and walked into the kitchen with Theo perched high on his shoulders, baby no longer but grave-faced toddler, outwardly as serious and solemn as his father had been. Placing both hands on Theo's waist Chuck swung him down on to Alma's lap. As Alma's hands closed around her child, Bethan saw Chuck watching them and realised that he too was aware of Alma's desperate state of mind.

'Don't suppose there's a cup of whatever you're drinking going spare for a man who's bushed? Junior here dragged me around the park twice this morning. And that's without all the pushes he had to have on the swings and lifts on to the slide . . .'

'You didn't let him go on that slide by himself?' Alma broke in anxiously.

'Of course not. We went down together didn't we, buddy?' He made a sweeping motion with his hand and Theo chuckled. 'So now you've got one more thing to write to my wife about to prove I'm a good father.'

'I've been writing and swapping photographs with Chuck's wife,' Alma explained. 'His son is only three months younger than Theo. They seem to be doing all the same things.'

'And, in gratitude for convincing my family what a fine father I'll make when I get a chance, they sent you a parcel of tinned goodies. I've left it on the stairs to your apartment.'

'There was no need.'

'Oh, but there was. I had visions of Marilyn keeping me away from Chuck junior when I got home, at least until I relearned my manners. Living with men sure does roughen up the edges. I'm glad you were around to polish them off, Mrs Raschenko.'

'I hope Charlie has had a chance to make friends with someone with children. But then, he didn't even know I was pregnant when he left.' Alma gripped Theo so tightly, he prised open her fingers and wriggled off her lap.

'Then he sure is going to be one surprised man when he gets back here.'

Sensing that Chuck wanted to say his final goodbyes to Alma, Bethan took her cup to the sink and gathered her nurse's bag and handbag. 'Goodbye, Major Reynolds.' She held out her hand.

'And goodbye to you, Nurse John.' He lowered his voice. 'Look after these two for me until Charlie gets home? I may never get a chance to meet him, so tell him from one happily married man to another, he sure is one lucky guy.'

'Where's the fire, honey?' Richard Reide slid into the booth alongside Anthea. They were in a cafe they'd never visited before, principally because it had been adopted by the enlisted men.

'I need to talk to you.'

'Then how about we go to Ronconi's restaurant? I could buy you a proper meal there.'

'I haven't time. I have to be back in work in three-quarters of an hour.'

'Come on,' he nodded towards the door. 'This place is too public. Let's pick up a couple of pies and I'll walk you round the park.'

Alma had no pies left, she never did after ten o'clock in the morning, and as the bright summer sunshine had brought out the crowds, Anthea didn't dare take up his suggestion that they visit his rooms. Not in the middle of the day. There were too many people who would like nothing better than to carry tales to her father before she even got back to work.

Hungry, and slightly queasy, she allowed Richard to lead her past the Park Cinema, through the park gates and down to the river. They left the path and moved into the shrubbery. There was a small, secluded area behind a copse of bushes that screened it from the path, but the flattened state of the grass suggested that it was known to other courting couples besides them. As soon as they sat down, Richard started fumbling with the buttons on her blouse.

'Please, don't.'

'Come on, honey, no one can see us and one glimpse isn't going to hurt.'

'Please, Richard,' she snapped. 'I have to talk to you, and I can't while you do that.'

Miffed by her refusal, he locked his hands behind his head and lay back on the grass. 'You want to talk. OK, talk.'

'I'm going to have a baby.'

'You're what!' He spat out the piece of grass he'd been chewing.

'I'm sorry.' She started to cry when she saw the look on his face.

'You can't be sure?'

'I've been sure for weeks. When it . . . something . . . something didn't happen last month . . . I thought it was that cold I had. I even put the sickness down to it. But it's gone on too long. It's been awful, Richard. I'm sure my mother suspects. I've tried to hide it, but she's heard me being sick, and I've caught her watching me.'

'Your mother knows you've missed your period?'

She stared at him, horrified that a man should know about such things.

'Come on, honey, I have three sisters. What I don't understand is why you waited until now to tell me?'

'I didn't want to worry you. You've been working so

hard lately, and you've been expecting permission to come through any day for us to get married. I hoped it would have happened by now and then we could have arranged the wedding quickly using the excuse that you could be sent overseas at any time. That way no one would have had to know ... and now ... now ... everyone is going to know ... and I won't be able to wear white or have a big wedding ...' She burst into tears.

He wrapped his arm around her shoulders. 'Leave everything to me, honey. I'll sort it out.'

She drew away from him. 'How can you?'

'Dry your tears, go back to work, and tell your father that I'm taking you out for a very special dinner tonight and you'll be home late.'

'And the special dinner?'

'I'll meet you after work. Six o'clock outside the bank.'

'But I'll have to go home to change.'

'You won't need to. Just be there, honey. And wait for me.'

'Mr Ronconi to see you, sir.'

'Show him in, Lieutenant Rivers.' David Ford left his chair and walked to the window. Summer had finally arrived and most of the people in the town who weren't working had turned out to enjoy it. Taff Street was crowded with mothers with babies, women queuing at the doors of half-empty shops, workers using their lunch break to bask in the sunshine, all of them simply enjoying life. He only wished he was free to do the same. He heard the door opening.

'You sent for me, Colonel Ford?'

'Sent is a strong word.' He turned to Ronnie. 'But please, sit down, Mr Ronconi.'

'When someone calls me "Mr" it usually means they want something I'm reluctant to give.'

'I have no power to make you give me anything, Mr Ronconi.' Sitting behind his desk, David opened a file.

Ronnie started in surprise when he saw his photograph pinned to the right-hand corner of the topmost sheet. 'Correct me if any of this is wrong. You were born in a small village outside the town of Bardi in northern Italy. You lived there with your mother and paternal grand-parents until you left with your mother at the age of six to join your father who had opened a cafe in Pontypridd. Until then, Italian was your first language?' He looked up, and when Ronnie gave no indication either way, he returned to the file. 'You worked alongside your father, building up his businesses in the town until 1936 when you married Maud Powell. She was suffering from tuberculosis, so you took her to Italy in the hope that the climate would improve her condition, and there she made a partial recovery. You worked on your grand-father's farm until Mussolini conscripted all able-bodied men, at which point you and your wife took to the hills and joined the partisans. After her death you agreed to guide two downed RAF pilots through the Alps into Switzerland, suffering severe injuries as a result of a skirmish with German troops you encountered on the way.'

'I'd argue the severe. I've made a full recovery.'

'Back in Britain you drew maps for the RAF before returning to Pontypridd. Last year you took a job in a munitions factory. You married your first wife's cousin eight months ago, you have a two–year-old stepson, and your wife is expecting your first child any day.'

'And you're a damned snoop.'

'That's part of my job, Mr Ronconi.' He closed the file. 'I have to remind you that everything said between us is covered by the Official Secrets Act.'

'I've signed it.'

'On March the first, 1941.'

'Do you know how many times I visit the ty bach in a day?'

'How would you like to go back to Italy, Mr Ronconi?'

'You can't find any other targets for the Germans to shoot at?'

'We need interpreters and guides who know the country and the people. Who can tell us who to trust and who to arrest.'

'That's a tall order, given what's happened and is happening there.'

'Are you interested?'

'On spying for the Allies after they interned my father, and drowned him on a ship heading for Canada?'

'That was unfortunate.'

'Damned right it was. I have a brother fighting in North Africa, another stuck in a German prison camp since Dunkirk, three British brothers-in-law, two conscripted into the army, the third in the pits and my mother and younger brothers and sisters are still not allowed to visit Pontypridd. They have to remain in exile in, and I quote, "an area more than a hundred miles from the sea".'

'I might be able to do something about that.'

'Bribery, Colonel Ford?'

'The Allies need you.'

'I lost everything once in Italy. It wasn't easy to rebuild my life and I've no intention of throwing it away on any false heroics now.'

'There'll be no false heroics, Mr Ronconi, not this time. The invading Allied troops will need interpreters and guides. You fit the bill. I can't promise that you will come out alive if you do decide to join us. But I can promise you a chance to strike a blow against the Nazis.'

'The Allies are invading Italy in force? How soon?'

'You don't really expect me to answer that, do you?'

'Do I have to give you my answer now?'

'Yes.'

'Supposing I agree to this proposal of yours, when would I have to leave?'

'Tonight.'

'And my wife?'

'We would give you an hour to say goodbye, but only on condition you didn't tell her where you were going. What's it to be, Mr Ronconi? Yes, or no?'

Tomas D'Este stood in the foyer of the hospital waiting for Jane, as he did every time she visited the wards. And Jane's heart gave the same somersault it always did whenever she saw him. She couldn't help herself. She only had to gaze into the depths of his black eyes for her emotions to spiral out of control. It made no difference that he had a fiancee, or she a husband, albeit an unfaithful one she'd rather not think about.

Her relationship with Tomas was nothing to do with Haydn or anyone else. He was simply there. A fantasy lover come miraculously to life. A daydream she could actually live for a few short hours once a week.

She had assumed that their meetings were accidental. She had no idea that he worked late every other day of the week just so he could steal a few hours with her whenever she visited. Or how she had begun to monopolise his waking thoughts as well as his dreams.

'Would the lady like a ride home?'

'Yes, please.'

'I visited Gaynor in the kitchens, and guess what?'

'You've finally discovered what goes into the savoury rolls?'

'I persuaded her to give us the ingredients for a picnic.'

'Woolton pie sandwiches?'

'Very possibly, I haven't investigated what's in the bag.'

'I guarantee whatever it is, it will give us indigestion.'

'And I guarantee half an hour's fresh air, birdsong and peace and quiet. Sometimes I think the countryside exists only in memory.'

'You too?' She took the bag from him as she climbed on to the back of his bike. It was hard to believe that she had once been terrified of riding behind him. Now, as they raced along the road past trees and bushes, and the wind snarled and twisted in her hair, she tightened her grip on his chest, taking a secret delight in the warmth radiating from beneath his jacket. Her imagination conjured images that brought hot, shameful colour to her cheeks.

Tomas kissing her . . . Tomas undressing . . . she knew from a day when one of his shirt buttons had been missing that his chest was covered in thick, black hair. She imagined both of them naked, rolling around on a bed, and hastily tried to supplant it with a vision of her and Haydn. But try as she might she couldn't. Every time she had pictured Haydn since his last leave, he'd been in bed with a peroxide blonde, and there'd been no room for her.

'We're here.'

Tomas's voice intruded on her thoughts as he slowed the bike to a halt. Ahead was a gate, and beyond it a field of waist-high grass dotted with poppies.

'I found this spot the other day. I was coming back from work tired, late and grouchy . . .'

'Grouchy?'

'Angry, irritable . . .'

'I know what it means, I just can't imagine you angry.'

'I have a foul temper.'

'Thank you for the warning.'

'But never with beautiful young girls.'

'Or older married women?'

Taking the bag from her, he walked ahead. He jumped over the gate, then helped her to climb over before turning to the right. Shrugging off his jacket he spread it beneath an oak tree. 'Your couch, madam.'

She fell in with his mood, play-acting princess to his courtier but there was an undercurrent between them that prevented her from meeting his eye. Turning away, she opened the paper bag.

'Do you want the broken sandwich or the squashed one?'

'Ladies should have first choice.' His hand closed over hers as she handed him the broken one. She leaned towards him, and both sandwiches fell to the ground as they kissed. Her lips parted beneath the pressure from his, her hands went to his face as he pulled her closer, gently lowering her on to his coat as he continued to kiss her. An American truck roaring past out of sight but not out of hearing, brought her abruptly to her senses.

'No!' She pushed him away.

'Jane, I'm sorry. Oh, Holy Mother of God, I didn't mean for that to happen!' Sitting up, he buried his head in his hands.

'It was as much my fault as yours.' She straightened her skirt and busied herself with scooping the remains of the food into the bag. 'It was only a kiss. There's no harm done.'

'No harm?' Kneeling beside her, he stroked the side of her face with the tips of his fingers. 'Even you can't be that innocent, my love.'

'I am not your love, I'm married, you are engaged . . .'

'And absolutely, hopelessly in love with you.'

'You can't mean that?'

'Oh, but I do. When I told you that one glimpse of your smile, the night we met, suggested that I'd reached civilisation, it was much more than that. I knew then. I know now. I've just been fighting it, and so have you.'

'I won't listen to this. There's Haydn and Anne . . .'

'And us?'

'Tomas, I'm *married*. I can't offer you anything more than friendship.'

'I know.'

'We shouldn't see one another again, at least not like this.'

'Is that what you want?'

When she didn't answer he slipped his fingers beneath her chin and lifted her face, forcing her to look at him. 'I'm glad, because I couldn't bear that either.' He tried to imagine living and working in Pontypridd and not seeing her, and shuddered at the bleak thought.

'But you must never, *never* kiss me again. And when I visit the hospital you must take me straight home. If you want to talk to me, it must be in front of Bethan or Maisie.'

'Yes,' he agreed hollowly.

'Do you understand what I said?'

'Everything. But that's next time. Can't we stay together for now? I'll tell you about Cuba, and America and my family and we'll pretend – '

'That I'm not married and you're not engaged?'

'Yes – no – and that there isn't a war and we're just two *compadres* – comrades, friends, who meet once a week to talk.'

'Only if we go somewhere where there are other people.'

'The New Inn?'

'The cafe,' she said, thinking of their bank balances.

'I think we should go to the New Inn. A little luxury would help me to forget the hospital for a while, and you the factory.'

'And that we kissed.' But as she grasped the bag of crumbs and followed him back to his bike she knew that she would never forget that kiss. Not as long as she lived.

Anthea made an excuse to go to the door of the bank at five minutes to six. When she couldn't see Richard waiting for her, she returned to her cashier's station, and took her time over clearing her drawer of money and papers. When she'd finished all her essential work, she began to lay out her pencils and pens in neat, symmetrical order.

'Aren't you ready yet, Miss Llewellyn Jones?' her father barked as he walked out of his office to oversee the staff filing into the cloakroom to fetch their coats and bags.

'I saw Richard at lunchtime, he asked me to have dinner with him.'

'Tonight! You could have given your mother more warning.'

'He said it's a special occasion.'

'Perhaps permission's finally come through?'

'I hope so.'

He gave her a tight smile. His wife had become so obsessed by wedding etiquette, dress patterns and trousseau collections that he'd already resolved to have a few words with Richard to see if there was anything he could do to expedite permission from the American army.

He hadn't needed his wife to warn him that a wartime wedding wouldn't bring Anthea anything like the quality or quantity of gifts they'd received when they had married back in 1910, but rather than delay the ceremony and risk Anthea reaching the landmark age of thirty a spinster, he'd resolved to suggest to their closest friends, like the Johns, that war bonds that could be cashed after hostilities had ceased might make suitably patriotic presents for the happy couple. That way Anthea wouldn't miss out too much on what should be the most profitable day in a girl's life.

The one thing he was concerned about was the lack of communication from America. Richard had made excuses about the mail, but he still felt that his parents should have written to welcome Anthea into their family by now. He had a presentiment it wasn't entirely down to the mail. Kurt Schaffer was forever walking in from headquarters with letters and parcels, the contents of which he often shared with them. Was Richard keeping something from them? Had his parents expected him to marry an American girl? He looked down at his daughter. Richard would only have to introduce Anthea to his family for them to see she was far superior to any contender for the position of daughter-in-law that they might have had in mind.

'Special occasion or not. No later than twelve. It's a working day tomorrow,' he said, noticing that Anthea wasn't looking as well as she might. He hoped she wasn't losing her bloom. Richard might be hooked, but he wasn't landed. Not yet.

'We might be going to Cardiff.'

'Have a good time.' Pecking her cheek, he lifted his hat and coat from the stand in his private office and walked out of the door. She saw him talking to the security guard, then he left. She couldn't put it off any longer. Checking her hair and make-up in the staff room, she picked up her cardigan, lightweight jacket and handbag and followed him out. But there was still no sign of Richard.

'Looks like he can't make it.' He father appeared beside her.

'Something must have held him up. You know how hard he works.'

'I don't want you standing on the street, not with the town full of American soldiers. If you insist on waiting I'll wait with you.'

'I'll be fine, Daddy, it's light for hours yet.' She looked around anxiously. An American officer was walking down Taff Street. His shoulders were broad, but not broad enough. And as he drew closer she could see that the hair beneath his cap was blond, not brown.

'Lieutenant Schaffer? Just the man we want to see.'

'Really, sir?' Kurt looked at Mr Llewellyn Jones not knowing what to expect.

'Anthea's waiting for Richard. I don't suppose you've seen him?'

'Richard?'

'Yes, Richard Reide,' Mr Llewellyn Jones repeated testily.

'He promised to meet me here at six o'clock,' Anthea interposed. 'There must have been a hold-up . . .'

'You don't know?' Kurt looked from Anthea to her father. There was no way he could soften the blow, so he didn't even try. 'Captain Reide and Major Reynolds shipped out two hours ago with most of the regiment, sir. I'm sorry. I can't tell you where they were going. It's classified.'

Anthea stared at him as though he'd gone stark, raving mad. Then as the full import of his words sank in, she swayed on her feet, registering the feel of Kurt's strong arms around her just before she fell.

Chapter Sixteen

KURT STOPPED A passing enlisted man and sent him to get a car. Maurice arrived with a Jeep a few moments later. After helping Anthea and her father in, and giving Maurice strict instructions to drive slowly, he headed back to HQ where he found George Rivers sitting behind a desk covered in papers.

'I need to see the old man.'

'And I'd like a date with Princess Elizabeth,' George retorted flippantly.

'Move it. It's important.'

'He doesn't want to be disturbed.'

Kurt stepped towards the door.

'Walk in if you want to lose your commission. He's on the telephone to Command.'

'Why didn't you say so?' Kurt demanded irritably.

'Because the boss is not the only one who's up to his neck in work. Look at it.' He picked up a handful of forms and scattered them over the mess on his desk.

'I see chaos, not work.'

'We've got over a thousand men coming in tomorrow. There's billets to sort, feeding arrangements to be made . . .'

'Chuck Reynolds sorted the accommodation and canteen facilities for the incoming troops last week.'

'That was before we were tipped off as to what exactly was coming in.'

'Northerners?'

'Worse.'

'There isn't anything worse.'

'Try niggers.'

'Here, in Pontypridd?'

Rivers nodded. 'And with a quarter of the white boys

left behind, that means trouble. The colonel's trying to sort it now.'

'I'll wait.' Picking up a copy of the *Stars and Stripes*, Kurt sat at Chuck's abandoned desk.

'He'll be in a foul mood when he's through.'

'And he'll be in a fouler one when he's heard what I have to tell him,' Kurt predicted gloomily.

After twenty minutes David Ford appeared in the outer office.

'I didn't see your name on the duty roster, Schaffer.'

Kurt jumped to his feet and saluted. 'It isn't, sir. I was hoping for a private word.'

Ford glanced at his watch. 'Will it take long?'

'Five minutes, sir.'

'Then you'd better come into the office. At ease,' he ordered as he walked in behind him and closed the door. 'I hope this isn't going to be a request for permission to marry a local girl, Schaffer,' he warned him abruptly. 'Officially we're processing all such requests. Unofficially, marriages between American military personnel and British civilians are being severely discouraged.'

'It's not my personal affair, sir. It's Captain Reide's.'

'Carry on, Lieutenant.'

'He got engaged to a local girl at Christmas, sir.'

'First I've heard of it.'

'Most of the officers knew. He gave her a ring.'

'Very generous of him,' David Ford commented sardonically, wishing Schaffer would hurry up and come out with whatever he wanted to say.

'I just saw her and her father in town, sir. Captain Reide had arranged to meet them. I had to tell them that he shipped out this afternoon. Apparently he didn't even leave her a forwarding address. Her father asked if I could find one. I thought perhaps you could . . .'

'Captain Reide's personal affairs are his own concern, Lieutenant Schaffer. If he'd wanted the girl to have a forwarding address, he would have given her one.'

'I agree, sir. It's just that I'm in an awkward position. I promised the family . . .'

'You know this girl?'

'Yes, sir, she's my landlady's daughter.'

'Mrs Llewellyn Jones?' David Ford turned on his heel and stared at Kurt, showing the first signs of animation since they'd walked into the room.

'Yes, sir.'

'Then we have trouble.'

'That's why I came to see you, sir.'

'Why didn't you tell me this was going on between Captain Reide and Miss Llewellyn Jones earlier, Lieutenant?'

'Because it was none of my business, sir.'

'You trying to be smart?'

'No, sir.'

'What have you told the family?'

'Only that Captain Reide and Major Reynolds have left town, sir.'

'Nothing else?'

'No, sir. I wouldn't have bothered you, but Mr Llewellyn Jones intends to visit you in the morning.'

'And you thought I'd like some advance warning?'

'Something like that, sir.'

'And,' Ford lifted his eyebrows as he looked enquiringly at Schaffer, 'American servicemen aren't going to be too popular in the Llewellyn Jones household tonight?'

'Or any other night, sir.'

'You want to leave your billet?'

'I could move into the vestry, sir.'

'Reide and Reynolds's rooms are empty, ask Rivers if he can fit you in with one of the incoming officers.'

'Thank you, sir.'

'You'd better pick up your things right away. Tell Mrs Llewellyn Jones that you've been moved into town for military reasons.'

'Sir.' Assuming he'd been dismissed, Kurt snapped to attention.

'One more thing, Schaffer. Do you know if the girl's pregnant?'

Typical of the colonel, Kurt thought. No euphemisms, coy words or hints, along the lines of 'could she be in trouble?' Just straight out with it.

'I have no idea, sir.'

'I'd appreciate the truth, Schaffer, man to man, not officer to CO. I need to know what I'm up against.'

'I do know that she visited Reide in his rooms.'

'And he really bought her a ring?'

'I don't know where he got it from, sir, but it looked pretty good to me.'

'How were the family when you left them?'

'I only saw Anthea and her father, sir. She was in quite a state. But it's my guess that Mrs Llewellyn Jones is going to be the one most upset by all this. She's been planning the wedding since Christmas.'

'Perhaps I'd better drive up there with you when you pick up your things, Lieutenant.'

'I'd appreciate the support, sir,' Schaffer answered, and he meant it. He had a feeling that battle was going to be an anticlimax compared to his forthcoming confrontation with his landlady.

'I need to know, Anthea. What exactly did Richard do to you?'

Anthea buried her face in her pillow and pulled the bedclothes over her head.

'Did he ever try to do more than kiss you?' her mother demanded. 'Well, did he?'

'He behaved like an officer and a gentleman at all times,' Anthea mumbled from beneath the blankets, realising that her mother wouldn't leave her alone until she answered.

'Did he ever touch you in a way you didn't like, or put his hand up your skirt?' Furious when Anthea continued to ignore her, she raised her voice. 'You're not a child. You know what I'm asking. Did he ever do anything to you that was wrong? Because if he did I could call Dr John back . . .'

'There's no need.'

Suspicions aroused by Anthea's fainting fit, her father had sent for the doctor as soon as they reached home. She had been truly petrified when he had walked into her bedroom with her mother, but all he had done was look at her tongue, take her pulse and leave her a couple of tablets he assured her would help her sleep. Only she couldn't sleep. Her mother wouldn't let her. And all she could think of was the baby growing inside her and Richard not being there.

She refused to believe that he had deliberately abandoned her. Kurt had to be mistaken. Something must have happened between their meeting at lunchtime and his leaving. Richard couldn't have known he was going – not when he last spoke to her in the park. Perhaps he took the place of another officer at the last minute . . .

'Perhaps we should ask him to give you a thorough examination anyway.'

'Please, Mother, just leave me alone.' Anthea burrowed even deeper under the bedclothes. She wanted to scream that she had liked everything Richard had done to her. Very much indeed.

Her face burned with shame when she remembered all the times she had lain naked on his bed, allowing him to arrange her body into any pose he chose. How he had gazed at her, kissed and fondled every inch of her. How they had done things she had never even heard other girls whispering about. How she had not only become accustomed to his lovemaking, but had looked forward to the stolen hours in his rooms when they had both taken off their clothes, and romped naked in and on his bed.

'Well, if you're absolutely sure that he didn't do anything wrong, or hurt you in any way, I suppose I'll have to take your word for it.' Her mother hesitated at the door, wanting to believe that her daughter was physically unscathed by her association with Richard Reide, if not mentally.

'I'm fine, Mother,' Anthea lied. 'Please leave me alone. I haven't had a minute to myself since I've been home.'

'Very well. But I'll be back later with some warm milk.'

'I don't want warm milk.'

The doorbell rang and Anthea almost shot out of bed. Her mother patted her back, the only part of her she could reach.

'That sounds like Colonel Ford's voice. I'll go and see what he wants.' She opened the door. 'I'm sorry if I upset you, Anthea. But I had to know. I'm your mother. I care about you, and Richard deceived not only you, but all of us. I promise you, he won't get away with this. Not with my daughter. Your father will see a solicitor first thing in the morning. We'll sue for breach of promise. He's going to learn that he can't treat an innocent girl the way he's treated you and get away with it.'

The door closed and Anthea clutched her pillow all the tighter. Who could she turn to now? For all her mother's show of concern, she knew her parents would throw her out of the house the moment they discovered she was pregnant. Her mother would never compromise her high moral standards. She had cut close friends from her visiting list, simply because their daughters had been seen talking to a boy from the wrong side of Pontypridd.

Even her parents' closest friends, the Johns, had suffered temporary social ostracism when Andrew had married Bethan. And when her parents had discovered that Bethan was pregnant before the wedding, her mother had made a point of visiting Mrs John to inform her that she'd heard Bethan Powell was a hussy who had deliberately set out to seduce and get impregnated by a doctor – any doctor – to better herself. And the rumours her mother had initiated hadn't stopped there. She had overheard her telling someone at a golf club Christmas party before the war, that Andrew's wife had once worked as a prostitute, rumours that had backfired after the birth of Rachel, when the Johns had finally capitulated and accepted their daughter-in-law. But then, Andrew had stood by Bethan. What if Richard never came back? It was too dreadful to contemplate.

She recalled the advertisements she and her friends had giggled over in the *Pontypridd Observer* for 'Blanchard's Female Pills'. She could even remember some of the claims made by the manufacturers. 'Cures all irregularities.' Could they be used to get rid of a baby, as one of her schoolfriends had suggested? Did they really work?

She could send for them – but her mother opened all her mail. A Post Office number was no good, everyone knew her family and she was bound to be recognised picking up the parcel. She pressed her hands over her stomach. Was it her imagination or was it already showing?

Her mother had urged her to take the week off. But going into work would be her only chance to meet someone who could help her. Perhaps one of the girls in the office? But if they spoke to her father . . . it was then she remembered someone who would know what to do. Someone who might even help her. All she had to do was get away from her parents for an hour or two.

Kurt Schaffer dumped his kitbag on a narrow, canvas cot that had been set up in a side cubicle in the vestry. His heart sank as he looked around at the peeling paint and damp patches on the walls. George Rivers had taken great delight in telling him that there was no other accommodation available. Every spare room and bed in the town had been earmarked for incoming officers and he could either take this, or leave it. Perhaps he should leave it? Even a park bench looked preferable to this place.

He reached for his jacket. The air was freezing despite the summer warmth outside, and if he was shivering now, what would it be like in winter? But whatever else, it had to be better than the Llewellyn Joneses' house right now. As he'd predicted, Mrs Llewellyn Jones had been hysterical, and her husband wasn't much better. They had ranted and raved at Colonel Ford about Richard Reide's lack of integrity and the invidious position he had put them in. Getting engaged to their daughter and then running out on her, leaving them in the middle of expensive wedding preparations. Turning them into the laughing stock of the neighbourhood after they had taken him into their home and treated him like the son they'd never had.

Their list of grievances had been infinite, but he couldn't help noticing that they had only spoken about their own situation. Neither of them had mentioned Anthea's feelings. And although he had originally pegged the girl as a rather obvious manhunter, he pitied her now. If he had been born female with parents like hers, he would probably have tried to grab any man who came along just to get away from home, too.

Glancing at his watch he realised it was almost time to meet Jenny. Leaving his kitbag, he climbed the steps and walked along to Ronconi's cafe. As usual Tina was presiding behind the counter, and he wondered if it was his imagination or if she was being marginally friendlier towards the Americans sitting at the tables.

Perhaps her change of heart had something to do with the men who had been shipped out. Now that they were being lined up to die, it just might make things right in Tina's eyes.

'Lieutenant Schaffer, how nice to see you.'

'Is that another example of British sarcasm?' he asked as he climbed on to a stool in front of the counter.

'No, now that I've found out that you've come over here to do more than sit around on your backsides in Pontypridd, I'll even give you a cup of tea on the house.'

'I don't suppose you'd stretch that to coffee?'

'No chance, unless you pay the extra twopence. Tell me, when are you leaving?'

'Ah, the coffee's a goodbye present?'

'Intelligent too. What more could a grateful civilian want from an American soldier than his absence?'

He was rummaging in his pants pocket for the coins when Jenny walked in with Judy.

'Hi, sweetheart.' He left the stool to kiss her cheek.

'As you can see, the lieutenant's still here. For now,' Tina added, as Jenny sat on the stool next to Kurt's.

'I heard some of the regiment shipped out.' Jenny took a pack of cigarettes from his shirt pocket and helped herself.

'That information's supposed to be classified.'

'With half the girls in the factory crying over their benches because their boyfriends have gone, who do you think you're fooling?'

'Evidently no one.'

'So when is it going to be your turn?'

'Can't wait to get rid of me, can you, Tina?'

'No.'

'You disapprove of my fraternising with the natives?' he asked, trying to keep the conversation light.

'Only the natives I care about, like Jenny.'

Jenny laughed. 'Come on, Tina, I can take care of myself.'

'Can you? This is the sixth time I've seen you two together in here in the last month.'

'So?'

'Take a good look. He's here today, but he'll be gone tomorrow, and in my opinion the last thing you need is a Yank who only wants to brighten up his evenings while he's in town.'

'Perhaps I only want to brighten up my own evenings,' Jenny responded carelessly.

'It's your funeral.' Tina banged a couple of cups down in front of them.

Kurt glanced at the enlisted men who were taking too much of an interest in their conversation for his liking. 'We're both adults, Tina. Don't you think Jenny's old enough to make her own decisions?'

'Frankly, no. Not when she's decided on a "love them and leave them" Romeo like you.'

'You don't know the first thing about me.'

'I know all that I want to.'

Kurt dug in his pocket for enough money to cover the cost of the coffee. 'You're wrong, Tina,' he said as he handed her the coins.

'Time will tell,' she bit back as she rang up the till.

'You're not going. I absolutely refuse to let you.' Diana stood with her back to the door.

'Di, *I* don't want to go, but there's a job that needs doing.'

'And I refuse to believe that you're the only man who can do it.' She eyed Ronnie sceptically. 'It's dangerous, isn't it? You'll be fighting again . . .'

'Diana, they won't allow me to tell you where I'll be going, or what I'll be doing, but I promise you it's safe. And no, I won't be fighting.'

'And that's supposed to make it all right? You're leaving me when I'm about to have your baby, and it's fine because you'll be safe?'

'I wouldn't go if I didn't have to.' He laid his hand on her stomach before kissing the tears from her eyes.

'You'll come back when the baby is born?' she pleaded.

'If I can, but I've no idea how long this will take.'

'Ronnie . . .'

'I know, Di.' He wrapped his arms around her and held her tight. 'I feel the same way too. Come on, let's pack your things and I'll get a taxi to take you and Billy to your mother's.'

'In Myrtle and Huw's house? Ronnie, I can't live there. It would feel strange to move back in with my first husband's sister after being married to you.'

'Someone has to look after you, and I won't leave you here on your own with Billy.'

'Good. In that case, I'm not going anywhere.' She

manoeuvred her swollen body into the armchair next to the range.

'Very funny,' he smiled. 'Come on, you have to go somewhere. Where's it to be? Bethan's?'

'Her house is full to bursting now that Jane and Anne are living there.'

'Graig Avenue?'

'It's as much as Phyllis can do to cope with Uncle Evan the way he is.'

'You're being deliberately difficult.'

'No, I'm not. I suppose I could ask Mam to come here.'

'And Myrtle?'

'Mam said she's been feeling a bit of a gooseberry since Myrtle's father died. Myrtle's coping better all the time, and she could stay here when Uncle Huw's on night shift if she wants to. I know this is your sister's house, Ronnie, but it feels like ours. And I'd rather stay in it until you get back. And so would Billy.'

'I'll call in at your mother's and Tina's before I catch the train and tell both of them to keep an eye on you. I don't want you to spend a single night alone here.'

'I won't.' She fought back her tears as she looked at him. 'Just you be sure that you come back from wherever you're going in one piece, Ronnie Ronconi, or I'll brain you.'

'The lady of the house all alone?' David Ford called out as he parked his Jeep in the drive of Bethan's house and walked over to the vegetable garden she was watering.

'It's good to be alone sometimes.'

'As I'm finding out.'

'You don't have to keep driving yourself so Maurice and Dino can go out with Liza and my aunt.'

'Yes I do. Who knows how much longer they'll be able to see one another? Three-quarters of the men shipped out this afternoon, but then you probably already know that. It seems to be the worst kept secret in town.'

'And the rest?'

'I don't make those kinds of decisions. Tomorrow I'll have another load of raw recruits to knock into shape. It's anyone's guess when they'll be needed.' He followed her to a small bench below the drawing room window.

'You'd rather have gone with your men?'

'I'd rather be doing some real soldiering instead of sitting up to my neck in billeting and supply lists and organising route marches. But then,' he gazed up at the setting sun, 'on a lovely summer evening like this with a beautiful woman at my side it's difficult to imagine that there's such a thing as war.'

Bethan glanced up at the window of the bedroom where her children were sleeping. She had allowed all of them to run around the garden until nine o'clock and by then even the older ones were too exhausted to protest that it was bedtime.

'I have a bottle of Maisie's elderflower wine that I've been saving for a special occasion. I can't think of a better time. Would you like to share it?'

'I'd prefer bourbon.'

'Too strong for me.'

'Not if you water it down. Stay there, you look exhausted. I'll get it.'

She settled back, listening to his quiet tread on the stairs as he climbed to the top floor. She felt more at peace than she had since the autumn. Andrew might still be imprisoned in Germany, but she had other things to be grateful for. The house in Graig Avenue was secured for Phyllis and Brian, her father was crippled but alive, and looking forward to work that exercised more brain than brawn; perhaps he should have done something like it years ago.

Haydn's last words, *'Enjoy what you have while you have it. That's what I do, sis'*, still bothered her, as did his continued absence and Jane's reluctance to talk about him. But at least he was alive and working in comparative safety.

She looked across at the trees, their thick, summer

leaves bathed in the soft golden light of the dying sun. Penycoedcae hadn't changed, and wasn't likely to. The vegetables were growing, a miracle of nature that never failed to thrill her: crops that would feed the whole household through the winter, raised from small, shrivelled roots and seeds. She and the children were well, she was too busy to see much of her mother-in-law, and relations between her and Andrew's father were better than ever. Life was bearable.

'One bourbon and branch water for madam.'

David walked out of the house carrying a tray like an experienced waiter, a cloth folded over his arm, the tray laid out with a bottle, glasses, a jug of water and, miracle of miracles, a bag of peanuts.

'Wherever did you get these?' she asked, fingering them.

'Not one of your shops. And before you count them and divide them up for the children, there's a bag ten times that size in the kitchen, so you can eat them without feeling in the slightest bit guilty.' Setting the tray down on a low wall, he poured a large whiskey for himself and a smaller, weaker one for her.

'To summer and light evenings.' He touched his glass to hers. 'How is your father?'

'I was just thinking about him and all the family. He's coping, thank you.'

'Have you heard from your brother lately?'

'You're thinking of Jane and Captain D'Este?'

'I ran into them the other day in the New Inn. They seem to be spending a lot of time together.'

'He works such long hours she hardly ever sees him except when he brings her home after her weekly visit to the hospital.'

'Some would argue that's all it takes.'

'I don't think there's any more to their relationship than there was with Alma and Chuck Reynolds, or us,' she added evenly.

'The loyal sister-in-law?'

'I've grown close to Jane. She would never do anything to jeopardise her marriage.'

'She must have been very young when she and Haydn walked up the aisle.'

'Eighteen, but that's not to say their marriage won't survive. Things will be different after the war.'

'Perhaps Britain will acquire the same high divorce rate as America?'

'You're a cynic.'

'I wasn't when I was a kid, but you – ' he shook his head admiringly. 'I don't know how you do it. Looking after a house full of kids, taking on four orphaned girls as well as your own two, working full time, nursing your crippled father, surviving the loss of a brother and sister and your husband's imprisonment. Tell me, where do you get your serenity from?'

'Serenity! Take a good look at me the next time I'm shouting at the children.'

'I've never seen you anything but patient.' He sat beside her on the bench. 'You remind me of my mother. She was an oasis of calm. All of us rushing around like madmen, my father screaming for a clean shirt, or his keys and papers, my sisters demanding new clothes, my brothers and I sports wear, and somehow, with no apparent effort she conjured everything we wanted, before returning to the swing on the porch and carrying on with her embroidery. I've seen you do the same thing. Walk in after a twelve-hour day that would flatten most men, and pick up conversations, solving domestic problems, soothing children . . .'

'What a wonderful portrait you've drawn of me, Colonel. I assume you've only ever seen me at the beginning and end of the day when I'm less fraught than usual.'

'No one in the house sees you any other time.'

'True.' She sipped her drink. 'This tastes like I'll regret drinking it in the morning.'

'If you finished the bottle it might.'

She smiled at him, mischief glowing in her eyes. 'Now that might be a hangover worth having.'

'So, you didn't get sent out with the others?'

'Don't you think I would have told you if I was going to be?'

'It wasn't part of our agreement. "Love me and leave me", remember?'

'That's what you wanted, Jenny, not me.'

Following her around the side of the shop he stood back while she unlocked the storeroom door.

'You coming in?'

'Am I invited?'

'For the present.'

'What Tina said tonight about me loving and leaving . . .'

'Is exactly what I want and expect from you.'

'Maybe I did too, when I first met you,' he qualified, as he followed her inside. 'But not any more.'

'Not another word.'

'You don't know what I'm going to say,' he protested indignantly.

'No? You want to marry me?'

'You guessed?'

'I don't have to guess, Kurt. Eddie asked me once. Alexander used to propose at least twice a week. The last thing I need is another husband, particularly a soldier who is going to get himself killed.'

'I love you.'

'You love my body.' She brushed her hand over the front of his trousers.

'No.' He gripped her hands and looked into her eyes. 'I love *you*. Your mind, your soul . . . whatever it is that's inside your head . . .'

'Thoughts of an empty stomach right now.' Turning, she ran up the stairs ahead of him. 'What do you want, a dried egg omelette, or mock goose?'

'Both sound disgusting.'

'An omelette it is.'

He followed her into the kitchen. Leaning against the door frame, he watched as she opened cupboards.

'I'm moving out of my billet,' he announced, giving up on trying to convince her that he loved her.

'Mrs Llewellyn Jones fed up with you?'

'She's been fed up with me since the day I moved in.'

'Where are you moving to?'

'Ebenezer Chapel.'

'With the men?'

'There's a sort of private cubicle.'

'How private?'

'Not enough for you to visit.'

'You could move in here.'

The offer came so quickly, so unexpectedly, he couldn't be sure he'd heard her correctly.

She continued to measure spoonfuls of egg powder into a bowl. 'I have a spare bedroom, use of a bathroom and kitchen.'

'What about the neighbours?'

'What about them? I'm a respectable widow.'

'And how long do you think you'll stay respectable after I move in?'

'Who cares?'

'I care about your reputation.'

'My reputation won't matter when we're all dead.'

'Will you stop talking about death! We have a lot of living to do first.'

'Perhaps, perhaps not. Do you want to move in or not?'

He knew he should check out her offer with Colonel Ford before accepting, but the thought of sleeping in a damp basement that stank of unwashed underwear, socks and male sweat as opposed to between the clean, white sheets, thick blankets and eiderdown on Jenny's bed, made the decision for him. It wasn't just the comfort and warmth, or even her soft, willing body. It was the prospect of living with her, seeing her every day, perhaps even the hope of persuading her that he really did love her. He gazed into her blue eyes, wanting to hold on to her and the way she made him feel.

'Yes.'

'Move in whenever you like, as long as you understand nothing's changed between us. I'll make up a bed in the front room over the shop. You'll close the blackout in there every night for appearances' sake, but if you want, you can share my bed. You know me, or you should by now. I'm game for a good time, but this arrangement means nothing more than that. And when it's your turn to be shipped out, I'll expect you to recommend another officer to take your place.'

'Jenny . . .' he laid his hand over hers. She shrugged it off.

'And as I'm putting myself out by having you here, you can start by assembling the bed.'

He screwed the bed together, fetched his things from the vestry, and shared a scrap meal of dried egg and tinned beans with her, but he couldn't help but notice that as soon as he'd agreed to move in with her, she'd fallen unusually quiet.

He helped her wash up after they'd eaten, then he moved his clothes into the wardrobe in the front bedroom that had once held her husband's things. She didn't offer to help. By the time he'd finished she'd gone to bed.

He joined her, and their lovemaking was as good and adventurous as it had ever been. Afterwards she rolled away from him, and when he heard her breathing steady to a quiet, even pace he assumed she was asleep.

It was later, much later, when he was dozing in a half drowsy, half awake, state that he heard a catch in her throat. He realised then that she was crying. He put his hand on her shoulder and whispered her name into the darkness.

'Leave me alone,' came the angry reply.

For the first time he ignored what she said. Drawing

her close, he held her, letting her tears fall on to his chest. And eventually, exhausted, they both slept.

Chapter Seventeen

JANE WALKED DOWN the stairs and into the kitchen. Picking up the bundle of letters Maisie had collected from behind the door, she flicked through them. There was one envelope addressed to her in Haydn's handwriting. Leaving it on the table, she lifted Anne into her high chair, and reached for the saucepan to make porridge.

'I'll do that, Mrs Powell. You read your letter,' Maisie offered as she bustled in from the pantry.

'I could save it until break time in the factory.'

'Why, when you're early for once? Sit down while I make the breakfast. If there's any news from your husband, Mrs John will be pleased to hear it. She worries so much about everyone.'

Sitting down at the table, Jane took a knife from the drawer and slit open the airmail envelope.

Dear Jane,
The tour will have finished by the time you read this, and I'll be on my way back to Britain. I'm heading for Bristol again, and I intend to go straight there and sort out rooms suitable for all of us so you can bring Anne down to stay for a few days, that's if you want to. As soon as I've done that, I'll try to wangle a couple of days' leave.
We have to talk,
Love, Haydn

'From Haydn?' Bethan asked as she walked in with Eddie and Rachel.

'His tour has finished and he's on his way back to Bristol.'

'Will he get leave?'

'He doesn't know yet.'

'Let's hope he can manage it. My father was only saying yesterday that it seems like years, not months since he was home.'

Jane stared down at the plate of porridge Phyllis had placed in front of her, remembered the kiss Tomas had given her only yesterday, and didn't know what to hope for.

'I don't think you should go into work.'

'I'm not ill, Mother. Just jilted.' Anthea handed her untouched breakfast plate back to the maid.

'I do wish you wouldn't talk like that in front of the staff,' Mrs Llewellyn Jones reprimanded as the maid carried the plates out of the dining room.

'Why? If they don't know Richard's left me by now, they will soon enough. I must be the talk of the town.'

Her mother reached out and stroked her hair in a rare maternal gesture. 'You don't look at all well to me. It's a pity Fiona's left London for Scotland. You could have gone to stay with her until all this has blown over.'

'London's a bomb site, not the hub of social life it was before the war. Besides, I'm needed in the bank.' She looked to her father for support.

'We can manage without you for a day or two, Anthea.'

'Will you both stop fussing,' she snapped. 'I'll be fine.'

'You won't be fine. Not while you're still wearing Richard's ring.'

Anthea removed it and stuffed it into her pocket. 'Satisfied?' she demanded of her mother.

'I'll take care of it for you, Anthea.'

'We may need it as evidence, for the breach of promise action,' her father explained.

'Richard gave it to me, and I intend to keep it.'

'Anthea . . .'

'I'll see you in the bank, Daddy.' Running into the hall she grabbed her cardigan and opened the door. The sooner she solved her immediate problem, the sooner she could get on with living the rest of her life and leave Richard Reide's desertion and betrayal behind her.

Anthea knew that all the staff were talking about her and the American captain who had duped her and her parents. There was an inordinate amount of whispering going on, and whenever she or her father approached, everyone fell silent, offering her sympathetic glances that set her teeth on edge. But swallowing her pride, she took her colleagues up on their suggestion that she visit the White Palace with them after work. Realising that his wife wasn't making the situation any easier for their daughter, Mr Llewellyn Jones was only too delighted to see her go.

As they entered the cinema Anthea excused herself, pleading a headache. Two of the girls offered to take her home, but she refused. Insisting all she needed was fresh air, she waited in the foyer until they went in, then she left.

After glancing up and down the Tumble to make sure no one was watching her, she made a bee-line for the White Hart. At that time in the evening the back room was almost deserted. Two Negro soldiers were sitting at a table in the corner, eyeing four girls who had commandeered the central table.

The girls were wearing too few clothes and too much make-up, and one had instantly recognisable curly brown hair. Weak with relief at finding Vera so easily, Anthea went to the bar and asked for a lemonade. The barman stared at her as though she were a German spy, but he served her without comment. Taking her drink, she walked over to the girls' table.

'Lost your Yank?' Vera asked as she stood awkwardly beside them.

'He left with the others.'

'I heard. Want to join us?' Vera pushed out a chair, and Anthea took it gratefully. 'I know what a dirty trick he played on you. I'm sorry.'

Anthea looked into Vera's eyes. There was compassion not mockery in them. 'I was hoping to find you here.'

'You, looking for me? Don't tell me, your mother's thrown you out and you're desperate for advice on how to play the field?' Vera nudged Anthea with her elbow as she hooted with laughter.

'You want me to throw you out again, Vera?' the landlord warned sternly from behind the bar.

'Sorry, Fred, bad joke. Just got carried away. I'm only having a quiet drink here with my friend.'

'You know Vera?' he asked Anthea sceptically, eyeing her bank 'uniform' of blue serge skirt and high-necked white blouse.

'We were in school together,' she lied.

He moved out of earshot, but continued to watch them from a distance.

'Seven o'clock train's due in, Vera.' The other three girls left the table.

'Got to go, duty's calling.' Vera finished her drink.

'Please, stay. I really do need to talk to you.'

'Look, love, if you think I can get George Rivers to tell me where that rat of a boyfriend of yours has gone, forget it. George never tells me anything . . . well, anything important.'

'It's not that.'

Vera studied her for a moment. Anthea looked ill as well as shell-shocked, and she kept glancing at the door as though she was terrified of seeing someone she knew walking through it. 'See you over there, girls,' Vera called as her companions left. 'I can't stay long,' she warned Anthea. 'Time is money. And I meant what I said about George. I haven't seen him in days.' She sat back, hitching her skirt higher for the benefit of the two Americans she knew were watching her every move. 'So, you've joined the pudding club?'

'How did you know?'

'It's obvious, isn't it? Girl like you coming in here, looking for me.'

'I'm desperate.'

'I bet you are. Well don't worry. Auntie Vera will sort you out, but it's going to cost. Did that bastard leave you any money?'

'No.'

'I don't know why I even bothered to ask. George said his wife has expensive tastes.'

'His wife?' Anthea gripped the table as the room whirled around her.

'He's married with four kids and from what the boys told me, you're not the first girl he's pulled that engagement stunt on. He reckons it's cheaper to fork out for a ring than pay a professional for services rendered. Tight bugger. According to George he finds himself a nice, willing virgin wherever he goes, and Bob's your uncle. For him, but not for you. You're the one left holding the baby. Literally.'

'You knew he was married that night we met in here?'

'It was obvious. I can spot them a mile off.'

'Why didn't you tell me?'

'Would you have listened?' Vera offered her a cigarette. 'Look, love, I'd like to stay and chat, but as I said, time's money.'

'But you will help me?'

'At a price. A tenner for the room, and fifty for the operator.'

'Fifty – '

'Not so loud. If word of this gets around we'll all be for it. Besides, what's the problem? You can afford it?'

Anthea swallowed hard. 'I have some jewellery I can pawn.'

'When do you want it done?'

'Now?'

'Don't be stupid. You haven't got the money, and it won't be like having a tooth pulled. We're talking about an all-night job.'

'I can't stay out all night, my parents wouldn't let me.'

'All right, all day. When?'

'I have next Wednesday off. I'll tell my mother I'm going shopping in Cardiff.'

'Whatever.' Vera glanced at her watch and left her seat. 'Just be at this address with the money.' She whispered in Anthea's ear. 'Got that?'

'Yes.'

'Ten o'clock, no earlier. I hate mornings, and don't forget the cash. No money, no deal.'

Two days later Anthea took her father up on his offer of time off and went into Cardiff. Believing shopping to be a cure for all ills, especially a broken heart, her mother would have liked to accompany her but she had a committee meeting. Anthea already knew. She had studied her mother's diary and deliberately picked a day when she would be busy.

There were plenty of pawnbrokers in Pontypridd, but she didn't want to run the risk of her parents recognising the ring Richard had given her in one of their windows. She fingered it as she walked up to the platform to wait for the train. She was loath to sell it. It was the only proof she had that a man had desired her enough to ask her to marry him, even if he hadn't really meant it. But after what her father had said about needing it as evidence for a breach of promise action, she knew she had to get rid of it. She could never go to court and publicly expose the humiliation of Richard's deception and desertion for the benefit of the *Pontypridd Observer* and her mother's friends and acquaintances. Especially now, when she knew he'd been married all along. And there wasn't any other way to raise the money. If she withdrew it from her bank account her father would see the transaction on her statement. Then again, perhaps there was something fitting about Richard's ring paying for the operation. When they reached Cardiff, she ignored a request for help from a woman burdened with a pram, a toddler and a baby, and walked briskly towards the arcade that housed the best-known pawnbroker in the city. She had to keep thinking about what was going to happen as a surgical operation. A quick, clean procedure no different from the removal of an appendix. She simply had to.

'Sorry, miss, I don't want it.' The wizened old man removed the eyeglass he'd used to examine the stones, and handed the ring back to her.

'I'd settle for less than the full value.'

'I bet you wouldn't, miss. That's worth about one pound five shillings.'

'It's gold set with diamonds and sapphires.'

'What you've got there, miss, is what's known in the trade as paste. Glass, to the uninitiated. Some clear, some coloured a very pretty blue, set in a gold-plated mount. Probably a copy of a valuable original the owners had made rather than risk taking the genuine piece out of the vault for the lady of the house to wear.'

'You don't understand. I need sixty pounds,' she pleaded.

He looked at her thoughtfully. 'I could give you fifty off that watch.'

She wrapped her fingers around it. 'I couldn't possibly. My grandmother left this gold watch to me when she died. It's been valued at a hundred and fifty pounds.'

'All right, seeing as how I've got a soft heart, sixty, and I'll throw in a passable copy for free. You won't get better than that anywhere in the city. What do you say?'

Bethan smiled and murmured 'Good morning' to the queue of Negroes snaking out of Alma's shop as she called in for her mid-morning tea. Opening the kitchen door, she crouched down beside Theo and kissed him, before straightening her back and looking at Alma.

'You're busy?'

'I'm not complaining.'

'Any problems?'

'With the Negroes? None. If anything, they're more polite than the white GIs.' Alma tipped a pile of cold mashed potato into a pie filling she was mixing.

'You've talked to them?'

'The two sergeants and a few of the boys staying in the chapel. Theo's never been so spoilt. They love him.'

'Everyone loves Theo.' Bethan tickled him, then joined Alma at the table.

'I did see Mrs Llewellyn Jones scurrying into the bank with an extremely indignant look on her face the day they arrived, possibly because she can't view any of them as a replacement bridegroom for Anthea, poor girl.'

'My father-in-law was telling me this morning that the Llewellyn Joneses have visited a solicitor. They're threatening to sue Richard Reide for breach of promise. Like you, I feel sorry for Anthea. It must be hard enough to lose a fiance without going through all the embarrassment of a court case.'

'They'll have to catch Richard Reide to sue him. And the Americans are refusing to give out any addresses.'

'How do you know?'

'Captain Reide wasn't the only one to love, leave and disappear. Mrs Lane told me this morning that there's four other girls in the same position as Anthea. Two of them pregnant. She also said that Richard Reide is married with four children, but don't ask me if that's true. I've no idea where half the stories going around the town come from. And I only repeat them to you in the hope that you'll either confirm or deny them.'

'I wish I could help Anthea,' Bethan mused.

'After all the things the Llewellyn Joneses have said and done to you over the years?'

'That's just the trouble, if I go to her now, she'll think I'm trying to get back at her, and it's not like that. She and Andrew were good friends when they were children.'

'And she did her damnedest to get him away from you, even after you were married.'

'That's water under the bridge.'

'You're more forgiving than I would be if she'd set her sights on Charlie.'

'As if Charlie would even notice another woman making eyes at him,' Bethan laughed.

'I also heard this morning that Kurt Schaffer moved in with Jenny a couple of days ago.'

'He's lodging with her. I have the colonel and his staff lodging with me.'

'That's what I told Mrs Lane, but she doesn't see it quite that way. If there is anything going on between Jenny and Kurt, I'm glad for her. She deserves some happiness after losing Eddie and then Alexander. I'm just trying to warn you that you'll both need to thicken your skins, because the gossips have their claws out.'

'I know.'

'They've had a go at you already?'

'Mrs Richards. A full ten minutes on how Jenny's blackening my dead brother's name.'

'That's sick.'

'Jenny visited my father to tell him Kurt had moved in, before he had a chance to hear it from anyone else.'

'Does he mind?'

'No. But he is worried about her. Not because of what people are saying, heaven only knows there's been enough talk about him and Phyllis over the years. I think he actually admires her for not giving a damn about the gossips, but what does bother him is that she hasn't given herself any time to grieve for Alexander. She's desperately trying to carry on as though she's immune to emotion. And it is a pretence. When Eddie was killed she was shattered. If it hadn't been for the job in munitions I think she might have had a breakdown.'

'Let's hope Kurt can help her come to terms with what happened to Eddie and Alexander. He seems a nice man.'

'He is. My father asked her to bring him to meet us.' Bethan smiled wryly. 'All we need to do now is silence the gossips. If only people would accept that Jenny has her own code of morals that don't quite coincide with everyone else's.'

'Especially Mrs Llewellyn Jones's?'

'No one can measure up to her ideals. But as far as I know, Jenny was faithful to both Eddie and Alexander while they were alive, and there's not many women in the town who can say that.'

'Bethan!'

'It's true. Ask the chemist. The demand for laxatives and quack abortion remedies has rocketed since the Americans have been billeted here. Unfortunately so has the incidence of VD, and there's more than one wife praying for a quick leave soon. The parish guardians are already looking at ways to increase the number of places in the orphanages.'

'I can't imagine any woman giving up a child.' Alma looked fondly at Theo.

'I can if they're desperate enough.'

'Talking about babies, I had a letter from Chuck's wife this morning. You can read it if you like. She said how glad she was that Chuck had someone like me to talk to while he was here, and she is praying that my Charlie will come home safely soon.'

'That was nice of her.'

'She also sent a box of sweets and clothes for Theo. I'll bring it up on Sunday so we can share it out. Do you think the Americans have gone into France?'

'I don't know. But with Ronnie gone . . .'

'It could be Italy?'

'I really don't know, and it doesn't do any good to speculate. Whenever and wherever it happens we'll find out. Eventually,' she added drily.

Anthea left the house early on the appointed day. Fortunately, her mother was still too incensed by the presence of Negro troops in Pontypridd and the colonel's refusal to give her Richard Reide's address to pay much attention to her family.

'Have a good time in Cardiff with Katherine,' Mrs Llewellyn Jones muttered absently as she checked the minutes of the last WI meeting, clucking over the fact that they had run to two pages, despite paper shortages and the need to conserve resources.

Feeling like a criminal, Anthea ran from the house and walked quickly down the hill. Taking a detour through the park, she rejoined the main thoroughfare close to the bank. Breathing slowly and deeply in an attempt to steady her nerves, she looked around. Most of the people in town were already queuing in the shops or searching the market for bargains. When she was sure no one was watching her, she carried on up Taff Street and down Broadway.

Paint was peeling on the door, windows and fascia boards at the address Vera had given her. Filthy lace curtains hung lopsided at even filthier windows. As she walked up the steps she heard voices raised in anger. Knocking tentatively, she stepped back.

'Yes?' A woman with her hair in curlers, and stockings rolled down around her ankles, wrenched open the door.

'I'm calling on Vera.'

'Calling!' The woman snorted in amusement. 'Then you'd better come in, Your Ladyship.' She stepped back to allow Anthea to walk through. There was an over-whelming smell of damp washing, sour milk and cheap perfume. 'The girls are downstairs,' the woman barked as Anthea glanced through an open door at a row of unmade beds.

She walked to the end of the passage and saw a flight of rickety wooden stairs leading down to a basement.

'The door's straight in front of you at the bottom. You can't miss it.'

'Thank you.' Anthea gripped the handrail as she entrusted her weight to the top stair. It creaked, pro-testing alarmingly, but held firm. The basement was dark and gloomy, the floor covered with cracked, blue and brown linoleum. She knocked on the door at the foot of the stairs. Wrapped in a flimsy rayon robe, cigarette in hand, Vera opened it.

'I hope I'm not too early,' Anthea apologised.

'You're on time. Got the money?' She opened the

door wider, revealing a crumpled double bed, and a floor strewn with clothes.

'Here.' Anthea delved in her handbag and handed over an envelope.

Vera flicked the top open and counted the notes before pocketing it. 'Come on through to the kitchen. It's behind you. I've just made tea.'

'I've had breakfast, thank you,' Anthea whispered hoarsely, suddenly terrified of what was about to happen.

'Suit yourself.' Vera went to the stove. It was obvious that she wasn't wearing anything beneath the robe, and Anthea was shocked by a glimpse of bare, white thigh, dark pubic hair, and the tip of one breast. Vera wrapped the gown closer to her before retying the belt.

'You look as if you haven't slept.'

'I haven't,' Anthea confessed.

'I was like that before my first.'

'You've done this?'

'Twice. Once after my old man threw me out, and once since. He already had his suspicions about our son. With good cause,' she admitted. 'The old bugger couldn't get it up, much less father anything. Then he heard me being sick one morning and as we hadn't done it in months he knew it couldn't be his, so he threw me out of the house and kept the boy.'

'I'm sorry.'

'What for? I'm better off without him. When I was with him I had no money other than what he gave me, which meant I had to do whatever he told me, including washing his dirty underclothes and cooking his tea. My sister was already living here. She got me a room and I've been as free as a bird ever since. I do what I like, see who I like, and bugger housework. I'm slave to no man. Most nights I eat out, I've got enough money to buy what I want when it's in the shops, and when it isn't, there's always a black-marketeer willing to trade favours with an independent working girl. So you see, Miss High-and-mighty, I'm better off than you.'

'You hear . . . I mean, I've heard such awful stories.'

'Most of them put about by men who like to keep all the fallen women and unmarried mothers in the workhouse so they can spend all day, every day, scrubbing it clean. Think what that must save the parish on labour costs. Here – ' she returned from the stove with two cups of strong tea and a couple of slices of heavily salted bread and dripping. 'I know you're not hungry, but try to get it down you. You'll need your strength.'

'Is it going to be very painful?'

'It's no picnic.' Vera tipped a generous measure of whiskey into both cups.

As soon as Anthea tasted it she began to cry.

'Hey, it's not that bad . . .'

'It's not that. It's this.' Anthea pointed to the cup. 'It's bourbon, the whiskey Richard used to drink.'

'Oh God, not waterworks over that rat. He's gone and you're better off without him. Come on, a couple of hours from now and it will all be over. Where is that bloody woman?'

'Language, Vera,' a sharp voice reprimanded from the door.

Anthea looked up and blanched. The nurse was a friend of her mother's and well known in the town before she had retired five or six years before. She wondered if she'd tell her mother she had seen her here . . . then she realised. She had been expecting a doctor, or a midwife who worked the slums, not this brisk, neat, little old lady who went to the same tea parties and fundraisers as her mother.

Taking off her coat, the nurse handed it to Vera. 'I want it hung away properly, on a hanger,' she ordered, glaring disapprovingly at the whiskey bottle. 'You've brought the money, dear?'

'I've given it to Vera.'

'I'll take it before we start.' She held out her hand and Vera counted out ten five-pound notes before handing them over. 'Right.' She pocketed them briskly. 'Vera, sort out the bed and put the kettle on. Make sure it's full and take it to the boil.'

'Yes, Nurse – '

'No names,' she interrupted swiftly. 'And if anyone asks, neither of you saw me. I wasn't here. Understand?'

'What if this doesn't work?' Anthea asked.

'It will work. It always does. Now go into the other room and strip off.'

'You want me to take off all my clothes?' Anthea asked, horrified at the thought of undressing in front of the two women.

'This baby has to come out the way it got in. If there's another way, I haven't heard of it.'

Anthea walked into Vera's bedroom. The bedclothes had been heaped on a chair and Vera was tucking rubber sheets over the mattress. Anthea started to fiddle with the buttons at the neck of her blouse.

'Come on, I'll help you.'

'No, it's all right, really,' Anthea demurred.

'You haven't got anything I haven't, have you?'

The nurse bustled in with her bag. Opening it, she removed a tin and began placing instruments in it. She stood back, watching as Anthea removed the last of her clothes.

'Lie down, dear.'

Humiliated and feeling totally vulnerable, Anthea did as she asked.

'Take this – ' the nurse handed Vera the tin – 'and fill it with boiling water. Boiling, and to the brim, mind you.'

Vera left, closing the door behind her.

Anthea began to panic.

'Deep breaths, dear. Slowly, one at a time. Breathe in, slowly, deeply, that's it. Now I need to examine you before we start. Just to check how far along you've gone.' To Anthea's mortification the nurse pinched her nipples between her finger and thumb. 'Oh yes, you're well on the way aren't you, dear? Bend your knees and open your legs.'

Anthea closed her eyes as the nurse painfully probed and poked her. 'Three months, I'd say. You agree?'

'I didn't think it was that far.'

'Take my word for it, dear. You are.'

The door opened and closed again, but Anthea kept her eyes shut.

'That's it, fill it to the top, Vera. Now this is going to hurt, but it will soon be over.'

Anthea opened her eyes to see the old woman holding an enormous syringe. 'Bend your knees and open your legs again, wider this time, dear.'

'No!' Anthea turned on her side and buried her face in her hands.

'Well, I've been paid, so I really don't care whether you go through with this or not. I'm asking for the last time. Do you want my help or not?'

Reluctantly Anthea did as she asked.

'Now hold still. Completely still. Vera, lean on her shoulders, keep them down, there's a good girl.'

An agonising pain shot through Anthea's abdomen. She opened her mouth ready to scream.

'The stick,' the nurse said urgently. 'Give her the stick.'

A wooden rod was pushed between her teeth.

'Bite down hard, dear.'

She heard Vera's voice: 'Do as she says, it helps.'

She could feel the syringe, hard, icy cold, nosing inside her. Then the pain came again, racking, sharp, excruciating like nothing else she had ever experienced. She opened her mouth and the stick fell from her lips. A hand clamped over her teeth.

'No noise, for God's sake. No screams. Keep it quiet. If anyone should hear we'll all be looking out from behind bars.'

It went on . . . and on . . . and on . . . until in the end she was pain. A single, total mass of pain from her breasts down, and it simply wouldn't stop.

Chapter Eighteen

THE PAIN WASHED over Anthea in tides. Ebbing and flowing . . . ebbing and flowing . . . buffeting her like a piece of useless flotsam on the crest of a wave, before dragging her down to cold, grey, suffocating depths where an all-consuming agony blotted everything from sight, sound and mind. Everything except the stabbing hurt that was tearing her insides apart. And just when she thought she could bear it no longer, she floated upwards again. There was light, concerned faces, disconnected snatches of conversation that made little sense.

' . . . something's wrong . . .'

' . . . of course something's wrong, you stupid girl. She's further along than she told me . . .'

' . . . can't you do something . . .'

' . . . now it's started it will have to run its course . . .'

' . . . how much longer . . .'

' . . . how much longer . . . how long . . . how long . . .' the words tumbled through Anthea's head. A cool hand pressed down on her face.

'Push! When you feel a pain, push!'

There's pain all the time. She tried to speak but the words remained imprisoned in her mind.

'You've got to do more to help yourself.'

Anthea summoned the last of her strength and tried to do as they asked. A scream filled the air. Shrill, racking, the bestial cry of animal suffering.

' . . . someone must have heard that . . .'

' . . . I have to go . . .'

' . . . you can't leave her like that . . .'

' . . . I've done all I can . . .'

'. . . There has to be something more you can do. There has to be . . .'

'Get me some more hot water, I'll take a look.'

This time it didn't matter that she was naked, her legs splayed wide apart.

'. . . get her walking, it will speed things up . . .'

'. . . don't leave . . . you leave and I'll call an ambulance . . .'

'. . . you wouldn't dare . . .'

Strong hands locked behind Anthea's back and lifted her from the bed.

'Try and walk around, dear. Once you're on your feet the pain will stop. Come along now.'

Wanting the pain to stop Anthea tried to obey. Arms supported her as she walked every step of the way to Cardiff and back. And when she reeled, no longer able to put one foot in front of the other, they laid her back on the bed.

The voice again, husky with fear.

'There's nothing for it but to try another syringe.'

'That was a good movie.' Kurt Schaffer folded Jenny's hand into the crook of his elbow as they stood outside the White Palace.

'You like weepies?'

'Yeah, sure, why not? Although that guy was a total dimwit. Not seeing that his girl had taken to the streets. I mean, what kind of an idiot was he?'

'So you think he shouldn't have taken her back?'

'Nope, he should have taken the girl away from his family, and interfering women, and as far from Waterloo Bridge as possible. Then married her.'

'She was a streetwalker.'

'Hardly her fault if she couldn't support herself any other way.'

'Are you serious, Kurt?'

'Sure. Hell I'd forgive a looker like her anything, even murder. And pinches,' he added as Jenny caught his finger between her nails.

'You can make eyes at any women you want, when you're not with me.'

'Goddammit, she was on a cinema screen. Now, landlady, how about a little supper?'

'You're prepared to face Tina?'

'I called in there earlier with an olive branch. We're the best of friends.'

'Really?' she enquired sceptically.

'Really. Besides, there isn't anywhere else to eat at this time of night.'

'She won't have food, only tea, coffee and cocoa.'

'And national loaf. I sure could go a bundle on a slice of wood and sawdust topped with fish oil margarine.'

Tina insisted they sit at a table in the far corner of the back room. When she served them, Jenny understood why. As well as coffee, Tina produced sandwiches, real sandwiches made with white bread, butter and Spam.

'Where on earth did you get these?' she demanded after Tina ordered the cook to cover for her, poured herself a tea and joined them.

'Ask no questions and I'll tell you no lies.'

Picking up a sandwich Jenny opened it. 'It's not just the meat and butter, it's this bread! It's so soft and white.'

'Why should the Yanks have all the good rations?'

'Why indeed?' Kurt winked at Tina.

'Don't tell me you're doing business with the Americans after all you've said about them?'

'Some of them aren't so bad. Especially the ones who provide me with chocolate bars and cigarettes that I can send to Will.'

'I see.' Jenny looked at Kurt.

'There's a way to every British woman's heart if only you know how to find it.'

Tina watched them as she ate a sandwich. She wouldn't have taken the chocolate if Kurt hadn't insisted that he was serious about Jenny, very serious, and he'd appreciate any advice she could give him on persuading

Jenny to marry him. She began to wonder what exactly it was that Jenny had to make every man who spent any time with her fall head over heels in love.

They were still sitting at the table eating when the door opened and a party of six Negro soldiers walked in.

'No peace for the wicked.' Tina left her chair.

'Stay there, I'll put them out for you.'

'What?' Jenny glared at him as he left his seat.

'You'll do no such thing, Kurt.' Tina stepped in front of him.

'But they're black.'

'So?'

'Don't you understand? Blacks don't go to the same places as white people.'

'They do in Pontypridd.' Turning to the counter, Tina shouted down to the cook, 'I'll come and give you a hand.'

'Are there any other troops in here?' Kurt asked, trying to look past Tina into the front room.

'No, but it wouldn't make any difference if there were.'

'It would, Tina. It would make a great deal of difference to Southerners. If you must throw your cafe open to both races, take my advice: keep one room for blacks, the other for whites.'

'You're being quite ridiculous,' Tina said heatedly, putting on her best smile as she went to the counter. 'You gentlemen all right?'

'Yes, ma'am,' a burly sergeant answered warily, as he reached into his pocket for money to pay for their coffees.

'That's all right, Sergeant, first cup is on me. Least I can do for men who've come to help us win this war.'

Kurt returned to the table and put his head in his hands.

'What's the matter?' Jenny asked indignantly.

'You and Tina. You have absolutely no idea what you're doing,' he muttered. 'No idea at all.'

*

Jenny and Kurt were still arguing about racial segregation when they left the cafe an hour later. Unaccustomed to such attention or freedom in their own country, the coloured soldiers had repaid Tina's hospitality by regaling the late-night stragglers in the cafe with tales of life in the American Southern States from the black point of view. Starting with their great-grandparents' memories of slavery. Jenny had listened, fascinated, but she couldn't help noticing that as soon as Kurt stepped out from the back room, they had all jumped smartly to attention, and although she couldn't swear to it, she thought she saw fear in their eyes.

Kurt had acknowledged their salute and walked out, Jenny had followed, and that's when the argument had started.

'Tina's right. You are being ridiculous. They're no different from us.'

'They're a different colour.'

'So? What would you do if Britain passed a law forbidding all blond men from going into pubs?'

'I don't disagree with your reasoning. All I'm saying is that some white Americans won't see it that way.'

'Then they're fools.'

'Maybe. But they're troublesome fools.'

'And you'll let them create trouble?'

'It's not a question of letting them.'

'You're an officer . . .'

'Who can't be everywhere at once. All I'm saying is that if Tina's not careful she's going to get that place smashed up.'

'Then the American army will have to pay for the smashing.'

'And the locals who get hurt?' He took Jenny's arm as they crossed the road into station yard, where he had parked his Jeep. Noticing a woman weaving her way unsteadily towards them, he veered sharply to the left to avoid her. 'The tarts in this town can't hold their drink,' he muttered, as she swayed and fell in front of the wall that separated the yard from the pavement.

'We can't leave her there.'

'The police will pick her up. Jenny, you've looked for enough trouble for one night.'

The moon broke out from behind a cloud as Jenny bent over the body slumped on the ground. 'Her legs are covered in blood. She's hurt, Kurt. Oh my God, look who it is!'

'Hey, you!' Kurt called to a porter who had come out of the booking office to see what the commotion was about. 'Call an ambulance.'

'And the duty nurse,' Jenny cried. 'Quick as you can.'

'I don't want that woman near my daughter.' Mrs Llewellyn Jones's high-pitched, hysterical tones reverberated down the corridor of the infirmary wing of the Graig Hospital.

'If Bethan hadn't got to Anthea when she did, your daughter would be in the mortuary, not a hospital bed,' Dr John informed her brusquely.

'And if it wasn't for her, Anthea would have married your son years ago.'

'Can we see her?' Anthea's father was as dazed and devastated as his wife, but mercifully calmer.

'There's no point. She's sleeping off the anaesthetic.'

'I want to see her. Just for a moment,' he pleaded.

'I'm her mother. If anyone should see her, I should.'

'You can both see her,' Dr John capitulated, 'but you will have to be very, very quiet. Anthea needs to rest. The slightest disturbance is likely to upset her.'

Mr Llewellyn Jones took his wife's hand as Dr John led them down the corridor away from the bench where Bethan had joined Jenny, Kurt Schaffer and Huw Davies. The constable had set his helmet aside, but his pencil and notebook were out, and he was obviously there in his official capacity.

'Is she going to be all right?' Jenny asked Bethan anxiously.

'She'll live, thanks to you two finding her when you

did,' Bethan answered briefly, unwilling to disclose any more information about a patient.

'Thank God for that,' Kurt murmured, watching the Llewellyn Joneses disappearing around the corner of the corridor. 'You look exhausted, Nurse John. I could give you a lift home.'

'That's kind of you, Lieutenant Schaffer, but I have my car.'

'In that case, if you don't need us any more, Constable Davies, I'll take Mrs Powell home.'

'Take care, both of you.' Bethan kissed Jenny's cheek and shook Kurt's hand before he led her away.

'When can we talk to Anthea?' Huw asked, putting away his notebook.

'That's for Dr John to say, but probably not for a couple of days.'

'How many cases does this make this year?'

'More than I care to think about. You really have no idea who's doing this?'

'None. We've been looking for leads since the first woman died nearly five years ago, but between you and me, we're no further forward now, than when we started. Nobody will talk to us. Not even the women who've ended up in here. They're too terrified of someone or something to tell us anything.'

'Can you blame them when they know you're going to arrest them?'

'I don't make the laws, Bethan, only enforce them.'

'I'm sorry, Uncle Huw. It's just so unfair. No woman would consider an abortion unless she was desperate. And then, after suffering all the pain and agony that goes with it, to face prosecution and jail.'

'That lieutenant is right, love. You do look exhausted.'

'I am. I'll go home as soon as I've sorted the paperwork with Dr John. Are you going to prosecute Anthea?'

'Not my decision, love.' Picking up his helmet he pushed it down firmly on to his bald head. 'You're sure she is going to live?'

'Unless there's unforeseen complications. But what I

didn't tell Kurt and Jenny was that Dr John had to perform a hysterectomy.'

'Then she'll never have children?'

'He had no choice. The abortionist ruptured her uterus. If we hadn't removed it, we would have lost her.'

'Poor kid. I wouldn't like to be the one to tell her that when she does come round. Look after yourself, Bethan.'

'I will.' Pulling off her cap and operating gown she went into the deserted office. Sinking down on to a chair she closed her eyes and tried to forget Anthea's pale and pain-racked face.

'Someone must have attacked her!' Mrs Llewellyn Jones's hysteria escalated into a frenzy of denial as she refused to believe what Dr John was telling her.

'I'm sorry, Dorothy,' he countered, 'but it's better you know the facts now, before Anthea comes round, so you can adjust to them. Then you can help her come to terms with what's happened.'

'But how can you be sure?' Anthea's father seemed to have aged twenty years in just a few hours.

'All the signs were there. They're unmistakable. I don't want to go into graphic details, but I can tell you that her uterus was ruptured when someone tried to perform an illegal abortion on her. There's no doubt about it. I've no idea how far advanced her pregnancy was, but from the damage inflicted I'd say three to four months. I had no choice but to perform a complete hysterectomy. She'll live, but she's very weak, and she'll be that way for some time. She's lost a great deal of blood, but with care and rest she should make a full recovery.'

'Are you trying to say that my daughter was pregnant?'

'Dr John's already told us that, Dorothy.'

Mrs Llewellyn Jones's face contorted in rage.

'She was engaged, Dorothy,' Dr John reminded her quietly.

'Engaged is not the same as married.'

'It's wartime. None of us know if we even have a

future. Think how that must feel to a girl of Anthea's age.'

'War is no excuse for stooping to the level of an animal.'

'She's suffered a lot of pain, don't be too harsh on her,' Dr John pleaded.

'She broke one of the Lord's commandments.'

'Isn't it enough that the poor girl nearly died? That she'll never have children? Please, Dorothy, Alfred, we've known one another all our lives. This isn't Anthea's fault. If you want to blame anyone, blame whoever performed that botched abortion. I met Captain Reide, and I was as taken in by him as you were. And if he fooled us, at our age, think how he made Anthea feel.'

'I *am* thinking. She never got over losing Andrew.'

'Andrew never asked her to marry him, Dorothy.'

'If you'd stopped him from marrying that worthless slut, Bethan Powell, Anthea would never have looked at Richard Reide and none of this would have happened,' Mrs Llewellyn Jones rounded on him. 'She would have been happily married to your son. I would have grandchildren. Well, I hope Anthea does die. I never want to hear her name again. Tonight I lost not only my daughter but all the future generations of my family. As far as I'm concerned she is dead.'

'She's not dead, Dorothy,' Dr John contradicted her vehemently. 'She's ill and she needs you.'

Mrs Llewellyn Jones looked from Dr John to her husband. 'I want to go home.'

Dr John knew it was useless to remonstrate. He stood back and watched them walk away. Mrs Llewellyn Jones paused at the office door where Bethan was sitting.

'You'll be sorry for this. You may have fooled everyone else into thinking that you're better than you are, but not me. And I'll see that you get what you deserve.'

'Dorothy, please, Anthea's condition is hardly Bethan's fault.' Dr John ran down the corridor after her, but she swept out of the door without a backward glance.

Bethan emerged from the sister's office to face her father-in-law.

'I hope you didn't hear all of that,' he said.

'Unfortunately I did.'

'I'm sorry she turned on you. The only excuse I can offer is that she's overwhelmed by what's happened.'

'It doesn't matter. Mrs Llewellyn Jones never has liked me, but what does matter is Anthea. What's going to happen to her?'

'She'll stay here until she's fit enough to be moved.'

'And then?'

'I'll have a word with Isabel but frankly I can't see her taking her in, and after what Dorothy said to you, don't you dare try it either.'

'Even if I wanted to I'd be hard pressed. The colonel has asked if I can find room for a sixth officer.'

'Whatever happens to Anthea, it's not your problem.'

'Someone has to talk to her when she comes round.'

'As I brought her into the world I rather think that's my responsibility. Go home and sleep while you can.'

Bethan nodded. She understood only too well. Perhaps it wasn't only the Llewellyn Joneses who blamed her for marrying Andrew and taking him away from his own kind.

By the time she closed her front door behind her, Bethan was so tired she could barely put one foot in front of the other. After checking that the blackout was in place she switched on the light and looked at the clock. Four, and Eddie would no doubt be up at six as usual. She climbed the stairs, threw off her clothes and crawled into bed. But tired as she was, sleep eluded her. She was plagued by images that had haunted her ever since Andrew had first taken her to meet his family.

Anthea Llewellyn Jones, radiant in white silk, lace and satin, smiling as she walked down the aisle of St Catherine's church beside Andrew. A very different affair to their hole in the corner wedding in a London register office, with her six months pregnant and Andrew's colleague and his wife as their only witnesses.

His parents had barely spoken to her before Rachel's birth: a few words at the funeral of their first child, that was all. Perhaps Mrs Llewellyn Jones was right. Perhaps she shouldn't have married Andrew John. If only she could see him, talk to him, discover if there really was anything other than the children left between them.

'Mrs John . . . Mrs John . . .'

Bethan opened her eyes sleepily, waking with a start when she saw the alarm on the bedside table. Ten o'clock!

'Maisie, why didn't you wake me earlier?'

'Dr John telephoned at half-past five this morning. He said you'd been up half the night, and not to wake you because he's arranged for you to do the afternoon shift.'

Bethan groaned inwardly. She hated working two till ten because it meant that she couldn't put the children to bed.

'I've brought you some tea, and you're not to worry about the children. I saw Mrs Phyllis when I took Rachel to school and she took Eddie and Anne. They wanted to go with her.'

'They know it's her baking day, and they'll get first pick of any treats she makes. I'll call in Graig Avenue on my way into town. Did Dr John say anything else?'

'Only that your patient is holding her own.'

Bethan sat up and drank the tea. Maisie had brought the post as well. There was a letter from Andrew. She opened it, but there were only the usual stories about what the men were doing to fill up their time, and fervent hopes and wishes that he'd be home soon – and his love. She wondered if he really did still love her, or if it was simply a meaningless phrase to be tacked on to the end of every letter.

She couldn't get Anthea Llewellyn Jones out of her mind. She knew only too well how desperate she must have been to place herself in the hands of a backstreet abortionist. When Andrew had left her pregnant in Pontypridd and gone to London, as she had thought at the time, for ever, she would have done the same thing if she had known where to go.

As it was, unable to bear the thought of her mother's reproaches and the shame she would bring on her family, she had tried to get rid of the baby herself. Fortunately for her, the doctor who had cared for her after her failed attempt had known both Andrew and herself, and kept the information from the authorities.

She wondered if Anthea knew that trying to abort a child was a criminal offence. Would the police prosecute, or would it be hushed up because Anthea was the daughter of two pillars of the community? Then she remembered the other women who had died and realised that neither Dr John nor the police would allow a cover-up. Not while there was a risk of more women dying or suffering as Anthea had done.

As she had plenty of time, she drew double the patriotic allocation of four inches of hot water, wallowing in the luxury of a deep bath, before dressing and going downstairs, where Maisie had made her porridge and toast.

'I timed it from the bath water running out, Mrs John. If there's nothing else I'll go shopping.'

'If you wait ten minutes I'll give you a lift down the hill.'

'Mr James is taking his horse and trap into town. He offered to take me, so I said yes. That is all right?'

'Of course, Maisie.' She heard steps on the gravel outside and looked through the window. Albert James, dressed in his Sunday suit, his red face ruddier than ever, was walking to the front door. A widower with three grown children, it was his youngest son Malcolm that she had assumed had a crush on Maisie. Suddenly she realised it wasn't Malcolm at all, but his father.

Typical farmer to pick out a good housekeeper and hard-working wife, but then, she reflected, it wouldn't be such a bad match for Maisie either. She and her daughter would get security, something that Bethan might not be able to offer them after the war.

'And you are certain of this?'

'As I said, I found her, sir. And then I went to the hospital.'

David Ford left his desk and walked to the window. He looked down at the crowds milling below him. A scandal involving Mrs Llewellyn Jones's daughter was all he needed just as a regiment of black soldiers had come in to be trained. He could almost hear the gossips as he looked down on them:

'If a white officer can seduce a well-brought-up girl like Anthea Llewellyn Jones and almost kill her, what will a black man do?'

'Do you think Richard Reide knew she was pregnant, Schaffer?'

'I don't know, sir.'

'Goddammit, Lieutenant, relations between us and the natives in this backwater are tricky enough without you playing dumb.'

Kurt hesitated for a moment before pulling an envelope from his pocket. 'I found some of the men looking at these, sir. I thought I should confiscate them.'

David opened the envelope. Several glossy black and white photographs spilled out on to the forms on his desk. They were of a girl, naked, amateurishly posed, but indecent and lewd enough to fetch a few dollars from sexually naive, frustrated soldiers deprived of female companionship.

'Is this who I think it is?'

'It's Anthea Llewellyn Jones all right, sir. I should know, I lived in her house for long enough.'

'And she's still in the hospital?'

'She was when I left there with my fiancee last night, sir.'

'Your what?'

'My fiancee, sir. That's my application to get married.'
He pointed to a form beneath the photographs.

'Damn and blast it, not you too! What the hell are
we running here, an army or a marriage broker's?' David
Ford turned to him in exasperation.

Feeling that the colonel didn't really expect him to
answer his question, Kurt turned back to the subject of
Anthea. 'A constable called on us this morning to see if
we'd remembered anything more. He told us that
although Miss Llewellyn Jones will almost certainly
recover, she'll never have any children.'

David Ford thought rapidly. He could blame
American army policy, the official discouragement of
marriages between USAAF military personnel and UK
civilians, or he could blame himself for burying his head
in the sand and ignoring the inevitable. But however he
considered the situation, Richard Reide had no business
getting engaged to anyone, not when he was married
with four children.

Bethan John had been right. She had tried to warn
him that something like this was going to happen the
night he had moved into her house. And all he had done
was talk sanctimoniously about the whores in station
yard.

He glanced at the photographs of Anthea Llewellyn
Jones as he pushed them back into the envelope. Whatever else, this girl hadn't been a whore before they had
come into town and Richard Reide had made her one.

'Tell the clerk to get me the Llewellyn Jones home
on the telephone.'

'Yes, sir.'

'And Schaffer? Warn your fiancee that she faces an
interview with a social welfare officer.'

'Do you have to do that, sir?'

'It's standard procedure.'

'In that case I withdraw my application.'

'Problems, soldier?'

'I haven't quite got her to agree to marry me yet, sir.
But I will.'

*

Isabel John felt as though she was presiding over a house of death. A sense of bereavement hung, heavy and foreboding over every room. Dorothy Llewellyn Jones insisted on lying on her bed, fully dressed in black. After taking the sedative prescribed for her, she had refused to allow anyone except her sister and oldest friend into the house.

It was a disloyal thought, but Isabel suspected that Dorothy was secretly wallowing in her daughter's disgrace. Her moans about never being able to hold up her head in the town again, and never knowing the thrill of holding a grandchild, rang selfish and hollow when she recalled her husband's description of the damage done to Anthea by the butcher who had tried to abort her child.

The telephone clamoured into the silence. Ordering the cook and maid to remain in the kitchen, Isabel closed all the doors in the hall before answering it. Leaving the receiver on the hall table she walked up the stairs and knocked on Dorothy's door.

'I can't talk to anyone.'

'It's Colonel Ford. He wants to speak to you about Anthea.'

'Tell him I don't know anyone of that name,' came the curt reply.

Chapter Nineteen

BETHAN PICKED UP her nurse's bag and glanced around the surgery to check if she'd forgotten anything.

'Going home?' her father-in-law asked.

'In time to put Rachel and Eddie to bed, if I'm lucky.'

'Isabel asked me to invite you and the children to tea on Sunday. You are free?'

'I'm free.' She was only confirming information he already knew. The timetable for staff shifts was pinned to the board above his desk. 'And we'd love to,' she replied, unable to think of a good excuse for not going.

'There'll only be us.'

'I'll look forward to it.' She only just stopped herself from heaving an audible sigh of relief. She knew that her mother-in-law still spent part of every day with Dorothy Llewellyn Jones, who persisted in playing the role of bereaved invalid a month after Anthea had been hospitalised.

'And, just in case you didn't know, Anthea's leaving hospital tomorrow morning.'

'She's made a full recovery?'

'As full as she's ever likely to. She's decided to join up.'

'The services?'

'WAACs.'

'Mrs Llewellyn Jones still refuses to see her?'

'Or even acknowledge her existence.'

'Poor Anthea.' Bethan suffered a twinge of conscience. She hadn't visited Anthea since the night she'd been admitted to the Graig Infirmary, justifying her absence with the excuse that her sympathy might be misunderstood.

'Give the children a hug from me.'

'I will.'

She went to her car and drove directly to the hospital. The sister was on break, but the staff nurse called out a friendly greeting as she made her way to the cubicle Anthea had been wheeled into on the night of her arrival. Fortunately she was still there, lying on the bed, listlessly flicking through the pages of a wartime thinned copy of *Good Housekeeping*. She glanced up at Bethan as she walked in.

'If you're expecting me to thank you for saving my life, don't hold your breath.'

'I've come to wish you luck. Dr John told me you're joining up.'

'Wish me luck, or gloat?' Anthea's mouth twisted into a thin, hard line and Bethan saw that her eyes were full of bitterness.

'Wish you luck,' she responded evenly, sitting on the chair at the side of the bed.

'Luck? What have I got to look forward to? No man will touch me now.'

'You're an attractive girl. You'll find one. The right one this time.'

'I'll never have children, you do know that?'

'You can adopt.'

'That's an easy thing for a woman with two children and a husband who adores her to say.'

'Anthea, I didn't come here to upset you. I really would like to help. You and Andrew were friends for a long time. He – '

'Loves you,' Anthea broke in acidly. 'Dear God, when I think of all the times he promised to marry me when we were children, I could scream. I always knew that we'd be separated when he went away to college, but I waited. And how I waited – for six long years, only seeing him at holidays and weekends and then when he came back, all he could think and talk about was you. I tried everything. I called into his house every time I saw his car turning in through the gates, persuaded my mother to invite him to dinner practically every night of the week, lowered myself to plead to be included in every invitation that was sent his way. I even wrote to his sister, inviting myself to her house in London when he went back there, but it was hopeless. From the minute he saw you there was no other woman for him.'

'I always thought he married me because of the baby,' Bethan murmured without thinking what she was saying, or who she was saying it to.

'He would have walked from here to Timbuctoo for you, even if there hadn't been a baby.'

'I didn't know.'

'You didn't recognise love when it was staring you in the face?'

'You must think I'm a fool.'

'A lucky one.'

'Anthea, I'm sorry.'

'I don't want your pity.' Anthea dropped the magazine and swung her legs over the side of the bed. 'Then again, perhaps I only ever loved the boy, not the man. Andrew seemed like a stranger when he came back from London after he'd qualified. An eligible stranger that both our families expected me to marry.'

'Family pressure can make things difficult,' Bethan agreed warily, conscious of Anthea's brittle mood.

'You know how it is.' She smiled too brightly, ashamed of having said more than she'd intended. 'I couldn't wait to fall in love, and he was the most convenient and obvious candidate at the time. Like Richard.' The fragile façade finally broke and tears started into her eyes.

Bethan sat on the bed and hugged her. 'I want you to know that you'll always have friends here. And not just Andrew.'

'Not to mention a mother who'll make my life hell if I stay in Pontypridd.' Reaching for a handkerchief, she broke free. 'I'm not going to be charged with anything. Did you know that?'

'No.'

'It seems wrong. I murdered my baby.'

'You did what you thought you had to at the time. You can't blame yourself for taking a desperate way out of an impossible situation.'

'You have no idea what I went through. What it's like . . .'

'I tried to do exactly the same before Andrew married me. Not with a backstreet abortionist, although I probably would have, if I'd known where to go. I had just enough nursing knowledge to attempt it myself, and if I'd succeeded no doubt I'd have ended up in here, like you. As it was, Edmund was born with horrendous problems and died when he was only a few months old. And I have to go through the rest of my life not knowing whether his defects were the result of what I did, or not.'

'You tried to get rid of your baby?'

'My first,' Bethan confessed, noticing that Anthea's eyes were as moist as her own.

'But you have two children now. And Andrew . . .'

'Who I haven't seen for three and a half years, and am not likely to see for God knows how many more.'

'But he's yours.'

'If there's anything I can do to help you, Anthea, I will,' Bethan answered, deliberately steering the conversation away from her husband. 'You could stay with me. I can't promise you peace and quiet. The house is crowded with evacuees and GIs.'

'Thank you, but no. I know what my mother would do to you if you took me in.'

'I could give you money. A loan until you get on your feet.'

'I have plenty. But thank you for the offer.' Anthea opened the locker at the side of the bed and pulled out her handbag. 'I'm a banker's daughter, and I'm over age. My mother might like to see me destitute, but she can't stop me from using my savings or the money my grandmother left me. Dr John has pulled some strings and arranged for me to join the WAACs. And once I'm there, no one will know who I am, what I've done, or where I come from. In my new condition, I can sleep with an entire American regiment without having to worry about getting into trouble. So you see, from now on, my life is going to be one big party.'

Bethan kissed her cheek, before rising to her feet.

'Perhaps if I'd made an effort we might have been friends,' Anthea said, leaning back on her pillows.

'It's as much my fault as yours that we weren't. I used to tell Andrew that the bridge between the Graig and the Common hadn't been built and never would. Take care of yourself. If you like, we could write to one another.'

'I would like that. Christmas cards and things.' Opening her handbag she took out the small leather-covered boxes Richard had given her. 'Please take these.'

Bethan opened them. 'I couldn't possibly.'

'They look good but they're not worth anything. Just a gold-plated shank set with glass stones, and gold plated hooks set with imitation sapphires. Not the real thing at all. Just like the man who gave them to me. When Rachel is old enough, give them to her and explain their history. Warn her to be a lot more careful than I was with the company she keeps. That way they might do some good after all.'

'And here's to the success of our boys and the downfall of all dictators.' George Rivers held up his glass.

'May they all topple and resign as easily as Mussolini.' Kurt Schaffer tightened his hold around Jenny's waist.

'And here's to everyone who is fighting in Italy coming home safely.' Diana gave David Ford a searing glance.

The garden party had been the idea of the Americans. But it had grown out of all proportion to the simple cook-out Dino had envisaged to celebrate the Allied successes in the invasion of Italy. David Ford had invited the town councillors and the officers of his own and every regiment within travelling distance of Pontypridd. The rest he had left to Bethan. She had asked her family, her in-laws and most of the people she worked with.

Secure in the knowledge that the Llewellyn Joneses were still refusing all social invitations, she had even dared to send them a card in the colonel's name. As a result of their combined efforts they had ended up with a guest list of over a hundred. Concerned about the safety of her vegetables, she had moved the venue from her garden into the field that Andrew rented out to Albert James.

The food had proved a great success; the hastily improvised band Kurt had cobbled together from all the Negroes in the regiment who had any pretensions to musical talent, even more of a triumph. The afternoon had flown past, and as the bright July day had dimmed into romantic twilight and several of the older guests had left and the younger ones been put to bed, the Americans had produced bourbon and beer. But it was the dancing not the drink that had proved the biggest attraction, and the small wooden platform Kurt Schaffer had erected close to the band was packed with couples by the time the moon rose, full and bright in the clear, night sky.

After the toasts had been drunk, the band struck up a slow waltz. David Ford left Bethan's side and sought out Diana, who was sitting on one of the chairs Dino had carried out of the house.

'Congratulations on your new baby, Mrs Ronconi.' He looked down at the bundle in her arms, but all he could see was a clump of dark hair shadowing the edge of a white shawl.

'I got your letter, and your cheque, Colonel Ford. I've put it into an account for her future.'

'I'm sure your husband will be very proud.'

'When he gets home.'

He picked up on the barb in her voice. 'He's doing essential work.'

'In a war zone where he's running the risk of getting killed. Hadn't he done enough, Colonel Ford, that you had to ask him to go back there?'

'I'm sorry, Mrs Ronconi. But he has unique abilities.

316

Without the help of people with his experience and command of the language we'd be hard pressed to know who to fire our guns at over there.'

'If you'd like to dance with Colonel Ford, Diana, I'll take my granddaughter,' Megan offered.

'I'd be honoured. Mrs Ronconi?' David hadn't been about to ask Diana to dance, but taking the expedient way out of what was threatening to turn into a sticky situation, he offered her his arm and led her on to the boards.

'It's amazing that the band can play like this without music,' Bethan said as she walked across to join Megan and Dino.

'Natural flair,' Dino observed, packing utensils and dishes into enamel bowls ready to carry back into Bethan's kitchen.

'They're nice boys.'

'Very.'

'You don't think they should be kept away from white people, Dino?' Alma asked, playing devil's advocate.

'Not me.'

'But most of the other officers in your regiment do.'

'One, I'm a sergeant not an officer, and two, I'm from the North of the States not the South.'

'There's a difference?'

'Give me an hour or two and I'll explain it to you,' he joked as the band finished their number. 'But right now, I'd like to ask Megan here to dance.'

'Is he serious about your mother?' Alma asked Diana after David Ford had escorted her back to her seat and led Bethan on to the staging.

'He's asked her to marry him.'

'Di, that's marvellous.'

'I think it is. I've almost persuaded her to say yes.'

'Who would have thought that something as good as that could come out of this war?'

'Or trouble like that.' Diana nodded towards the gloom that surrounded the makeshift staging.

Alma could make out Jenny's blonde head resting

317

on Kurt Schaffer's shoulder, and behind her, the dark, entwined figures of Tomas D'Este and Jane, and the colonel and Bethan.

'Haydn!' Bethan stared in disbelief at her brother as he walked into the kitchen where Maurice and Liza were helping her to wash dishes. 'Why didn't you tell us you had leave?'

'Thought I'd surprise you. Don't tell me that wife of mine is working?'

'No, she's in the field.'

'Digging it?'

'We've had a garden party to celebrate the invasion of Italy.'

'I thought I could hear music.'

'Come on, I'll take you to her.'

'Is Anne out there?'

'Don't be silly, she went to bed hours ago.'

'Can I see her?'

'If you're quiet. Between my own, Alma's, yours, Diana's children and the evacuees there's so many sleeping upstairs it feels as though I'm running an orphanage.'

'How's Dad?' he whispered as they walked up the stairs.

'He's here too, in the garden with Phyllis and Megan. You'll see him in a minute. Physically he's fine and he seems to be a lot happier since he started back to work.'

'You're not just saying that, Beth?'

She shook her head. 'I won't pretend it's been easy on any of us, but Phyllis took the brunt of his depression. That's why Jane and Anne stayed here with me. We thought it would give Dad and Phyllis time to adjust. He's still not his old self, but he's getting there.' Turning the handle, she opened the bedroom door. Putting her finger to her lips she led him into a room lit by a ceramic toadstool nightlight and crammed with cots and makeshift beds. She tiptoed softly to a cot in the far corner. Following her, Haydn looked down on a pink, sleep-flushed face, topped by a mop of blonde curls.

'She's grown so much, I wouldn't have recognised her,' he said as they walked down the stairs.

'But she recognises her daddy's photograph,' Bethan consoled him.

'Photographs can't make up for all the time I've missed.'

'It's the same for everyone.'

'Not everyone. Ronnie . . .'

'Is in Italy.'

'What!'

'They asked, he went.'

'I never had him down as a hero.'

'A reluctant one, according to the letters he sends Diana.'

The strains of 'Don't sit under the apple tree with anyone else but me' wafted towards them on the cool night air as they opened the small gate at the bottom of the garden.

'How is Jane, Beth?' he asked seriously as she paused to listen to the music.

'She seems fine. Busy, between work and taking care of Anne. We don't have much time to talk. You know how it is.'

'No, but I can imagine.'

'It's not easy on any of us.'

'I don't need you to tell me we have problems, sis. Her letters have got shorter and shorter since my last leave.'

'And yours are long?'

'She's showed them to you?'

'No. But I think I know what you're going through. Sometimes when I read what Andrew's written I wonder if we'll have enough in common to pass the time of day when the war is over.'

'You've nothing to worry about with cashmere coat, Beth. He knows he's on to a good thing with you. He'll jump through hoops to keep you happy when it's over.'

'And if I don't want him to jump through hoops?'

'Typical woman. Never satisfied, no matter what a man does for her.'

He blinked hard as his eyes adjusted to the darkness. Two couples were dancing in the moonlight. He recognised Jenny's blonde hair, shining silver in the half-light. There was no mistaking the slender frame, height or size of the other woman. As he watched, she stretched upwards to receive the kiss of her partner. Heart thundering, Haydn took a step forward. Wrenching the couple apart, he didn't even look at the woman. Swinging back his fist he knocked the man clear from the staging.

'After Eddie was killed, I thought we'd put this sort of thing behind us.' Evan poured out two brandies from the bottle Bethan had unearthed, and handed Haydn one.

'And I never thought I'd come home to find my wife kissing another man.'

'Seems to me you two have some sorting out to do.' Evan sat on the sofa in Andrew's study and looked up at his son.

'What's the point?' Haydn paced restlessly to the window. The blackout had been pulled but he remained there, his back turned to his father, fingering the cloth.

'She's your wife.'

'You wouldn't think it, the way she carried on over that Yank doctor after I hit him.'

'Probably because she didn't know who you were. A fist coming out of the darkness can be pretty anonymous when you're not expecting it.'

'I saw the look on her face when the Yanks carried him into the kitchen.'

'She was concerned. You'd just put him flat on his back.'

'What about me?' He held up his bruised and swollen knuckles.

'Haydn, it's not just you and Jane here,' Evan said

forcefully. 'You have a daughter to consider. Jane's your wife. All I'm saying is talk to her.'

'The way you talk to Mam?'

'I'm not making excuses for the mess I made of my marriage to your mother, but we never loved one another. Not the way you love Jane. And we didn't need a war to wreck our marriage. We did it all by ourselves. You and Jane might have been married for three years, but how long have you been together in all that time? Ten months? Son – '

'Can I stay with you tonight?' Haydn broke in abruptly.

'You don't need to ask. It's your home, Haydn.'

The door opened and Bethan walked in. 'There's no bones broken, but he's going to have a sore head and a wonderful shiner in the morning.'

'Right, that's all I've been waiting to hear. I'll see you back at the house, Dad.' Haydn finished his drink and set his glass on the desk.

'Aren't you going to see Jane?' Bethan asked.

'I've no reason to.'

'Haydn, don't be stubborn, not now. She's in a terrible state.'

'My heart bleeds for her.'

'And my heart bleeds for both of you,' Bethan retorted angrily. 'I've put her in my bedroom. I'll sleep with the children tonight. Please, go and see her, take all the time you want, but sort out your problems once and for all. Right now, she's feeling pretty wretched.'

'And how do you think I feel!' he shouted. 'All that nonsense about staying with you, so Dad and Phyllis could have time alone together, when all she wanted to be was here, in the same house as that . . .'

'If you think that's why she stayed here, Haydn, you're mistaken.'

'And I suppose I didn't see what I did?'

'Go upstairs and talk to her. If you are man enough,' Bethan added, taking a calculated risk that the taunt might override his anger and obstinacy.

'I'll talk to her. But only to discuss a divorce. I'll see you down the house, Dad.'

Evan looked helplessly at Bethan as Haydn left the room.

Haydn walked across the hall and up the stairs. He could hear muffled whisperings and movements behind closed doors as he passed, but he met no one. Reaching Bethan's bedroom door, he knocked quietly, opening it when he heard a strained 'Come in.'

Jane was sitting on the bed, her face turned away from him. He looked past her at the furnishings. The severity of a pale wood, art deco bedroom suite was offset by crisp, cream lace curtains and bedspread and deep blue satin drapes. He found himself wondering if Bethan or Andrew had furnished the room. The plain wallpaper and furniture looked like Andrew's taste, but he could imagine his sister picking out the lace and satin.

'I'm sorry.' Jane made a valiant effort to keep her voice steady. 'I didn't mean for it to happen.'

'You just thought you'd get your own back on me?'

'It wasn't like that.'

'Then what was it like, Jane? Tell me. I'm listening.' He leaned against the door and crossed his arms.

'How can you expect me to explain when you're in that mood?'

'The music, the moonlight . . . the romance of the moment. Just like in the films?'

'Something like that,' she confessed miserably.

'And how often has it happened before?'

'Once, only once. I swear it, Haydn. I told him then he could never kiss me again . . .'

'But it didn't stop him, did it?'

'No more than the thought of Anne and me stopped you with that chorus girl?'

Suddenly exhausted, not only by the events of the day but the futility of their conversation he picked up a chair and moved it as far from the bed as the confines of the room would allow, before sitting down.

'It doesn't matter what I've done or haven't done, does it, Jane? Not any more.'

'What do you mean?' Her red-rimmed eyes widened in fear.

'You're in love with D'Este.' It was a statement, not a question.

'Nothing's happened between us, Haydn. Only two kisses . . .'

'But in your mind you've already made love to him a hundred times over. Kissed him the way he kissed you. Imagined yourself in his arms . . .' He had to stop himself from crossing the room and touching her in an effort to make her forget that there was a man called Tomas D'Este.

'I don't even know him, Haydn.'

'But you will.' He rose to his feet. 'Let's cut our losses, Jane, and get a divorce. I'll admit adultery. That should speed things up and give you all the grounds you'll need.'

'And Anne?' She lifted her tear-stained face to his.

'Touring with a singer is no life for a kid. You'd better keep her,' he said harshly, gripping the door handle. 'This D'Este,' he looked back at her, 'he will marry you?'

'I don't know.'

'I've got two days' leave. I'll be staying with my father until tomorrow. Unless there's something you can think of that's relevant to the divorce, I'd rather not see you.' Closing the door he looked up the narrow staircase that led to the top floor. Eighteen steps later he was on the landing.

'Captain Powell?' David Ford, no longer the immaculately turned out colonel, but half dressed in braces and shirt-sleeves, opened a door and stepped out to meet him.

'I'm here to see D'Este.'

'I'm not sure that Captain D'Este wants to see you.'

'He will, once he's heard what I've got to say.'

'I take it you do just want to talk?'

'In private.'

'I owe the man an explanation, David.' Tomas D'Este stood in the doorway, a bandage holding a cold compress on his head, the bruise that had spread halfway across his face already deep purple.

'If you want to throw any more punches, might I recommend you take it outside again, gentlemen, rather than risk disturbing the household and breaking the furniture,' David suggested drily.

Tomas opened the door wider and stepped back. Haydn followed him into a small room furnished with a canvas army cot and a trunk. An ashtray and a framed photograph of a middle-aged couple surrounded by children of various ages stood on a small folding table set in front of the window. Apart from the trunk, a canvas chair and regulation-issue canvas washing and toilet bags, and an open book on the bed, the place was bare. Not even a rug to cover the floorboards. It reminded Haydn of a monk's cell.

'Please, sit down.' Tomas indicated the chair. 'Would you like a cigarette?'

'I'd prefer my own, thank you.' Haydn tapped one out of the packet he took from his breast pocket.

'I'm sorry for what happened, Captain Powell. It's not Jane's fault. I lost my head.'

'I haven't come for explanations. Are you prepared to look after her and Anne? Marry her when I divorce her?' He wanted to add 'because if you're not, leave her alone . . .' but the proviso remained unspoken.

'I love her. I want nothing more than to spend the rest of my life with her.' D'Este's frank reply took Haydn by surprise. He'd expected refusal, or at best evasion.

'And Anne?'

'She's Jane's daughter. I'd treat her like my own.'

'Be sure you do.' Haydn pulled out his lighter and lit his cigarette.

'That's it?' Tomas stared at Haydn incredulously. 'You

hit me, then you come up here and hand your wife over to me as though she's a piece of livestock.'

'You don't know Jane very well if you think she'd allow anyone to treat her like a piece of merchandise.'

'If you're doing this because you assume that we've been having an affair, you couldn't be more wrong. Jane would never do anything to compromise her marriage. She's the most honest and decent woman I've ever met.'

'I know.' Haydn left the chair. 'Which is why I've got more sense than to try and hold on to her when she loves you, not me.'

'Captain Powell . . .' Tomas stood looking helplessly at him. 'I never thought this would happen to me. Not with another man's wife.'

'None of us knew what was coming when war broke out and our governments sent us careering all over the world, D'Este. Just take care of them. That's all I ask.'

'Don't you want to stay in touch with Anne? You're her father. The most important figure in a girl's life.'

'She doesn't even know who I am,' he said flatly. 'She cries every time I go near her. You see her every day, D'Este. It would be easier all round if you take on that responsibility.'

Chapter Twenty

'YOU'RE BEING STUPID and stubborn. You just can't walk away from your responsibilities, Haydn. Jane's *your* wife. Anne's *your* child.'

'And D'Este has promised to take care of them.'

Bethan stared at her brother in exasperation. 'Then you don't love them any more?'

'You know me, sis. Footloose and fancy free. A girl in every show.'

'You don't mean that?'

'Oh, but I do.' He kissed her cheek before climbing out of the passenger seat of her car.

'She hasn't left the bedroom since you walked out of the house. I know that if you saw her just one more time, you could – '

'I could do a great many things, Bethan, but I won't.' Pulling his railway warrant from his top pocket, he turned, leaned on top of the car and faced her.

'You said yourself that you don't have to go until tomorrow. Dad . . .'

'Dad is going to be all right. You and Phyllis will make sure of that. I saw what I came to see, you and him. And now,' he gave a wry smile as he heaved his kitbag from the back of her car, 'it's time to go to Bristol and sort myself some female companionship for the duration of my stay there.'

'Tit for tat. Is that it?'

'Retaliation doesn't come into it. Chastity is for wives and monks. Not red-blooded males. Didn't you know that if we don't get our regular quota we go raving mad?'

'That's rubbish.'

'Not so,' he assured her gravely.

'Then what about all the men in prison camps?'

'They'll need a great deal of care and attention when they are released. Better start preserving your strength for when cashmere coat comes home now, Beth. You're going to need it.'

Bethan stared at her brother, wishing he'd drop the bravado for a moment, so she could reach out and talk to him the way she wanted to.

'Take care of yourself, sis.' He stepped forward and kissed her again. 'And enjoy your fling with your colonel. Remember, what the eye doesn't see the heart doesn't grieve.'

'Haydn . . .'

'There's no need to get on your moral high horse. You're a woman of the world. And this war isn't won yet, no matter what's happening in Italy. Live for today, for tomorrow we may die. There's nothing wrong with that philosophy provided you're discreet. Jane and I made the mistake of conducting our affairs in public.'

'There's nothing going on between me and David Ford.'

'The same nothing that's been going on between Jane and D'Este, and Aunt Megan and that cook?'

'None of us are jumping into bed with the Yanks, if that's what you think.'

'I know you aren't. That's what's so sad. If you did, you'd get it out of your system. Instead, you allow obsolete Victorian moral principles to rule your lives, and spend all your time brooding and regretting what can never be, because none of you have the courage to follow your instincts. Sleep with the colonel, Bethan. Who's to know or care? Cashmere coat certainly won't, stuck behind bars in Germany.'

'But I would, Haydn. And when he comes back I want to be able to look him in the eye.'

'Then brush up on your acting skills. Don't you think he'd prefer a happy, fulfilled wife to one who's going to spend the rest of her life sleeping beside him every night and wondering what it would have been like to take a tumble between the sheets with a handsome American?'

'I take it you've never spent a sleepless night wondering?'

'Never.' He flashed her a wide and shallow, theatrical smile.

'And you're happy?'

'I'm never lonely.'

'And love?'

'Is something that comes with lights out, and leaves before breakfast. You should try it. That way your days will never be complicated by excess emotion.'

'You think you have all the answers, don't you?'

'Just some of them.'

'Would you give Jane the same advice?'

'I already have.'

'And the thought of her with another man doesn't bother you?' she asked, deliberately trying to provoke him into revealing his real feelings.

'Jane's made her choice. I've left my address with Dad. I'll be there for the next six weeks. After that I'll be touring. I'll let you know where, once I start.'

'And if Jane wants to get in touch?'

'She can write.'

'Then you'll give your marriage another chance?'

'I'll sign the divorce papers, Bethan. That's all she wants from me. As I said, take care of yourself. And don't forget to "gather ye rosebuds while ye may".'

'Poetry from you?'

'School was good for something.'

He hugged her and she clung to him. 'Whether you like it or not, I'll take care of your wife and daughter.'

'Get D'Este to relieve you of that load, sis. You can't look after the whole of Pontypridd.' Swinging his kitbag on to his shoulder he turned his back and walked towards the entrance.

'It's Haydn Powell! . . . Haydn . . . our Haydn!'

Bethan heard the cries and saw half a dozen girls rush up to him. As they intercepted him at the entrance to the booking office he smiled, greeting them as though he hadn't a care in the world. When the prettiest held up her face, he kissed her cheek.

Bethan turned away bewildered and hurt by his cavalier attitude to his broken marriage. As she opened the car door she racked her brains trying to think of something she could do, something she could say to Haydn or Jane to make it come right again.

'Mrs John, this is a pleasant surprise.' David Ford opened the door to his office and ushered her in. 'I'm sorry I can't offer you tea, but we do have excellent coffee. And food.' He offered her a plate heaped high with meat and real butter sandwiches.

'Coffee would be fine, thank you.' She sat in the chair he pulled out for her. 'But I didn't come here to eat.'

'It's lunchtime, and they brought me more than I need or want.' He sat in his chair and looked at her. 'This isn't a social call, is it?'

'I was hoping you could do something about the situation between Captain D'Este and my sister-in-law.'

'I've found him a temporary billet closer to the hospital.'

'That's not what I meant.'

'It wasn't my suggestion. Under the circumstances he thought it would be best to move out of your house, and I didn't disagree with him. What happened last night . . .' he paused to pour and hand her coffee ' . . . was extremely regrettable.'

'It wasn't your fault.'

'You warned me that my men were going to play havoc with the women of the town.' He pointed to a pile of papers on his desk. 'Applications for permission to get married. And that's without the ones who have asked me informally for advice. Including Maurice Duval.'

'Don't tell me he wants to marry Liza. She's only seventeen.'

'Soon to be eighteen, according to the information he's given me.'

'And she's agreed to marry him?'

'He hasn't asked her – yet. But he will.'

'That's ridiculous, they're children. There's her sisters to consider.'

'All of which I pointed out to him. But he remains undeterred. Sergeant Morelli and your Aunt Megan aren't helping.'

'No one can accuse them of letting their hearts rule their heads at their age.'

'No?' He continued to look at her and she turned away uneasily. 'The problem is, Mrs John, I understand the reasoning behind each and every one of these applications. Italy is just the beginning. It's inevitable that we're going to move out of here soon, and when we do, some of us will get killed. In the meantime we're living amongst pretty and lonely women. What could be more natural than falling in love, particularly when it may be your last chance to do so?'

'Nothing, provided both parties are free.' She had the oddest feeling that they were no longer talking about Tomas and Jane.

'If it's any consolation, as well as battered and bruised, Tomas is also feeling extremely guilty at the thought of breaking up a marriage.'

'It's no consolation.' She rose to her feet. 'I'm sorry, I don't know why I came here. If I'd thought about it I would have realised that there was nothing you could do.'

'I only wish there were something.' He left his chair and opened the door. 'You will tell Mrs Powell that Captain D'Este has moved?'

'I'll tell her.'

'I have his address . . .'

'He knows hers, Colonel. If he wants to get in touch with her no doubt he will. Shall we leave it at that?'

*

'She's here.'

Tomas D'Este fingered his blackened and swollen face as he looked at his colleague.

'You're sure?'

'Absolutely. I don't know why you thought she wouldn't come. You should have known that she wouldn't let the boys down.'

'No. I suppose she wouldn't,' he said slowly, thinking of Peter Greaves and all the others she'd helped over the past months. He'd been a fool to think that she'd come to the hospital just in the hope of seeing him again.

'You've got yourself into a right mess over her, haven't you?'

'Yes.'

'If it's any help . . .'

'Take my word for it, whatever you were about to say, won't be any help at all. I keep telling myself she's married with a daughter. That I had no right to kiss her much less break up her marriage, but I can't help myself.'

'You have got it bad.'

'I never knew love could hurt so much.'

'In that case, how about trying to take your mind off Jane Powell by rebuilding a shattered jaw?'

'Greaves?'

'Evan's. There was a time when you would have known who was on the list without any prompting.'

Crumpling the wrapper of the Baker's chocolate bar he'd just eaten, Tomas tossed it into the wastebin and followed Higgins out through the door.

Jane had never had such difficulty in concentrating on a conversation. Every time the door to the ward opened, she looked up expecting to see Tomas. She strained her ears, listening to voices drift in from the garden outside, but none had his Spanish lilt. The hands on the ward clock crawled sluggishly round, marking off seconds that dragged past more slowly than days, as she struggled in vain to understand what Peter was telling her.

'You got problems, Jane?' he asked after she'd ignored his third direct question.

'No.'

'Liar,' he contradicted her fondly. 'I've just asked you what you thought about the Russians invading Australia and all you did was murmur "Mmm".'

'I'm sorry. I'll try to pay more attention.'

'This isn't school.'

'I'm interested in what you're saying.'

'No, you're not. And I don't mind, really. I don't expect even the most perfect visitor to be perfect all the time. It's not your husband, is it?'

'What do you mean?' she asked quickly, wondering if gossip about the fight between Haydn and Tomas had reached the hospital.

'He's in a war zone?'

'No, Bristol.'

'And your little girl is all right?'

'Wonderful.'

'Then everything is OK?'

'As OK as it can be in wartime.'

'And it's still all right for me to come and stay with you and your sister-in-law at the end of the month?'

'Of course,' she lied, crossing her fingers behind her back. She and Bethan had hardly spoken since Haydn had left, and she had no idea how Bethan felt about her and Anne staying on in her home now that Haydn was divorcing her, let alone a strange man she had befriended. The one time she had dared broach the subject over a hurried breakfast, Bethan had been most insistent that as far as she was concerned nothing had changed, and Haydn would come to his senses, sooner or later. But then Bethan hadn't seen Haydn's face when he had told her he would admit adultery to speed their divorce. She dreaded the time when she would have to face the situation, because it would mean losing not only

Haydn, but also the family she had come to regard as her own.

'Sorry, I was a bit preoccupied.' She squeezed Peter's hand. 'I promise I'll be back to my normal self next week.'

'This visiting lark can cut both ways, you know. You helped me with my problems. I could help you with yours, if you let me.'

'I wish you could.'

'Try me?'

'Perhaps I will, but not now. There isn't time.' She smiled in relief as the sister rang the bell for the end of visiting.

'It's nothing to do with Captain D'Este, is it?'

She stared at him, wondering if his question was a roundabout way of confirming rumours, or if she and Tomas had made their attraction to one another that obvious.

'We've all seen the way he looks at you,' he explained.

'Mrs Powell, it's time,' the sister called.

'See you next week.' Glad of an excuse to get away, she almost ran down the ward and into the foyer where Tomas was waiting for her.

'Want a ride?'

She shook her head.

'You can't avoid me for ever, Jane.' He dropped his voice to a whisper as he drew closer. 'We need to talk.'

'I don't want to go to the New Inn.'

'I wasn't suggesting we should. Come on.'

He drove to the field where he had kissed her for the first time. Then it had been high summer, now there was a chill in the air that portended autumn. Driving across the verge, he parked the bike and waited to help her over the gate. She hesitated for a moment before taking his hand.

'I'm sorry about your face,' she apologised, moving away from him as soon as her feet touched the ground.

'I would have done the same if I was your husband and caught a stranger kissing you.'

'But you're not my husband.'

'No.' He touched her hair gently, and she turned to look at him. 'But I could be.'

'No, Tomas. You couldn't.'

'Jane, I didn't want to fall in love with you. But it's happened. We can't ignore it.'

'Nothing can change the fact that I'm married.'

'Didn't Haydn tell you that he came to see me that night?'

'After the fight?'

'He asked me if I intended to marry you when you were free.'

'And what did you say?'

'That I loved you and if I was given the chance I'd marry you and bring up Anne as if she was my own child.'

'But she's not your child, and I'm not your wife.'

'But you could be.' He moved away, sensing that it would be better not to touch her again lest she think he was trying to pressurise her into making a decision she wasn't ready to make.

'Tomas, whatever I feel for you, and whatever Haydn said, I can't just walk away from him and pretend that we were never married.'

'I don't expect you to. After all, there's Anne. Whatever happens between us, Haydn will always be her father. The only question is, are you going to stay with him?'

'How can I when he's divorcing me? I know Haydn, he won't change his mind, not now. And after what we did, who can blame him?'

'It isn't as if we've done anything serious,' he said angrily. 'Just two damned kisses.'

'It's not the kisses, Tomas. I think if I'd asked him, he would have forgiven me if we'd made love. It would even up the score.'

'He's been unfaithful to you and you're worried about what we haven't even done!'

'I can't be sure, but I think from the way Haydn behaved before we married he's never set great store by fidelity, certainly not his own. Before he asked me out, I watched him work his way through an entire line of chorus girls. He spends his working life surrounded by beautiful, half-naked women, and most of them mean nothing to him, not even when he sleeps with them. He knew I'd be upset at the thought of him having an affair, no matter how fleeting, but guilt still drove him to confess. But that's Haydn. Honest to the point of reck-lessness. He'd rather risk our marriage than live a lie. And the problem is he's seen through me. It's not the thought of us having an affair that drove him to ask for a divorce. He would forgive me anything, except my falling love with you.'

'Then you do love me?'

'Did you ever doubt it?'

'I was beginning to wonder.'

'I think I fell in love with you the moment we met.'

'This is getting too complicated for me. I love you, you love me, Haydn knows and is prepared to divorce you, yet you won't marry me?'

'No.'

'Holy Mother of God, I'll never understand women.'

'But I will make love with you, if that's what you want.'

He stared at her in disbelief. 'Are you serious? You'll make love to me, just like that? What are we supposed to do? Go to my room, or some seedy hotel? You'll play the part of the whore and I'll be your client. We'll undress and spend twenty minutes grappling around in a strange bed, then afterwards, we'll put our clothes back on and go our separate ways?'

'Hopefully it won't be like that.'

He knelt beside her and laid his hands gently on her head, pulling it close to his, gazing into her clear, brown eyes. 'Don't you understand? I love you. I worship and adore you, I want you to be my wife.'

'I'm not a Madonna, Tomas, but a flesh and blood woman.'

'Then marry me!'

'And your fiancee?'

'I've already written to her.'

'Tomas . . .'

'No, you listen to me for once. I want you. Do you understand – *you* and no one else. I could never settle for Conchita, not now I've known you and what love can be like between a man and a woman. Life with her would be second best and she deserves a husband who will love her as much as I love you. So, will you marry me?'

She shook her head.

'And that's your final answer?'

'I'm married to Haydn.'

'Who doesn't want or deserve you,' he retorted impatiently.

'If he doesn't want me then perhaps it's time I lived alone for a while.'

'What have you been doing?'

'Not living alone. Haydn might have been away, but he's always been there in the background. Try to understand, Tomas, for most of my life people have made my decisions for me. The workhouse, the homes – I couldn't even choose what time to get up in the morning or when to go to bed. I had the use of only one dress a week so I didn't know what it was to stand in front of a wardrobe and pick out clothes for the day. And even when I left, there wasn't time for anything except earning the money I needed to survive. Not until Haydn came along. He gave me everything . . .' She turned away as her voice trembled.

Taking her in his arms, Tomas held her close. Her body was soft, unresisting.

'Take me to your rooms?'

'Now?'

'Right now, Tomas. Please?'

'And afterwards?'

'I don't know about afterwards. I only know that I want you. And perhaps Haydn is right. It would be more honest of us to make love than dream about it. It's what we both want, isn't it?'

He drove towards Llantwit Fardre, slowing down in front of an old pub that fronted the road. Driving around the back, he parked his bike, unstrapped his bag and walked to a kitchen entrance.

'There shouldn't be anyone here at this time of day. I assume you don't want to go through the bar?'

She hung back and shook her head.

Taking a key from his pocket, he unlocked the door and showed her into a whitewashed passageway.

'Is that you, Captain D'Este?'

'It is, Mrs Jones.'

'I wasn't expecting you this early. Will you be wanting anything to eat?' A large, blowsy woman with frizzy hair stopped in her tracks when she saw Jane.

'This is a friend of mine, Mrs Jones.'

'Well.' She eyed Jane, staring at her wedding ring.

'There's no problem with my having visitors in my room?'

'None at all, Captain D'Este, as long as they're out by ten o'clock.'

'I won't be staying that long,' Jane said quietly.

'Well, if you do, I'll be charging double for the room.'

'We'll be eating out, Mrs Jones.'

'That suits me, Captain. It's the darts championship tonight, we'll be run off our feet in the bar. What did you say your name was?' she asked Jane.

'We didn't, Mrs Jones. See you in the morning.' Pushing Jane ahead of him, Tomas ran up the stairs behind her. 'It's not too late to change your mind,' he whispered.

'I won't.'

'It's a pity she saw you.' Tomas unlocked his door

and showed Jane into a large, square room that looked as though it had been furnished at the beginning of Victoria's reign and not cleaned since. Brocade drapes thick with dust, spiders' webs and dirt hung at grimy windows. The bed was huge, with massive, mahogany head and footboards, and judging by the state of the faded satin cover, a lumpy mattress.

'You could have told Mrs Jones my name was Smith. I wouldn't have minded.'

'I would. You're not just some girl I picked up to have sex with. I love you, I'm proud of you. And I won't tell lies about who you are.'

'How many bodies do you keep in the wardrobe?' she joked clumsily, feeling suddenly shy now that they were alone in his bedroom.

'Dozens.' Closing the door he turned the key in the lock and tossed his bag into the corner. 'We could just sit and talk.'

'No.'

'You do realise she'll tell everyone in the bar that I've brought a woman to my rooms? It won't take much for my fellow officers to work out exactly who that woman is.'

'It doesn't matter. After the night of the garden party everyone thinks the worst of us anyway.'

'I don't want it to be like this between us, Jane.'

'You want me in a virginal white dress with orange blossom in my hair?'

He stood before her and removed her hat, running his fingers through her soft, brown hair. 'Yes.'

'You wouldn't get that, even if I was free.'

'No. I suppose I wouldn't.' Leaving her, he went to the window and looked out at the surrounding rooftops. Dusk was gathering. 'The nights are drawing in.'

'Winter will soon be here.'

As he turned, his breath caught in his throat. She had slipped off her dress and was standing next to the bed in a white, silk petticoat.

'This is as virginal and bride-like as you're going to

get. But I warn you, I'm very skinny and not at all attractive.'

'You're beautiful,' he murmured, taking a step towards her.

She opened her arms and he went to her. Suddenly nothing mattered. Not the dingy room with its ugly furniture, rickety gas fire and damp-stained wallpaper. Not that she had a husband, or he a fiancee. Nothing except his fierce, all-consuming hunger for her body and hers for his.

'I never knew it could be like that.'

They were lying side by side in the bed, her head pillowed on his shoulder. When she didn't answer he looked down and saw that her eyes were moist.

'Jane, I'm sorry.' He wiped her tears away with a corner of the sheet. 'I only meant that it was the first time I felt as though I was making love. Really making love with a woman instead of just sex.'

'You've slept with many women?' she questioned, hoping he wouldn't ask her about Haydn.

'Two.'

'And you didn't love either of them?'

'One was a widow. A friend of my parents. I was seventeen, a real man of the world,' he mocked deprecatingly, as he recalled his other, younger self. 'Now I realise she seduced me, not the other way around.'

'And the other?'

'A nurse at the hospital. It happened after a party. We were both drunk, and neither of us could look the other in the eye afterwards.'

'And here's me thinking that all Latin men have lovers lined up like dominoes before a game.'

'Not this Latin lover.' He leaned over and kissed her tenderly on the lips. 'I love you, Jane, and I want to marry you, no matter how long we have to wait. What do you say to my marriage proposal now?'

'Some would say you have me at an unfair advantage.'

'That's why I'm asking.' Leaving the bed he closed the blackout and switched on the light.

'What did you do that for?'

'So I could read the expression in your eyes. 'Well, will you marry me?' he repeated intently.

'I'm not free.'

'But you will be, and until then you could move in with me.'

'How can I? There's Anne and Haydn's family to consider.'

'There's you, Anne and me. Your new family, Jane. And that's all that's going to be important from now on. Believe me.'

'I won't move in with you. Not before the divorce.'

'Please . . .'

She laid her finger over his lips. 'But I will visit. As often as I can,' she murmured, pushing aside the bedclothes and pulling him close to her.

Chapter Twenty-One

SNOW WHIRLED DOWN, catching in small flurries that banked up in between the skeletal frames of the fruit bushes and trees and formed drifts against the garden walls. Bethan stood with her face pressed to the glass of the drawing room window, watching as Jane took the letters from the postman at the entrance to the drive. It hadn't been easy to persuade her sister-in-law to stay with her after Haydn's last leave, and she doubted that she would have succeeded, if it hadn't been for Anne. The little girl adored Eddie and dogged his footsteps wherever he went. They had become inseparable, much closer even than Eddie and Rachel because they were the same age. Maisie had helped make up Jane's mind by insisting that it was easier looking after two toddlers than one, because they played together, leaving her free to get on with the housework.

Eventually, and Bethan felt rather reluctantly, after weighing up all the considerations, Jane had decided to carry on doing 'her bit' for the war by continuing to work in munitions, and undoubtedly the easiest way for her to do that was by remaining where she was.

They had never discussed Tomas D'Este after the night of the garden party. Bethan knew that Jane still visited the hospital because she talked about the patients, and occasionally brought one home for a day or a weekend break. Maimed and injured men, who were pathetically grateful for a small glimpse of family life, and men her father empathised with only too well.

Jane also stayed out late on the days she visited, but if she was with Tomas D'Este, she never mentioned his name. And as Bethan never heard any rumours that linked her sister-in-law's name with D'Este after the night of the party, she hoped that their brief association was over. She preferred to believe that, than listen to David Ford's hints that if Jane and Tomas were still seeing one another, they were too discreet to go anywhere where they might be seen.

As Bethan left the window, Bing Crosby's new recording of 'White Christmas' rang out from the wireless set in the kitchen, where Maisie, Eddie and Anne were baking Christmas biscuits with spices that had come courtesy of the Americans.

'Anything?' she asked hopefully as she opened the front door for Jane.

The frown deepened on Jane's face as she flicked through the bundle of envelopes. 'Christmas cards, but nothing for you from Andrew, I'm afraid.'

'That makes it over four months.'

'I think it's time you contacted the Red Cross again.'

'I will. Today,' Bethan added decisively.

'There's one for me from a London solicitor. I can guess what that is about,' she tossed it down on to a side table, 'and this.' She held up a small parcel addressed to Anne in Haydn's writing, with DO NOT OPEN UNTIL CHRISTMAS DAY emblazoned across the top in red ink.

'Nothing for you from Haydn?'

'My Christmas present is the solicitor's letter.'

Bethan suppressed the urge to press her further. She had told Jane when she had finally decided to stay, that whatever happened between her and Haydn was their business, but that didn't stop her from hoping that they would get back together – eventually.

She returned to the drawing room and the window. She had been half out of her mind with worry for the past three months. When the erratic flow of Andrew's letters had dribbled to a halt four months ago, she had put it down to the vagaries of prisoner-of-war mail. Then, after making discreet enquiries among the relatives of other prisoners, like Mrs Richards and Tina, she had discovered that Andrew was the only one who had stopped writing home.

Clinging to the hope that his letters were simply going astray, she had begun to write to him every day instead of three or four times a week, then twice a day. Her concern intensified when her father-in-law confided that they hadn't heard from him either. Letters to the Red Cross only brought back confirmation that a man of Andrew's name, rank and serial number was being held in an officers' camp in the Reich.

'Shall we start decorating the Christmas tree?'

'Yes,' Bethan agreed absently, still watching the snow.

'Are the boxes under the stairs?'

'Yes.' Bethan turned around with a more determined look on her face. 'And if we get them out now, while Eddie and Anne are with Maisie, we stand a chance of saving the more delicate glass baubles from their marauding hands.'

Jane looked at the tree Albert James had cut down and carried into the house for them. Its topmost branches brushed the ceiling. Over sixteen feet high, just the sight of it undecorated had excited the children.

'I wonder . . .'

'. . . if this will be the last Christmas of the war?' Bethan finished for her.

'How did you know what I was going to say?'

'Because I've been wondering the same thing myself. Who would have thought in 1939 that we'd still be fighting four years later?' Going into the hall she opened the cupboard door and threw out half a dozen pairs of wellington boots and a pile of old coats that had been crammed in on top of the rows of boxes. 'Why do I keep all this junk?' She held up a pair of rubber boots that were too big for any of the children and too small for an adult.

'Because you'll need them if the war goes on for another ten years?' Jane suggested. 'Any more cutbacks in clothing coupons and we'll be snipping off the toes so they fit us.'

'You're a proper Job's comforter.'

'I'm glad Anne and I are spending Christmas here,' Jane said suddenly, squeezing Bethan's hand.

'Me too.' Afraid to say any more lest Jane tell her something about her and Haydn she didn't want to hear, Bethan crawled back into the cupboard. 'First box coming up.'

There were seven boxes of decorations, and they seemed to get progressively heavier.

'It feels like there's last year's Christmas tree in here,' Jane complained as she staggered into the drawing room with a small, but surprisingly heavy parcel.

'That one holds all the wooden table centres, and metal candle holders that Mrs John gave me.' She lowered her voice. 'Don't tell anyone, they bought them in Germany on their honeymoon before the Great War. Between you and me, I think she thought it was unpatri-otic to keep or use them, so she salved her conscience by passing them on to me.'

The doorbell rang just as they manhandled the last of the decorations into the drawing room.

'Expecting anyone?' Jane asked as she tackled the string on a box marked GLASS BAUBLES.

'No, and if it's anyone wanting a nurse, they'd better be on their last legs. I booked this day off weeks ago.' Rising from her knees, she shouted, 'It's all right, Maisie, I'll get it.' To her surprise her father-in-law was standing, shivering on the doorstep.

'I'm sorry to disturb you.'

'You're welcome any time, Dr John, you know that. Come in, you look frozen, and your trousers are soaking wet.'

'I didn't attempt to bring the car down your drive, I thought if I did I'd never get it back out into the lane again.'

'The snow's that bad?' she asked anxiously, thinking of the children having to walk home from school.

'And getting worse.' He followed her into the drawing room.

'Hello, Jane.' He greeted Bethan's sister-in-law awkwardly. It was well known in Pontypridd that Haydn was divorcing his wife and he couldn't understand why she was still living in Bethan's house.

'Excuse the mess. As you can see, we're decorating the tree.' Bethan helped him off with his coat. Putting it and his hat on a side table, close, but not too close to the fire to dry, she pushed an easy chair near the hearth. 'Sit down. If you want to change your trousers, you can have a pair of Andrew's. They'll only take a few minutes to air.'

'No it's all right. I can't stop. I came up to talk to you.'

'Would you like some tea, Dr John?' Jane asked as she went to the door.

'That would be nice, thank you.'

Jane closed the door behind her.

'I take it you still haven't heard from Andrew?' he asked as Bethan sat in the chair opposite his.

'Nothing. You?' she asked eagerly.

'Yes.'

'Is he all right? Why hasn't he written . . .'

'He's all right, Bethan, at least physically he's all right. Now,' he added acidly.

'But something is wrong?'

'I wish I didn't have to tell you.' Rummaging in his pocket he produced a creased blue envelope. 'Perhaps you'd better see for yourself. That way you can draw your own conclusions.' He handed it to her. She tore it open and began to read.

Dear Dad,

I'm sorry I haven't written for so long. I know you and Mother must have been worried about me, but I couldn't bring myself to write to anyone at home, not after getting Mrs Llewellyn Jones's letter . . .

'Mrs Llewellyn Jones wrote to him?' Bethan looked up quizzically.

'If you read on, you'll understand what she said, and why Andrew hasn't written to either of us in months.'

... about Bethan's affair with the American colonel who's moved into the house. You can have no idea of the effect the news had on me. I think I went insane for a while.

Bethan keeps writing, but I can't bring myself to open, let alone reply to her letters. And the damned XXXXXXXXXXXXXXXXXXXXXX don't help. All we hear on the radio and from our guards is how the Americans are sleeping with our women while we're stuck in here and can't do a thing about it.

What I can't understand is why you didn't tell me what was going on. If I had to hear it from anyone, I would have much rather it had been you than Mrs Llewellyn Jones.

This brings me to my reason for writing now. Can you start divorce proceedings and get the children away from Bethan? Mrs Llewellyn Jones says they are calling this colonel Daddy. I can't bear the thought of my children being brought up by another man and not even knowing who their father is. I'd appreciate it if you and Mother could look after them until I get home, and then I'll make other arrangements.

And I will be home, just as soon as this is all over. There was a time a few weeks back when I thought I wouldn't. I behaved rather stupidly, and if it hadn't been for a couple of the men in here with me, I would be buried in the camp cemetery right now. But as they reminded me, I have a son and daughter who need looking after.

Andrew

Bethan dropped the letter on to her lap.

'I've already written, telling him everything.'

'Everything,' Bethan echoed dully.

'About Anthea, and Mrs Llewellyn Jones's threat to get back at you. I contacted the Red Cross and told them it was important that Andrew get the letter as soon as possible, in the hope that they'd have some way of sending it through quickly, but all they could suggest was that I put "urgent" on the envelope.'

'What exactly did you tell him?'

'The facts. That Mrs Llewellyn Jones's letter was a pack of lies. That she became deranged after Anthea's broken engagement and backstreet abortion. It's short but to the point. I thought long and hard about putting more, but I knew that if I wrote too much, the censor wouldn't allow it through. Those German bastards seem to like nothing better than destroying the morale of our boys. By right they should never have allowed any letter through with a reference to Americans.'

'No, they shouldn't have,' Bethan agreed, thinking of the sections that had been blacked out by the censor's pen in Andrew's letters to her.

'I thought you might like to elaborate on my explanation.'

'There's no point in my even trying. Andrew said he doesn't even open my letters.'

'Rachel can write legibly now, can't she?'

'Yes.'

'Then get her to address the envelope. What father could resist his child's handwriting?' He looked up as Jane carried in a tray of tea and home-made biscuits.'

'Would you like to see the children, Dr John?'

'We'll see them later, Jane, if that's all right.'

'I'll be in the kitchen with Maisie if you need me.'

'Is everything all right?' Bethan asked anxiously.

'Apart from the children discovering how to make flour bombs, fine,' Jane reassured her before closing the door.

'There's just one more thing,' Dr John said as soon as they were alone again. 'Telephone Isabel as soon as you can and tell her that you've heard from Andrew.'

'You haven't told her about this?' Bethan held up the letter.

'I thought it better not to, until I'd seen you and Mrs Llewellyn Jones. You know how highly strung she is.'

'Yes, but she should know . . .'

'That Andrew tried to kill himself because her best friend wrote a pack of lies about you and one of your lodgers?'

'Oh God, put like that it sounds appalling.'

'What other way is there to put it? Fortunately, I was up before her this morning, so I got to the letter first. And you can leave Dorothy Llewellyn Jones to me. I'm going up there to see her as soon as I leave here.'

'What I can't understand is how she got Andrew's address?'

'Isabel gave it to her. She's been sending him birthday and Christmas cards.'

'He never told me.'

'He wouldn't. You two never got on well, even before the war.'

'But she is a family friend.'

'She's always been more Isabel's friend than mine.'

'Did you keep the letter from Mrs John because you think she'd believe what Mrs Llewellyn Jones said about me and the colonel?'

He looked at Bethan a long time before answering. 'People in this town have always gossiped too much.'

'I'm not having an affair with anyone, American or British.'

'I never thought for a minute that you were. For one thing I barely give you enough time to run this house in your free time, let alone entertain gentlemen friends. The only question is, how do we get Andrew to believe it when we can't even talk to him?'

'Bad news about Andrew?' Jane asked when she returned to the drawing room after the doctor left.

'He hasn't written because he thinks I'm having an affair with David Ford.'

'What?' Jane almost dropped the silvered glass ball in her hand.

'Mrs Llewellyn Jones wrote to him. I told you she threatened me the night Anthea was taken into the Graig Hospital.'

'This is all my fault, Beth.'

'Don't be ridiculous.'

'Don't you see? I'm having an affair with Tomas, so you must be having one with the colonel. That's the way people's minds work around here.'

'And no doubt Alma had an affair with Chuck Reynolds before he left too. It's hard enough trying to keep everyone in this house happy and healthy, and everything running smoothly without holding myself responsible for what people think of us.'

'But I am having an affair with Tomas D'Este, so I should go.'

Taken aback by Jane's honesty, Bethan stared at her in bewilderment.

'I'm sorry, I thought you realised.'

'I had hoped that you and Haydn would patch things up.'

'He made it plain the night of the party that he didn't want me any more. Did you know he asked Tomas to take care of me and Anne?'

'No. But you know how proud Haydn is. He was probably so hurt and angry, he did and said the first thing that came into his head. And it wasn't the right thing.'

'Neither is my being here. You and Haydn are close. He relies on you, Beth, and your father, much more than you'll ever know. Oh, outwardly he's the handsome, debonair man about town. The showbusiness personality with enough confidence to sink a battleship, but underneath all that . . .'

'He's a frightened little boy playing the part of the celebrity and absolutely terrified of getting caught out.'

'You've realised?'

'Of course. I was the one who wiped his nose, bandaged his knees and covered up for him every time he tore his trousers or smashed something in the house.

My father wasn't strict with us, but my mother broke nine stair rods on his and Eddie's backs. Not that beating either of them did any good. But don't you see, Jane, that's why he married you, not one of his leading ladies? He knows just how false and hollow the theatrical world is. He wants someone real, someone who will love him in spite of all his faults and someone he can love in return.' She fell silent, aware that she'd said more than she'd intended.

'But he doesn't need me any more.'

'And Tomas does?'

'He's asked me to marry him as soon as I'm free.'

'I see.'

'I haven't given him an answer. Let's face it, none of us can make plans for next week let alone next month. Only for when the war is over, whenever that will be.'

'And until then, I need you,' Bethan said forcefully. 'And with this awful business with Andrew, now more than ever.'

'Do you mean that?'

'Who else am I going to talk to? Maisie treats me as though I'm her boss.'

'Could it be because you are?'

'And Liza's so wrapped up in work and Maurice she has no time for anyone else. The children are wonderful, but I can hardly confide in them. That leaves you. And,' she smiled wryly, 'you know exactly what it's like to have a husband who thinks you're unfaithful.'

'Unfortunately.'

'So, let's concentrate on giving the children the best Christmas we can, and forget things we have no control over.'

'And Andrew?'

'His father has already written to him. I'll write tonight.'

'You're lucky to have Dr John on your side.'

'I know,' Bethan mused. 'Very lucky indeed.'

*

The windscreen wipers on Dr John's car bowed beneath the weight of the falling snow as he drove cautiously up the hill to the Common. It lay thick and heavy on the bonnet and boot, piling high, blocking the rear window. Hoping that no one would need his professional services until the storm eased, he parked the car in his garage and tramped the short distance to the Llewellyn Joneses' house.

Their drive was almost impassable, and he recalled last winter when Mrs Llewellyn Jones had been out supervising her cook and maid's clearing operations while the snow was still falling. Stamping his boots to shake off the worst, he rang the bell and checked his watch, hoping that his wife had left for the day. He was in luck, the young girl who opened the door told him that Mrs Llewellyn Jones was alone, resting, and had given strict instructions that she wasn't to be disturbed.

'She has a headache, that's why she sent for me,' he said abruptly, pushing past her into the hall. 'Don't bother to show me up, I know the way.' Brushing the snow from his coat, he hung it on the hall stand before climbing the stairs.

Dressed in a cream satin robe, Dorothy Llewellyn Jones was lying on a chaise-longue in her pink and cream decorated bedroom. A box of chocolates was open on a sofa table beside her, a book on her lap. She looked up in surprise as he walked in.

'Is something wrong? Is Isabel . . .'

'Isabel is fine, Dorothy. Which is more than can be said for my son.'

'Andrew? Have those beasts hurt him?'

'Not as much as you have.' Without waiting to be asked, he sat on a Lloyd Loom chair.

'I don't understand,' she said coldly, glancing down at her book.

'I had a letter from him this morning.'

'You must have been pleased. Isabel said you hadn't heard from him for months.'

'We hadn't heard because he tried to kill himself after receiving a letter from you.'

'Kill himself? Andrew? Surely you must be mistaken. He would never do a thing like that!'

He could see that she was genuinely shocked at the news, but that only made him all the more determined to bring home to her the magnitude of what she had done.

'Have you any idea what it must be like for the men who were captured at Dunkirk? To be incarcerated behind bars in Germany for year after year with no sign of respite, no sign of the war coming to an end.'

'Of course. That's why I wrote to him.'

'To tell him a pack of lies?'

'I told him what everyone in the town is saying. That your daughter-in-law is having an affair with Colonel Ford. She's been seen, Frederick. Going into his office at all hours of the day.'

'A lot of people go into David Ford's office. Are they all having affairs with him?'

'It's common knowledge. Besides, you can't deny that they spend their nights together.'

'In the same house as six other adults, and God alone knows how many children.'

'They talk . . .'

'We are talking now, and in your bedroom.'

'You are a doctor.'

'For pity's sake, this affair was born in your sick and twisted imagination, Dorothy. Have you any idea of the damage your gossip-mongering has done this time? Not only to Andrew, but to Bethan and the children? She's been absolutely distraught the last four months.'

'And what do you think I've been! If it wasn't for that slut, Bethan, Anthea . . .'

'So you do remember ycu have a daughter?'

'I remember, and I remember how Bethan took your son away from her.'

'Andrew would never have married Anthea. He didn't

love her. He loves Bethan and you've done your damn-edest to ruin their lives.'

'I won't allow language like that in this house.'

'And I won't allow you to poison my son's life, such as it is at the moment. If his suicide attempt had succeeded, I think I might have killed you myself, Dorothy. Hanging would be a small price to rid the world of a venomous, frustrated woman like you.' He spoke so softly, she couldn't believe what she was hearing.

'Unlike you, he'll thank me for having the courage to tell him the truth.'

'He'll despise you for lying to him. And as for the truth, I've already written to him to tell him that.'

'Then I'll write again. I'll – '

'You'll do nothing, because if you do, I'll tell the whole town exactly what happened to Anthea. How she was forced to turn to a backstreet abortionist because she knew her own parents would fail her.'

'You wouldn't dare!'

'Wouldn't I? The file is still open in the police station. Anthea gave us the name of the retired nurse who carried out the operation on her. When she comes to trial I'll see your name dragged through the mud.'

'You mean you'll see your own god-daughter's name dragged through the mud?'

'Anthea's well away from Pontypridd and all its mud, Dorothy.'

'You know where she is?' Her eyes blazed in anger.

'I write to her every week. Someone has to,' he added, not telling her that he also passed on Anthea's letters to her father. 'This is no idle threat, Dorothy. And one more word from you about my daughter-in-law and the Americans lodging in her house to anyone, and I'll have you in court for slander.' He left his seat. 'And if the damage you've done can't be repaired, this won't be the last you'll hear of this.'

'Isabel . . .'

'Won't be visiting here any more. Goodbye, Dorothy.' Wrenching open the door, he walked on to the landing and down the stairs. He could hear her shouting behind him, but for once he didn't even pay lip service to the courtesy that had been instilled into him during his upbringing. All he had to do now was convince Isabel that he had done the right thing, and once she knew that Andrew had tried to commit suicide, he didn't think he'd have too much of a problem.

The *Pontypridd Observer* lay open on the kitchen table beside Bethan. She looked at the photograph of Haydn with the tall, curvaceous blonde, and re-read the caption.

PONTYPRIDD'S GOLDEN BOY STRIKES LUCKY ON TOUR. As you see, Haydn Powell gets on extraordinarily well with his co-star, Lucy Langdon. When asked if their on-stage romance extended to their off-stage lives, all our Haydn would say is that some things are best kept private.

Jane had pretended that the photograph and article meant nothing to her, but Bethan had seen her lip trembling when she'd read the page. A short while ago she wouldn't have believed it possible for any woman to be in love with two men at the same time; now she wasn't so sure.

Some time soon she would have to ask Jane if she'd given any thought to Tomas D'Este's proposal. But not now, she reflected as she stared at the blank letter in front of her.

For now she had enough problems of her own to sort out. Picking up her pen she began to write.

Dear Andrew,
Your father brought me the letter you wrote to him today. Colonel David Ford along with four other GIs have taken over the top floor of our house. We are friends, and that is all.

She chewed the end of her pen. Why should she apologise when she hadn't even done anything . . .?

I am angry that you think so little of me, to take Mrs Llewellyn Jones's word that we have been having an affair. I know it can't be easy for you, being locked up all this time, but if you have nothing else to do, you could try thinking of me and the children and what the war is like for us at home.

The Americans are just as confused and lonely as you. They've left their families in America and haven't a clue what is happening to them over there. The mail to America, if anything, is even slower than the mail to the POW camps.

David has a family, and a son of seventeen he is desperately hoping won't have to fight in this war. He's not a father to Rachel and Eddie, no one could ever be that except you, but like all his staff, he is a first-rate uncle. All the children, ours as well as the evacuees', look forward to what little time they can spare to tell them about another country, teach them baseball, and cook them food they wouldn't even know existed if it wasn't for the rations that come out of the American PX.

I find it devastating to think that we've drifted so far apart that you'd rather believe a poisonous gossip like Mrs Llewellyn Jones, before your own wife, to the extent that you even tried to kill yourself. Don't you realise how much the children and I are relying on and looking forward to your homecoming? How difficult it has been for us to survive without you?

If I ever do decide to have an affair I promise you now, you'll be the first to know. But I suppose I'll carry on waiting and hoping that one day we'll be together again and there really is a future for all of us – together.

Your father has told me that he has written to you about what happened to Anthea, but Anthea aside, Mrs Llewellyn Jones has always disliked me, and it has grown into outright hatred since I stopped her from putting four of my evacuees into the homes. I should have told you, but I didn't want you worrying about domestic things you couldn't help with. Here's another bombshell. Alma and I adopted the four girls ranging in ages from seventeen down to ten rather than see Mrs Llewellyn Jones put them out to service and in the workhouse.

I'm doing my bit in keeping the home fires burning, Andrew, it would be comforting to think that you are doing your bit and keeping safe until you can come home.

Your loving and faithful wife,
Bethan

She looked at what she'd written. It might not be the most tactful letter to send to a husband incarcerated for the duration, but she meant every word. Folding the letter in on itself she gummed down the flap. There was a postbox at the top of the lane by the Queen's Hotel. It was late, it was dark, still snowing and freezing, but she reached for her coat. If she didn't post it now, she never might.

Chapter Twenty-Two

'I'M SORRY IF I've inconvenienced you by asking you to call in at short notice, Mrs Powell. Sergeant Morelli.' David Ford pulled out a chair for Megan as Dino snapped to attention.

'You haven't inconvenienced me at all, Colonel,' Megan murmured apprehensively.

'At ease, Sergeant.'

Dino relaxed to the point where he dared broach the question uppermost in his mind. 'Is this about our application for permission to marry, sir?'

The colonel offered him the chair alongside Megan's. 'Yes, Sergeant. I had a memo from HQ yesterday and I wanted to inform you of the contents myself. I regret having to tell you this, Mrs Powell, but your application has been refused. The authorities will not grant you US citizenship.'

'That's crazy!' Dino exclaimed hotly. 'She's going to be my wife.'

'You have my sympathy, Sergeant Morelli.'

'They can't refuse an application just like that. There has to be grounds.'

David Ford flipped over the papers on his desk. 'You have a criminal record, Mrs Powell?'

'Megan never made any secret of it. We put it on the form. She told me she'd been in prison the first time I asked her out. It's plain to anyone who knows her she'll never do anything like that again. She was desperate. A war widow left with two young children to bring up on her own.'

'Dino, please.' Unlike the sergeant, Megan had been watching David Ford and knew there was nothing to be gained from pleading. The decision had very obviously been taken out of his hands.

'She sold stolen goods to pay her rent and put food on the table,' Dino continued, much to Megan's embarrassment. 'She didn't steal anything herself. She did wrong, did time for it and it's over. In the past.'

'I agree, Sergeant Morelli. But unfortunately the people who make the rules don't see it that way.'

'Then they're idiots, begging your pardon, sir.' Dino threw the cap that he had been rolling into a ball on top of the mess of papers on the desk. 'I have money, property. I pay my taxes. I'm an honest citizen and if I say so myself, a damned good judge of character. If I want to marry Megan, I will.'

'No one can stop you from marrying once you've been demobbed, Sergeant, only Mrs Powell from entering the States.'

'Then to hell with the States. We'll live here.'

'Dino.' Megan laid her hand on his arm. 'You can't give up your country. Your businesses, your family are all in America.'

'I have no children, only nieces and nephews. And as for my businesses, I'll sell them. I want no part of any country that doesn't want you.'

'Dino . . .'

'We'll talk about this later. Thank you, Colonel Ford. I'm sorry I lost my temper there for a moment. I know you did what you could for us.' Picking up his cap he left his chair and snapped to attention.

David held out his hand to Megan. 'I congratulate you on your choice of husband, Mrs Powell. When this is all over, I hope to get an invitation to the wedding.'

'You will, sir,' Dino said firmly. 'And if I have anything to say about it, it will take place the day I'm demobbed.'

'I've run you a bath, put some of those salts you like in it, and as soon as you've finished, I'll serve dinner. Steaks *a la* Schaffer with french fries and green salad.'

'Steaks. Real steaks?'

'Real honest to goodness, American beef off the hoof.'

'If I ever knew, I've forgotten what it tastes like.' Jenny gazed, dumbfounded at the table in her living room. Kurt had found her mother's best damask tablecloth, napkins and china, he'd also put red candles in a silver holder that was new to her. Next to it stood a vase of hothouse flowers and a bowl of exotic fruit that shone as though it had been polished. 'What's the occasion?' she asked suspiciously.

'If you need one, call it a late Easter celebration.'

'Easter was weeks ago. You're not going to . . .'

'I'm not going to do anything other than look after the steaks. You've no idea how many favours I had to promise the cook to get them, and that was in addition to a week's crap winnings. Bath, woman! I refuse to eat this sensational dinner opposite anyone with a munition-yellow face.'

Bemused and bewildered, Jenny went into the bathroom. Kurt had not only run and scented her bath, but also laid out her robe and slippers. After the long day in the factory, it looked warm, relaxing and luxurious. Five minutes later she was lying back, up to her neck in water with her eyes closed. Kurt knocked the door.

'Is it time to eat?' she asked sleepily.

'I thought you might like some wine.' He stuck his head round the door and handed her a glass.

'Wine as well. Wherever did you get it?'

'HQ's secret store. It was marked "For the use of Generals only." ' He touched his glass to hers.

'You'll be court-martialled.'

'Possibly, but it will be worth it.'

'What are we toasting?' she asked, her misgivings resurfacing.

'The evening ahead and my seduction techniques?'

'And that's all?' She studied him over the rim of her glass.

'Does there need to be more?'

'Not for me.'

'You have five minutes. Any longer and the steaks will burn.'

She pulled the plug on the bath, wrapped herself in a towel and went into her bedroom. Falling in with his celebratory mood she dressed carefully in her one good set of silk and lace underwear and a pre-war blue dress that matched her eyes. Brushing out her hair until it fell, soft and curling on to her shoulders, she applied a touch of make-up, and a liberal splash of scent. Knowing she looked good, she wandered into the kitchen.

'I've never seen a man in a frilly apron before. It won't catch on as part of a military uniform.'

'You're right.' He glanced down at the pink gingham print. 'It's the wrong colour.' He handed her a bread mixing bowl filled to the brim with thin, chipped potatoes. 'If you take that in I'll bring the steaks.'

'How many are coming?'

'Just us.'

'There's enough here to feed an army.'

Following her into the living room, he heaped an enormous steak on to her plate. 'You must be hungry after working all day.'

'There's hungry and there's gluttonous.' Taking her knife she cut the steak in two and replaced half of the portion he had given her on the serving dish.

He refilled her wine glass. 'Tell me about your day.'

'It was like every other day. Boring.'

'You forget I've never been in a munitions factory.'

Even as she recounted the strain that the step-up in production targets had put on all the workers, including her, she felt that there was something more, something he wasn't telling her. But whatever it was, she knew she'd never prise it out of him. She'd simply have to wait until he decided to tell her.

Bethan sat next to Alma on the sofa in the room above the shop.

'It's so unfair,' Alma protested. 'Chuck was only thirty. He had a wife and son, absolutely everything to live for . . .' the remainder of the sentence was lost in a torrent of tears and sobs as the reality of his death sank in.

'He was happy while he was alive, and he brought happiness into the lives of others. You have to think how much that means to everyone who knew him.' Bethan looked helplessly to David Ford.

'I'll make some tea,' he said awkwardly, retreating into the kitchen.

'But his wife . . . his son . . .' She extricated herself from Bethan's arms. 'I don't know how I'm going to bear this, and I only knew Chuck for a year. What must they be going through?'

'We can only imagine,' Bethan murmured, thinking of Andrew and hating herself for wondering how she would have reacted if he had succeeded in killing himself when he had received Mrs Llewellyn Jones's letter.

'I must write to her.'

'I've met Marilyn and I'm sure she'd appreciate hearing from you.' David Ford returned with a tray of cups that he set on the table. 'Kettle's on.'

'Do you know how Chuck died?' Alma asked.

'I know he's been mentioned in dispatches, and he'll get a posthumous medal. He saved an entire platoon by single-handedly attacking and disabling a German gun emplacement,' he answered, neatly evading her question. Chuck's commanding officer's letter hadn't made easy reading. The major had survived the attack, only to die four hours later from abdominal wounds in a makeshift, front-line aid station. David needed little imagination to picture the conditions, or Chuck's slow, painful death.

'I'm sorry.' Alma made an heroic effort to pull herself together as Bethan left to make the tea. 'I know how busy you must be. It's kind of you to bring me the news yourself, Colonel.'

'It was the least I could do under the circumstances. Chuck used to say that coming here to see you and Theo was like having a second home.'

'He was a good man, and a wonderful uncle to Theo.'

Bethan came in with the teapot. 'I could telephone home and stay here tonight?'

'No.' Alma shook her head. 'Please don't take this the wrong way, but I'd rather be alone.'

Bethan nodded as she poured the tea, but she couldn't help worrying at the effect the news was going to have on Alma once the initial shock had passed. Would Chuck's death finally bring home the realisation that there was no real hope for Charlie? And if Alma was this upset over the death of a close friend, what would she be like when she was forced to accept that her husband would never be coming home?

'Good meal?' Kurt asked Jenny as he cleared their plates.

'Unbelievable.'

'And you don't have to worry about cooking tomorrow, there's enough meat left over for cold steak sandwiches. They're delicious with mustard or horseradish.' He returned with plates and knives for the fruit, and a bottle of whiskey. 'Nightcap?'

'Yes, please. I can't remember when I last felt this full, contented and sleepy.'

'And that is exactly the mood I intended to get you in.' Pulling a small box from his pocket he went down on one knee. 'Will you marry me, Mrs Powell?'

'Kurt, I told you when you moved in that I didn't want a serious relationship.'

'That was before we'd lived together for six months. And you can't deny that I've kept to my side of the bargain. We've had a good time, haven't we? And I haven't plagued you with proposals.'

'So why spoil it now?'

'Because I want to apply to the army for permission for us to marry, and I can't do that without you knowing about it. As soon as the war is over, I intend to take you back to the States.'

'The States! Don't be ridiculous. I can't leave here.'

'Why?'

'I have the shop . . .'

'Sell it.'

'My father . . .'

'Didn't even recognise you the last time you went to see him.'

'I'm all he's got.'

'We'll pay someone to take care of him.'

'He's my father.'

'And the doctor told you to expect the worst at any time. Jenny, his life is over, ours is ahead of us.'

'You know I hate thinking about the future.'

'You can't drift on alone for ever.'

'Why not?'

'Because when the war is over – '

'You're leaving, aren't you?' she broke in suddenly.

'For a while,' he admitted reluctantly.

'So that's what all this is about. Instead of telling me that you're going off to fight, straight out, as any honest man would have done, you prettied it up with food, wine, candles and flowers.'

'It's not like that, Jenny,' he remonstrated. 'I love you . . .'

'Love!' she spat out the word as though it was an obscenity. 'You know you're going to die, and you want someone who'll wait for a telegram and shed tears every time she looks at your photograph. Well, if you think I'm your ticket to immortality and remembrance, Kurt, you've got the wrong girl. I've cried enough over men. No more. Go off and get yourself killed. I don't give a damn!'

'I'm going to retrain as an army photographer not tackle Hitler on my own.'

'Then you'll be in the front line of the invasion when it happens?'

'Ahead actually,' he said wryly, recalling the army directive ordering combat photographers to step off the landing crafts in advance of the troops so they could film them attacking the enemy.

'Is that supposed to be funny?'

'War isn't funny, Jenny, but I'll survive.'

'No you won't. And you're a selfish bastard for wanting me to agree to marry you when you know you're going to die!'

'I know no such thing,' he contradicted vehemently.

'And what makes you think you're so bloody special?'

'I've got my very own guardian angel.'

'Haven't you heard? All guardian angels have been given a sabbatical for the duration.'

'Darling, I've got far too much to live for to do something as stupid as die on a battlefield.'

'So did Eddie.'

'What can I say to convince you that this particular bad penny is going to keep on turning up?'

'Nothing. When are you leaving?'

'Tomorrow,' he admitted hesitantly.

'Good. You can start packing now. Tonight you sleep in the front bedroom.'

'Jenny, I'm not going to get killed, but I have no idea when I'll be back. I wanted tonight to be special.'

'It is, Kurt: the evening our relationship ended. Tell the billeting officer to send up a replacement tomorrow. Any young, good-looking officer who wants a good time will do. But the same rules apply. No strings attached.' She stormed out slamming the door behind her, leaving him staring down at the unopened ring box in his hand.

Maurice crept softly along the landing on the second floor of Bethan's house. Trembling at his own audacity, he laid his hand on the doorknob of the room Liza shared with her younger sisters and turned it, panicking when the hinges squeaked. He waited a moment. When all remained quiet he peeped around the door into the darkness.

'Who's there?' Liza's voice quavered, tremulous with fear.

'Me, Maurice. I have to see you. It can't wait.'

'I'll be out in a moment.'

He retreated to the foot of the staircase that led to the top floor. He could hear Liza whispering to her sisters. A few minutes later she appeared on the dimly lit landing, wearing a woollen dressing gown over her pyjamas. Glancing nervously over her shoulder, she joined him.

'It must be serious if it can't wait.'

'It is.' Taking her hand he led her up the stairs into the room he shared with Dino.

'Maurice, I can't come in here.'

'No one's in. Colonel Ford sent me home from town because he's going to be late, Dino's visiting Megan, and Lieutenant Rivers is on night duty.' Closing the door, he faced her. 'I'm not supposed to know, so don't tell a soul, but we're moving out tomorrow.'

'You're leaving Pontypridd?'

'The whole regiment is going. But I'll be back,' he assured her, his heart racing at the downcast expression on her face. 'First leave I get, we'll be married, I promise. I wrote to my folks about you. They'll love you as much as I do when they meet you, you'll see.'

She sank down on to the only chair in the room, shivering from a mixture of cold and shock.

'Here.' Taking a blanket from his bed he wrapped it around her.

'You'll take care of yourself?'

'You bet I will.'

She looked around the bare room. The few personal possessions, like combs and hairbrushes, that hadn't been packed into the bulging kitbags looked sad and pathetic. She stared at a highly coloured calendar picture of Betty Grable posing provocatively in a swimsuit.

'Dino's idea,' he muttered in embarrassment.

'Maurice, I've never done it. You know what I mean?'

'Neither have I,' he confessed.

'If you want to, we could do it now,' she suggested nervously.

'No. It wouldn't be right.'

'The nurses in the hospital talk about it all the time. You don't have to have a baby. There's ways of stopping it from happening. I hoped you'd know about them.'

'It's not that I don't want to,' he mumbled in embarrassment. 'But I promised the colonel and Dino I'd behave like a gentleman with you.'

'Then we could get into bed and just hold one another?'

'We could. But wouldn't you mind?'

'I love you, Maurice. And I want to give you something special before you go.' Without waiting for him to reply, she took the blanket from her shoulders and spread it over his bed. He hesitated for a moment, then locked the door. Untying her dressing gown, she turned her back and unbuttoned her pyjamas. His heart travelled to his throat and beat there while he watched her undress.

'I've never seen a woman naked before,' he said huskily as she dropped her jacket and trousers on top of her dressing gown.

'And I've never seen a naked man.' She slipped between the sheets as he shrugged off his jacket. In shirt-sleeves and braces he sat on the bed beside her.

'You can't come in like that.'

'You want me to undress too?' His face flamed at the thought.

'At least take your boots off.'

He bent down to untie them, glad of an excuse to hide his blushes.

'If you're shy you could put your pyjamas on. It would make it more like we were married.'

'They're under the pillow.'

She took them out, but held them back. 'Maurice, this is the same for both of us. I love you. We shouldn't be ashamed of our bodies. My mother used to tell me that the right kind of love between a man and a woman is the most important thing in life.'

'I bet she also used to tell you that it should come after the wedding.'

'But we're not going to do anything wrong. You promised.' She tossed his pyjamas on to the floor. Unable to meet her eyes, he stripped down to his shorts, folding

366

his uniform neatly over the chair before turning to the bed. She moved away from the edge, holding back the sheet as he lay rigidly next to her.

'You look as though you're lying to attention,' she joked in an attempt to dispel the tension between them.

'I was afraid you'd laugh at me.'

'I thought you would laugh at me.'

'Why should I?' He turned to face her. 'You're beautiful, Liza.'

'I'm not. I've got fat legs and no bust . . .'

'You look just perfect to me.'

'Do you really think so?'

'The perfect girl for me.' He risked putting his hands around her waist and pulling her close.

'I never thought it would feel like this,' she breathed headily.

'Nor me. You sure you don't mind?' he asked, folding down the sheet so he could see more of her.

'No. This feels right. As though we were meant to be with one another like this.'

'I never imagined that just holding you could make me feel so good.'

She hugged him tight. 'You could . . .'

'I will, but after we're married. When we can lie like this every night.' Unable to trust himself to honour the promise he'd made to his commanding officer if he remained next to her any longer, he left the bed.

'I didn't realise how beautiful a man's body could be.'

Disconcerted by her admiration he pulled on his trousers and buttoned the flies. 'Men aren't beautiful.'

'You are.'

He sat beside her. 'I love you. And I can't wait until we can be alone together every night.'

'After the war.' She closed her hand over his as he touched her breasts through the sheet.

'The minute I get permission. You'll see.'

*

'Thank you for coming to see Mrs Raschenko with me.'
David Ford offered Bethan his arm as they walked up
Taff Street.

'Thank you for going to see her. It would have been
terrible if she'd heard about Chuck's death from a
customer.'

'I could see that the news about Chuck reminded her
of her husband.'

'Alma doesn't need anything to remind her of Charlie.
I doubt a minute goes by without her thinking of him.'

'Is there any hope that he's still alive?'

'After three years? You're the soldier, you tell me.'

'I wish I could reassure you. But it seems that Mrs
Raschenko doesn't need any help to keep her faith.'

'No, she doesn't. When the telegram came to notify
her that Charlie was officially declared dead, three
months after he was posted missing, my father and I
went to see her. We took some brandy to toast his
memory. Alma refused to touch her glass. What worries
me is what's going to happen after the war when she
may be forced to give up hope.'

'There were hundreds of cases of men reported dead
in the last war who turned up alive after the peace
treaties were signed.'

'And this war?'

'Time will tell.'

She stopped at her car. 'Thank you for walking me
back.'

'I was going to beg a lift home. Not knowing how
long we'd be with Mrs Raschenko, I gave Maurice the
night off.'

'Jump in.' She unlocked the door.

'The end of the war may come sooner than you think,
Mrs John,' he said when the doors were closed and
there was no danger of anyone overhearing them. 'The
regiment is pulling out tomorrow.'

'All of you?'

'Yes, but before you breathe a sigh of relief, another
will be coming in.'

'Then the invasion – '

'My orders are to relocate to the south of England for more training,' he interrupted pointedly. 'Did I tell you that my son is on his way over here?'

'No.'

'I'm still hoping he'll be too late for the worst of the fighting.'

'It's strange, for the last eighteen months we've been such good friends. Yet now you tell me this I don't know what to say.'

' "Goodbye" does seem rather inadequate,' he agreed.

'I could write.'

'I'd like that, although I can't promise to be a good correspondent.'

'You'll be busy.'

'The army has plans for me.'

Taking the silhouette of the massive, old chestnut tree in her garden as a marker, she slowed the car, turned into her drive and switched off the ignition.

'I'm going to miss you.'

'And I you, Mrs John. Especially our late-night talks.' Slipping his fingers beneath her chin he lifted her face to his and kissed her lightly on the lips. 'It was the wrong time and place for us.'

'I . . .'

'No, please. I have no right to ask anything of you. But I do envy your husband. You're a woman worth coming home to.'

Kurt tossed and turned on the cold, damp bed in the front bedroom for an hour before giving up trying to sleep. Pulling on his shorts, he went into the kitchen in search of a glass of water. He was rinsing the glass when he heard something that sounded suspiciously like a sob.

He crept to Jenny's door. Tapping lightly, he called out,

'Are you all right?'

When there was no reply, he opened it.

'Jenny?' he whispered into the pitch darkness.

'Go away,' came the muffled reply.

'I will tomorrow.' Feeling his way slowly across the room, he reached the bed.

'I don't want you near me.'

'Who are you kidding?' Ignoring her anger he stroked the tumble of hair on the pillow. She sat up and grasped him, fiercely, savagely, kissing him with an intensity that bordered on brutality.

'This changes nothing,' she said when she released him.

'Of course it doesn't.' Kicking off his shorts he climbed in beside her.

'Don't you mock me, Kurt Schaffer.'

'I wouldn't dare. But would it be so awful of you to admit, just for this one night, that you love me back?'

Chapter Twenty-Three

BETHAN SWITCHED ON the light as she walked into the kitchen. It wasn't even five o'clock. She could have stayed in bed another half-hour – if she'd been able to rest. She sat at the table, picked up yesterday's newspaper from the chair beside her, and reread the article that had prevented her from sleeping.

> Forty-seven British and Allied airmen have been shot by the Gestapo after escaping from their prison camp. Ninety-six officers tunnelled their way out of the camp. Fourteen are still at large.

'They were airmen in a Stalag Luft, not army officers in an Oflag. So Andrew definitely wasn't among them. And even if by some miracle he had been, you would have heard from the War Office by now.'

'Possibly not, if he was one of the fourteen still at large.' Bethan looked up at Jane as she folded the paper.

'Wherever he is, I'm sure he's fine,' Jane reassured her as she filled the kettle. 'I take it you couldn't sleep either?'

'I don't know what's the matter with me.'

'Everyone's marking time. You only have to read the papers to know that the invasion of France is going to happen any minute. All those notices about coastal areas being banned to visitors, and that American General with the German name . . .'

'Eisenhower,' Bethan supplied.

'That's the one . . . being put in charge. The sooner they go over there the better. Five years is quite long enough for any war.'

'They'll still have to fight when they get to France.'

'It's strange to think of boys like Maurice killing people.'

The letterbox rattled. Bethan suppressed her initial reaction to run to the door. Jane went instead. She knew that Bethan had written to Andrew every day since Dr John had visited before Christmas, but she still hadn't had a reply.

Bethan continued to sit and wait, superstitiously believing that if she didn't go into the hall herself, something would be there. Knowing that Andrew wouldn't have had her letter until the end of March at the earliest, she couldn't reasonably expect an answer until the end of June, and that's if he'd opened it and replied by return. She had weeks more of waiting – but she could almost see the blue envelope addressed to her in Andrew's sloping hand – hear the crackle of the paper as she picked it up . . .

'Is this what you've been hoping for?' Jane teased gently as she dropped it on to her lap. 'I'll make the tea. If you go into the drawing room to read it, I'll bring you some in when it's ready. But take a blanket,' she warned as Bethan left her chair. 'It's always cold in there until the sun moves round.'

Shivering, Bethan curled up on the sofa, draped the blanket around her shoulders and slid her thumbnail beneath the gummed section. Flattening the paper on her knee she began to read.

Dear Bethan,

I've tried to reply to the letter you wrote a dozen times this morning, but I was so ashamed of myself I didn't know where to start. So, I'm determined that no matter how this turns out, you will read it, otherwise the war will be over before you hear from me. Now there's a thought!

I'm grateful that you, my darling, never stopped writing in all the time I behaved so stupidly. After I read the letter you so cleverly got Rachel to address to me, I read everything else you'd written over the last eight months. You see, I kept every one of your letters. Even after Mrs Llewellyn Jones wrote, I couldn't bring myself to destroy them. I don't know why, unless a part of me couldn't really believe, even then, that you had been unfaithful.

If I'd had the sense to open them when they'd arrived I would have seen straight away that Mrs Llewellyn Jones was lying, because, as ever, in them is the strength I need to keep on living from day to day, and hour to tedious hour in this place.

My father has written explaining everything that you didn't. I can understand Mrs Llewellyn Jones's bitterness over what happened to Anthea, but I will never forgive her for what she did to us. You were right to be angry with me. For almost four years I have been preoccupied with my own problems to the exclusion of everyone and everything else. But your letters and my father's have shown me that you have suffered as much, if not more.

You have forced me to look at a side of my character I have always chosen to ignore, and have come to hate. Now I realise I am a selfish, egotistical man who only sees things as they affect himself, not the people around him. It amazes me that someone as kind and generous as you has put up with me all these years. I promise you I'll change, Bethan. When we are together again, I'll be a different man.

When I behaved so stupidly after receiving Mrs Llewellyn Jones's letter, one of the lieutenants looked after me. I think the consensus of opinion was he was the best man for the job. His wife had a baby two years after he last saw her. Unlike most of the other officers in here who've been through the same thing, he forgave her. He's of the opinion that if she'd been locked up for five years no one would have expected him to live like a monk, so why should she live like a nun? His favourite saying is 'if you still love and want the woman, what the hell's another kid in the family?' I wish I had his outlook on life and had listened to him instead of reading and *rereading Mrs Llewellyn Jones's letter until it drove me mad.*

I'm running out of room to write. I love you, I need you, please don't ever give up on me, and kiss and hug the children. All of them including my new daughters. Why didn't you tell me that you and Alma had adopted them? Surely you didn't think I'd be angry? I know you well enough to realise that you would never turn your back on anyone in real need, especially a child.

All my love now and for ever,
Andrew

'Tea?' Jane pushed the door open to see Bethan staring down at the letter. 'Is everything all right?'

'Thanks to Dr John he no longer believes that I had an affair with David Ford.'

'That's good news.'

'I suppose so.'

'You're still worried about him?'

'No, just angry that he didn't trust me.' Bethan curled her fingers around the cup Jane handed her, siphoning off the warmth. 'And then what if I'd had an affair? Made the mistake of looking for consolation with another man for a short while. He's been away for nearly five years.'

'But you didn't have an affair,' Jane interrupted firmly.

'I wanted to.'

The silence between the two women was palpable.

'I'm sorry, that was tactless of me,' Bethan apologised.

'When I married Haydn I never thought I'd look at another man, much less fall in love with one.'

'Then you really do love Tomas?'

Jane nodded. 'Yes, but I can't simply forget Haydn. Even without Anne there is so much between us.'

'What are you going to do?'

'What can I do? The divorce will be final in another few months. Haydn can't make it any plainer that he regards our marriage as finished.'

'Haydn's stubborn. You hurt his pride, but he still loves you. I know he does.'

'He'll never admit it, Beth. Not again.'

'And Anne?'

'Haydn wants me to keep her because he intends to carry on touring after the war is over. I promised Tomas that I'd give him an answer to his proposal when the divorce is finalised. If it's yes, he'll want us to go to America with him.'

'And will you say yes?'

'I don't know. I love him, Beth, but I love . . . loved Haydn and that wasn't enough for either of us. I've made a mess of one marriage, will I do the same again?'

'What happened between you and Haydn isn't your fault.'

'I can't blame everything on the war. Haydn has his faults but basically he's a kind, wonderful man. I'd like to settle everything between us amicably. If I could only be sure that marrying Tomas is the right, not selfish thing to do, for Anne and Haydn as well as myself, I would do it.'

'Only you can know what's right.'

'At the moment I'm incapable of deciding whether to make toast or porridge for breakfast, let alone anything as monumental as reply to a marriage proposal.'

'So, nothing is resolved between you and Tomas, any more than it is between Andrew and me. This – ' Bethan folded the letter – 'doesn't solve anything. We're back to where we were last year. Neither really knowing the other, both of us trying to please too hard. The latest is that he's promised to change. Be a different man when he comes home. Why can't he see that it was the old Andrew, flaws and all, that I married?'

'And it's the old Andrew you still love?'

Bethan stared at the photograph of Andrew on the mantelpiece.

'I don't think so,' she said seriously. 'But I can't picture him any more. I look at his photograph and I see a stranger's face. An arrangement of light and dark that could be anyone's likeness. I've forgotten his voice, his presence. I can tell you what his taste in food and clothes used to be, but if I ever knew what made him laugh, I no longer know what it was. And I can't help feeling that he doesn't want *me*, Bethan, the person I am now, but the good, faithful wife he's established I've been. So, we're back to writing meaningless, polite letters full of trivia.'

'It will be different when you finally see him.' Jane reached out and touched Bethan's hand. It was icy cold. 'And it can't be much longer.'

'I hope so,' Bethan said fervently. 'And you?'

'I'm seeing Tomas this afternoon.'

'Whatever you decide I know it will be right for you and Anne.'

'I wish I had your faith in me, Bethan.'

'Damn this war!'

'Now, that is one sentiment I can agree with.'

A year of clandestine meetings in Tomas's room hadn't dulled or diminished the magnetism between them. Jane only had to catch a glimpse of his tall, olive-skinned figure striding down the hospital corridors for her heart to start pounding, just as it had the night they had met. She only felt truly alive when she was with him. But her love for Tomas couldn't blot out the look on Haydn's face as he had walked out on her. It was ingrained in her subconscious, and intruded even when she was alone with Tomas. That afternoon was no different. It was almost as though Haydn was there, in Tomas's room with them.

'This may be the last afternoon we'll spend together here.' Tomas closed the door and locked it. 'I've been transferred to the south of England. They're relocating most of the medical centres.'

'Ready for the invasion?'

'Probably. Come with me?' Taking her hand he pulled her down on to the bed beside him.

'To England? How can I?' she pleaded, gazing into his dark eyes. 'I've my job and Anne to consider.'

'Exactly, you're a mother. You don't have to work. Haydn's pushing through the divorce. I can take care of you and Anne until everything's finalised, and then we'll get married.' He ran his fingertips lightly over the contours of her face. 'As soon as the war is over we'll go to America.'

'You make it all sound so simple.'

'It is.'

She plucked nervously at the bedcover. 'There's still Haydn.'

'Do I have to remind you that he's divorcing you? In a few months you'll be free.'

'I think he still loves me.'

'And you?' he asked quietly, looking into her eyes. 'Who do you love, Jane? Him or me?'

'I feel so guilty I don't know what to think or do any more,' she confessed wretchedly. 'When we're apart I think I should run back to Haydn, if only for the sake of Anne and the family we were, then when you're close enough to hold me, like now, I can't imagine life without you.'

'Then I'll keep on holding you.' He kissed her, his moustache grazing her cheek, his arms, warm and comforting around her back. When he released her she picked up his hand and caressed his long, tapering fingers.

'I can't go with you, Tomas. Not now. Not without knowing what's going to happen to Haydn. I can't bear the thought of him hating me for the rest of his life. Please, try to understand.'

'I understand that you won't even give us a chance.' Leaving the bed he paced restlessly to the window.

'If Anne and I do go to America with you, I want us to start out fresh and clean, with no regrets.'

'And Haydn's blessing?' he asked tersely.

'Would that be so terrible?'

'Yes, because you're not going to get it, Jane. You

were married to the man for three years. After being here with you just a few hours a week I can imagine what that must feel like. And if I was him, I would never give you up. Never!'

'You're not Haydn.'

He stepped closer and cradled her head in his hands. 'Leave with me next week?'

'No.' She moved away from him and went to the door. 'I'm going back to Bethan's.'

'Stay, just a little while. We don't have to make love, or even talk. I need to be with you, Jane.'

'And I need to think, Tomas, and I can't do that here.'

'And us?

'You'll write?'

'Oh yes, I'll write,' he agreed bitterly. 'If your address is all you'll give me, I'll write.'

The new troops, who moved into Pontypridd a week after David Ford's South Carolina Regiment shipped out, did not take the place of those who had left. There were fewer of them and the rooms on the top floor of Bethan's house remained empty. Some went to church and attended socials, but they were in the minority. Most spent their free time in the pubs and organising crap games amongst themselves.

The townsfolk devised excuses for the lack of integration:

'They're not as nice as the other boys . . . not as friendly . . . not in the same class . . .'

But Bethan felt that it was not the troops who were at fault, but the people of Pontypridd. They had waved goodbye to their fathers, husbands, sons and brothers, then made friends with the Americans only to suffer the same indefinite, and possibly final parting. She sensed that she wasn't the only one in the town who had nothing left to give strangers.

And then there was the waiting. For almost a month life revolved around the wireless and newspapers until the warm, early June morning when she walked into the surgery to see everyone standing solemnly to attention as her father-in-law formally toasted the invasion of France.

Pontypridd erupted. Strangers hugged one another in the street as though the war was already won. But when the initial euphoria faded, the question on everyone's lips was, who had been in the front line of Eisenhower's D-Day landings? They soon found out. When the casualty lists were published, even the most vociferous anti-American critics had to concede that the Yanks were bystanders and good-time Joes no longer, but soldiers and victims of war, just like the Welsh boys who had gone into Europe and died alongside them.

'Everyone's right, these new troops really aren't a patch on the ones who left,' Dr John complained one dark November morning when Bethan walked into the surgery.

'I take it there's been more trouble?'

'Last night. Fourth fight this week in the Horse and Groom. The landlord's threatening to ban the coloured troops from the premises.'

'He can't blame them.'

'As no one else was involved I don't see how he can blame anyone else, and when the police followed the troublemakers back to their chapel billet they found four workhouse girls who'd escaped over the wall, hiding there. I had to go to the station to examine them. They had one vest between them. You should have seen your Uncle Huw's blushes.'

'I wish I had,' Bethan smiled.

'Nothing but fist fights and prostitutes. I don't know what the world is coming to.'

'Peace, I hope. Since the Allies took Paris most of the news has been good.'

'Apart from Hitler's silent bombs falling on the south-east, the Nazis reducing Warsaw to rubble . . .' he gazed at her as he picked up the paper on his desk. 'You haven't seen today's *Times?*'

'No.' Usually her father-in-law understated disasters but she had a presentiment that this was something too serious to dismiss. He handed her the paper. 'Bottom left-hand corner. You'd better read it for yourself, then visit your friend Alma.'

'I was going to fill my case.'

'Restocking can wait.'

As she started to read she sank down into the chair in front of his desk. 'Where is Maidenek?'

'Poland.'

'This has to be Soviet propaganda.' She stared at him, wanting him to confirm that the account she had just read of a camp where men, women and children were methodically stripped, gassed and cremated on arrival, could not possibly be true. 'No one, not even the Nazis, would kill one and a half million people this way.'

'I agree, it's hard to believe. But if Alma reads this it may make her realise just how futile it is to hope that Charlie is still alive. I saw her last week. The waiting has exacted a toll on her health. For three years she's clung to the belief that Charlie has been locked up by the Germans in a Russian prisoner of war camp somewhere in Eastern Europe. This place was found by the Soviets and they said that all nationalities had been murdered there. Presumably that includes Russians. Take the morning off and go and see her.'

'I will.' She handed him back the paper. 'Do you think it will be over by Christmas?'

'More like next Christmas,' he answered gloomily. 'And sometimes I wonder if it will ever be over.'

'Happy Christmas.' Skilfully using his one hand, Evan opened the bottles of beer he'd coaxed out of the land-lord of the Graig Hotel and divided the contents between the glasses on the table.

'Let's hope it's our last at war,' Mrs John said sol-emnly as she touched her glass to his.

'We'll all drink to that.' Dr John rose to his feet and glanced down the table to where Bethan was sitting.

'To peace,' Diana and Megan echoed the toast.

'Look at us,' Tina complained as they began to eat the Christmas dinner that Bethan, Jane and Maisie had cooked. 'Eleven women,' she winked at Liza who was grinning with pleasure at being counted a woman, 'a horde of children, and only two men between us. Not that you aren't both fine men,' she conceded with a smile at Evan and Dr John, 'but you can hardly cope with all of us.'

'I certainly wouldn't want to try and "cope" with you, as you put it, Mrs Powell,' Dr John responded, as his wife gave Tina a hard look. 'I've heard too much about your husband.'

'I wonder where William is right now?' Megan said thoughtfully, deliberately steering the conversation away from innuendo.

'The last battle in Italy was in a monastery.'

'I can't quite see William in a monastery, Alma.'

'Or Ronnie,' Diana added.

'Do you think he'll have managed Christmas dinner?' Tina asked, staring down at the roast potatoes, parsnips, chicken and stuffing on her plate.

'Knowing William, most definitely.' Bethan passed the gravy boat down the table to her in-laws. 'And if he's anywhere near Ronnie . . .'

'They'll have wheeled their way into the nearest wine cellar,' Diana suggested, her eyes moistening as she glanced across the room to the cot where her daughter was sleeping.

'How are you two adjusting to life without yellow skin?' Megan asked Jenny and Jane.

'As we were only given our cards two weeks ago, it's not easy to answer that, but I must admit I find running the shop easier than working long hours in the factory.'

'You haven't taken in any more lodgers, Mrs Powell?' Mrs John asked Jenny snidely.

'No. Now that the pressure's eased on accommodation in the town, I've discovered just how much I missed my privacy.'

'I haven't had time to discover anything, except full-time motherhood and housework, and believe it or not, after three and a half years working in a factory, I'm loving every minute,' Jane enthused.

'I'll talk to you again in six months.'

'If she can spare the time, Megan.' Bethan looked at Maisie, who blushed. 'Maisie is leaving us. She's marrying Mr James.'

As congratulations poured in from all sides, Bethan sat back and eyed her father who was watching Alma and Megan. Despite outward jocularity the strain of five years of war was beginning to tell on all of them, but most of all on the women like Diana, Tina, Liza and Megan whose men were involved in the fighting, and Alma – who grew more restless with every day that brought the end, and a truth she might not want to face, closer.

Bethan was loath to admit it, but she was actually glad when the Christmas holiday was over and she could return to what passed for normality. Only it wasn't normality. Everything was changing. In January all her evacuees except the Clark girls returned to London, and a week later Maisie married Albert James.

Although she only moved a few hundred yards away to the village, Bethan hardly saw her. Jane took over the housekeeping, and they began to chart the Allied advance into Germany, studying the atlas every night, ticking off the names of the towns the Russians liberated as they closed in from the east and the British and American forces from the west.

All POW mail was stopped, and Bethan spent minutes at a time staring blankly at the map wishing she knew exactly where Andrew was, wondering if the Russians would reach him first or the Americans and, what was more important, if he would be allowed to come straight home.

On 29 April the Germans in Italy surrendered to the Allied Forces, and as Tina and Diana sat poring over

Ronnie and William's last letters looking for clues as to whether they were anywhere near the last battles, Tina's brother Angelo and Mrs Richards's son Glan walked off the train and into the cafe – both of them freed after five years in POW camps. That night Tina and Gina threw a party for all of Pontypridd's returning POWs in the restaurant, and Bethan could only wonder why Andrew wasn't among them.

'Mrs Richards?' Bethan crossed to the table where her old neighbour was clinging to Glan's arm as though she wasn't prepared to let her son go anywhere without her, ever again. 'Do you mind if I talk to Glan and Angelo a moment?'

'You have one moment,' Angelo informed her solemnly. 'But only one. There's a girl standing over there a man who's been locked away from women for five years would give his right arm to talk to.'

'Liza's my adopted daughter.' Bethan gave him a warning look. The antics of the older Ronconi boys had been notorious before the war, and there was very little of the naive seventeen-year-old Angelo she remembered, in the confident young man facing her.

'You'll introduce me?'

'Only if you promise to behave yourself.'

'He doesn't know how,' Glan laughed, bringing the first smile to his mother's face since her husband had been killed.

'Look at them,' Mrs Richards said fondly, catching Angelo's hand as well as her son's. 'Both of them too skinny by half. I don't think they've had a decent scrap of food in five years. But here I am keeping you, when you want to talk to them about Dr John. I'll go and have a word with your Aunt Megan.'

'Mrs John,' Glan lifted his teacup in a toast.

'You used to call me Bethan when you worked as a porter in the Graig Hospital.'

'That was before you married into crache. Please, as you're obviously not too proud to join us, sit down.'

As she took the chair he pulled out for her, Bethan couldn't help noticing, like his mother, how thin they both were.

'You need feeding up.'

'Don't you start. Angelo was just saying his sisters are stuffing him like a Christmas chicken.'

'Tell me. What was it like?'

'We survived,' Angelo beamed, making her wonder what exactly was in his teacup.

'Please, Angelo. Andrew is still over there. Were you badly treated, beaten – '

'Why does everyone ask that?' Glan interrupted. 'Do you think we deserved a thrashing for past crimes?'

'I need to know what Andrew's been through.'

'Officers had it soft from what we heard, unlike Glan and me.' Angelo dug him in the ribs with his elbow.

'We were worked half to death in the early months, before we got ourselves a relatively . . .' Glan waited for a confirming nod from Angelo ' . . . cushy number on a farm where we ate almost as well as the natives.'

'Unlimited acorn coffee, black bread and cabbage soup,' Angelo elaborated, kissing his fingertips as though it had been gourmet fare.

'We were half starved for the last six months when our Red Cross parcels went astray.'

'But once the Allies began closing in, we were taken on a walking tour. Such pretty countryside, and I loved the bombed-out cities. They were a credit to our RAF boys.'

'You forgot the nine months we spent in chains.'

'They didn't go well with our uniform,' Angelo quipped.

'And through it all, this one here – ' Glan looked at Angelo – 'kept us all going. He's quite a character. He's got Ronnie's weird sense of humour.'

'I've noticed. Did either of you see or hear anything of Andrew?'

'They separated the officers from the men early on, Mrs John.'

'If you call me that once more, Glan, I'll brain you.'

'Vicious,' Angelo mocked, 'just like the Huns. Perhaps I don't want that introduction to your adopted daughter after all.'

'As Angelo said, if rumours are anything to go by, the officers had it a lot easier than us.' Glan reached for another sandwich.

'Most of the camps have been liberated. I can't understand why he isn't home.'

'They're still fighting in some areas, and . . .' Glan fell silent in response to a warning look from Angelo.

'And what?' Bethan pressed urgently.

'And nothing.' Glan reached for another sandwich.

'There's something you're not telling me, and I'm not moving from here until you do.'

'Bethan . . .'

'The truth, Glan.'

He looked around; only when he was sure no one was listening did he lower his voice and continue. 'We met a lieutenant who'd been in the same camp as Captain John. He said they'd been liberated two weeks before us.'

'Then why isn't he here?'

'They were desperate for doctors and Dr John volunteered.'

'Volunteered!' Bethan couldn't believe what she was hearing. 'Are you telling me he could have been home two weeks ago?'

'They really do need doctors, Bethan.'

'The invading force has its own medical personnel.'

'Not enough for all the camps.'

'The other camps,' Glan explained.

'Like that one that was in the paper. The camp in Poland?'

'I spoke to some of the boys who'd seen them, they said the conditions there were indescribable.'

'What's indescribable?' Mrs Richards asked as she rejoined them.

'All this food after five years of black bread and porridge,' Glan smiled at his mother. 'Dr John will be back soon, Bethan. The Germans wouldn't dare try to hang on to a Welshman. Even an officer,' he added deprecatingly.

'Did Angelo and Glan tell you anything about Andrew?' Jane asked as they drove up the hill after the party.

'Only that his camp was freed two weeks before theirs.'

'Then he'll be home any time,' Jane said brightly.

'He would be home right now if he hadn't volunteered for further duty,' Bethan responded acidly. 'I don't understand him. First he stays behind at Dunkirk . . . now this.'

'Someone's here,' Liza called out as Bethan pulled into the drive and her lights illuminated an American Jeep. 'I bet it's Maurice!' She jumped out of the car before it even stopped and ran to the door. It was opened by Dino, his arm in a sling.

'Is Maurice here?' Liza asked eagerly, charging up to him.

'No, Liza. I'm sorry . . .'

'What happened to your arm, Sergeant Morelli?'

'Slight accident. Nothing serious, just enough to get me a couple of days' leave.' He looked to Jane and Bethan as they walked in. 'I hope you don't mind, Mrs John. I sent Maisie home when I arrived. The children were all quiet and asleep and they've stayed that way.'

'You should have come down to the cafe, Dino,' Bethan said as he helped her off with her coat. 'Megan was there.'

'I didn't feel up to a party, and I'll see Megan in the morning. I was hoping I could stay here for tonight.'

'You're welcome to stay as long as you like. Your room is just as you left it. There's a young flyer convalescing in Captain D'Este's old room, but otherwise the top floor is all yours.'

'Thank you.'

'Maurice really isn't with you?' Liza complained

dejectedly as she trailed behind them into the drawing room. 'Did he give you a letter for me?'

'The convoy we were in was shelled. I'm sorry, Liza. Maurice didn't make it.'

Stunned, she stared at him in disbelief.

'There was nothing any of us could do,' Dino continued quietly. 'He never knew what hit him. I've brought you his last letter and some other things we found in his kitbag.'

Liza turned from the sergeant to Bethan to Jane. Then she began to scream.

'I've given her something to make her sleep. Jane will sit with her until it takes effect. Is there anything I can get you, Dino? You must be hungry.'

'No, thank you, Mrs John. I ate on the way here.'

'I'm sorry.' She grasped his hand. 'It must have been terrible.'

'It was,' he replied, returning the pressure.

'I didn't want to ask about Colonel Ford and Lieutenant Rivers in front of Liza.'

'George died with Maurice. The colonel was injured, worse than me, but he's going to make it. He's in a hospital in London. I came down here with Lieutenant Schaffer and a major who's been detailed to find the missing twenty million tons of army property that we apparently left in Wales.'

'They didn't want to stay here?'

'You wouldn't have wanted the major. He's left over from the first war and an absolute stickler for discipline. Lieutenant Schaffer offered to stay with him tonight in the officers' club in Cardiff so he can tell him everything he knows about our supply depots. He'll be free tomorrow. He has a week's leave coming and I think he intends to spend it with Mrs Powell.'

'Kurt's all right?'

'Not entirely. Like me, he caught a bullet. His was in the leg. But we solved Megan and Jenny's problems on the way here. I'm going to buy Jenny's shop from her as soon as I can get the money wired from the States, so Megan and I will have a business to run, and Jenny's going to the States as soon as Lieutenant Schaffer's demobbed, whenever that will be.'

'Do Jenny and Megan know any of this?'

'Not yet.'

'It will be interesting to see how they react to you two planning out their lives for them. You sure I can't get you anything?'

'I'm sure.'

'Get a good night's sleep, Dino.' She rose to her feet.

'You're going to sit with Liza?'

'Yes.'

'That girl's had more knocks in her short life than a bowling alley. Did I tell you I'm waiting to be demobbed too?'

'No.'

'I had money, and not much else when I came here. The reason I joined up was that I didn't want to live, not after my wife died of cancer back early in '39. Now I have Megan. Apart from my nieces and nephews I've never known what it is to have a family. I don't suppose you'd consider sharing one of the Clark girls with me and Megan? It's not that I'm muscling in, but I've been thinking about it a lot. Had nothing much else to do, I suppose. I know Megan's not that strong so I thought perhaps Polly would be company for her, maybe help her a bit around the house in return for a proper education. She's really bright, and I wouldn't expect her to do much because I intend to get Megan some paid help to do the heavy work.'

'You'll never get my aunt to agree to that.'

'We'll see. I intend to run the shop myself, but I don't want to live over it. I'd like something like this place. A house in the country with plenty of room for dogs, Polly, and Megan's grandchildren to run around in.'

'I think you need to talk to Megan and the Clark girls, especially Polly.'

'Then you'd have no objection to our offering her a home?'

'None if she agrees, Dino.'

'You wouldn't feel I was taking her away from you?'

'If you intend living in Pontypridd you wouldn't be.'

'No I suppose I wouldn't. See you in the morning, Mrs John.'

'You don't understand!' Liza shouted at Jane and Bethan. 'You can never understand. You're married, it's different for you. I wanted to give Maurice everything. I *wanted* him to make love to me, but he wouldn't. He said he'd promised the colonel he'd behave like a gentleman, and because of that he died without ever knowing what it was to be with a woman. He's dead and he'll never know . . .'

Bethan tried to hug her but the girl was frantic.

'Another pill?' Jane suggested quietly.

Bethan shook her head. 'She's had the maximum dose. And in this state nothing will have any effect.'

'Poor kid.'

'If you get some sleep now, you can take over later.'

'Promise you'll wake me?'

'If I stay awake myself.'

It was another hour before Liza's sobs finally began to quieten. Bethan stayed with her on the bed, holding her tight, and eventually Liza stopped thrashing round. Later, when she'd finally cried herself to sleep, Bethan still sat, stroking her hair, and thinking of Maurice dying before he even knew what it was to live. And Andrew, turning down an unmarried officer's offer to take his place in the medical station at Dunkirk, and how he'd done exactly the same again after five years of separation. Preferring to carry on working in Europe instead of coming home.

But it was David Ford who dominated her dreams when she closed her eyes. And when she woke, the first thing she did was find Dino and ask just how badly the colonel had been wounded.

Chapter Twenty-Four

D*EAR JANE,*
I am marrying my co-star Lucy Langdon in London on 7 May. I didn't want you to read about it in the press, hence this letter. I wish I had been the kind of husband you deserve. Better luck with Tomas.

I'd appreciate it if you'd pass on the enclosed letter to Anne when she is old enough to understand why we couldn't go on living together – or not living together – which I suppose was the real truth of our marriage. If you notify my father or Bethan with any change of address, I'll continue to pay maintenance for Anne and send her birthday and Christmas presents, unless you'd prefer me not to.

Thank you for three of the happiest years of my life,
Good luck in the future,
Haydn

Jane dropped the letter on to the bench beside her. She looked up as Bethan walked out of the kitchen to join her in the garden.

'Haydn's getting married again.'

'I know.' Bethan sat next to her. 'He sent railway warrants for my father and me. He's booked rooms for us in a hotel.'

'Are you going?'

'If I do, it will only be to try and talk some sense into him.'

'No, please don't.' Jane shook her head. 'And you should go. He needs you.'

'And you?'

'It's time I went south.'

'To Tomas?'

'I've saved enough to keep Anne and myself for a

while. I'll try and find rooms near where he's working. If we still feel the same about one another in a month or two, perhaps we'll marry.'

'And if you don't feel the same?'

'Then I'll build a life for myself and Anne. You know something? Now that I've finally made the decision, I'm looking forward to going. The war is nearly over. Anne will grow up in peaceful times.'

'And Haydn?'

'Will always be Anne's father.'

'You haven't seen the morning paper?'

'No.'

'They're already hailing Haydn and this Lucy Langdon as the Oliviers of musical comedy.'

'She's very pretty, Bethan. I hope he loves her.'

'I'm sorry.'

'What for? You've been the best possible sister-in-law, and,' Jane smiled determinedly, 'nothing can ever change that.'

'No.' Bethan hugged her. 'Not even the Atlantic between us can change that.'

'Come on,' Jane pulled Bethan's hand, 'I want you to drop me off at the station on your way to work. I have train tickets to buy.'

'Steak, french fries, salad and fresh pineapple, please, miss?'

Jenny looked up from the boxes she was dragging into the shop from the storeroom to see Kurt standing in front of the counter.

'You're hurt,' she snapped accusingly, when she realised he was leaning on a stick.

'I promised I'd come back, I didn't say anything about one piece. Besides, it's a blessing in disguise. They don't want men with bullet holes in the Pacific. And I've been given a whole week's leave.'

'Leave? Then you are going back?'

'Only as far as Cardiff to help a man look for all the vehicles and stores we've mislaid.'

'Some of those Cardiffians can be rough.'

'Not as rough as Germans, or Pontypridd women come to that. Now, will you marry me?'

She continued to stare at him as though she couldn't be sure he was really there.

'I need an answer if I'm going to get an application in before I'm demobbed. On the other hand we could wait until I'm a civilian and pay our own passage back to the States. In fact the more I think about it, the more I think it's a good idea. That way we won't have to be separated, ever again. Hey,' he opened the counter and walked towards her, 'are those tears I'm seeing?'

'I thought you'd be killed.'

'I told you I wouldn't be.'

'You don't have to go back?'

'It's all over in Europe bar the shouting. You can relax. I'm not going anywhere without you. Come here.' He pulled her towards him. 'I'm still waiting for my answer.'

'You really don't have to fight any more?'

'Only you,' he joked as he wrapped his arms around her. 'And you don't have to be afraid of being happy. I won't leave you again even if you throw stones. So, what's it to be?'

'I'll marry you.' Her voice was clotted with tears.

'And you'll come to the States with me?'

'Yes, please.'

'Boy oh boy, are my folks going to be surprised when they see you.' He kissed her, just once, before turning the sign on the door from OPEN to CLOSED.

'You sure you don't mind?'

'For the tenth time, no, I don't mind. Now go and enjoy yourself, will you?' Phyllis practically pushed Bethan out through the door.

'We'll look after the children, and the vegetable garden,' Evan said as he opened the back door of Bethan's car and lifted in her bag.

'And enjoy the Penycoedcae air while we're doing it,' Phyllis smiled.

'Don't forget to give Haydn our good wishes if this marriage is what he really wants.' Her father kissed her cheek.

'I will.' Bethan hugged Rachel, Eddie, Polly, Nelly and Brian one last time, closed the door, waved and drove out into the lane and down the hill towards the station. If anyone had to go to Haydn's wedding she would have much rather it had been her father, but he had been most insistent that she needed a break more than him; and he had used every excuse he could think of to get her to London, including the argument that Haydn was now closer to her than him. She only wished it was true.

'How long will you be leaving your car here, Mrs John?' the booking clerk asked, as she handed him the keys in case he had to move it.

'Three or four days at the most. Is that all right?'

'Fine. I'll look after it, never fear. And don't forget to give your brother our congratulations.'

'I won't.' Taking her bag she walked up to the platform.

The journey seemed endless. The hot, airless carriages were packed with servicemen and women wearing every conceivable uniform. The whole country seemed to be on the move. Evacuees going home, soldiers either heading for, or coming from leave, women taking children to visit relatives. And the timetable didn't help. They stopped at every small town and village *en route*. Then just before midday when they halted outside a country station festooned with flowers, the doors opened and they heard church bells. The stationmaster lifted his megaphone and shouted:

'It's over! The war's over in Europe! It's been announced on the radio.'

The echo of 'it's over', 'it's all over' was taken up by everyone on the train. Bethan sat back and watched strangers hugging, kissing and shaking hands. But she simply couldn't bring herself to join them.

She remembered her brother, Eddie, twenty-one, young and handsome in his uniform that last time he had come home on leave in 1940. Ronnie telling her how Maud had fallen sick living rough in the Italian hills, so they could escape the Fascist trawl for English aliens. Chuck Reynolds dying of wounds in an aid station at Monte Cassino. Maurice and George shot and killed on a road from France into Germany.

Someone touched her hand. She turned to see a woman dressed in black sitting next to her. Her eyes were dark, troubled.

'They gave their lives so no one else will have to die,' she whispered, pitching her voice below the noise in the carriage.

Bethan couldn't help asking, 'But was it worth it?'

'If it finally brings peace, lady, it was worth it,' an American serviceman standing in front of them declared flatly.

By the time the train pulled into Paddington station after ten and a half hot, sticky hours of travelling, all Bethan wanted was solitude and a long, cool bath.

'You came, sis!'

'Haydn, I didn't expect you to meet the train.'

'You know me, ever optimistic. I even hoped Dad might change his mind.'

'He . . .'

'You don't have to make excuses for him, Bethan. I know how fond he is of Jane. How fond you all are of her. I only hope you like Lucy half as much.' He picked up her bag. 'Come on, I've a car waiting.'

'How are Anne and Jane?' he asked as the driver inched his way out of the station into the stream of traffic.

'Both well.'

'She writes to you?'

'Yes.'

'When is she marrying D'Este?'

'She's not, at least she has no immediate plans to.'

'But she will,' he asserted firmly, as though he needed to convince himself.

'She left Pontypridd intending to build a new life for herself and Anne, I don't think D'Este came into it,' she murmured, stretching the truth.

'She never has had much of a life or a home. First the workhouse, then getting bombed out of London less than a year after we married.'

'It's not too late, Haydn. I have her address. It's not far from London, you could . . .'

He shook his head. 'You never give up do you, Beth? This time tomorrow I'll be a married man again, and a week later Lucy and I will be heading for America on the *Queen Mary*. We're making a film there.'

'Do you love her, Haydn?'

'Haven't you heard? The whole world loves Lucy Langdon.'

'That's not what I asked.'

'I'd be a fool not to. She understands me and show-business. We've lived together for nearly a year, and when we were touring, in the most primitive and disgusting conditions. I think we stand a chance of making it work.'

'And love?'

'I tried that once, I'm not in a hurry to do it again.'

'Haydn . . .'

'Please, Beth, I've made my decision. From now on my career comes first. That's the way it is and is going to be. Try and be happy for me.'

'I will if it's what you really want.'

'It's what I want,' he reiterated. 'Now about tonight. Lucy and I are in a show . . .'

'I can look after myself.'

'No doubt you can, but I've got you a ticket and an escort. Can you get ready in an hour?'

'If I have to.'

'The show isn't that bad, sis.'

'It's just that I'm tired.'

'You've got the rest of your life to sleep. Tonight we celebrate. Do you know the Prime Minister has designated tomorrow as Victory in Europe Day?'

'You'll have no excuse to forget this wedding anniversary.'

'No I won't.' He glanced out of the car window at a group of American servicemen dancing with a couple of WAACs in the street. 'But I still have difficulty in believing it's really over.'

The hairdresser and maid in the hotel performed miracles. Three-quarters of an hour after Bethan booked into reception she was standing on the staircase that led down to the foyer, bathed, perfumed and wearing a freshly pressed evening gown. Her breath caught in her throat as she saw a familiar figure standing in front of the desk. He looked older than when he'd left her house a year ago and there were lines of pain etched around his eyes. Steadying herself on the handrail she walked down to meet him.

'You're as beautiful as ever, Mrs Powell.' David Ford stepped forward and kissed her cheek.

'Haydn said he'd arranged an escort for me. I had no idea it would be you.'

'We met a couple of months back when he put on a concert in the hospital I was convalescing in. We kept in touch, and when he said you were coming here for the wedding, I offered.'

'Dino told me you'd been wounded. I meant to write . . .' Unable to think of an excuse as to why she hadn't, she found difficulty in meeting his eyes.

'Nice dress,' he complimented, offering her his arm.

'Same old velvet.'

'Ah, but you wear it with such style, it looks new.'

'You haven't forgotten how to flatter.'

The concierge held the door open for them and he walked her to the waiting car. She saw him grimace as he stepped into the back and sat beside her.

'Dino said you'd been badly wounded.'

'Dino exaggerated.'

'Judging by the way you look, not much.'

'A bullet in the chest. It's more or less healed.'

'I can tell by your breathing.'

'Stop being a nurse for five minutes and give me all the news. How is my sergeant?'

'Waiting to be demobbed so he can marry Megan.'

'Then he is staying in Pontypridd?'

'I'm afraid he's put my aunt before his country.'

'Lucky man to have that choice.'

Remembering a past conversation with Haydn, she wondered if her brother had deliberately engineered this meeting between her and David Ford. 'Kurt Schaffer and Jenny are marrying next month. He won't be demobbed for at least another year but they hope to settle in the States.'

'That's my country. Win some, lose some. And Liza and her sisters?'

'Are staying with me at present, but Dino and Megan have offered Polly a home.'

'Has Liza recovered from hearing about Maurice?'

'That depends on what you mean by "recovered". She'll never forget him, but there's a couple of young men who've come back from prison camps who are trying to help her come to terms with his death.'

'The young have had to grow up fast the last few years.'

'And your son?'

'He's mad because his old man pulled strings to organise a safe job for him.'

'Clever old man.'

'I told him I'd rather have him angry than dead. It didn't go down too well.'

'He'll forgive you.'

'I'm not so sure. Haydn's throwing a party after the show for everyone who can't go to the wedding tomorrow.'

'Are you going to the wedding?'

'Didn't he tell you? I'm best man.'

'No.'

'I was going to suggest that as we're both going, perhaps we could skip the party and have a quiet dinner?' When she hesitated, he murmured, 'Not even Mrs Llewellyn Jones's spies reach as far as London.'

'There's nothing I'd like better than a quiet dinner with you, Colonel Ford.'

'Good, because I've already booked the table. I just hope it holds good in all this bedlam of victory euphoria.'

'Lucy's beautiful and charming, isn't she?' David asked as he and Bethan sat across from one another in a crowded restaurant.

'Charming,' Bethan echoed, thinking of Jane and wishing her new sister-in-law was anything but.

'Your brother's a lucky man. First Jane, now Lucy.'

'He would have been luckier if he'd held on to Jane.'

'People and times change. I think both he and Jane will be happier the way they are now, than if they'd stayed together.'

'How can you say that?'

'Because I had a letter from Tomas D'Este yesterday. He seems pretty confident that he'll be able to get Jane to marry him before too long.' He tasted the wine the waiter poured into his glass, and nodded approval. 'So, we've talked about everyone except us.' He looked into her eyes. 'How is your husband?'

'I had a card two days ago to say he was well and free.'

'He's not home?'

'No. Although other POWs who were in the same area returned to Pontypridd in April. They told me that the camp he was in had been liberated two weeks before theirs.' She toyed nervously with her wine glass. 'You told me before you left that it wasn't the right time and place for us. Perhaps it could be now?'

'I'd like nothing better than to make you fall in love with me, but it would have to be for the right reasons.

Tell me truthfully, would you even be here having dinner with me if your husband had come home?'

'Probably not.'

'He's a doctor,' he said slowly, 'and there's a desperate shortage of medical personnel in Germany right now.'

'There's doctors with the invasion force, and in Europe.'

'Not enough. Finish your meal, Bethan. There's something I have to show you.'

Andrew sat back in the corner seat of the carriage and looked across at the passenger sitting opposite him. He searched for familiar lines in the face of the man he had known so well before the war, but the hunched skeletal figure, with close-cropped silver hair, looked nothing like the well-built, strong, dependable man, with the distinctive mop of thick, white blond hair, who had swept Alma off her feet and set up a successful business in Pontypridd at the height of the depression. He wondered if everyone else would have the same trouble in identifying Charlie.

'I wish you'd let me book us into a hotel in London for the night. It was crazy to come up on the milk train.' He stopped talking when he realised that Charlie wasn't listening. Most of the time the Russian scarcely seemed to notice what was happening around him, and Andrew wondered if mentally he was still in the hellish, nightmare world of the death camps he had been incarcerated in for so long.

He leaned back against the seat and looked out of the window. He could see nothing except his own and Charlie's reflections in the glass, but when he had tried to pull the blinds earlier, Charlie had stopped him. He knew why. The camp Charlie had been in had been very different to his, but when darkness had fallen both of them had been locked into wooden huts, the doors and shutters firmly secured from the outside.

He had thought nothing could be worse than the Oflag he had been confined in for five years, but then he'd been ignorant of the horrors of the concentration and forced labour camps. And according to one Russian doctor he had worked alongside, the camps in the east were even worse and more numerous than those in the areas that had been liberated by the British and Americans.

It was difficult to imagine anything worse than Belsen and Nordhausen. And both had been 'cleaned up', for want of a better word, before he'd arrived, but even now he couldn't get their foul stench out of his nostrils.

When the British army had reached the gates of his camp, he had been ecstatic. Every officer had packed his meagre belongings and was ready and waiting with one thought in mind. HOME. Then the CO had sent for him and the two orderlies he'd trained and asked if they would consider working in a camp they'd discovered a few miles to the south-east that was short of medical personnel. He'd asked if it was an order. The CO had admitted he couldn't order them to do anything, but their services were badly needed until more permanent arrangements could be made.

He'd refused, protesting that he had a wife and two children he hadn't seen in over five years waiting for him. The CO hadn't argued, simply pulled a few photographs from an envelope he was carrying. They had been given transport, and a few hours later he had been driven into Belsen.

He could even remember the date. 19 April. His birthday. Nothing had prepared him or the orderlies for the sight that met their eyes. They had been told the bare facts: ten thousand unburied corpses, evidence of cannibalism, atrocities, disease, systematic starvation, deliberate neglect – but those were concepts that could be put into words. A British doctor had come up to them and handed them pens. Red pens. He'd looked at him in bewilderment.

'Put a cross on the foreheads of those you think have a chance of surviving.'

Time became irrelevant, he scarcely slept or ate. The

stench hung heavy in the air, a foul odour he thought he'd never get used to, but somehow he did. The death rate dropped to three hundred a day. Men and women at the end of their strength who no longer had the will to carry on breathing. And in all that time he had scribbled only one postcard to Bethan.

Am well and free. Be home as soon as I can, but am needed here at present. All my love, as ever, Andrew

When ninety-eight fresh, keen medical students arrived from London he was asked if he'd move on to another camp. One where slave labourers had been held. That time he didn't argue. And there, in a corner of a typhus hut, a heap of rags had moved and he'd heard someone call his name.

He hadn't recognised Charlie. Not until the Russian had whispered his Welsh nickname, and even then he'd found it difficult to believe that the scarcely human wreck in front of him was his old friend. After making sure that the hut and everyone in it had been thoroughly deloused, he spent every minute he could with him. It had taken hours to get him to swallow the thin gruel the prisoners hated, but was the only food the emaciated could digest. Then had come the difficult part: convincing the authorities that Charlie wasn't Russian but a British soldier who'd been working behind enemy lines.

It had taken two weeks to get the confirmation they'd needed and new identity papers for Charlie. There had been more important messages on the wires, and more important concerns than the fate of one Russian-born British officer. But nothing was more important to Andrew. Distanced from Bethan by more than miles, terrified she'd no longer love him when he finally got home; in some, crazy, superstitious way he wanted to believe that if he saved Charlie and returned him alive to Alma, then it would be enough to safeguard his own marriage.

Crazy stupid superstition. And, at first Charlie had

refused even to talk about Alma, insisting that he had told her to build a new life and marry again if anything happened to him. Andrew had stolen minutes to sit by Charlie's bed – not minutes that belonged to other inmates, but precious minutes that he should have spent resting – talking, coaxing, reading every extract from Bethan's letters that related to Alma. But Charlie had been impervious to every mention of his wife, until by chance Andrew had read out an account of Ronnie and Diana's wedding. From that moment there had been a spark in Charlie's eyes. He had ransacked his bag and combed through all the photographs Bethan had sent until he found one of Alma with her son. That night while Charlie slept, he had pinned it to the wall above his bed.

The following day Charlie had left his bunk for the first time since liberation. Andrew had believed himself impervious to emotion after five years of imprisonment and almost a month working in the camps with the survivors, but that was before he had seen Charlie sway on his feet, his skin stretched like yellow parchment over his skeletal frame, his eyes sunk deep in their sockets, using what little strength remained to him to put one foot in front of the other.

'We'll be in Cardiff soon.' Charlie's voice, hoarse, cracked, intruded into his thoughts.

Andrew checked his watch. 'We'll be home in less than an hour. Alma will be up, working in the kitchen of the shop, although I doubt she still has the playpen in the corner. Your son, like mine, will be too big for it now. He's three and a half and Eddie four and a half, I've almost forgotten what boys of that age are like.'

Charlie pulled out the photograph Andrew had given him and studied it in the poor light. Andrew knew he didn't need to look, he could trace every line of the boy's face from memory. Those small blurred black and white figures had accelerated the Russian's recovery more than any food or medicine.

Andrew left the seat and lifted down the two kitbags.

They had both been issued with new bags but there was little in either. Charlie had only the shaving kit, soap, toothbrush and paste and uniform Andrew had scavenged for him. There had been an American in Nordhausen who had earned the nickname of 'the scrounger'. Andrew had told him his own and Charlie's stories. God knows where the man had got them from, but he had turned up with French perfume and silk lingerie for Bethan and Alma, and toys for the children, and although he had made Andrew pay handsomely for his presents, he had refused to take a penny from Charlie, although Charlie's back pay was already in hand, unlike Andrew's. His request had been turned down on the grounds that the Germans had paid him for his services as a doctor while he'd been imprisoned. The fact that neither he, nor any of the other medical personnel captured at Dunkirk had received a penny piece in five years, didn't affect the official ruling. And eventually, too happy in his new-found freedom to argue any more, he had let the matter drop.

As the lights on the platform drew closer, Charlie tried to lift his kitbag. Andrew took it from him and tossed both on to the platform as soon as the doors opened. When he turned back he saw that Charlie had managed to step down by himself. A workman tipped his hat to them, stopping and staring as they walked towards him.

'And there I was thinking I looked good,' Charlie complained in his guttural accent.

'Compared to a couple of weeks ago you look brilliant, but you should still be in a hospital bed.'

Charlie sank down weakly on to a bench. Andrew patted his pockets searching for the glucose tablets he'd packed.

'Here, suck a couple, they'll make you feel better.'

'Do you think I've done the right thing in coming home?'

'No. You should have stayed in the hospital at least another month.'

'I don't mean that. Look at me, Andrew, I can't even walk. Alma will have her hands full. A baby, the shops . . .'

'That she needs help with.'

'What help will I be able to give? I can't even carry myself.'

'You'll soon be able to carry an ox if you give yourself time to recover. You need food and rest, and as you won't listen to me, perhaps you'll listen to her. Come on.' Andrew picked up both kitbags. 'Let's see if there's a lift that will take us down, and up again to the Pontypridd platform.'

Dawn had broken when their train drew into Pontypridd. Andrew watched the familiar redbrick buildings draw into view and thought about how often he had dreamed of this moment.

'Dr John?' Dai Station held out his hand to take their travel warrants. 'Everyone's been wondering when you'd be coming home. Angelo Ronconi and Glan Richards turned up weeks ago, but then I suppose things are different for officers.'

'Not that different, Dai.' He saw Dai staring at Charlie, but there was no spark of recognition in his eyes.

'Would your friend like to go down in the lift?' Dai continued to gawk at his companion, wondering how anyone so thin could stand upright.

'I'll use the stairs,' Charlie answered in a surprisingly firm voice.

'Charlie . . .'

Andrew heard Dai gasp as he took Charlie's arm and helped him down the steps. The porter followed with their kitbags. He glanced around station yard. The taxi rank was empty, but he recognised the car parked in the corner.

'Want me to telephone for a taxi for you, Dr John?' Dai Station offered, running behind them.

'If you would, please.' Andrew led Charlie towards the seats in the tiled booking hall.

'Mrs John is away. She went to London the day before yesterday. But then you must know that her brother has married again.'

'Something happened to his first wife?' Andrew asked anxiously.

'Went off with a Yank. Like half the women in the town.'

Andrew's heart sank as he looked at Charlie, who seemed mercifully impervious to the man's babbling. 'Just get the taxi as quickly as possible.'

They sat side by side and waited. It wouldn't have taken Charlie more than five minutes to walk from the station to his shop in the old days, but neither of them suggested walking now. It seemed an eternity before the taxi with a huge gas balloon on the roof arrived. The porter stacked their bags in the luggage hold next to the driver while Andrew helped Charlie into the back. He saw him stagger and clutch the door handle as he climbed in. It was pointless to ask if he was all right. It was patently obvious he wasn't.

As they left station yard he saw a bus driver and conductor walk into Ronconi's cafe. A milk cart rattled down the Graig hill and under the railway bridge. They turned the corner past the New Theatre and there was a poster with Errol Flynn's name emblazoned across the top. This was his home town and he felt like a stranger. They carried on past the turn to Mill Street and the entrance to Market Square.

'You want the fountain, sir, is that right?'

'Please.' Andrew studied the driver. His face was unmarked, unlined, he was too young to have fought in the war. 'And if you could wait, please, I'd like you to take me up to Penycoedcae afterwards.'

'I'll wait, sir, but I'll have to leave the clock on.'

'I expect you to.'

There was a queue of tall, well-built Negroes outside Charlie's shop. They were talking and laughing quietly amongst themselves. All of them looked incredibly fit, healthy, clean and well fed after the people he had tended in the camps. One month – four short weeks – and he had almost forgotten about normality. What must it be like for Charlie who had lived for years in those conditions?

'Business is good, Charlie,' Andrew said, fighting a lump that had come into his throat.

Charlie nodded and Andrew realised that he wasn't looking at the men. A small boy was sitting on the shop doorstep. There was no mistaking his white-blond hair, or the deep blue eyes.

'Good God! It's you all over again, Charlie.' The toddler turned his head and gazed at Andrew as he opened the door of the taxi. Extracting Charlie's kitbag from the luggage hold, Andrew stood back and waited. Charlie stepped out and the men in the queue fell silent.

Andrew watched anxiously as Charlie leaned heavily against the cab. The men crowding into the shop moved away from the doorway. Alma walked out from behind the counter. Then, tears streaming down her cheeks, she ran forward.

'I think we'd better go inside,' Andrew suggested as she embraced her husband as though he were made of glass. He followed them back to the shop. A young girl had already opened the door to the stairs.

'It's all right, Theo, you can go too.' The girl gave the small boy a gentle push. Andrew held out his hand.

'Don't you want to come and meet your daddy?'

'My daddy?' The small boy's eyes grew round in wonder.

'He's come home, Theo.'

The boy took his hand and they walked behind Alma and Charlie up the stairs and into the living room.

'Alma, I don't want to intrude . . .'

'How could you, Andrew, you brought him home.' She was crying and laughing at the same time. Charlie patted her hand as he fell into his chair.

'Charlie's on a strict diet, simple foods that are easily

digested. Nothing too rich, oatmeal and the like. I'll be at home. Telephone, if you want any advice. If there's a problem, I'll come at once. I'll be down to see you tomorrow.'

'Andrew,' Charlie looked up at him.

'Yes?'

'Thank you.'

Chapter Twenty-Five

ANDREW CLOSED THE door of the living room behind him. Running down the stairs, he walked through the queue of servicemen to the taxi.

'Your friend looked rough, sir,' the taxi driver commented as he climbed back into the cab.

Andrew nodded, unwilling to elaborate.

The man drove up to the Fairfield, turned the car around and headed back through the town towards the Graig hill. Andrew checked his watch, a new one he'd been given to replace the officer issue that had been confiscated as British military property by the Germans, most likely to end up as loot in one of the guards' pockets.

As the car climbed the hill past the workhouse he noted the changes. The peeling paint on the shops and houses, the worn and mended clothes on the people walking up and down the hill, the shop windows filled with advertisements and empty cardboard boxes. No tins, no sweets, no goods to entice a casual passer-by.

'Home on leave, sir?'

'For good, I hope.'

'There were times when we wondered if it was ever going to end. My brother's in Singapore. We can't wait for that to finish so he can come home.'

'Let's hope it will be soon.' Andrew looked left up Graig Avenue, wondering if Evan and Phyllis were taking care of his children. Why hadn't he insisted that Charlie stay in London and rest in a hotel last night? He would have telephoned home, and found out that Bethan was there. He could have gone to see her. They might even have passed in the street.

'Where do you want to go in Penycoedcae, sir?'

'Do you know Ty Twyfe?'

'Nurse John's place.'

'That's it.'

'You know, Nurse John, sir?'

'Yes.'

'Nice lady. She looked after my mother when she got burned when the chip pan caught fire. Pity about her father losing an arm.'

'I didn't know.'

'It was a pit accident, sir. She's had a lot to put up with what with losing her brother and sister and her husband being a prisoner and everything, but it never seemed to get her down. Always has a smile for everyone.'

They left the houses behind them and Andrew looked out at the hedgerows and fields. The greenery was soft and lush, the morning colours fresh and brilliant, just as he'd imagined so many times when he'd been stuck behind barbed wire in the compound. He remembered writing a letter to Bethan . . .

The trees would be green, she'd be sitting on the lawn with the children . . .

'We're here, sir. Do you want me to turn into the drive?'

'No, thank you.' If there was no one in, it would be a long trek down to Graig Avenue, but he wanted to walk down the drive alone.

'That'll be five bob, sir.'

Andrew left the car, checked the fare and added a tip.

'Thank you, sir, have a good homecoming.'

As the car chugged up the road, Andrew turned and stepped on to the gravel drive.

The first thing he noticed was that the gates had gone. He fingered the rusty posts before moving on, then stopped in stunned amazement. There was no lawn, only neat rows of vegetables. At the bottom of the garden the shrubs had been pulled up and a chicken run installed in their place. Why hadn't Bethan told him? Then he remembered the food parcels and tins she'd sent. More than anyone else had received. He'd often wondered how she'd done it. Now he realised.

Then, suddenly there was the house, its once white walls green and weather-stained, the gloss on the doors and windows peeling, just like on every other building he'd seen. It wasn't only Germany that needed reconstruction, but then he was lucky, a coat of paint was trivial compared to rebuilding from rubble.

Shouldering his bag he walked to the front door. Feeling faintly ridiculous he rang his own doorbell. It echoed hollowly through the hall. He heard someone hushing small, shrill voices, then Phyllis opened the door. He looked past her to the three children standing behind her.

'Andrew?'

'I'm finally home.' He smiled at the children and they retreated.

'Bethan . . .'

' . . . is in London. I know, someone told me in the station.'

'She's going to be furious that she missed your homecoming. And you're here so early in the morning.'

'We caught the milk train.'

'You came home with someone?'

'Charlie.'

Phyllis turned white. 'Everyone except Alma thought he was dead, but she would never believe it.'

'I know. Bethan wrote to me.' He stepped inside and dropped his bag next to the coat hooks. Opening it, he extracted a bundle of parcels.

He glanced into the kitchen where the children had retreated.

'Rachel,' he called softly. She gazed back at him from beneath lowered lashes. Then he looked to her brother – they both had the same dark auburn hair, the same tawny eyes. Bethan was right, they resembled him far more than her.

He crouched down and offered her one of the parcels. She backed away.

'It's all right, Rachel,' Phyllis reassured her. 'This is your daddy.'

Rachel put her thumb in her mouth as she looked to Phyllis and Brian for reassurance, but Eddie continued to back away.

'You're not my daddy.'

'I am, Eddie, and I know your mummy told you about me.'

'You're not my daddy,' Eddie repeated stubbornly. 'I'll get my daddy and show you.' He rushed to a chair. Dragging it to the dresser he lifted down a photograph frame.

'This is my daddy.' He handed Andrew the photograph. Andrew smiled.

'This was taken before you were born. I didn't have any grey hairs then.' He touched the side of his head. 'Look I have something here for you too, and Brian, and – ' he looked at the two girls sitting at the table – 'my new, almost grown-up daughters.' He handed them two of the four headscarves the American had sold him, and gave his fountain pen to Brian.

The children perked up at the sight of his presents. Andrew gave Rachel a wooden peg doll and Eddie a wooden train. 'I hope you like them, you see I'm not sure what you do and don't like. We're going to have to spend a lot of time getting to know one another.'

As the children tore off the brown wrapping paper he turned to Phyllis. 'When are you expecting Bethan back?'

'She telephoned early this morning to say she'd be in on the last train tonight. You look exhausted, I could make you some breakfast. What would you like?'

'After what I've been eating the last five years, anything.'

He stepped back into the hall. The hat stand was festooned with large and small coats, a neat row of wellington boots and shoes laid out beneath it. The paintwork was clean but scuffed.

He glanced into the drawing room. Two cardboard

boxes held piles of home-made toys, there was no sign of his furniture and the place looked even worse than the hall.

'Bethan moved all the good furniture out when she took in evacuees. It's all safe and sound in the old stables,' Phyllis explained, seeing the crestfallen expression on his face.

'The house doesn't matter, I just wish Bethan was here.'

'I'll make you something to eat, then I'll take the children to school.'

'As I've just come home, can't we make it a holiday?'

'You'd be better off catching up on some sleep by the look of you.'

'I've five years of absence to catch up on, Phyllis, and the sooner I start the better.'

'Can we keep our new toys while we eat breakfast?' Rachel asked.

'Of course.' To his surprise they ran back into the kitchen. 'Bethan doesn't eat in the dining room any more?'

'She shut it up for the duration.'

'There's been a lot of changes.'

'If you sit with the children I'll make you an omelette.'

'With real eggs?'

'Didn't you see the chickens?'

He followed her into the kitchen where the two older girls were busy serving the younger ones porridge. 'Everything seems to have changed around here.' He looked at the apprehensive faces of the Clark girls and realised how his words might be misconstrued. 'My wife said she wouldn't have been able to manage without you.'

'None of us would have managed without her,' Phyllis said resolutely. 'And that's for sure.'

Bethan was exhausted, both physically and mentally, by the time the train crawled into Pontypridd. She walked down the steps into station yard and went to her car.

Home, just her and the children, and that was the way it was going to be until Andrew came home, whenever that might be.

All the way from London she hadn't been able to think of anything other than the films David Ford had shown her. Still immersed in them, she turned left instead of right out of station yard and drove down to the fountain. Parking the car outside Ronconi's restaurant she walked across the road and knocked at the door that led up to Alma's flat.

She stepped back as she heard Alma running down the stairs. The door flung open, 'Bethan? What a marvellous surprise.' Alma hugged and kissed her.

'I've only been gone a couple of days . . .'

'Come in.' Alma pulled her into the tiny hallway and dragged her up the stairs.

'Aren't you even going to ask how Haydn's wedding went?'

Alma held her finger to her lips and opened the living room door. Sitting in a chair, with Theo dressed in pyjamas on his lap, she saw what appeared to be a gaunt, elderly man. She stepped closer.

'Charlie?' she whispered uncertainly.

He glanced up at her. What little hair there was, was silver not white, his face was emaciated and haggard but there was no mistaking the eyes.

'Oh my God, Charlie, you were in one of those awful camps.'

'Andrew told you?'

'Andrew . . . how would he know?'

'Andrew brought Charlie home this morning,' Alma revealed.

'He's home?' Shocked at the sight of Charlie so soon after seeing the films, Bethan leaned back weakly against the wall. 'Oh God, Charlie, not you.'

'It's all right, Bethan. I'm home now. I can begin to put it behind me.'

'But you . . .'

'I'm fine.' He looked up at Alma and grasped her

413

hand. 'I wasn't, but I am now. How did you know about the camps?'

'I saw some films in London. They're going to show them to everyone. In the pictures . . . Alma always said you were still alive, Charlie. The rest of us never believed it, but she never gave up hope.'

'And I was right,' Alma smiled. 'You must be hungry and thirsty. Supper's all ready, we're going to eat when this young man goes to bed, which he's going to do right now.' She reached down and took Theo from Charlie, tickling him as she lifted him into her arms.

'No . . . no, thank you. If Andrew's home I'd better go.'

'Sit and talk to Charlie just for a minute while I put Theo to bed.'

'Please?' Charlie looked at her.

'Just for a minute,' she relented. Unbuttoning her jacket she sat down and studied him as Alma held Theo out, first for Charlie's kiss then hers.

'Stop staring at me like that, Bethan,' he said as Alma left the room.

'Sorry.'

'I have your husband's permission to live.'

'I've never seen anyone as thin as you.'

'I've put on weight the last three weeks. There are a lot worse off than me. I'm alive, I have a country, a home, and a wife and son who seem to want me.'

'There were times when I thought Alma would go crazy with wanting you. She's done nothing but talk about you since you went missing. And Theo . . . Charlie you've no idea what she went through when she was having Theo.'

'I know some of it, Andrew read me your letters while I was recuperating.'

Bethan reached out and touched his hand. 'It's so good to have you home. We'll see you soon?'

'Andrew's promised to call tomorrow. Come with him,' he pressed, not trying to detain her any longer.

'I will.'

She turned and walked quickly out of the room. Alma was closing Theo's door. She saw Bethan and held out her arms. They clung to one another for a moment.

'I'll look after him. Andrew told him there's no reason why he shouldn't make a full recovery. And he will, you'll see.'

'He'll be fine now he's with you,' Bethan reassured her. 'No, don't.' She stopped Alma from following her down the stairs. 'I'll see myself out.'

Alma waited until she heard the door close behind Bethan, then she walked into the living room. Charlie was standing at the window, watching Bethan cross the road to her car.

'I've been lucky to have a friend like her.'

'We both are.'

'I think you'd better sit down.'

'It's been a long day, even with that sleep this afternoon. And I still can't believe I'm really here. I'm terrified I'll wake up and find out it's a dream, like all the other times it was real enough to seem like torture when I was forced to finally stir myself.'

'It's no dream. And supper's ready. I made soup.'

'I can't eat all the time, Alma.'

'You can try.'

For the first time since he'd been home, he bent his head and kissed her. 'I've wanted to do that for a long, long time.'

'And so have I. God, Charlie, so have I.'

Bethan drove slowly up the hill. Dusk had fallen cloaking the lane in dense shadows. As she turned into the driveway and parked the car she saw the lights from the drawing room windows shining across the garden. She walked towards the front door, starting as someone rose from a chair that had been carried through the french windows.

She looked at her husband. There was no comparison between him and Charlie. He seemed much the same as he had done when he'd left. Perhaps there were a few more lines at the corners of his mouth and his eyes, and some grey hairs, but basically he was still the same old Andrew. How could she ever have thought that she wouldn't recognise him? She felt that she should have flung herself into his arms instead of standing and staring, but the moment had passed. It was too late.

'I called in on Alma and Charlie. They told me you were home.'

'I know Charlie looks dreadful, but he will make it.'

'You've seen the children?'

'I kept Eddie and Rachel off school for the day. I don't think Phyllis was impressed by the first decision I made as a father. They're fine children, Bethan. You've done a first-class job of bringing them up.'

'I'm glad you think so.'

'I have a bottle of wine I can open.'

'Wine? Wherever did you get it?'

'A looting shop called Europe.'

'Have you been to see your parents?'

'No, I wanted to see you first. Come and sit with me a while.' He went back into the room and carried a second chair close to his. 'Are you hungry? Phyllis made some sandwiches.'

'Is she still here?'

'No. Once Evan came back from work she insisted on going home. She took the Clark girls with her. Your father seems to think we need time on our own. Just the four of us.'

'I should kiss the children goodnight.'

'I read to them until they slept. I have a confession to make. I fell asleep in their bed.'

'I often do that.' She stood awkwardly for a moment not quite sure what to say next.

'We need to talk.'

'Yes. There's so much I need to explain.'

'You don't need to explain anything.' He looked into her eyes. 'Your letters . . . didn't it ever occur to you that I realised you were skating over all the problems? You didn't even mention your father's accident.'

'I didn't want to worry you.'

'I knew you were holding back. It's not much of an excuse but it's the only one I can offer for believing Mrs Llewellyn Jones's letter.'

'I'd like to see it.'

'I burned it. Unfortunately it wasn't thick enough to keep us warm for more than a few seconds.'

'Andrew . . .'

'You're my wife, I trust you.'

'And I need to explain what happened.'

'No, you don't.'

'Yes I do, because if I'm going to stay your wife I don't want anything left unsaid between us.'

'And I've told you I trust you.' His voice was husky, she couldn't tell whether it was from cold or emotion.

'Let me tell you about Alma first. She met an American major, he lived next door in Frank Clayton's shop. They used to spend hours together, he talking about his wife and son, and Alma talking about Charlie. He was killed in Italy. Alma's written to his wife ever since. It's the poor woman's last link to her husband. And that's what I was to the colonel who stayed here,' she insisted, thinking only of the first few months David Ford had spent in the house. 'A link with the family he left behind in America.'

'You didn't need to tell me that.'

'I want you to *know* that nothing happened between us. *Nothing*,' she asserted vehemently, wishing that she hadn't wanted it to. 'You weren't here, he was. He couldn't be with his own son but he could be with our children and me.'

'Those old cats really got to you didn't they, Beth?' Pulling the cork on the bottle he poured out two glasses of dark, red wine and handed her one. Taking it, she finally sat in the chair.

'Sometimes I think I would have gone mad if it hadn't been for your father. All the time, no matter what Mrs Llewellyn Jones tried to do or say, he always believed in me.'

'He wrote and told me what things were really like here.' Andrew gazed into her eyes, mysterious dark pools in the half-light. 'I would rather it had been you.'

'I didn't want to upset you. You were locked up hundreds of miles away. There was nothing you could do.'

'Except worry. And didn't it occur to you I was doing that anyway?'

'I've made a mess of it, haven't I?'

'I have no intention of repeating the experience so you can try and do better next time.'

'I know why you didn't come home with the others.'

'Charlie told you?'

'Not just Charlie. The colonel was at Haydn's wedding. He took me to see the films they made of those places.'

'You saw Belsen?'

'And Dachau. Was Charlie in one of those?'

'Nordhausen. But the name doesn't matter, they were all the same death factories.'

'Is he really going to live, Andrew?'

'Now he's with Alma, yes.'

'He looks frail.'

'Not to me, but then I saw tens of thousands of others. A living man looks healthy compared to a corpse.' He touched his glass to hers. 'Here's to life, recovery, us and a peaceful future.'

'You are back for good?'

'Most definitely.'

She looked at his clothes. They were ones he'd left in his wardrobe. They were loose on him. 'You changed out of uniform?'

'After I put the children to bed. It feels good to be a civilian again.'

She rested her arm on the table between them and he covered her hand with his own. 'You've had a tough war, Bethan.'

'No tougher than you.'

'Oh, yes. You had choices to make. I had none. They

were all made for me, all I had to do was sit and wait to be freed. It wasn't always easy but it taught me something I should have learned a long time ago.' He lifted her hand to his lips and kissed her fingers. 'Patience, and to value what I have. I love you, Bethan, and now we're finally together nothing else matters. You don't have to work tomorrow?'

She shook her head. 'I have a week off. I could have spent it in London, but after seeing that film it seemed more important to get back to the children.'

'And me?'

'I didn't know you'd be here.'

He rose to his feet, placed his glass quite deliberately on the table and stood in front of her. 'But I am. Let's take the wine and go to bed. Do you remember those letters I wrote, about the time we used to spend in the bedroom before going to bed?'

'I've been waiting for this moment for five years and now it's here . . .'

'You're shy and embarrassed?'

'How do you know?'

'Because I feel the same way. Ever since I've been home people have been telling me about my wife the miracle worker. Even my mother.'

'I thought you hadn't seen your parents?'

'They telephoned. Rumours had reached them of my being here.'

'And you didn't go to see them?'

'I said we'd call up later in the week. That I had my hands full with my children, and wanted to wait for my wife to come home.' Helping her to her feet, he held her close. 'Your hair is different and you've stopped wearing essence of violets.'

'We couldn't get it any more.'

'This is better.'

'It's French. Ronnie sent it from Italy.'

'Trust him.'

'It is going to be all right between us isn't it, Andrew?'

'It is.' He bent his head and kissed her. A long-drawn-out kiss that reminded her how much she had once loved him. 'Things won't be the same, Bethan, they can't be. Too much has changed, and too much has been lost, but there's a whole new world out there. I've had enough of war, separation and excitement to last me a lifetime. All I want are those two bundles sleeping upstairs, my new daughters, as quiet a life as a GP's can be in this town that, for all its faults, I've discovered I love more than any other place on earth, and – ' he paused and looked down at her – 'you. Please, Bethan, give me a chance to show you how much I love you.'

She wrapped her arms around him and held him close. 'I love you too,' she whispered softly, desperately wanting to believe it.

He took her hand. 'Then let's lock the doors and go to bed.'

All Orion/Phoenix titles are available at your local bookshop or from the following address:

Mail Order Department
Littlehampton Book Services
FREEPOST BR535
Worthing, West Sussex, BN13 3BR
telephone 01903 828503, *facsimile* 01903 828802
e-mail MailOrders@lbsltd.co.uk
(Please ensure that you include full postal address details)

Payment can be made either by credit/debit card (Visa, Mastercard, Access and Switch accepted) or by sending a £ Sterling cheque or postal order made payable to *Littlehampton Book Services*.
DO NOT SEND CASH OR CURRENCY.

Please add the following to cover postage and packing

UK and BFPO:
£1.50 for the first book, and 50p for each additional book to a maximum of £3.50

Overseas and Eire:
£2.50 for the first book plus £1.00 for the second book and 50p for each additional book ordered

---

BLOCK CAPITALS PLEASE

name of cardholder ....

address of cardholder ....

....

....

postcode ....

delivery address
(if different from cardholder)

....

....

....

postcode ....

☐ I enclose my remittance for £.......................................

☐ please debit my Mastercard/Visa/Access/Switch (delete as appropriate)

card number ☐☐☐☐ ☐☐☐☐ ☐☐☐☐ ☐☐☐☐

expiry date ☐☐☐☐   Switch issue no. ☐☐

signature ....

prices and availability are subject to change without notice